DEREK LAUFMAN

RUINWORLD

• EYE FOR AN EYE •

kaboom!

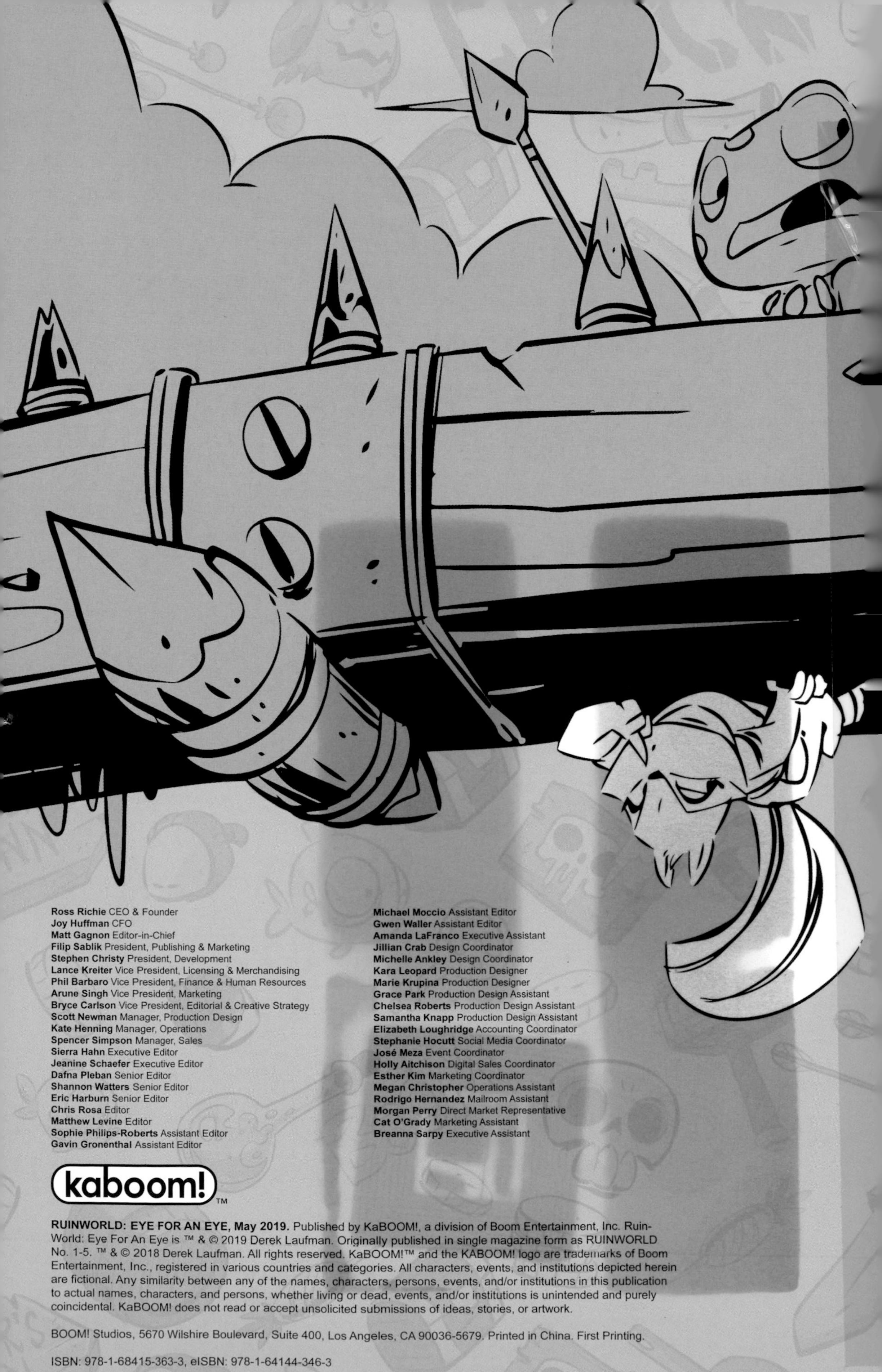

RUINWORLD: EYE FOR AN EYE, May 2019. Published by KaBOOM!, a division of Boom Entertainment, Inc. RuinWorld: Eye For An Eye is ™ & © 2019 Derek Laufman. Originally published in single magazine form as RUINWORLD No. 1-5. ™ & © 2018 Derek Laufman. All rights reserved. KaBOOM!™ and the KABOOM! logo are trademarks of Boom Entertainment, Inc., registered in various countries and categories. All characters, events, and institutions depicted herein are fictional. Any similarity between any of the names, characters, persons, events, and/or institutions in this publication to actual names, characters, and persons, whether living or dead, events, and/or institutions is unintended and purely coincidental. KaBOOM! does not read or accept unsolicited submissions of ideas, stories, or artwork.

BOOM! Studios, 5670 Wilshire Boulevard, Suite 400, Los Angeles, CA 90036-5679. Printed in China. First Printing.

ISBN: 978-1-68415-363-3, eISBN: 978-1-64144-346-3

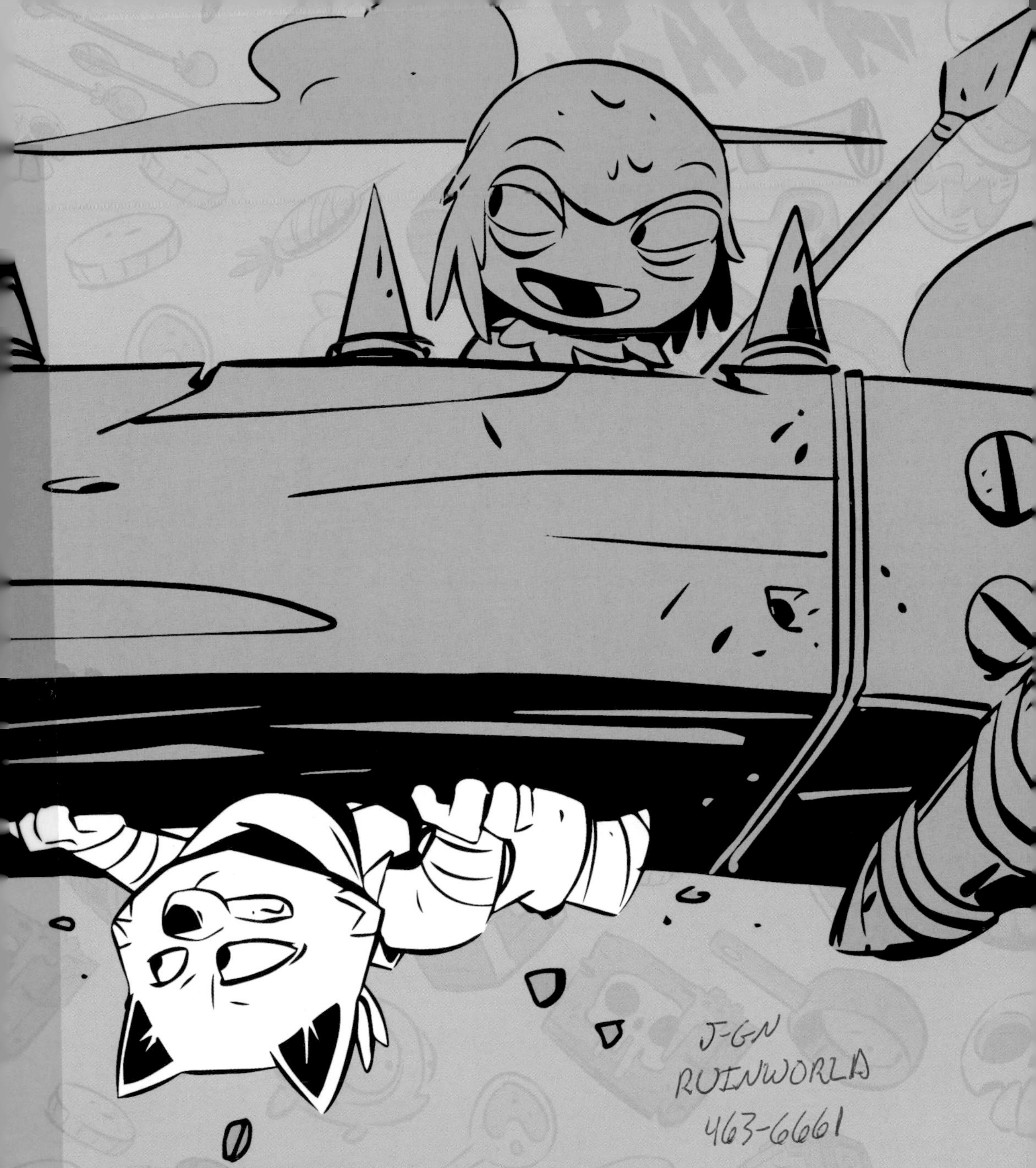

RUINWORLD IS DEDICATED TO MY AMAZING BOYS, BRODY AND OWEN, AND MY LOVING WIFE VALERIE.

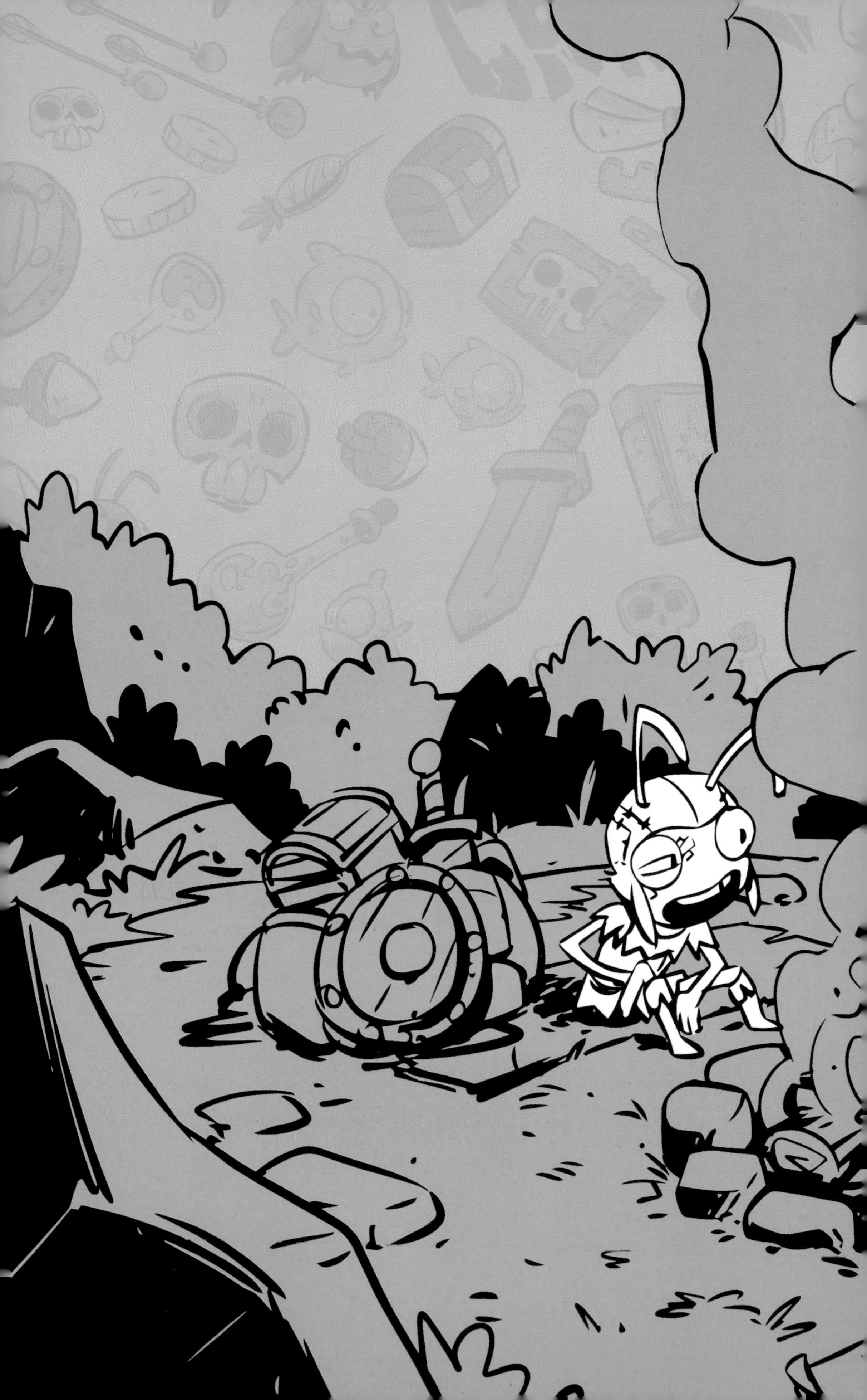

CREATED, WRITTEN & ILLUSTRATED BY
DEREK LAUFMAN

LETTERED BY
WARREN MONTGOMERY

COVER BY
DEREK LAUFMAN

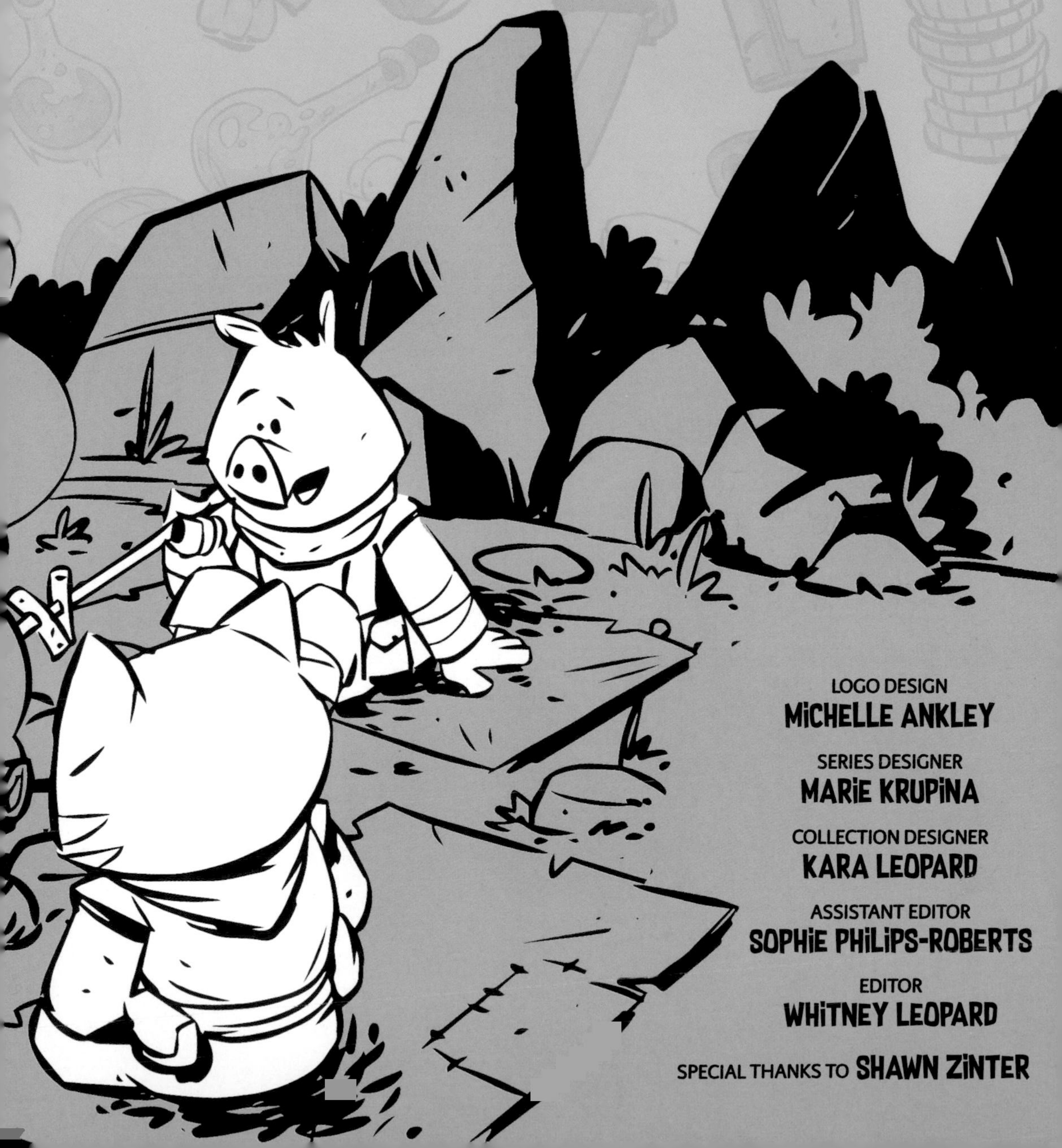

LOGO DESIGN
MICHELLE ANKLEY

SERIES DESIGNER
MARIE KRUPINA

COLLECTION DESIGNER
KARA LEOPARD

ASSISTANT EDITOR
SOPHIE PHILIPS-ROBERTS

EDITOR
WHITNEY LEOPARD

SPECIAL THANKS TO **SHAWN ZINTER**

ISSUE 1 COVER BY DEREK LAUFMAN

CHAPTER 1

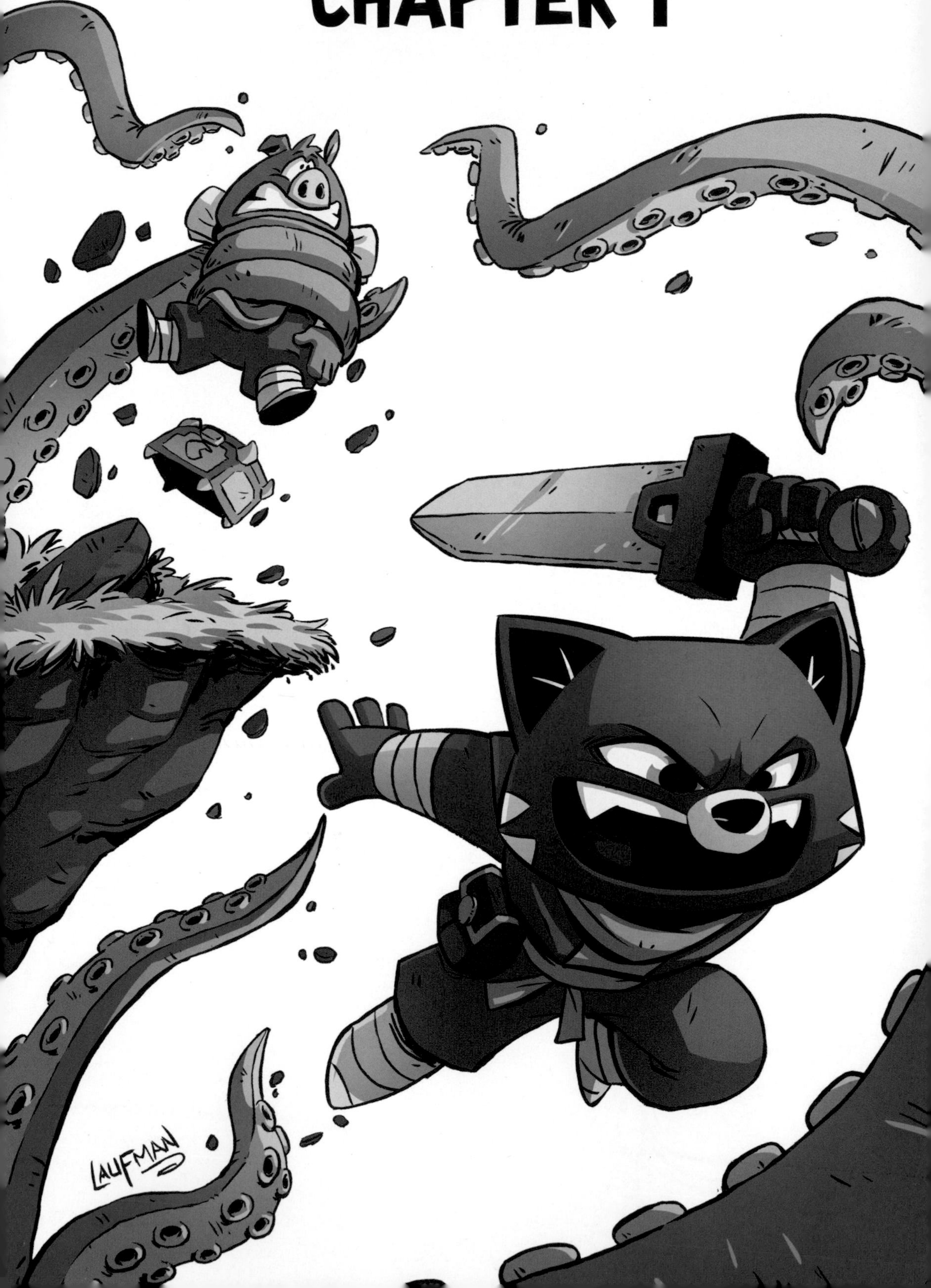
LAUFMAN

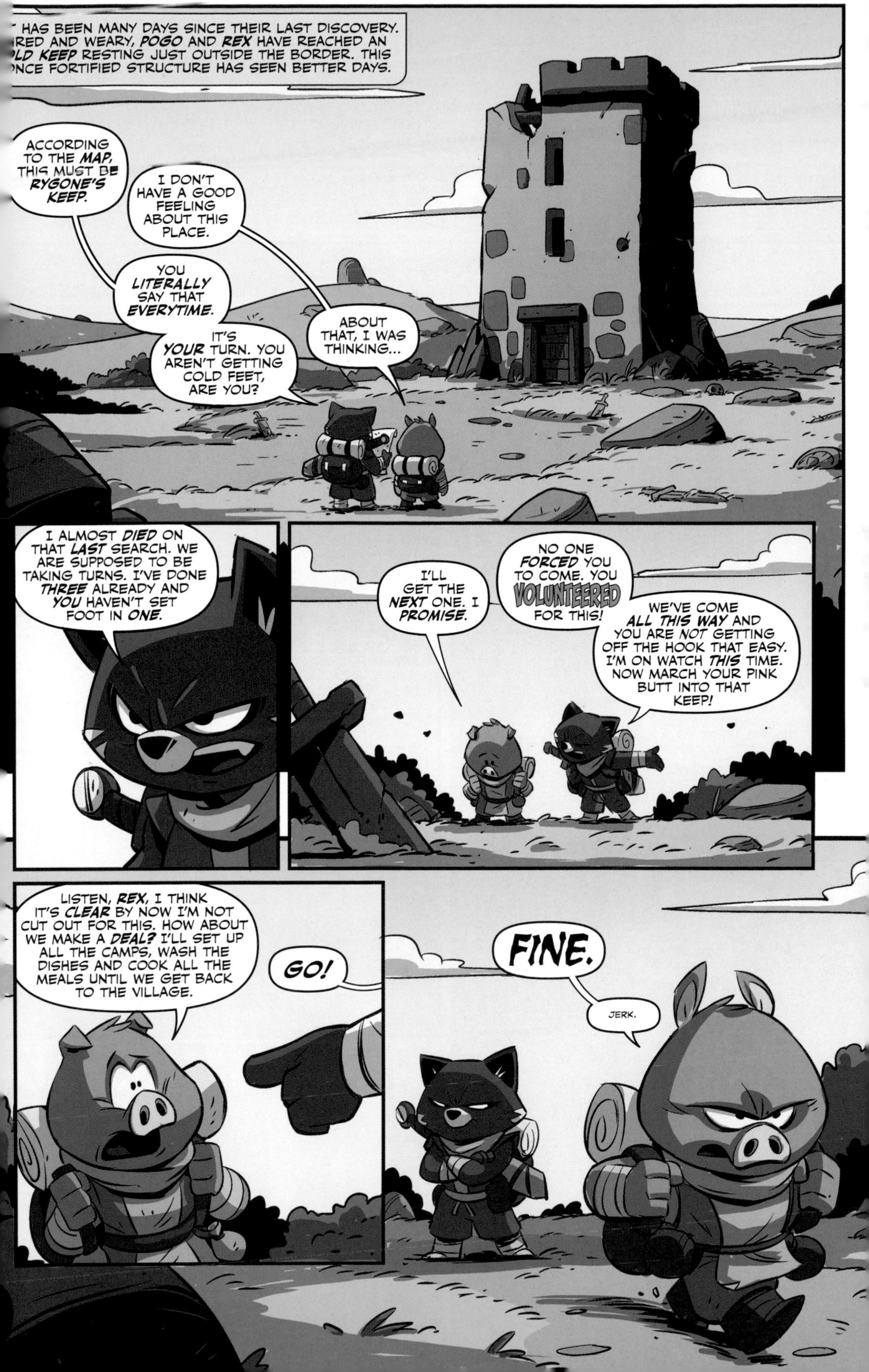
T HAS BEEN MANY DAYS SINCE THEIR LAST DISCOVERY. RED AND WEARY, POGO AND REX HAVE REACHED AN LD KEEP RESTING JUST OUTSIDE THE BORDER. THIS NCE FORTIFIED STRUCTURE HAS SEEN BETTER DAYS.
ACCORDING TO THE MAP, THIS MUST BE RYGONE'S KEEP.
I DON'T HAVE A GOOD FEELING ABOUT THIS PLACE.
YOU LITERALLY SAY THAT EVERYTIME.
IT'S YOUR TURN. YOU AREN'T GETTING COLD FEET, ARE YOU?
ABOUT THAT, I WAS THINKING...
I ALMOST DIED ON THAT LAST SEARCH. WE ARE SUPPOSED TO BE TAKING TURNS. I'VE DONE THREE ALREADY AND YOU HAVEN'T SET FOOT IN ONE.
I'LL GET THE NEXT ONE. I PROMISE.
NO ONE FORCED YOU TO COME. YOU VOLUNTEERED FOR THIS!
WE'VE COME ALL THIS WAY AND YOU ARE NOT GETTING OFF THE HOOK THAT EASY. I'M ON WATCH THIS TIME. NOW MARCH YOUR PINK BUTT INTO THAT KEEP!
LISTEN, REX, I THINK IT'S CLEAR BY NOW I'M NOT CUT OUT FOR THIS. HOW ABOUT WE MAKE A DEAL? I'LL SET UP ALL THE CAMPS, WASH THE DISHES AND COOK ALL THE MEALS UNTIL WE GET BACK TO THE VILLAGE.
GO!
FINE.
JERK.

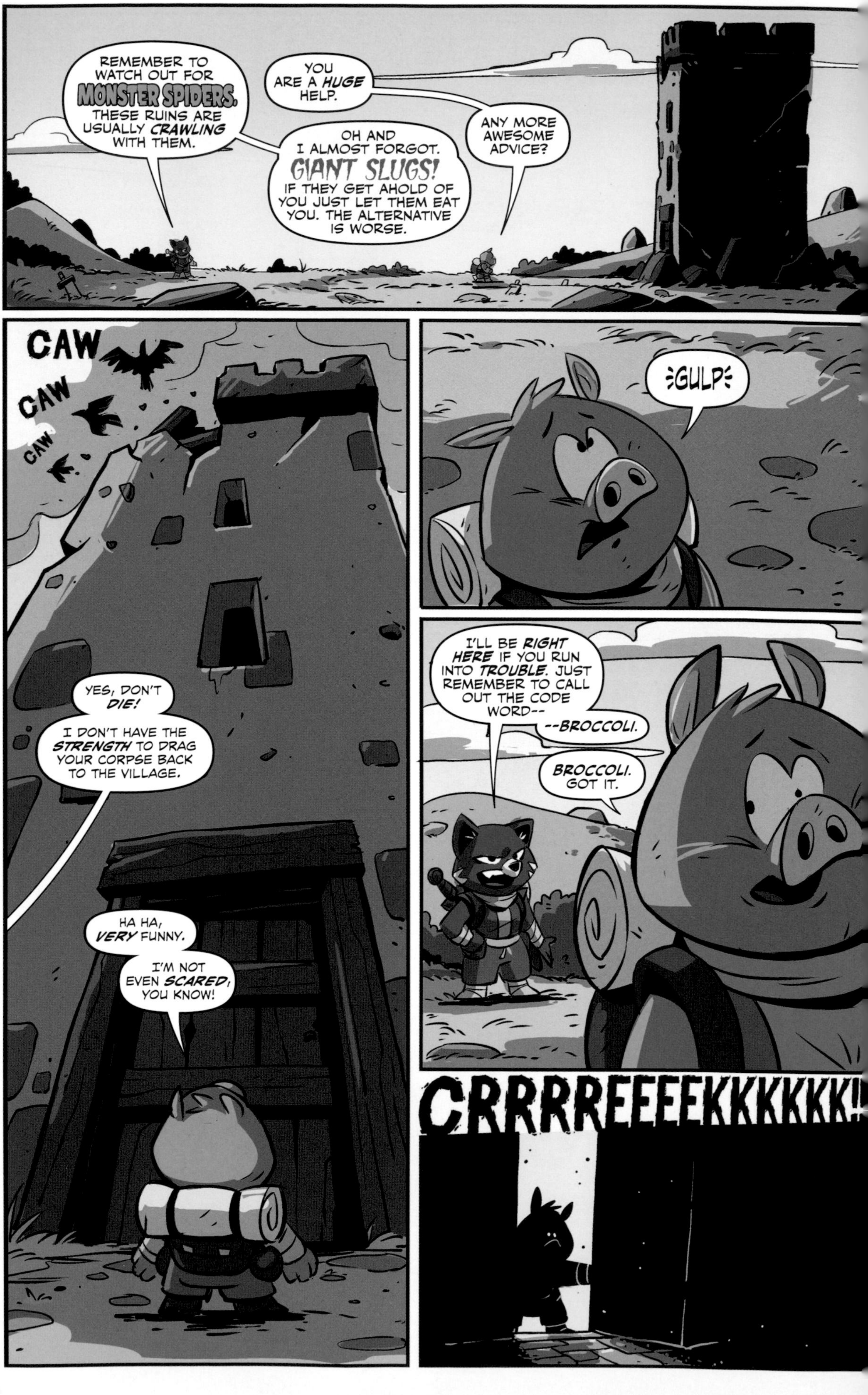
REMEMBER TO WATCH OUT FOR MONSTER SPIDERS. THESE RUINS ARE USUALLY CRAWLING WITH THEM.
OH AND I ALMOST FORGOT. GIANT SLUGS! IF THEY GET AHOLD OF YOU JUST LET THEM EAT YOU. THE ALTERNATIVE IS WORSE.
YOU ARE A HUGE HELP.
ANY MORE AWESOME ADVICE?
CAW
CAW
CAW
YES, DON'T DIE!
I DON'T HAVE THE STRENGTH TO DRAG YOUR CORPSE BACK TO THE VILLAGE.
HA HA, VERY FUNNY.
I'M NOT EVEN SCARED, YOU KNOW!
GULP
I'LL BE RIGHT HERE IF YOU RUN INTO TROUBLE. JUST REMEMBER TO CALL OUT THE CODE WORD--
--BROCCOLI.
BROCCOLI. GOT IT.
CRRRREEEEKKKKKK!!

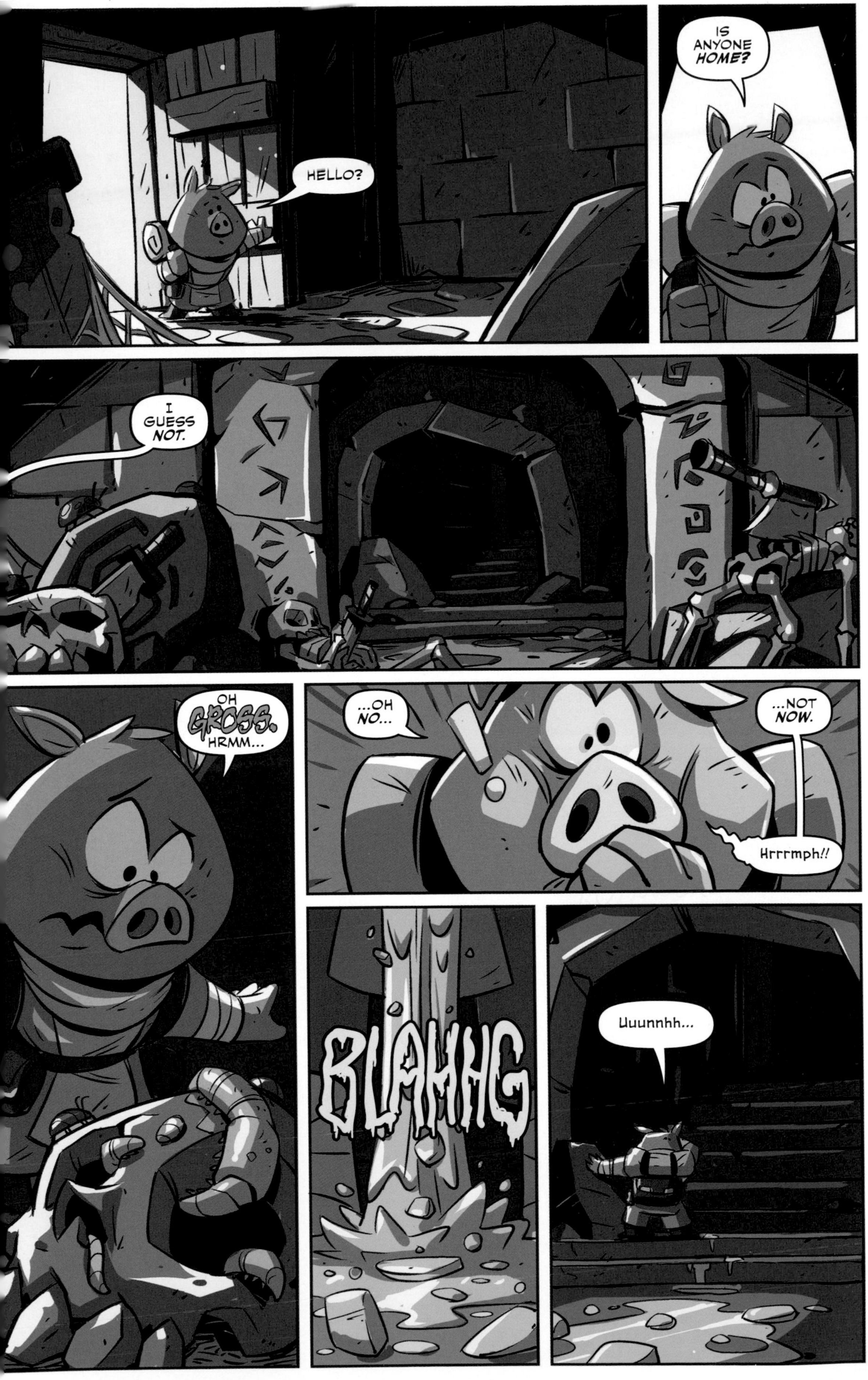
HELLO?
IS ANYONE HOME?
I GUESS NOT.
OH GROSS. HRMM...
...OH NO...
...NOT NOW.
Hrrrmph!!
BLAHHG
Uuunnhh...

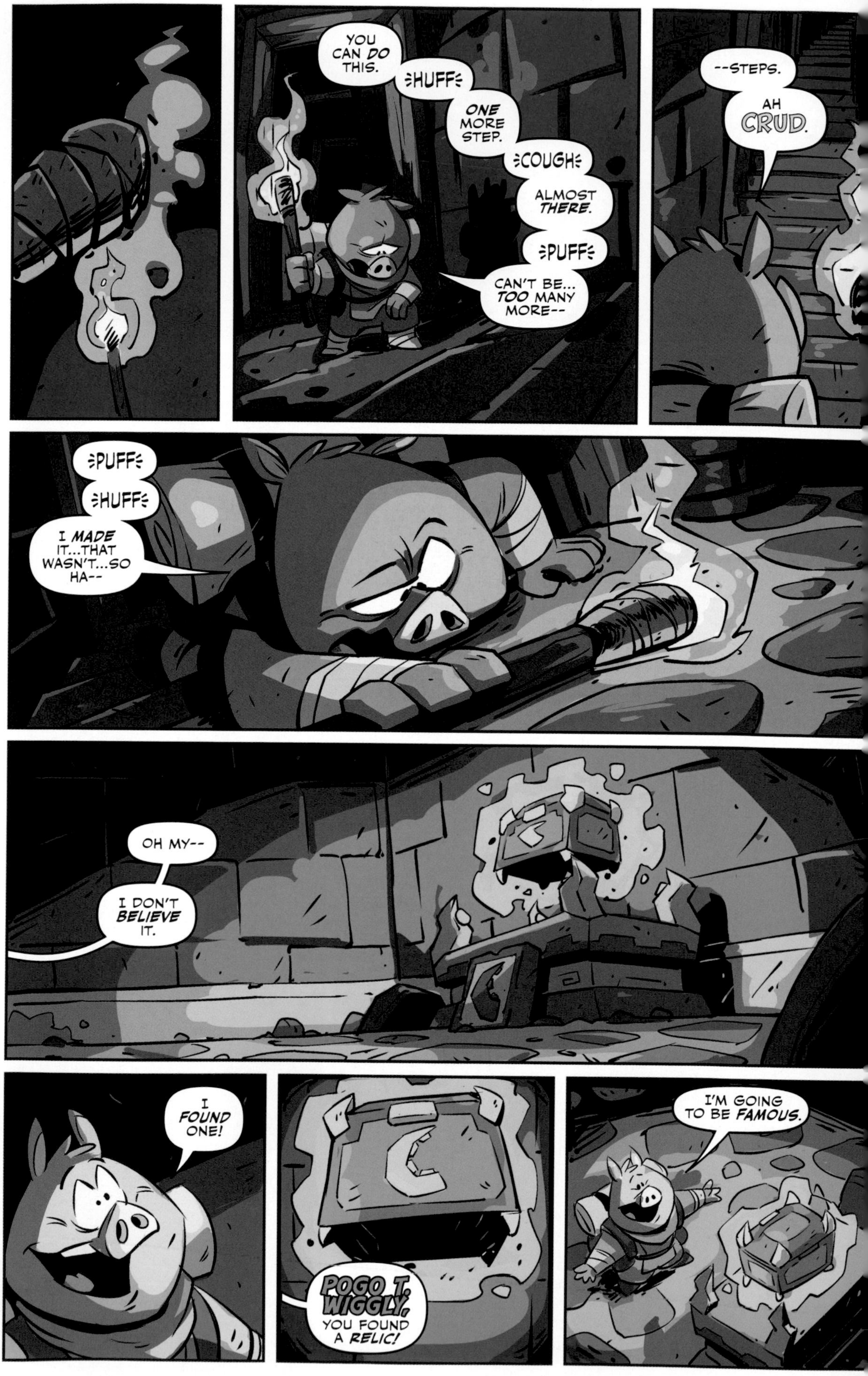
YOU CAN DO THIS.
HUFF
ONE MORE STEP.
COUGH
ALMOST THERE.
PUFF
CAN'T BE... TOO MANY MORE--
--STEPS.
AH CRUD.
PUFF
HUFF
I MADE IT...THAT WASN'T...SO HA--
OH MY--
I DON'T BELIEVE IT.
I FOUND ONE!
POGO T. WIGGLY, YOU FOUND A RELIC!
I'M GOING TO BE FAMOUS.

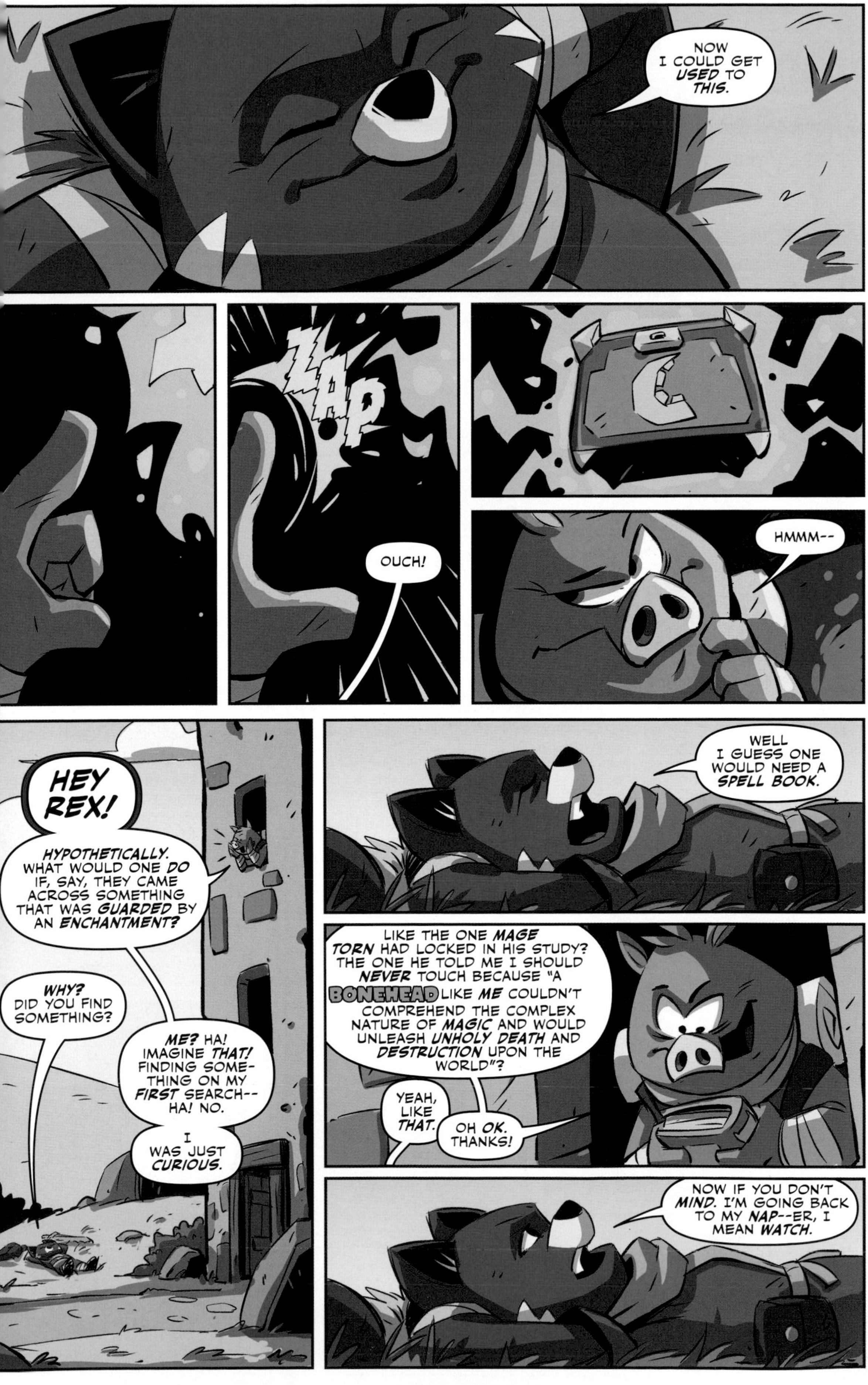
NOW I COULD GET USED TO THIS.
ZAP
OUCH!
HMMM--
HEY REX!
HYPOTHETICALLY. WHAT WOULD ONE DO IF, SAY, THEY CAME ACROSS SOMETHING THAT WAS GUARDED BY AN ENCHANTMENT?
WELL I GUESS ONE WOULD NEED A SPELL BOOK.
LIKE THE ONE MAGE TORN HAD LOCKED IN HIS STUDY? THE ONE HE TOLD ME I SHOULD NEVER TOUCH BECAUSE "A BONEHEAD LIKE ME COULDN'T COMPREHEND THE COMPLEX NATURE OF MAGIC AND WOULD UNLEASH UNHOLY DEATH AND DESTRUCTION UPON THE WORLD"?
YEAH, LIKE THAT.
OH OK. THANKS!
WHY? DID YOU FIND SOMETHING?
ME? HA! IMAGINE THAT! FINDING SOMETHING ON MY FIRST SEARCH-- HA! NO.
I WAS JUST CURIOUS.
NOW IF YOU DON'T MIND. I'M GOING BACK TO MY NAP--ER, I MEAN WATCH.

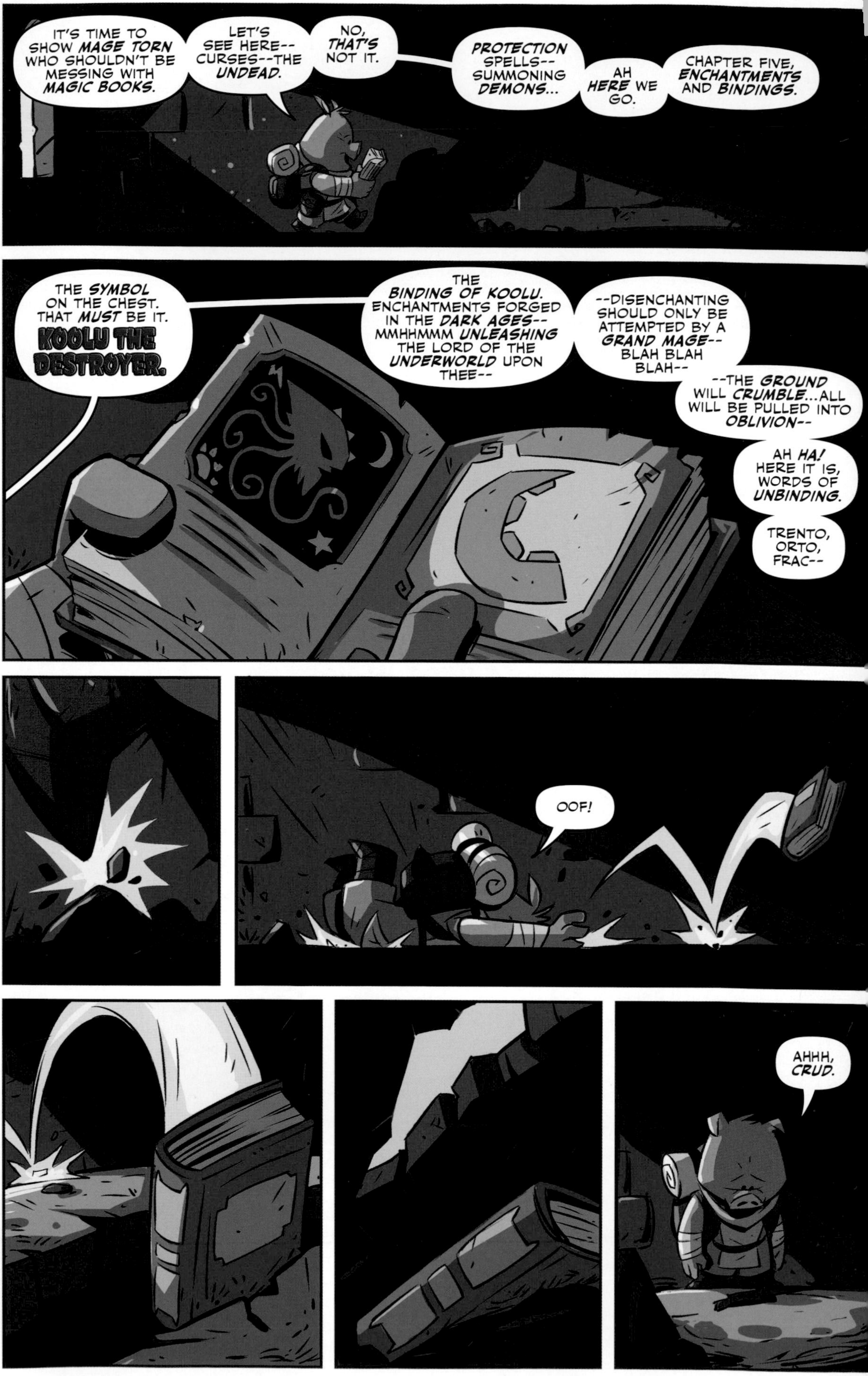
IT'S TIME TO SHOW MAGE TORN WHO SHOULDN'T BE MESSING WITH MAGIC BOOKS.
LET'S SEE HERE-- CURSES--THE UNDEAD.
NO, THAT'S NOT IT.
PROTECTION SPELLS-- SUMMONING DEMONS...
AH HERE WE GO.
CHAPTER FIVE, ENCHANTMENTS AND BINDINGS.
THE SYMBOL ON THE CHEST. THAT MUST BE IT. KOOLU THE DESTROYER.
THE BINDING OF KOOLU. ENCHANTMENTS FORGED IN THE DARK AGES-- MMHHMMM UNLEASHING THE LORD OF THE UNDERWORLD UPON THEE--
--DISENCHANTING SHOULD ONLY BE ATTEMPTED BY A GRAND MAGE-- BLAH BLAH BLAH--
--THE GROUND WILL CRUMBLE...ALL WILL BE PULLED INTO OBLIVION--
AH HA! HERE IT IS, WORDS OF UNBINDING.
TRENTO, ORTO, FRAC--
OOF!
AHHH, CRUD.

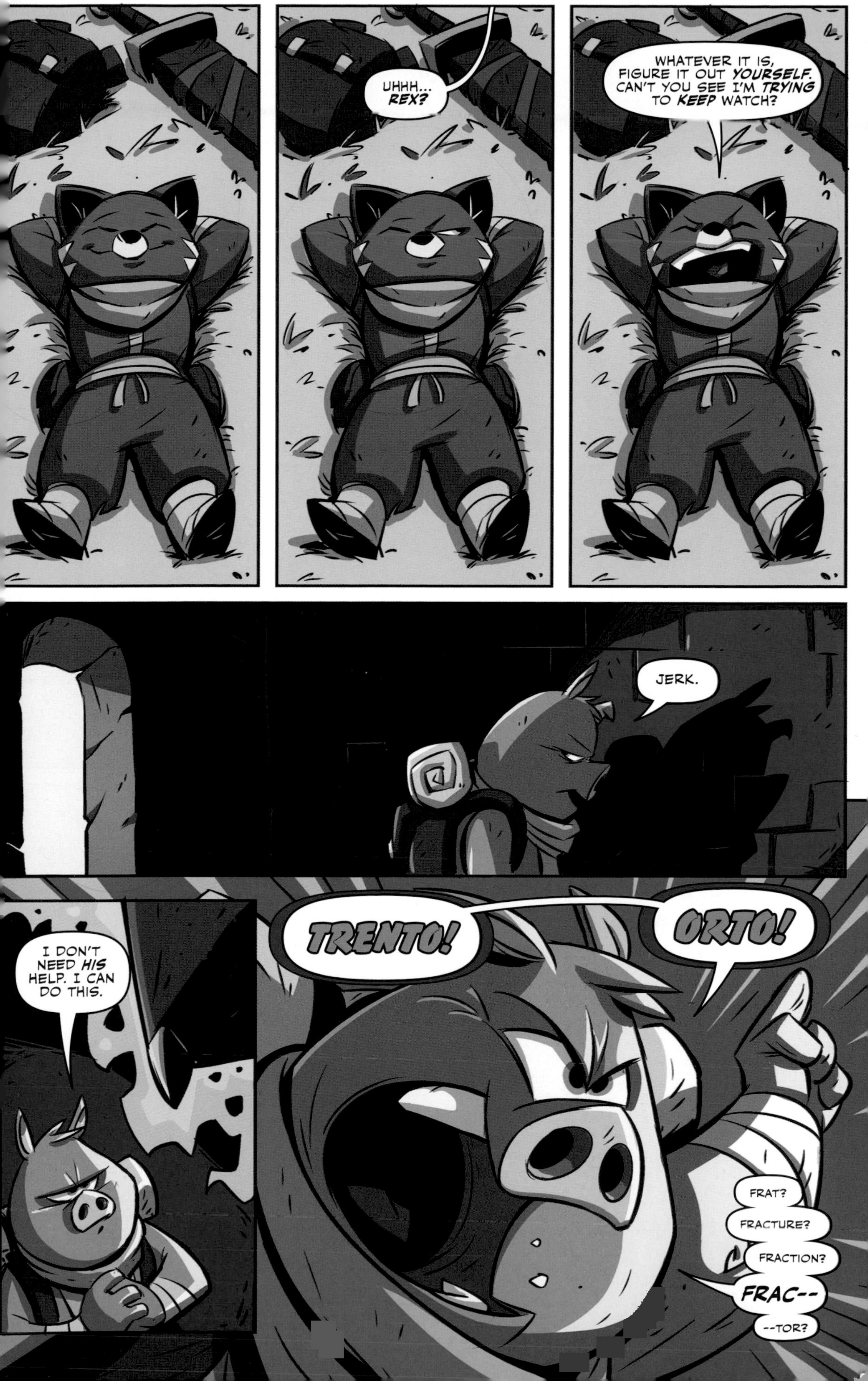
UHHH... REX?
WHATEVER IT IS, FIGURE IT OUT YOURSELF. CAN'T YOU SEE I'M TRYING TO KEEP WATCH?
JERK.
I DON'T NEED HIS HELP. I CAN DO THIS.
TRENTO!
ORTO!
FRAT?
FRACTURE?
FRACTION?
FRAC--
--TOR?

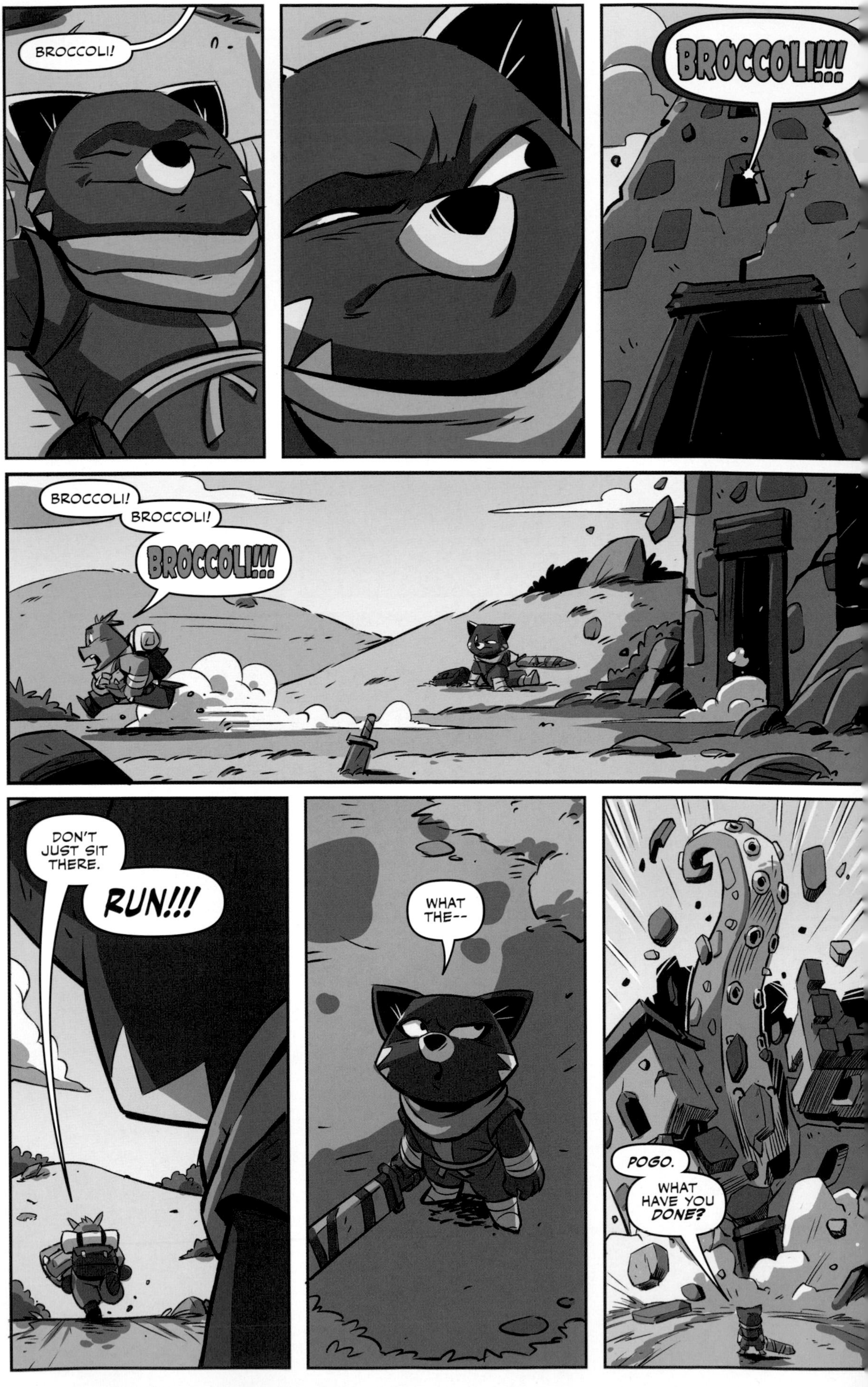
BROCCOLI!
BROCCOLI!!!
BROCCOLI!
BROCCOLI!
BROCCOLI!!!
DON'T JUST SIT THERE.
RUN!!!
WHAT THE--
POGO.
WHAT HAVE YOU DONE?

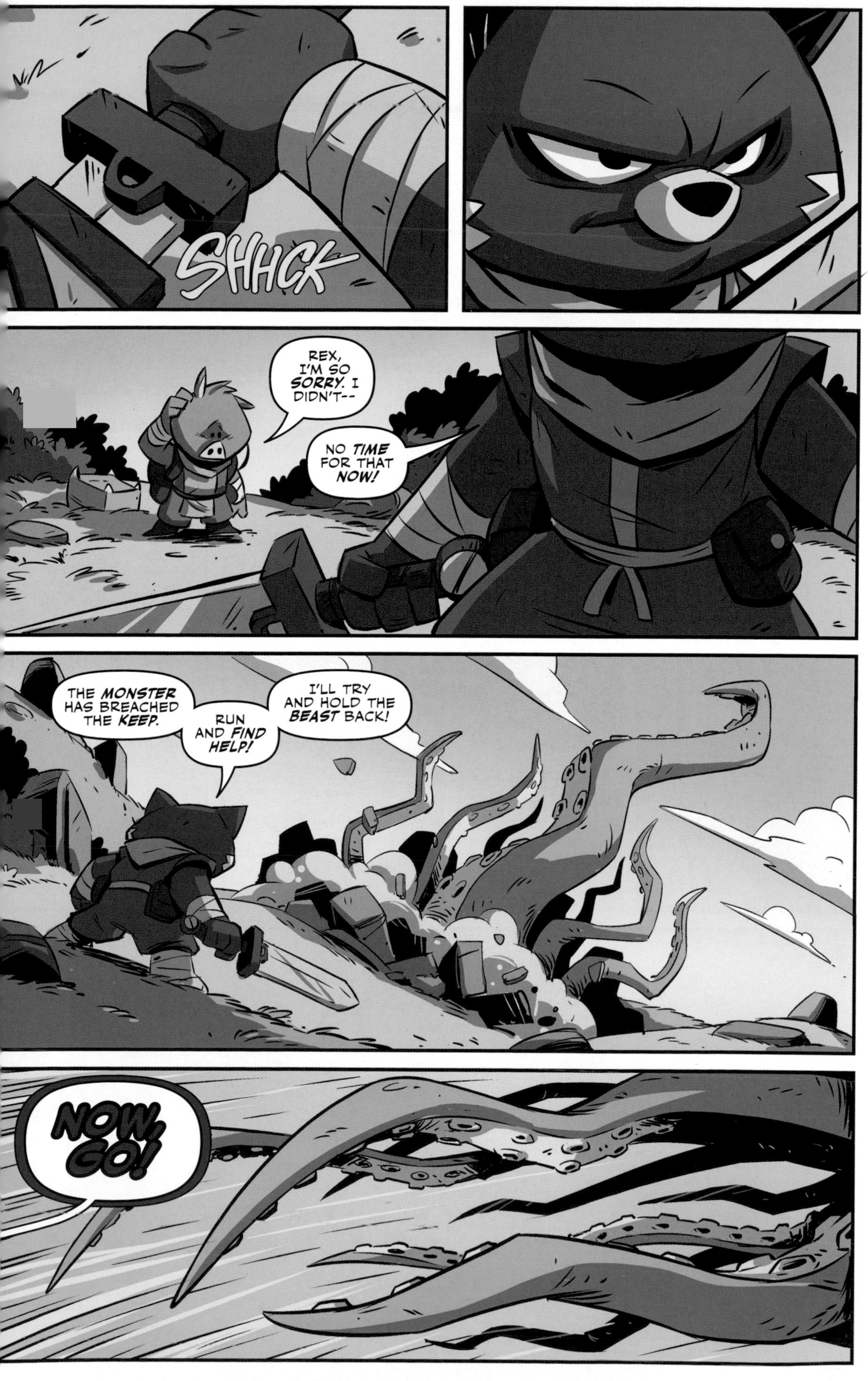
SHHCK
REX, I'M SO SORRY. I DIDN'T--
NO TIME FOR THAT NOW!
THE MONSTER HAS BREACHED THE KEEP.
RUN AND FIND HELP!
I'LL TRY AND HOLD THE BEAST BACK!
NOW, GO!

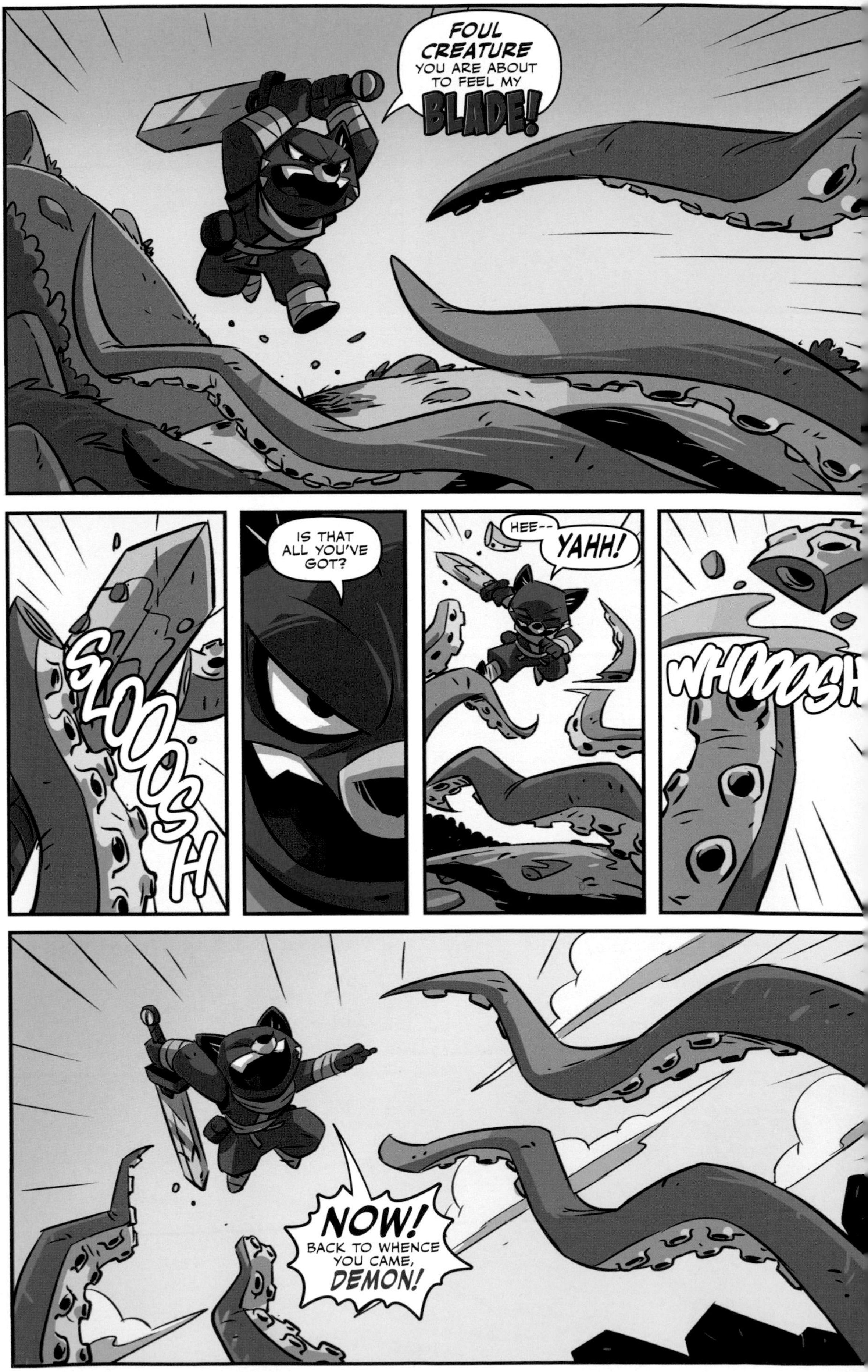
FOUL CREATURE YOU ARE ABOUT TO FEEL MY BLADE!
SLOOOSH
IS THAT ALL YOU'VE GOT?
HEE--
YAHH!
WHOOOOSH
NOW! BACK TO WHENCE YOU CAME, DEMON!

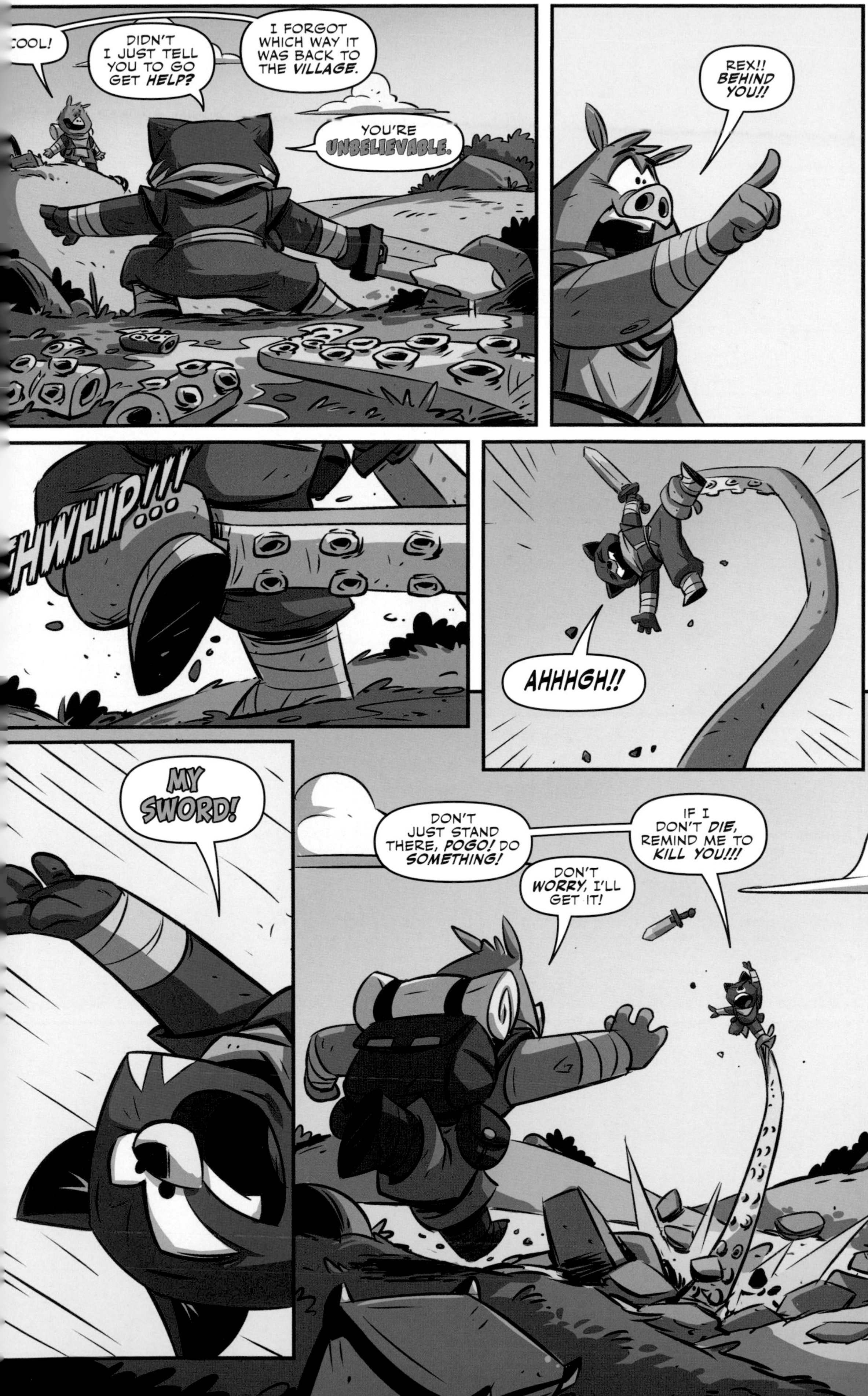
COOL!
DIDN'T I JUST TELL YOU TO GO GET *HELP?*
I FORGOT WHICH WAY IT WAS BACK TO THE *VILLAGE*.
YOU'RE UNBELIEVABLE.
REX!! *BEHIND YOU!!*
HWHIP!!!
AHHHGH!!
MY SWORD!
DON'T JUST STAND THERE, *POGO!* DO *SOMETHING!*
IF I DON'T *DIE*, REMIND ME TO *KILL YOU!!!*
DON'T *WORRY*, I'LL GET IT!

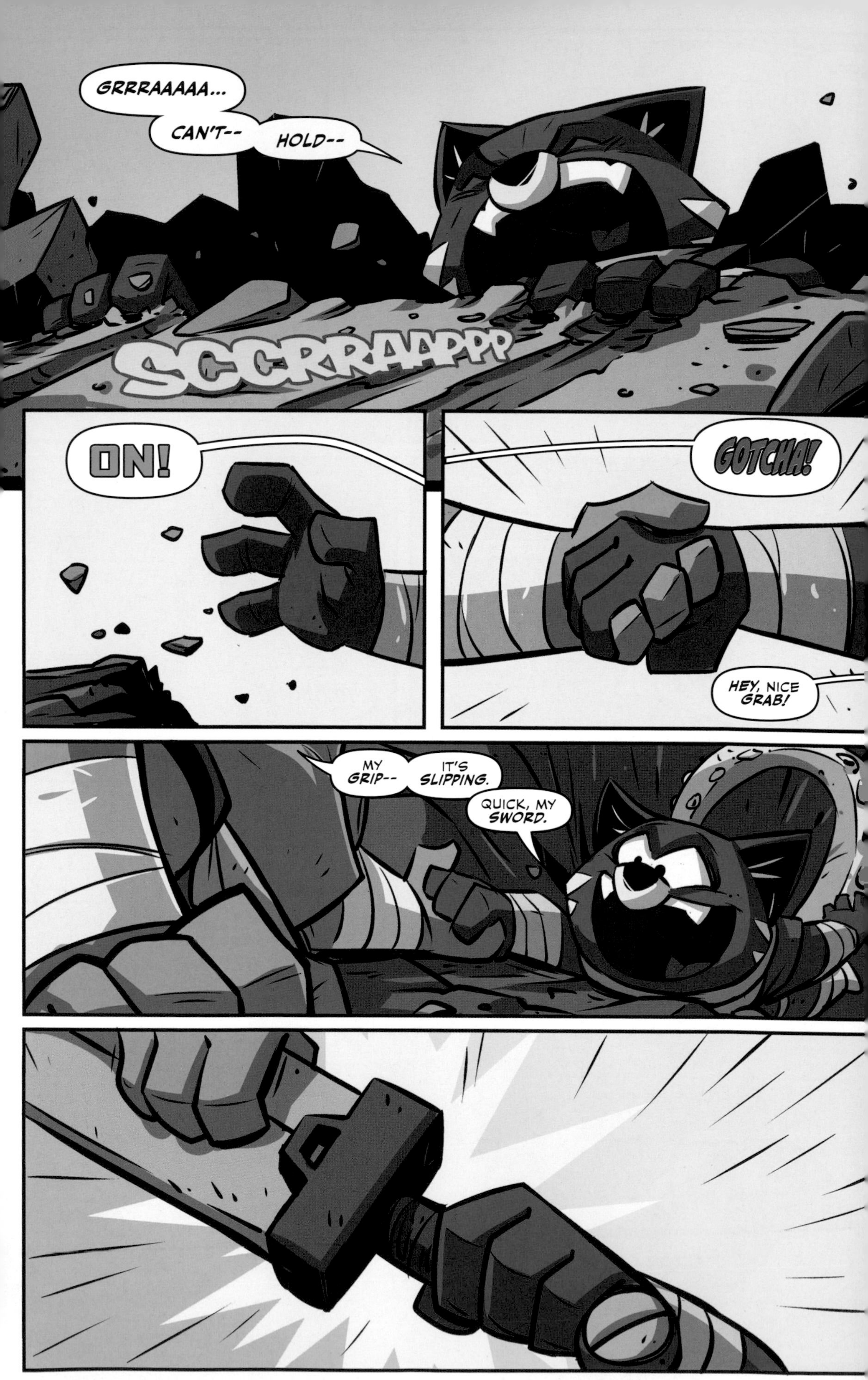
GRRRAAAAA...
CAN'T--
HOLD--
SCCRRAAPPP
ON!
GOTCHA!
HEY, NICE GRAB!
MY GRIP--
IT'S SLIPPING.
QUICK, MY SWORD.

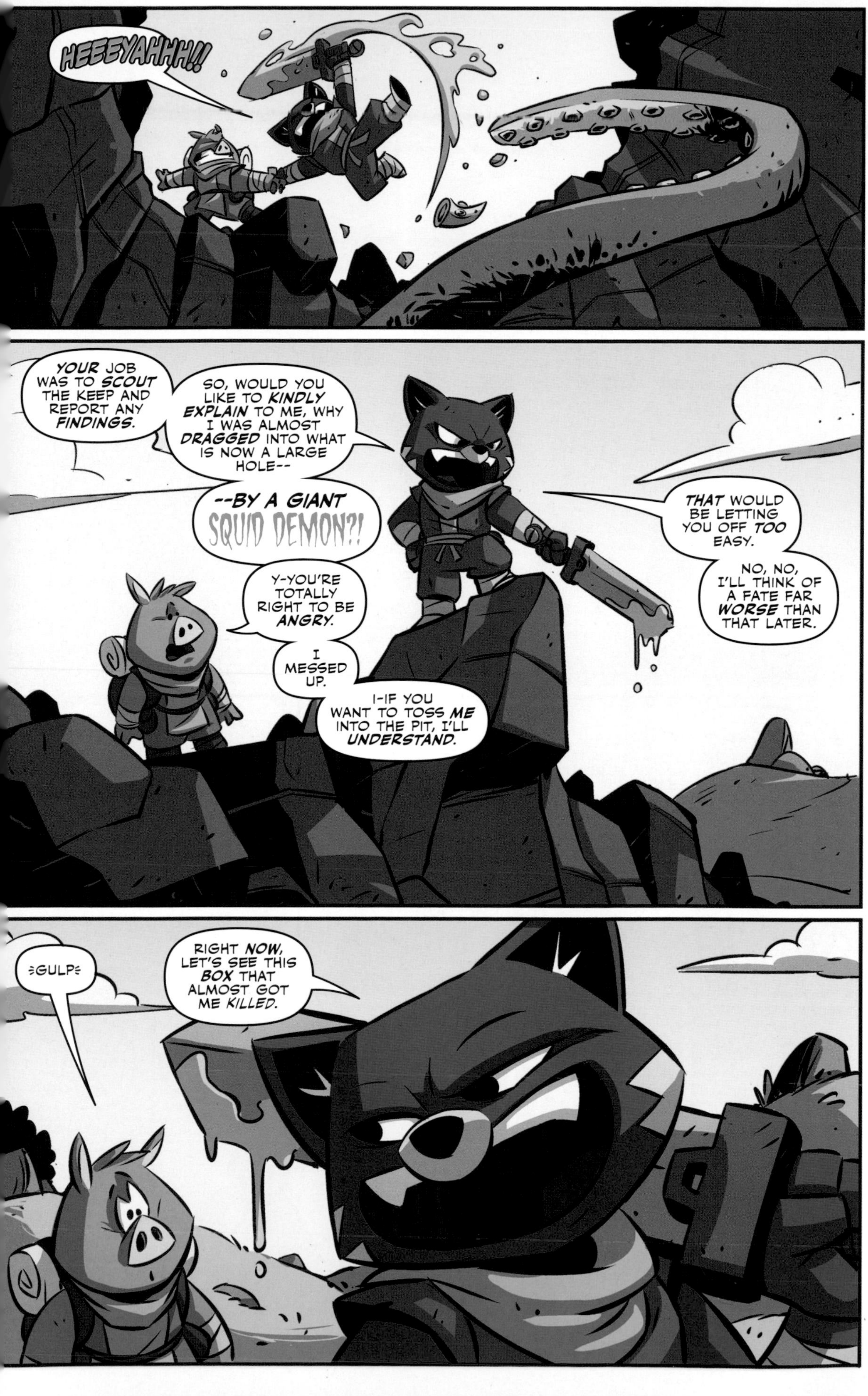
HEEEYAHHH!!
YOUR JOB WAS TO SCOUT THE KEEP AND REPORT ANY FINDINGS.
SO, WOULD YOU LIKE TO KINDLY EXPLAIN TO ME, WHY I WAS ALMOST DRAGGED INTO WHAT IS NOW A LARGE HOLE--
--BY A GIANT SQUID DEMON?!
Y-YOU'RE TOTALLY RIGHT TO BE ANGRY.
I MESSED UP.
I-IF YOU WANT TO TOSS ME INTO THE PIT, I'LL UNDERSTAND.
THAT WOULD BE LETTING YOU OFF TOO EASY.
NO, NO, I'LL THINK OF A FATE FAR WORSE THAN THAT LATER.
GULP
RIGHT NOW, LET'S SEE THIS BOX THAT ALMOST GOT ME KILLED.

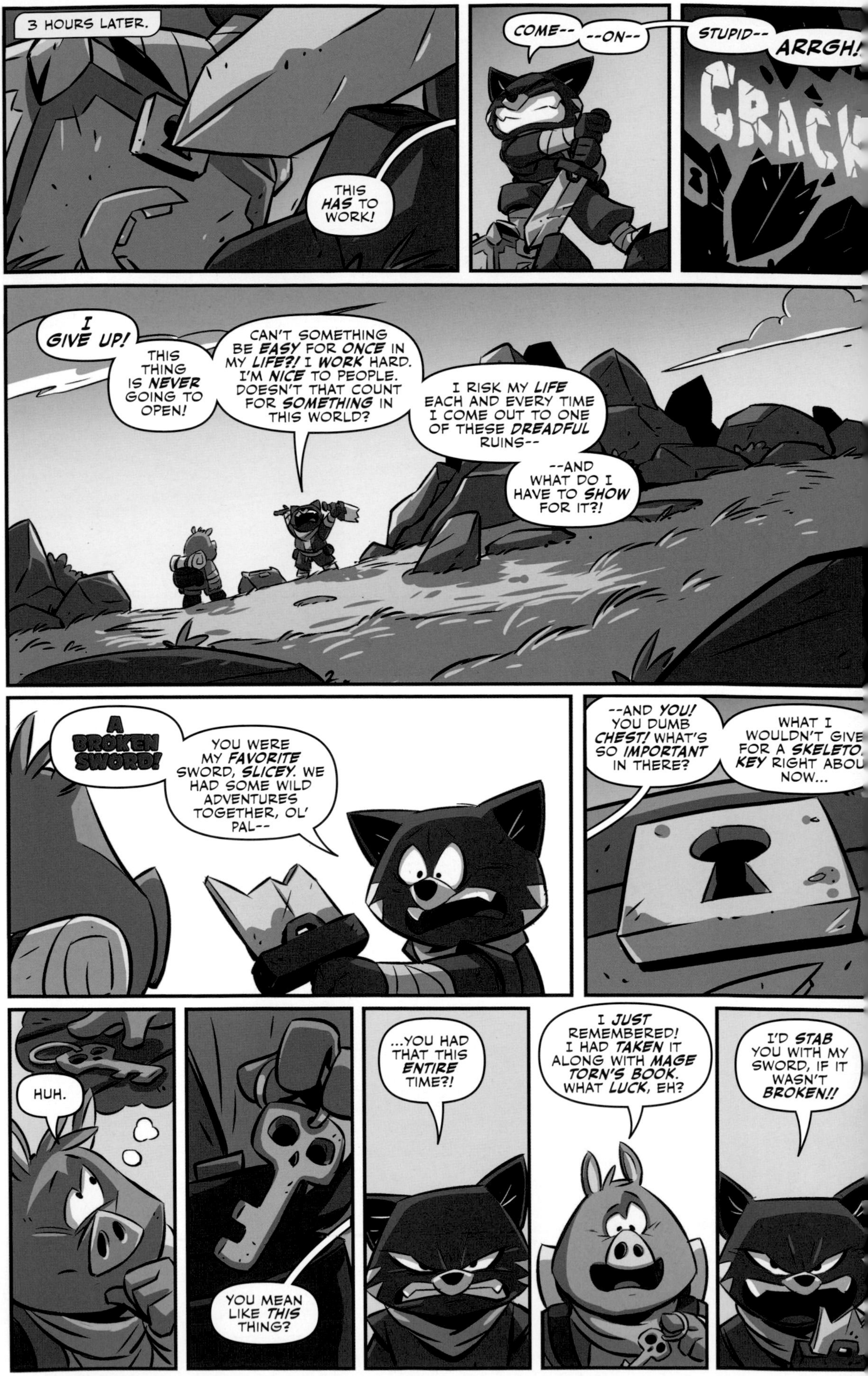
3 HOURS LATER.
THIS HAS TO WORK!
COME-- --ON--
STUPID-- ARRGH!
CRACK
I GIVE UP!
THIS THING IS NEVER GOING TO OPEN!
CAN'T SOMETHING BE EASY FOR ONCE IN MY LIFE?! I WORK HARD. I'M NICE TO PEOPLE. DOESN'T THAT COUNT FOR SOMETHING IN THIS WORLD?
I RISK MY LIFE EACH AND EVERY TIME I COME OUT TO ONE OF THESE DREADFUL RUINS--
--AND WHAT DO I HAVE TO SHOW FOR IT?!
A BROKEN SWORD!
YOU WERE MY FAVORITE SWORD, SLICEY. WE HAD SOME WILD ADVENTURES TOGETHER, OL' PAL--
--AND YOU! YOU DUMB CHEST! WHAT'S SO IMPORTANT IN THERE?
WHAT I WOULDN'T GIVE FOR A SKELETO KEY RIGHT ABOU NOW...
HUH.
YOU MEAN LIKE THIS THING?
...YOU HAD THAT THIS ENTIRE TIME?!
I JUST REMEMBERED! I HAD TAKEN IT ALONG WITH MAGE TORN'S BOOK. WHAT LUCK, EH?
I'D STAB YOU WITH MY SWORD, IF IT WASN'T BROKEN!!

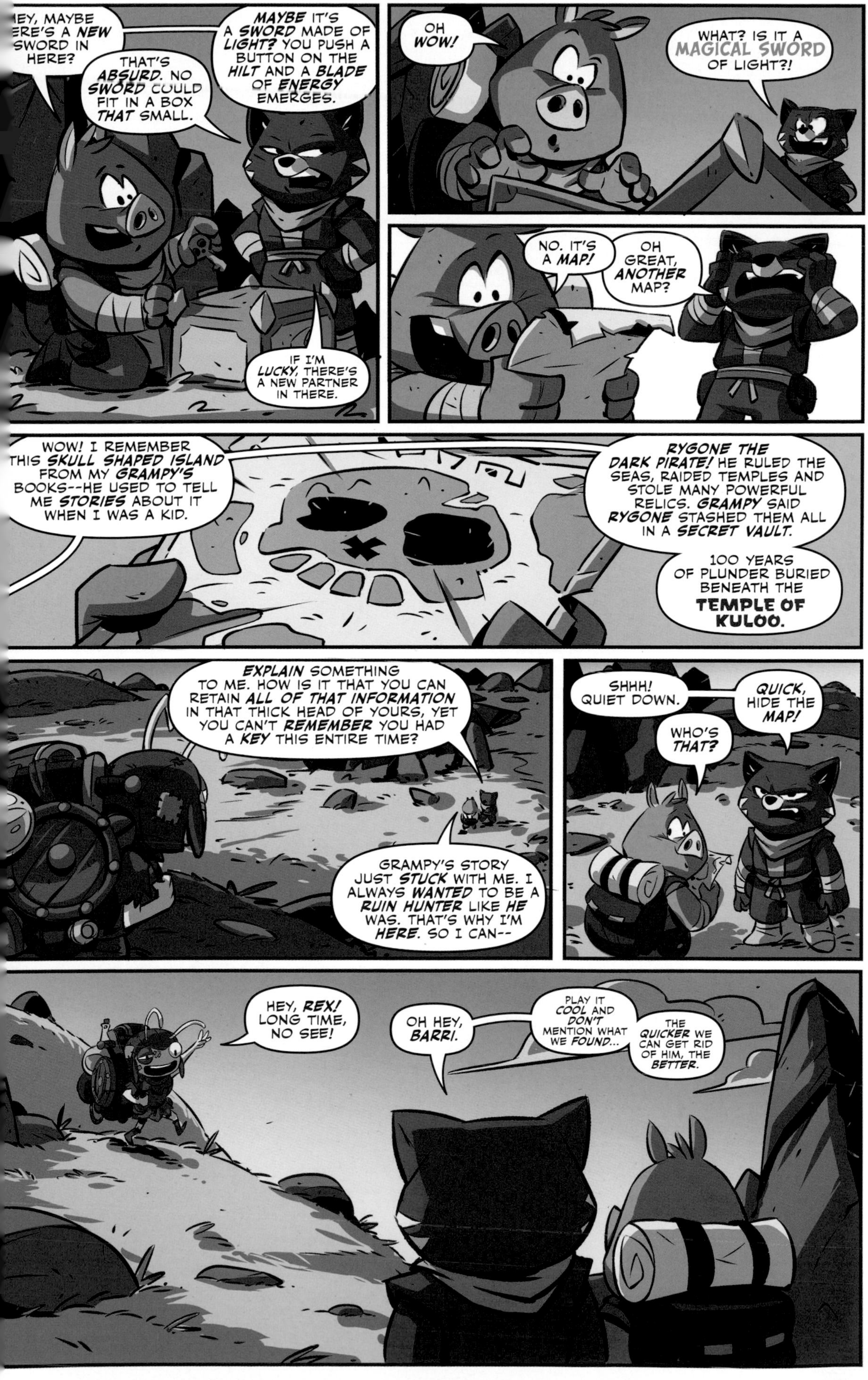

EY, MAYBE ERE'S A NEW SWORD IN HERE?
THAT'S ABSURD. NO SWORD COULD FIT IN A BOX THAT SMALL.
MAYBE IT'S A SWORD MADE OF LIGHT? YOU PUSH A BUTTON ON THE HILT AND A BLADE OF ENERGY EMERGES.
IF I'M LUCKY, THERE'S A NEW PARTNER IN THERE.
OH WOW!
WHAT? IS IT A MAGICAL SWORD OF LIGHT?!
NO. IT'S A MAP!
OH GREAT, ANOTHER MAP?
WOW! I REMEMBER THIS SKULL SHAPED ISLAND FROM MY GRAMPY'S BOOKS--HE USED TO TELL ME STORIES ABOUT IT WHEN I WAS A KID.
RYGONE THE DARK PIRATE! HE RULED THE SEAS, RAIDED TEMPLES AND STOLE MANY POWERFUL RELICS. GRAMPY SAID RYGONE STASHED THEM ALL IN A SECRET VAULT.
100 YEARS OF PLUNDER BURIED BENEATH THE TEMPLE OF KULOO.
EXPLAIN SOMETHING TO ME. HOW IS IT THAT YOU CAN RETAIN ALL OF THAT INFORMATION IN THAT THICK HEAD OF YOURS, YET YOU CAN'T REMEMBER YOU HAD A KEY THIS ENTIRE TIME?
GRAMPY'S STORY JUST STUCK WITH ME. I ALWAYS WANTED TO BE A RUIN HUNTER LIKE HE WAS. THAT'S WHY I'M HERE. SO I CAN--
SHHH! QUIET DOWN.
QUICK, HIDE THE MAP!
WHO'S THAT?
HEY, REX! LONG TIME, NO SEE!
OH HEY, BARRI.
PLAY IT COOL AND DON'T MENTION WHAT WE FOUND...
THE QUICKER WE CAN GET RID OF HIM, THE BETTER.

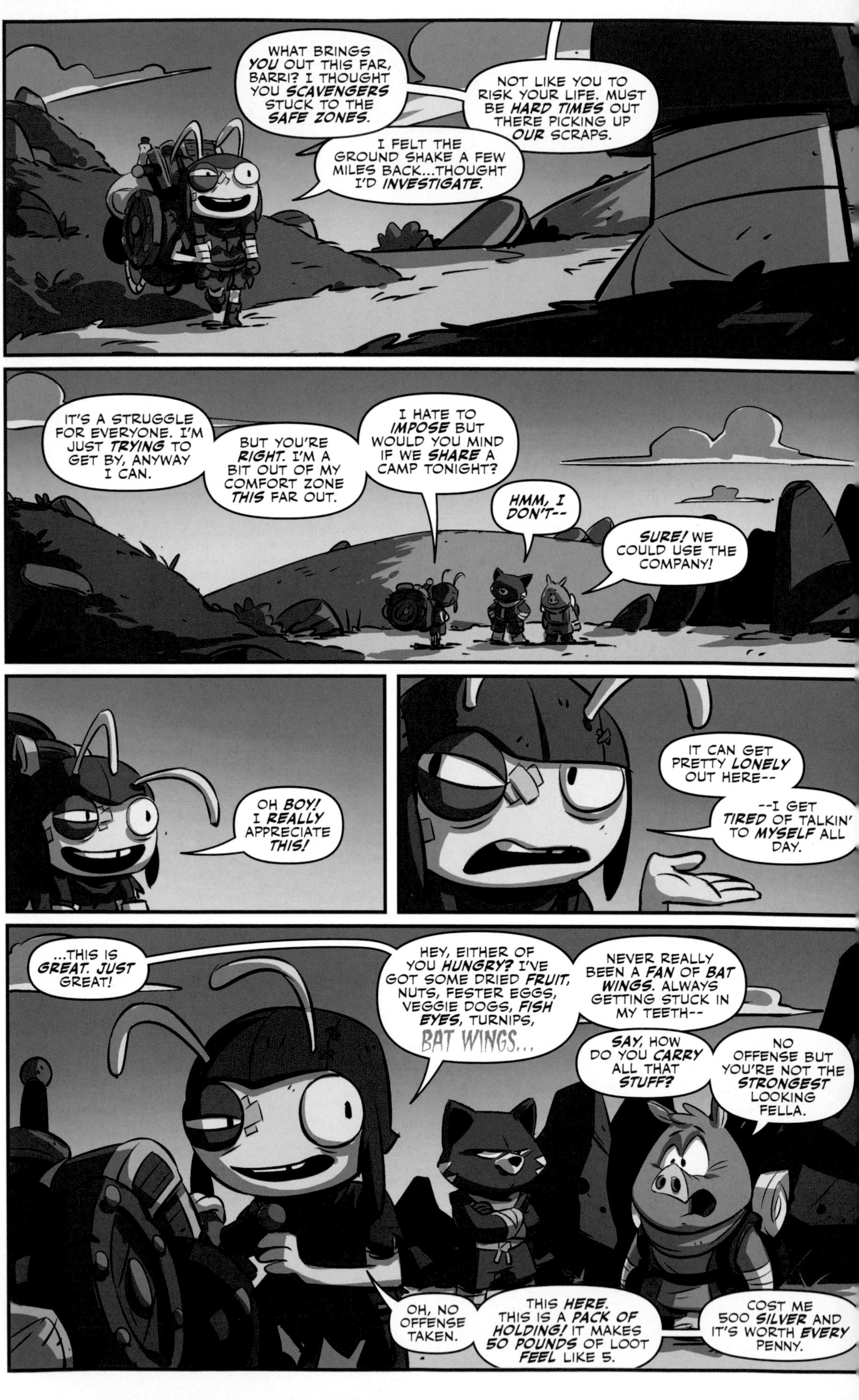
WHAT BRINGS YOU OUT THIS FAR, BARRI? I THOUGHT YOU SCAVENGERS STUCK TO THE SAFE ZONES.
NOT LIKE YOU TO RISK YOUR LIFE. MUST BE HARD TIMES OUT THERE PICKING UP OUR SCRAPS.
I FELT THE GROUND SHAKE A FEW MILES BACK...THOUGHT I'D INVESTIGATE.
IT'S A STRUGGLE FOR EVERYONE. I'M JUST TRYING TO GET BY, ANYWAY I CAN.
BUT YOU'RE RIGHT. I'M A BIT OUT OF MY COMFORT ZONE THIS FAR OUT.
I HATE TO IMPOSE BUT WOULD YOU MIND IF WE SHARE A CAMP TONIGHT?
HMM, I DON'T--
SURE! WE COULD USE THE COMPANY!
OH BOY! I REALLY APPRECIATE THIS!
IT CAN GET PRETTY LONELY OUT HERE--
--I GET TIRED OF TALKIN' TO MYSELF ALL DAY.
...THIS IS GREAT. JUST GREAT!
HEY, EITHER OF YOU HUNGRY? I'VE GOT SOME DRIED FRUIT, NUTS, FESTER EGGS, VEGGIE DOGS, FISH EYES, TURNIPS, BAT WINGS...
NEVER REALLY BEEN A FAN OF BAT WINGS. ALWAYS GETTING STUCK IN MY TEETH--
SAY, HOW DO YOU CARRY ALL THAT STUFF?
NO OFFENSE BUT YOU'RE NOT THE STRONGEST LOOKING FELLA.
OH, NO OFFENSE TAKEN.
THIS HERE. THIS IS A PACK OF HOLDING! IT MAKES 50 POUNDS OF LOOT FEEL LIKE 5.
COST ME 500 SILVER AND IT'S WORTH EVERY PENNY.

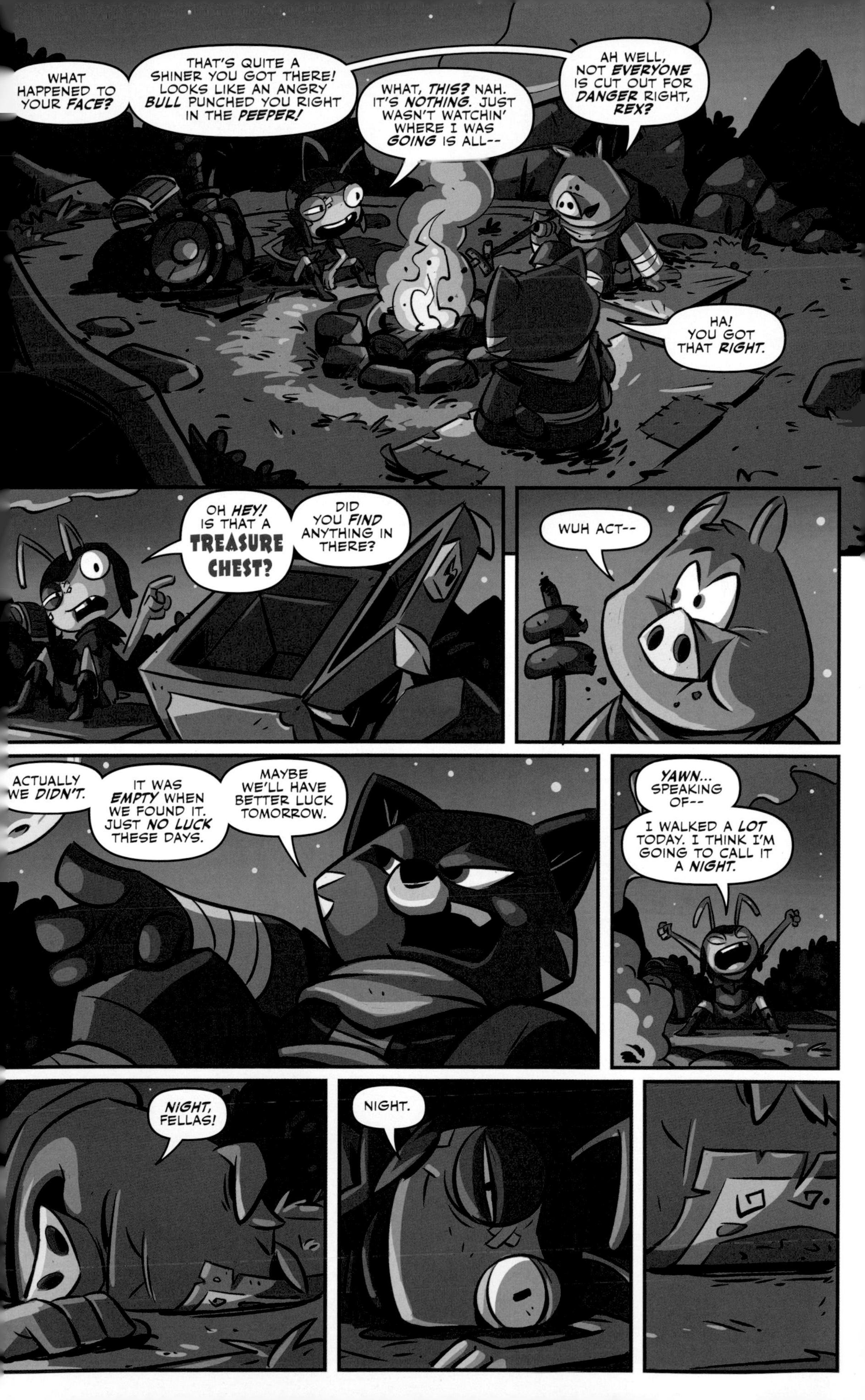
WHAT HAPPENED TO YOUR *FACE?*
THAT'S QUITE A SHINER YOU GOT THERE! LOOKS LIKE AN ANGRY *BULL* PUNCHED YOU RIGHT IN THE *PEEPER!*
WHAT, *THIS?* NAH. IT'S *NOTHING*. JUST WASN'T WATCHIN' WHERE I WAS *GOING* IS ALL--
AH WELL, NOT *EVERYONE* IS CUT OUT FOR *DANGER* RIGHT, *REX?*
HA! YOU GOT THAT *RIGHT*.
OH *HEY!* IS THAT A **TREASURE CHEST?**
DID YOU *FIND* ANYTHING IN THERE?
WUH ACT--
ACTUALLY WE *DIDN'T*.
IT WAS *EMPTY* WHEN WE FOUND IT. JUST *NO LUCK* THESE DAYS.
MAYBE WE'LL HAVE BETTER LUCK TOMORROW.
YAWN... SPEAKING OF--
I WALKED A *LOT* TODAY. I THINK I'M GOING TO CALL IT A *NIGHT*.
NIGHT, FELLAS!
NIGHT.

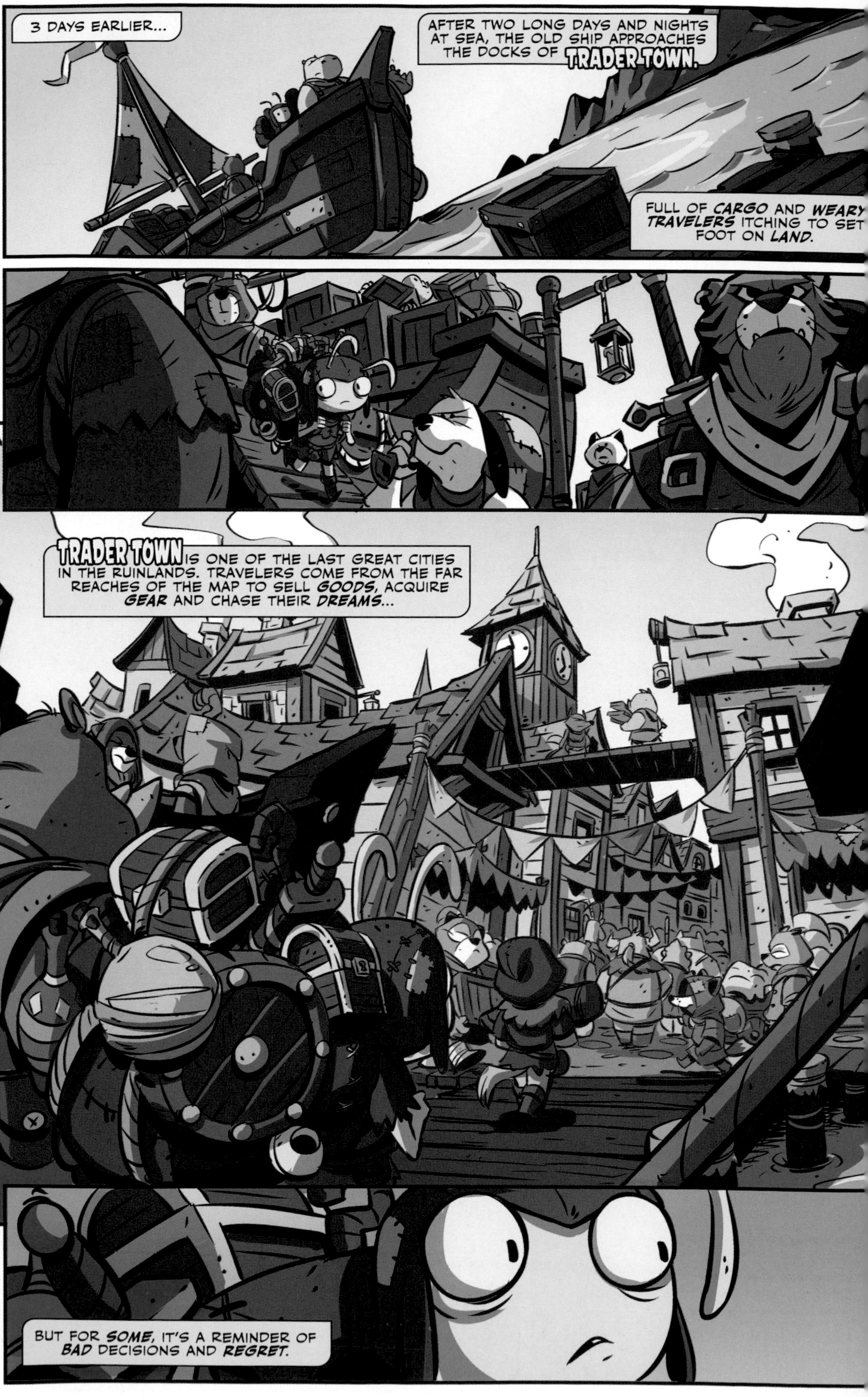
3 DAYS EARLIER...
AFTER TWO LONG DAYS AND NIGHTS AT SEA, THE OLD SHIP APPROACHES THE DOCKS OF TRADER TOWN.
FULL OF CARGO AND WEARY TRAVELERS ITCHING TO SET FOOT ON LAND.
TRADER TOWN IS ONE OF THE LAST GREAT CITIES IN THE RUINLANDS. TRAVELERS COME FROM THE FAR REACHES OF THE MAP TO SELL GOODS, ACQUIRE GEAR AND CHASE THEIR DREAMS...
BUT FOR SOME, IT'S A REMINDER OF BAD DECISIONS AND REGRET.

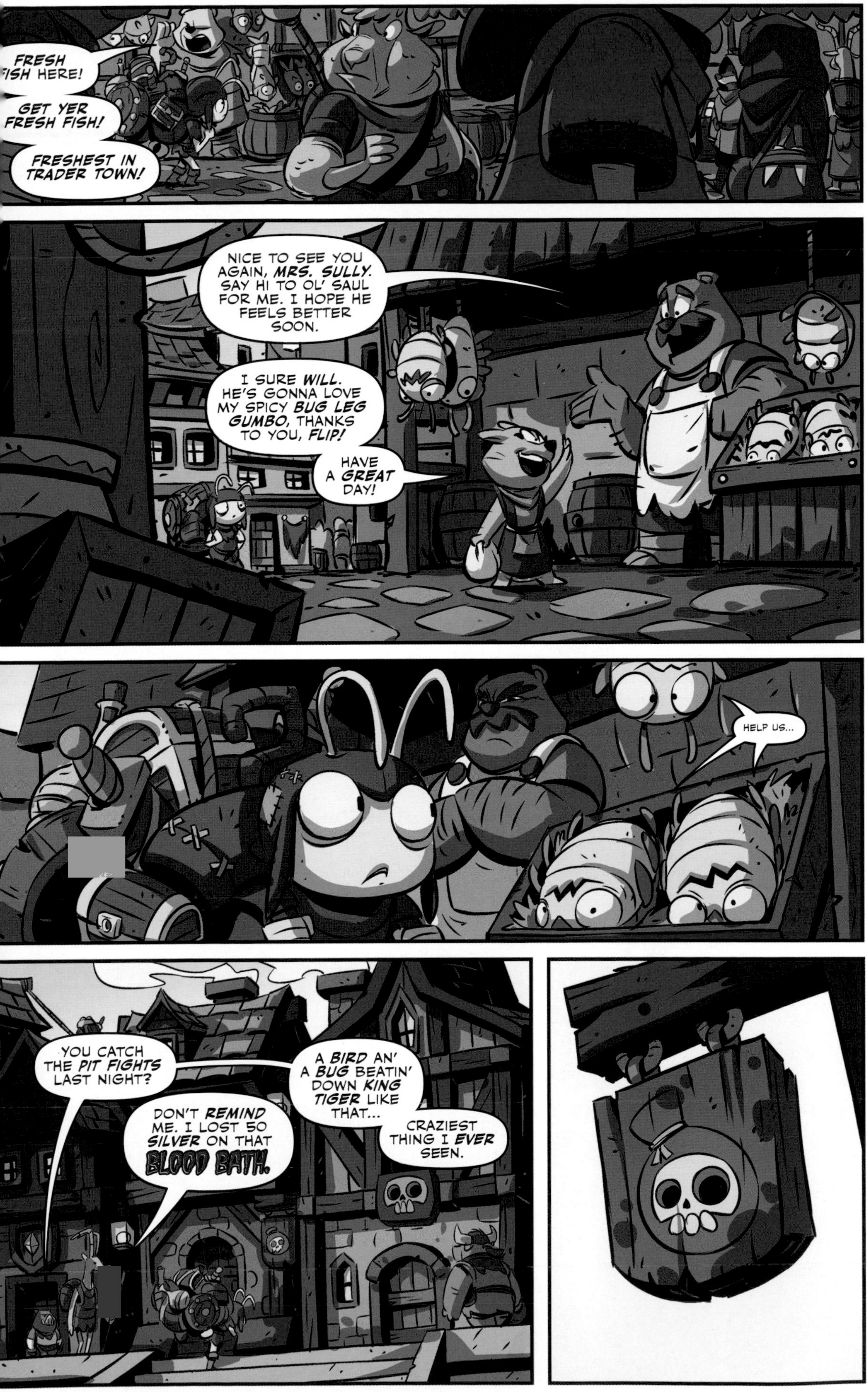
FRESH FISH HERE!
GET YER FRESH FISH!
FRESHEST IN TRADER TOWN!
NICE TO SEE YOU AGAIN, MRS. SULLY. SAY HI TO OL' SAUL FOR ME. I HOPE HE FEELS BETTER SOON.
I SURE WILL. HE'S GONNA LOVE MY SPICY BUG LEG GUMBO, THANKS TO YOU, FLIP!
HAVE A GREAT DAY!
HELP US...
YOU CATCH THE PIT FIGHTS LAST NIGHT?
DON'T REMIND ME. I LOST 50 SILVER ON THAT BLOOD BATH.
A BIRD AN' A BUG BEATIN' DOWN KING TIGER LIKE THAT...
CRAZIEST THING I EVER SEEN.

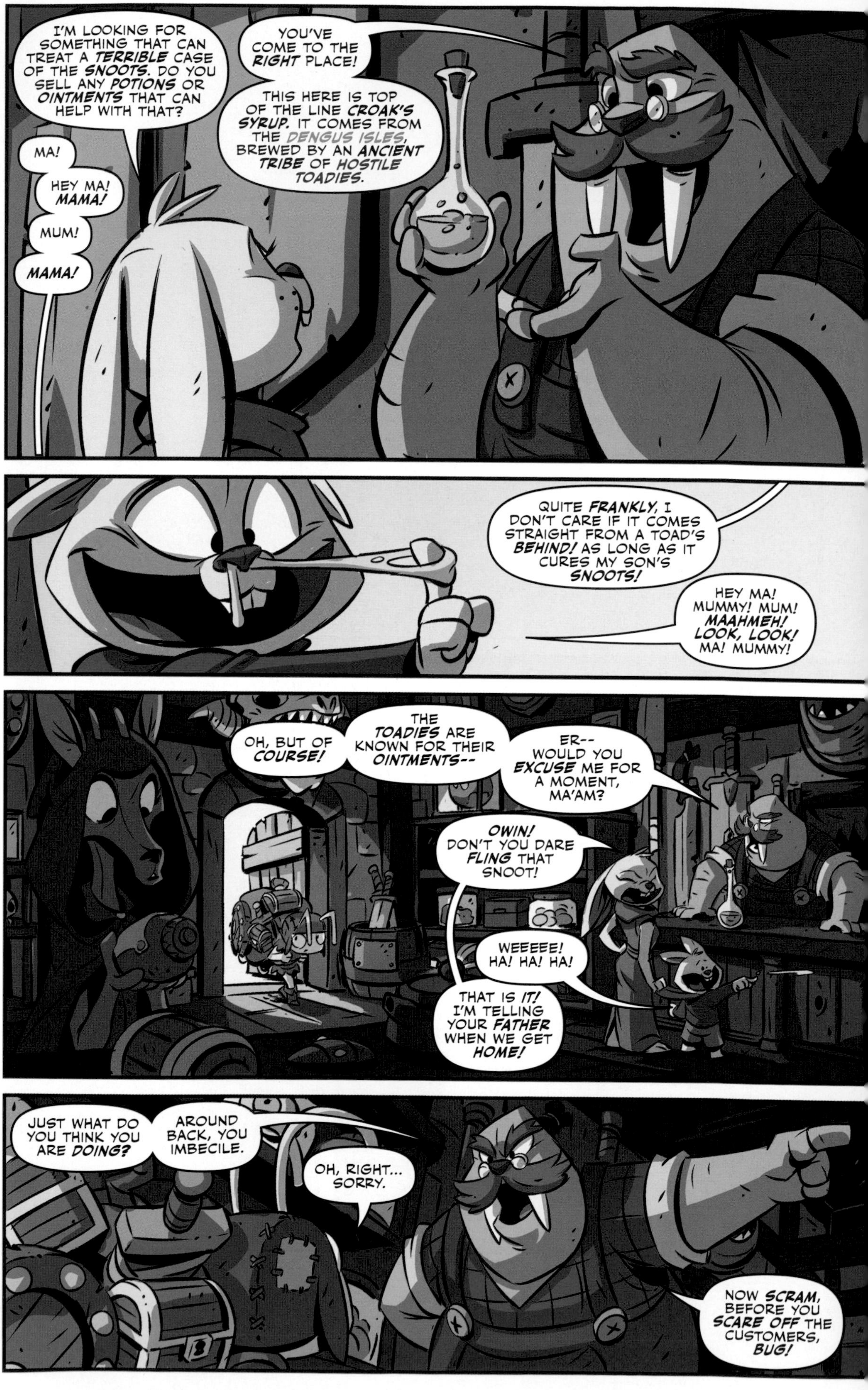
I'M LOOKING FOR SOMETHING THAT CAN TREAT A TERRIBLE CASE OF THE SNOOTS. DO YOU SELL ANY POTIONS OR OINTMENTS THAT CAN HELP WITH THAT?
YOU'VE COME TO THE RIGHT PLACE!
THIS HERE IS TOP OF THE LINE CROAK'S SYRUP. IT COMES FROM THE DENGUS ISLES, BREWED BY AN ANCIENT TRIBE OF HOSTILE TOADIES.
MA!
HEY MA! MAMA!
MUM!
MAMA!
QUITE FRANKLY, I DON'T CARE IF IT COMES STRAIGHT FROM A TOAD'S BEHIND! AS LONG AS IT CURES MY SON'S SNOOTS!
HEY MA! MUMMY! MUM! MAAHMEH! LOOK, LOOK! MA! MUMMY!
OH, BUT OF COURSE!
THE TOADIES ARE KNOWN FOR THEIR OINTMENTS--
ER-- WOULD YOU EXCUSE ME FOR A MOMENT, MA'AM?
OWIN! DON'T YOU DARE FLING THAT SNOOT!
WEEEEE! HA! HA! HA!
THAT IS IT! I'M TELLING YOUR FATHER WHEN WE GET HOME!
JUST WHAT DO YOU THINK YOU ARE DOING?
AROUND BACK, YOU IMBECILE.
OH, RIGHT... SORRY.
NOW SCRAM, BEFORE YOU SCARE OFF THE CUSTOMERS, BUG!

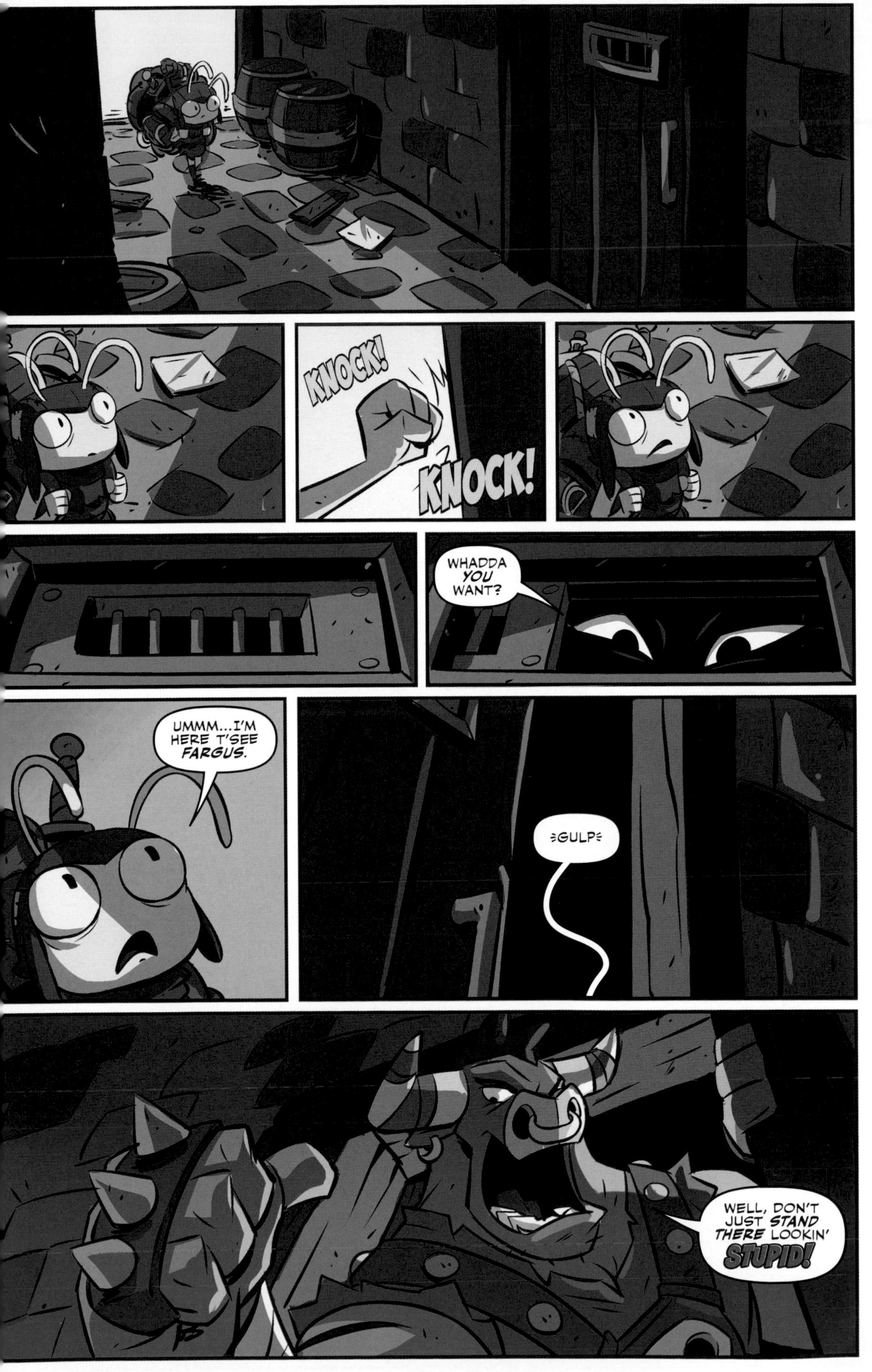
KNOCK!
KNOCK!
WHADDA YOU WANT?
UMMM...I'M HERE T'SEE FARGUS.
GULP
WELL, DON'T JUST STAND THERE LOOKIN' STUPID!

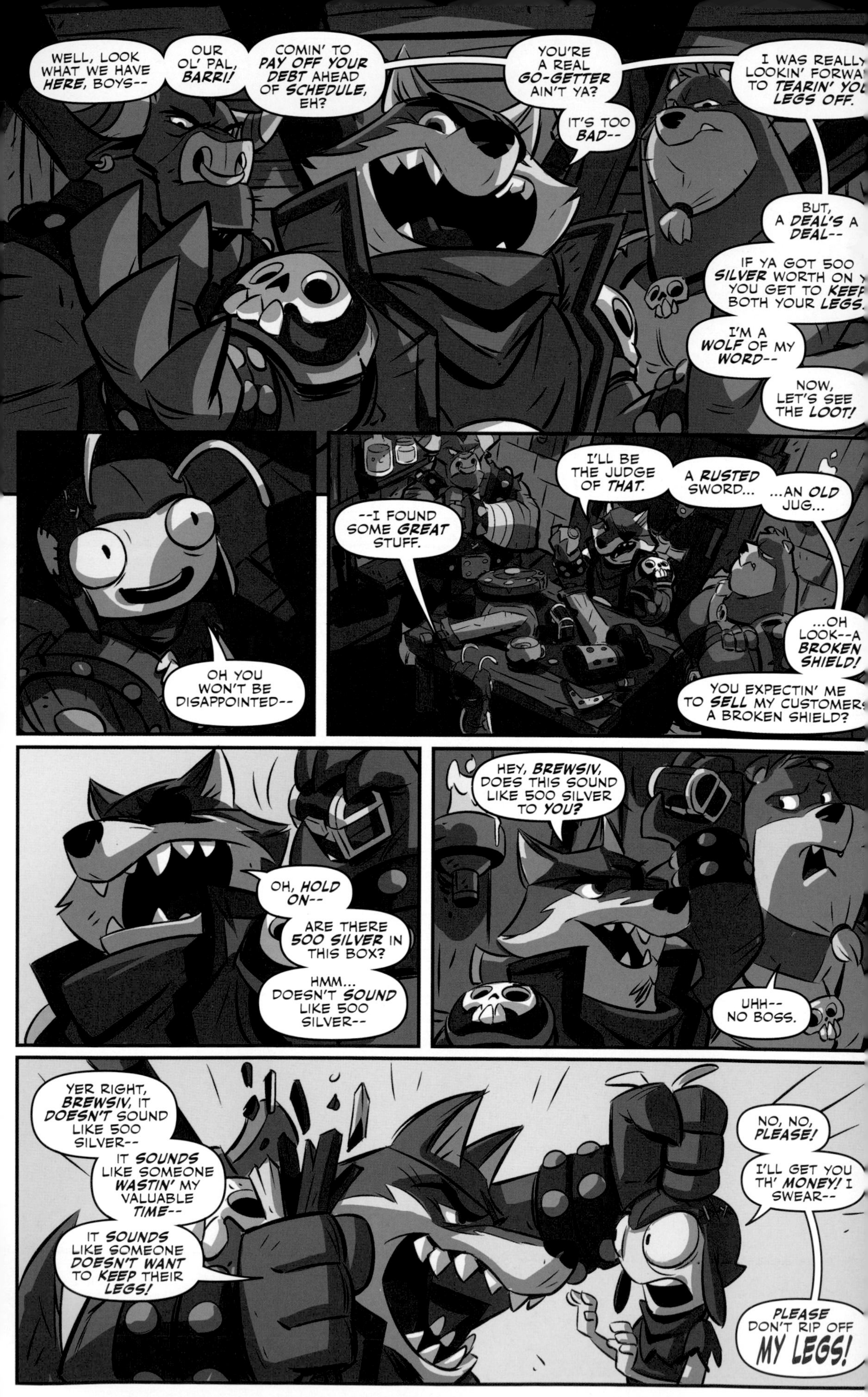
WELL, LOOK WHAT WE HAVE HERE, BOYS--
OUR OL' PAL, BARRI!
COMIN' TO PAY OFF YOUR DEBT AHEAD OF SCHEDULE, EH?
YOU'RE A REAL GO-GETTER AIN'T YA?
IT'S TOO BAD--
I WAS REALLY LOOKIN' FORWA TO TEARIN' YO LEGS OFF.
BUT, A DEAL'S A DEAL--
IF YA GOT 500 SILVER WORTH ON Y YOU GET TO KEEP BOTH YOUR LEGS.
I'M A WOLF OF MY WORD--
NOW, LET'S SEE THE LOOT!
OH YOU WON'T BE DISAPPOINTED--
--I FOUND SOME GREAT STUFF.
I'LL BE THE JUDGE OF THAT.
A RUSTED SWORD...
...AN OLD JUG...
...OH LOOK--A BROKEN SHIELD!
YOU EXPECTIN' ME TO SELL MY CUSTOMER A BROKEN SHIELD?
OH, HOLD ON--
ARE THERE 500 SILVER IN THIS BOX?
HMM... DOESN'T SOUND LIKE 500 SILVER--
HEY, BREWSIV, DOES THIS SOUND LIKE 500 SILVER TO YOU?
UHH-- NO BOSS.
YER RIGHT, BREWSIV, IT DOESN'T SOUND LIKE 500 SILVER--
IT SOUNDS LIKE SOMEONE WASTIN' MY VALUABLE TIME--
IT SOUNDS LIKE SOMEONE DOESN'T WANT TO KEEP THEIR LEGS!
NO, NO, PLEASE!
I'LL GET YOU TH' MONEY! I SWEAR--
PLEASE DON'T RIP OFF MY LEGS!

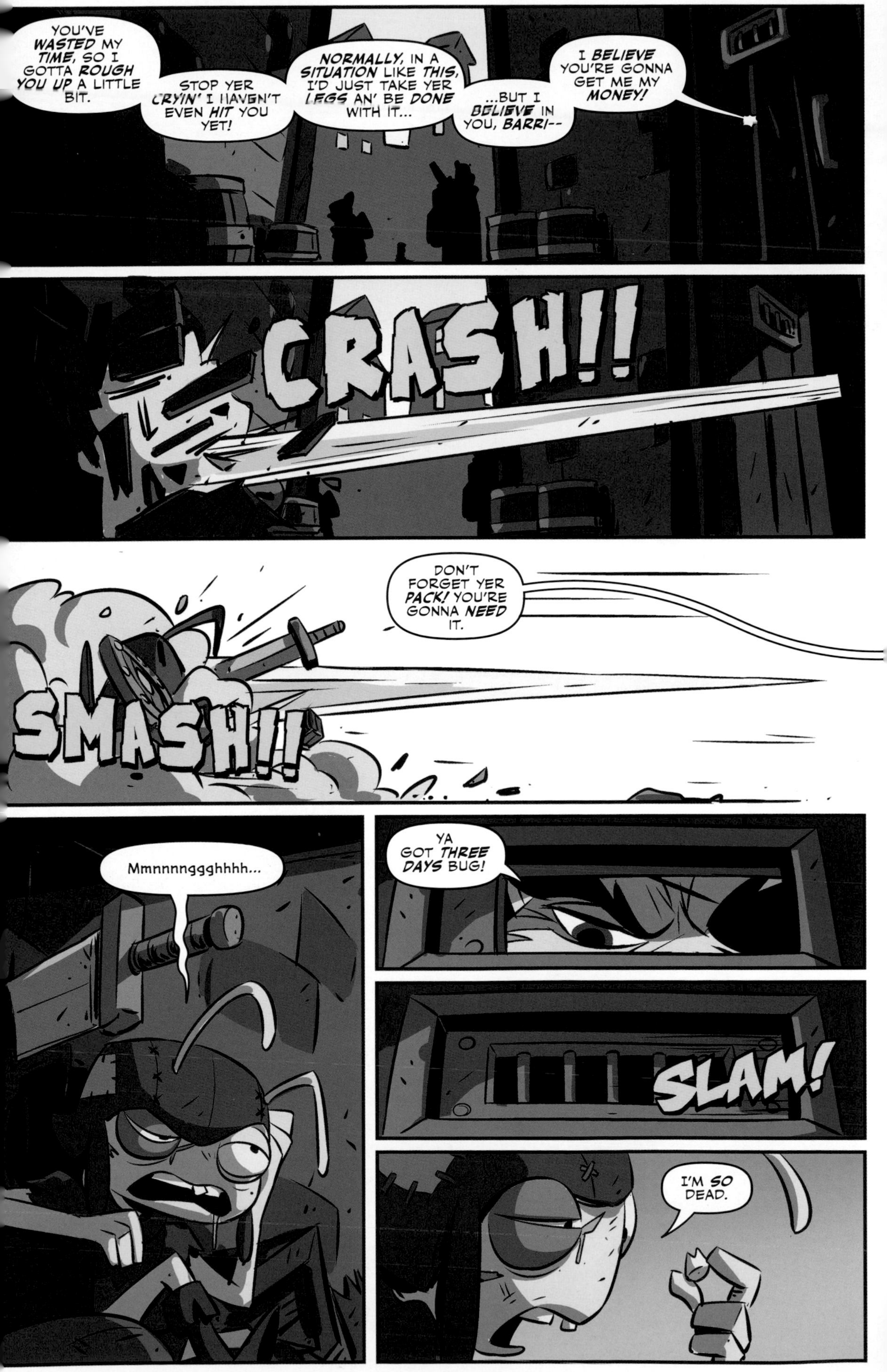
YOU'VE WASTED MY TIME, SO I GOTTA ROUGH YOU UP A LITTLE BIT.
STOP YER CRYIN' I HAVEN'T EVEN HIT YOU YET!
NORMALLY, IN A SITUATION LIKE THIS, I'D JUST TAKE YER LEGS AN' BE DONE WITH IT...
...BUT I BELIEVE IN YOU, BARRI--
I BELIEVE YOU'RE GONNA GET ME MY MONEY!
CRASH!!
DON'T FORGET YER PACK! YOU'RE GONNA NEED IT.
SMASH!!
Mmnnnnggghhhh...
YA GOT THREE DAYS BUG!
SLAM!
I'M SO DEAD.

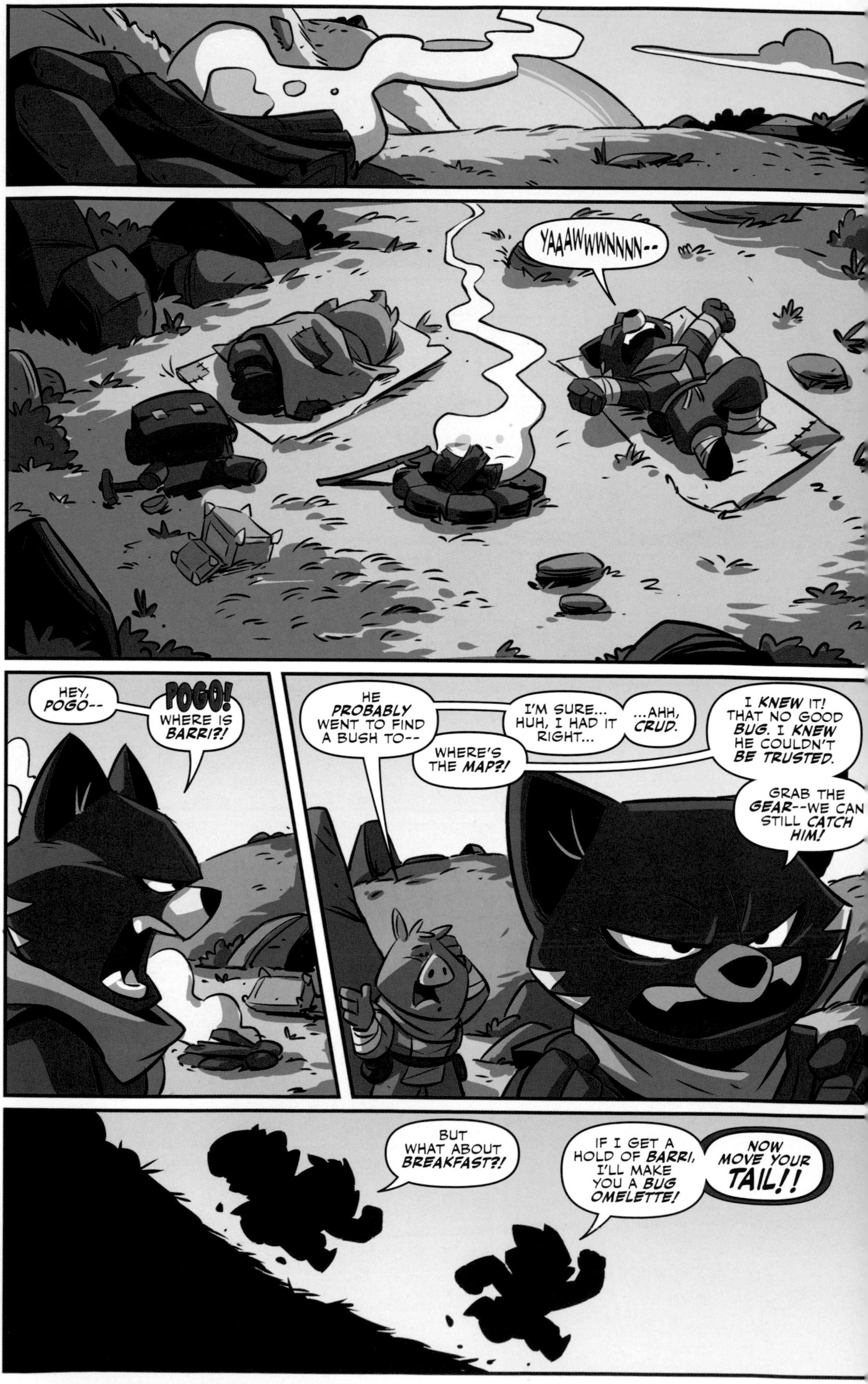
YAAAWWWNNNN--
HEY, POGO--
POGO! WHERE IS BARRI?!
HE PROBABLY WENT TO FIND A BUSH TO--
I'M SURE... HUH, I HAD IT RIGHT...
...AHH, CRUD.
WHERE'S THE MAP?!
I KNEW IT! THAT NO GOOD BUG. I KNEW HE COULDN'T BE TRUSTED.
GRAB THE GEAR--WE CAN STILL CATCH HIM!
BUT WHAT ABOUT BREAKFAST?!
IF I GET A HOLD OF BARRI, I'LL MAKE YOU A BUG OMELETTE!
NOW MOVE YOUR TAIL!!

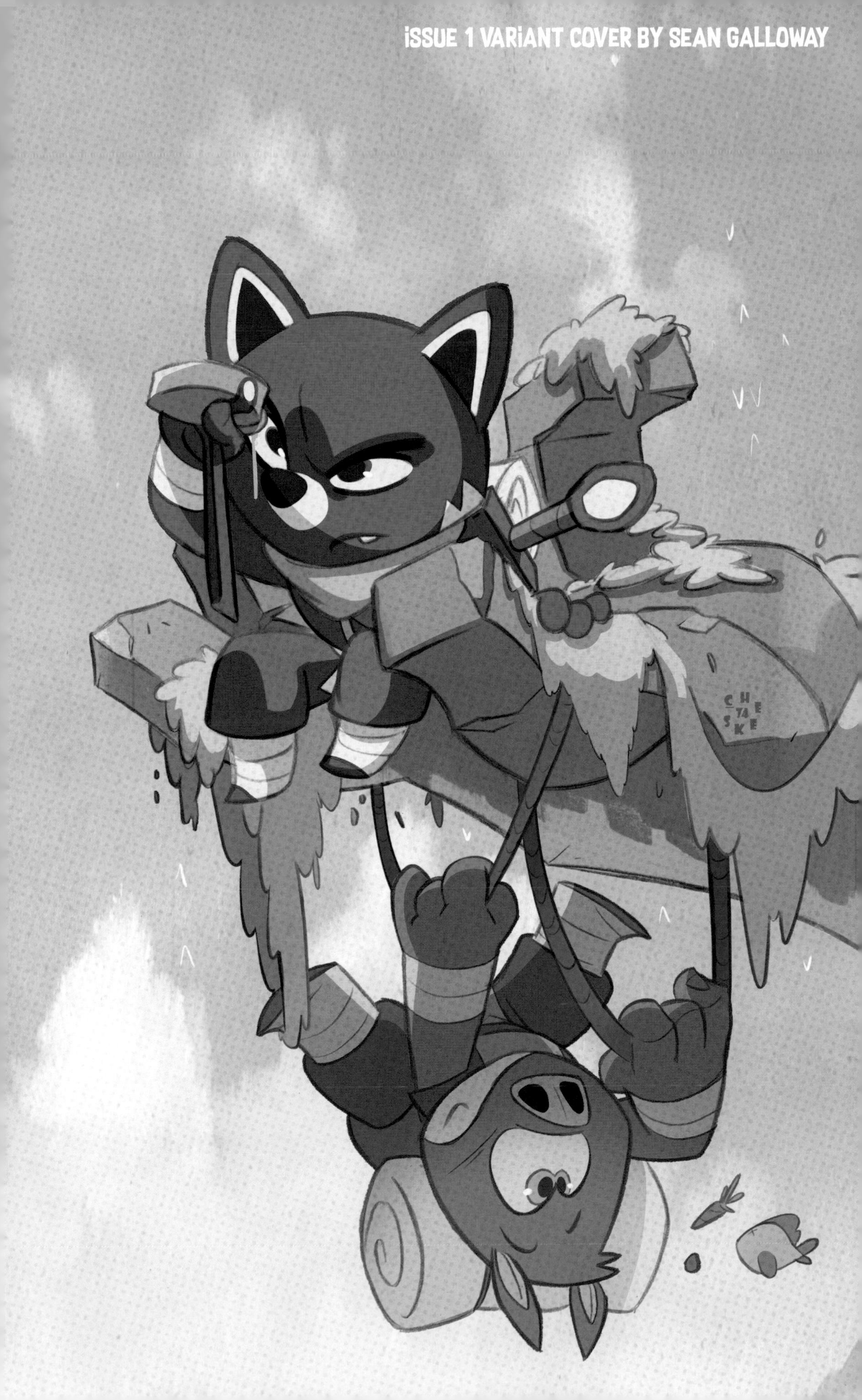

ISSUE 1 VARIANT COVER BY SEAN GALLOWAY

iSSUE 2 COVER BY DEREK LAUFMAN

CHAPTER 2

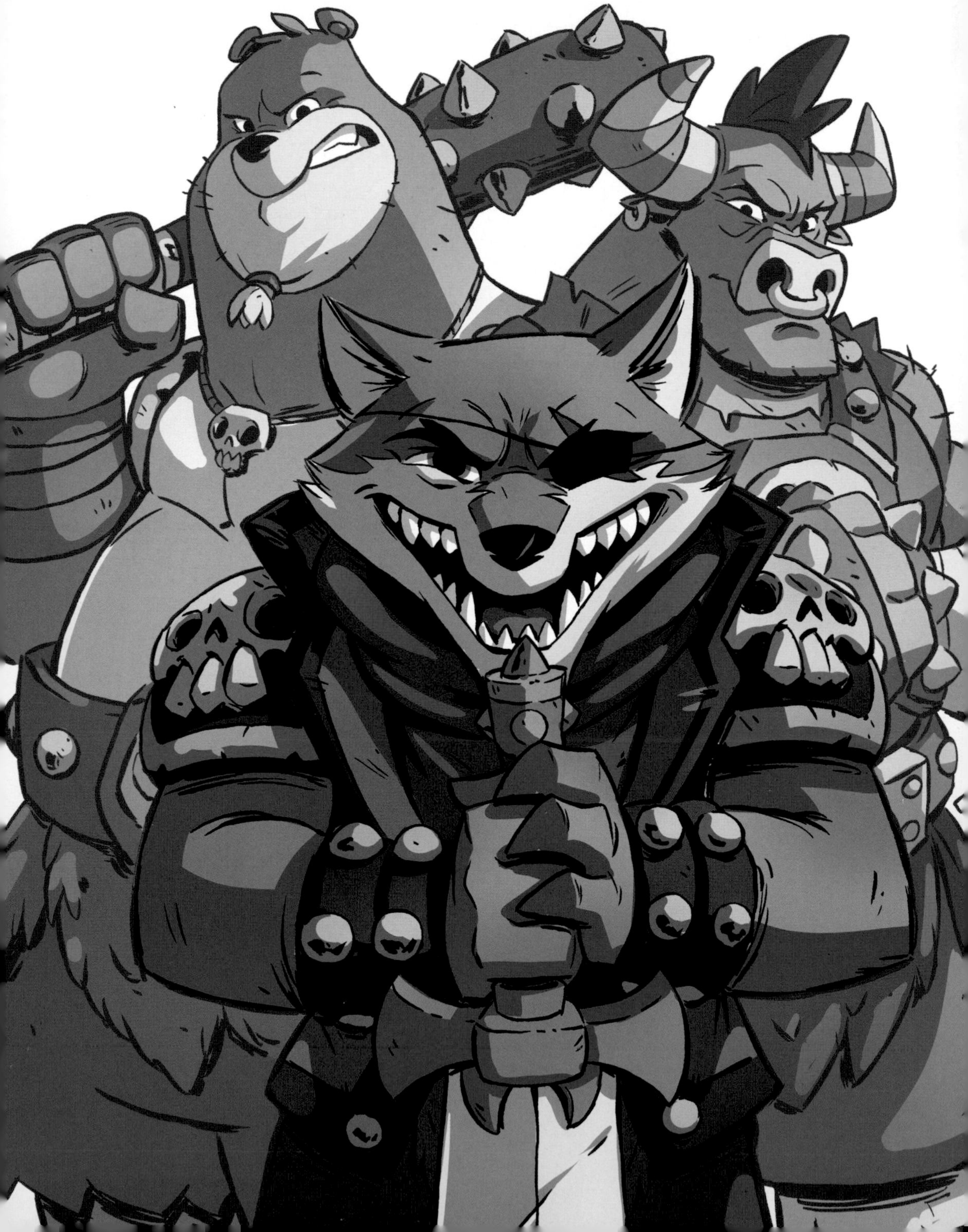

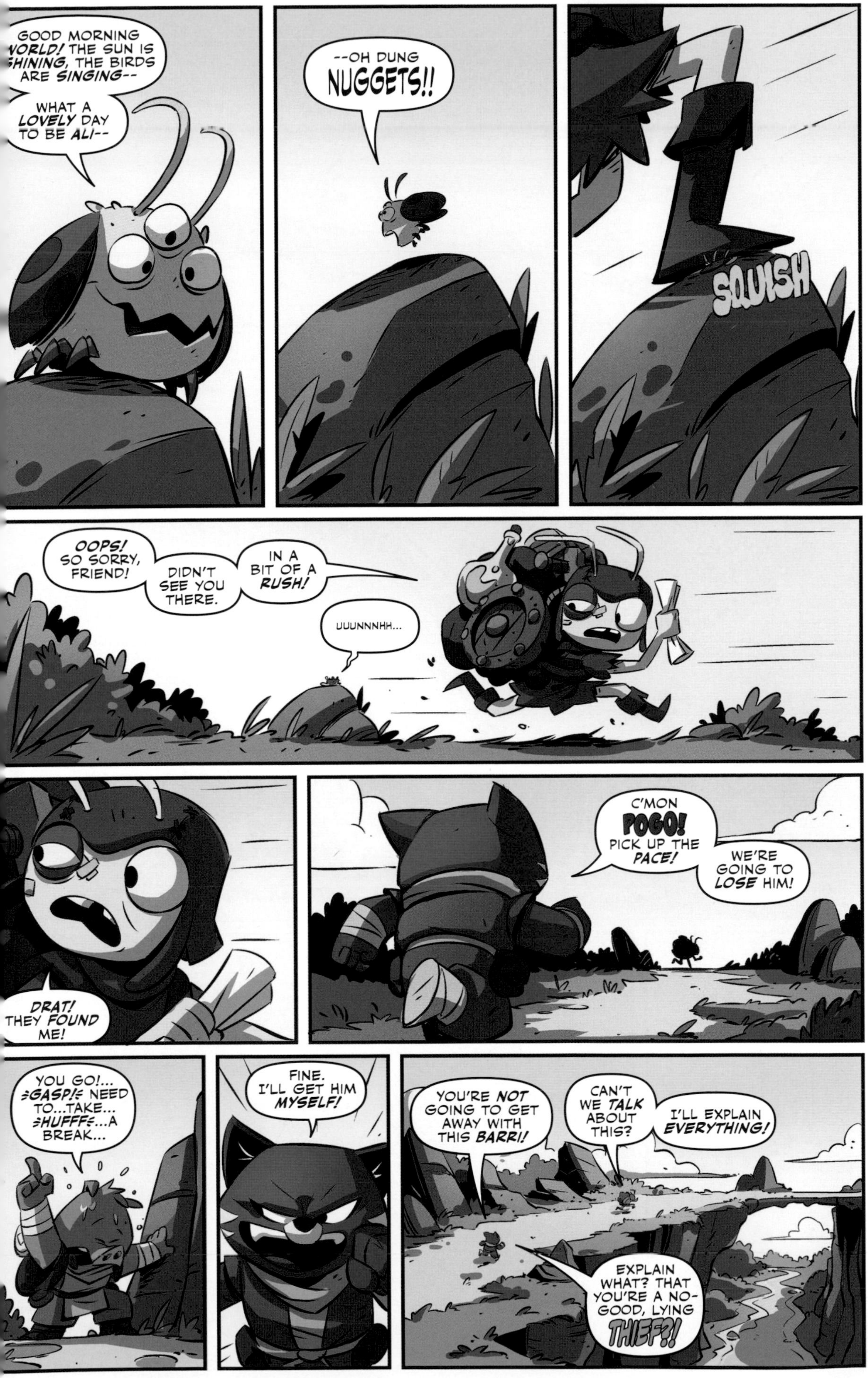

GOOD MORNING WORLD! THE SUN IS SHINING, THE BIRDS ARE SINGING--
WHAT A LOVELY DAY TO BE ALI--
--OH DUNG NUGGETS!!
SQUISH
OOPS! SO SORRY, FRIEND!
DIDN'T SEE YOU THERE.
IN A BIT OF A RUSH!
UUUNNNHH...
DRAT! THEY FOUND ME!
C'MON POGO! PICK UP THE PACE!
WE'RE GOING TO LOSE HIM!
YOU GO!... GASP! NEED TO...TAKE... HUFFF ...A BREAK...
FINE. I'LL GET HIM MYSELF!
YOU'RE NOT GOING TO GET AWAY WITH THIS BARRI!
CAN'T WE TALK ABOUT THIS?
I'LL EXPLAIN EVERYTHING!
EXPLAIN WHAT? THAT YOU'RE A NO-GOOD, LYING THIEF?!

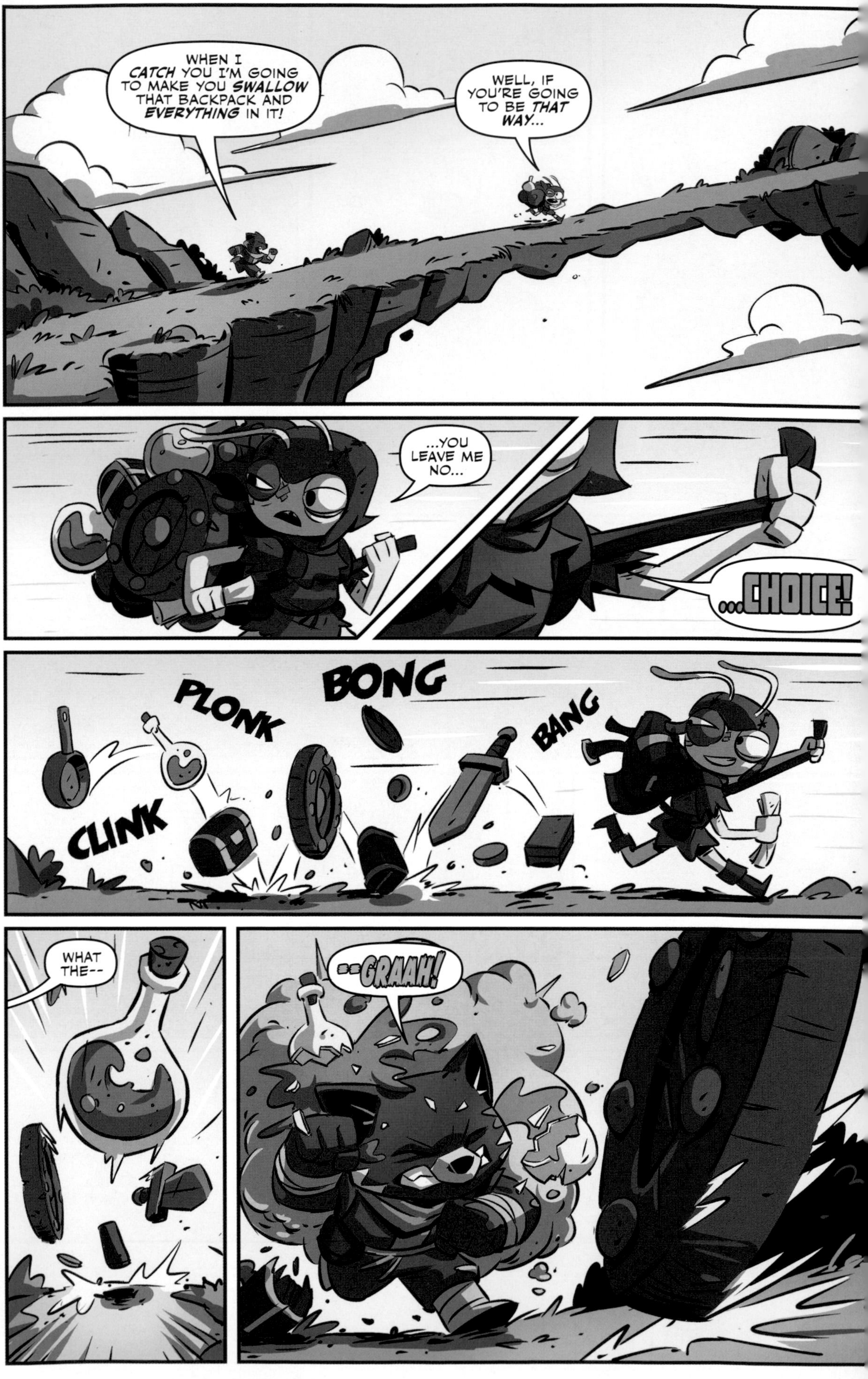

WHEN I CATCH YOU I'M GOING TO MAKE YOU SWALLOW THAT BACKPACK AND EVERYTHING IN IT!
WELL, IF YOU'RE GOING TO BE THAT WAY...
...YOU LEAVE ME NO...
...CHOICE!
PLONK
BONG
BANG
CLINK
WHAT THE--
--GRAAH!

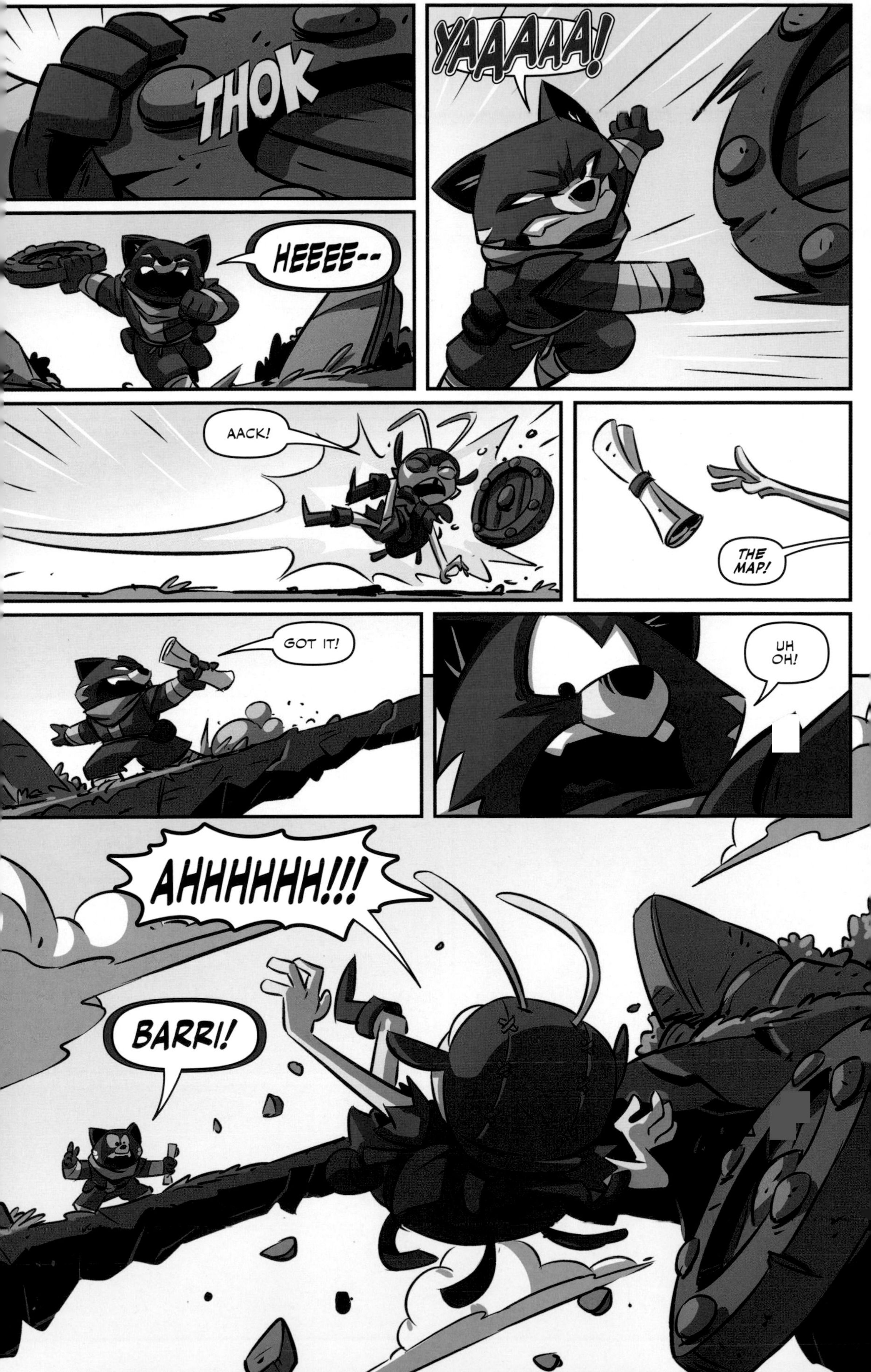
THOK
HEEEE--
YAAAAA!
AACK!
THE MAP!
GOT IT!
UH OH!
AHHHHHH!!!
BARRI!

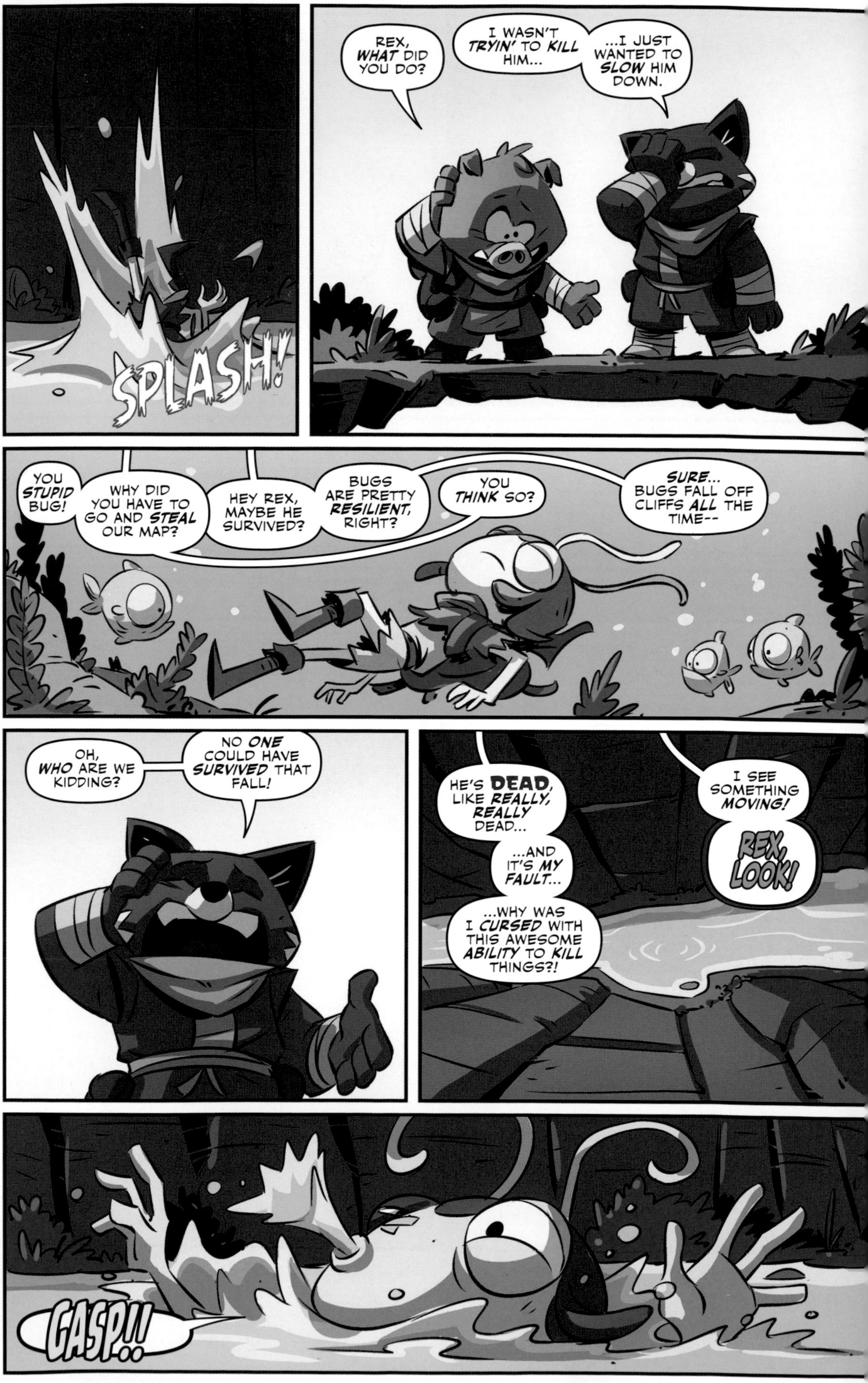
SPLASH!
REX, WHAT DID YOU DO?
I WASN'T TRYIN' TO KILL HIM...
...I JUST WANTED TO SLOW HIM DOWN.
YOU STUPID BUG!
WHY DID YOU HAVE TO GO AND STEAL OUR MAP?
HEY REX, MAYBE HE SURVIVED?
BUGS ARE PRETTY RESILIENT, RIGHT?
YOU THINK SO?
SURE... BUGS FALL OFF CLIFFS ALL THE TIME--
OH, WHO ARE WE KIDDING?
NO ONE COULD HAVE SURVIVED THAT FALL!
HE'S DEAD, LIKE REALLY, REALLY DEAD...
...AND IT'S MY FAULT...
...WHY WAS I CURSED WITH THIS AWESOME ABILITY TO KILL THINGS?!
I SEE SOMETHING MOVING!
REX, LOOK!
GASP!!

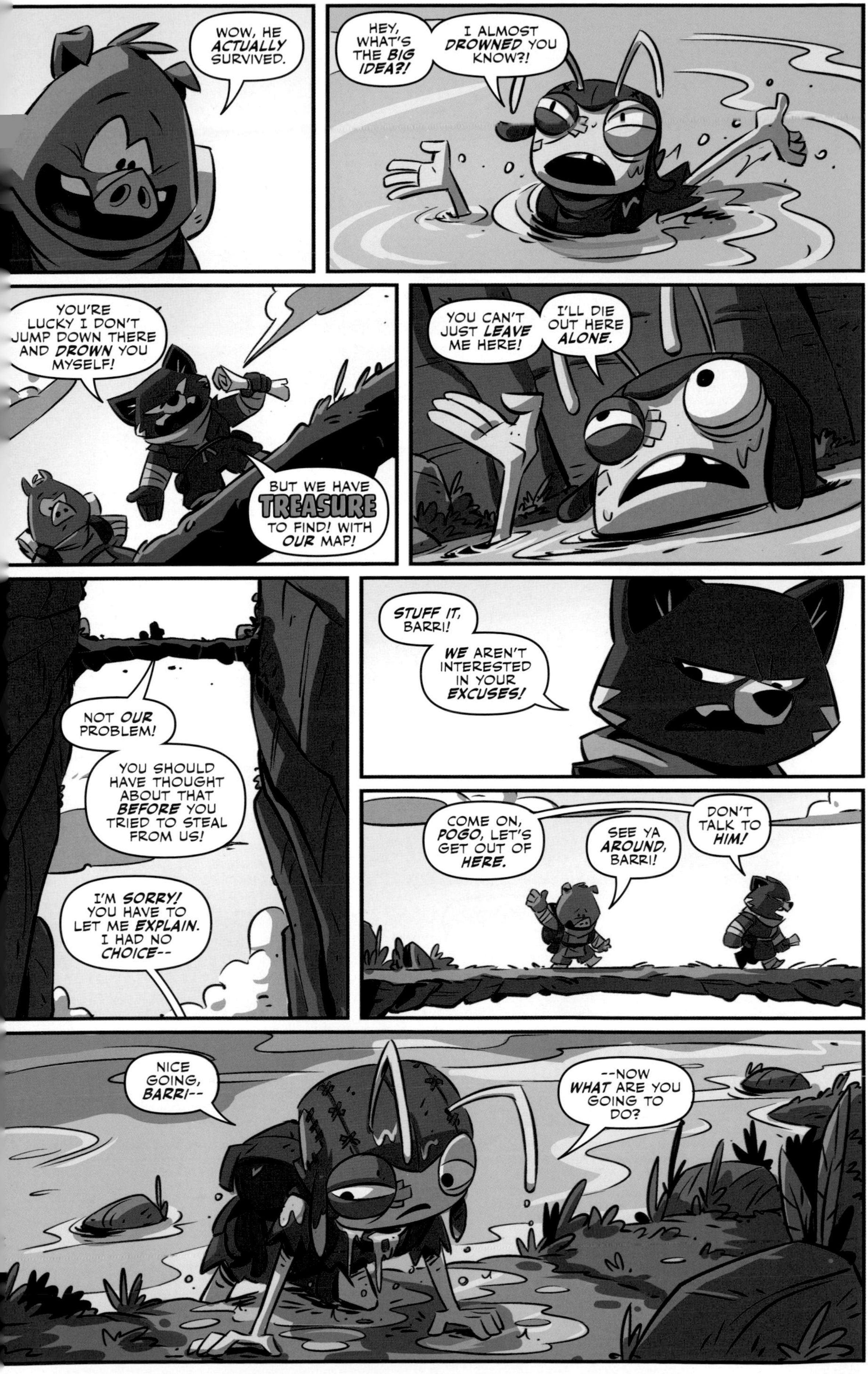
WOW, HE ACTUALLY SURVIVED.
HEY, WHAT'S THE BIG IDEA?!
I ALMOST DROWNED YOU KNOW?!
YOU'RE LUCKY I DON'T JUMP DOWN THERE AND DROWN YOU MYSELF!
BUT WE HAVE TREASURE TO FIND! WITH OUR MAP!
YOU CAN'T JUST LEAVE ME HERE!
I'LL DIE OUT HERE ALONE.
NOT OUR PROBLEM!
YOU SHOULD HAVE THOUGHT ABOUT THAT BEFORE YOU TRIED TO STEAL FROM US!
I'M SORRY! YOU HAVE TO LET ME EXPLAIN. I HAD NO CHOICE--
STUFF IT, BARRI!
WE AREN'T INTERESTED IN YOUR EXCUSES!
COME ON, POGO, LET'S GET OUT OF HERE.
SEE YA AROUND, BARRI!
DON'T TALK TO HIM!
NICE GOING, BARRI--
--NOW WHAT ARE YOU GOING TO DO?

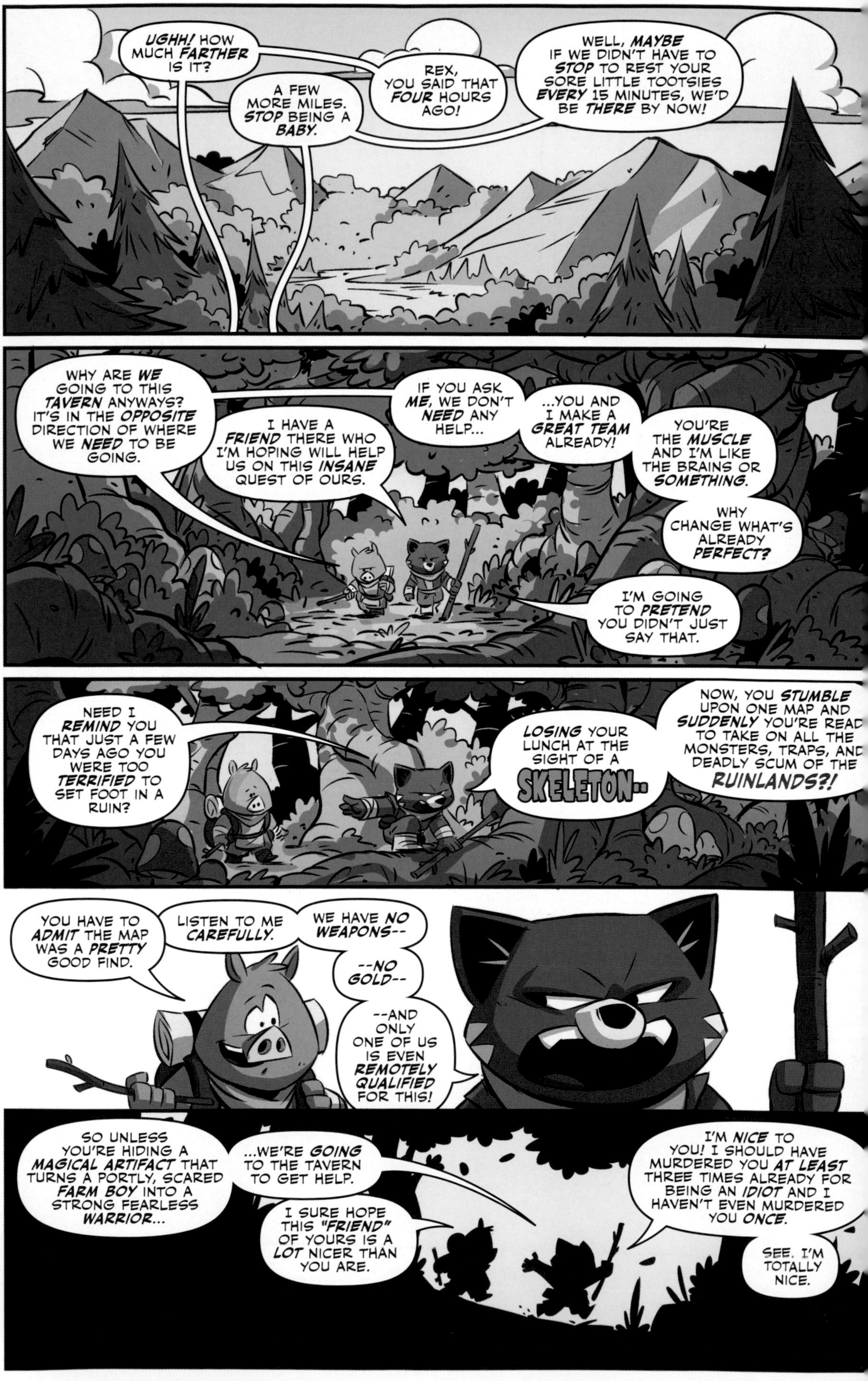
UGHH! HOW MUCH FARTHER IS IT?
A FEW MORE MILES. STOP BEING A BABY.
REX, YOU SAID THAT FOUR HOURS AGO!
WELL, MAYBE IF WE DIDN'T HAVE TO STOP TO REST YOUR SORE LITTLE TOOTSIES EVERY 15 MINUTES, WE'D BE THERE BY NOW!
WHY ARE WE GOING TO THIS TAVERN ANYWAYS? IT'S IN THE OPPOSITE DIRECTION OF WHERE WE NEED TO BE GOING.
I HAVE A FRIEND THERE WHO I'M HOPING WILL HELP US ON THIS INSANE QUEST OF OURS.
IF YOU ASK ME, WE DON'T NEED ANY HELP...
...YOU AND I MAKE A GREAT TEAM ALREADY!
YOU'RE THE MUSCLE AND I'M LIKE THE BRAINS OR SOMETHING.
WHY CHANGE WHAT'S ALREADY PERFECT?
I'M GOING TO PRETEND YOU DIDN'T JUST SAY THAT.
NEED I REMIND YOU THAT JUST A FEW DAYS AGO YOU WERE TOO TERRIFIED TO SET FOOT IN A RUIN?
LOSING YOUR LUNCH AT THE SIGHT OF A SKELETON..
NOW, YOU STUMBLE UPON ONE MAP AND SUDDENLY YOU'RE READ TO TAKE ON ALL THE MONSTERS, TRAPS, AND DEADLY SCUM OF THE RUINLANDS?!
YOU HAVE TO ADMIT THE MAP WAS A PRETTY GOOD FIND.
LISTEN TO ME CAREFULLY.
WE HAVE NO WEAPONS--
--NO GOLD--
--AND ONLY ONE OF US IS EVEN REMOTELY QUALIFIED FOR THIS!
SO UNLESS YOU'RE HIDING A MAGICAL ARTIFACT THAT TURNS A PORTLY, SCARED FARM BOY INTO A STRONG FEARLESS WARRIOR...
...WE'RE GOING TO THE TAVERN TO GET HELP.
I SURE HOPE THIS "FRIEND" OF YOURS IS A LOT NICER THAN YOU ARE.
I'M NICE TO YOU! I SHOULD HAVE MURDERED YOU AT LEAST THREE TIMES ALREADY FOR BEING AN IDIOT AND I HAVEN'T EVEN MURDERED YOU ONCE.
SEE. I'M TOTALLY NICE.

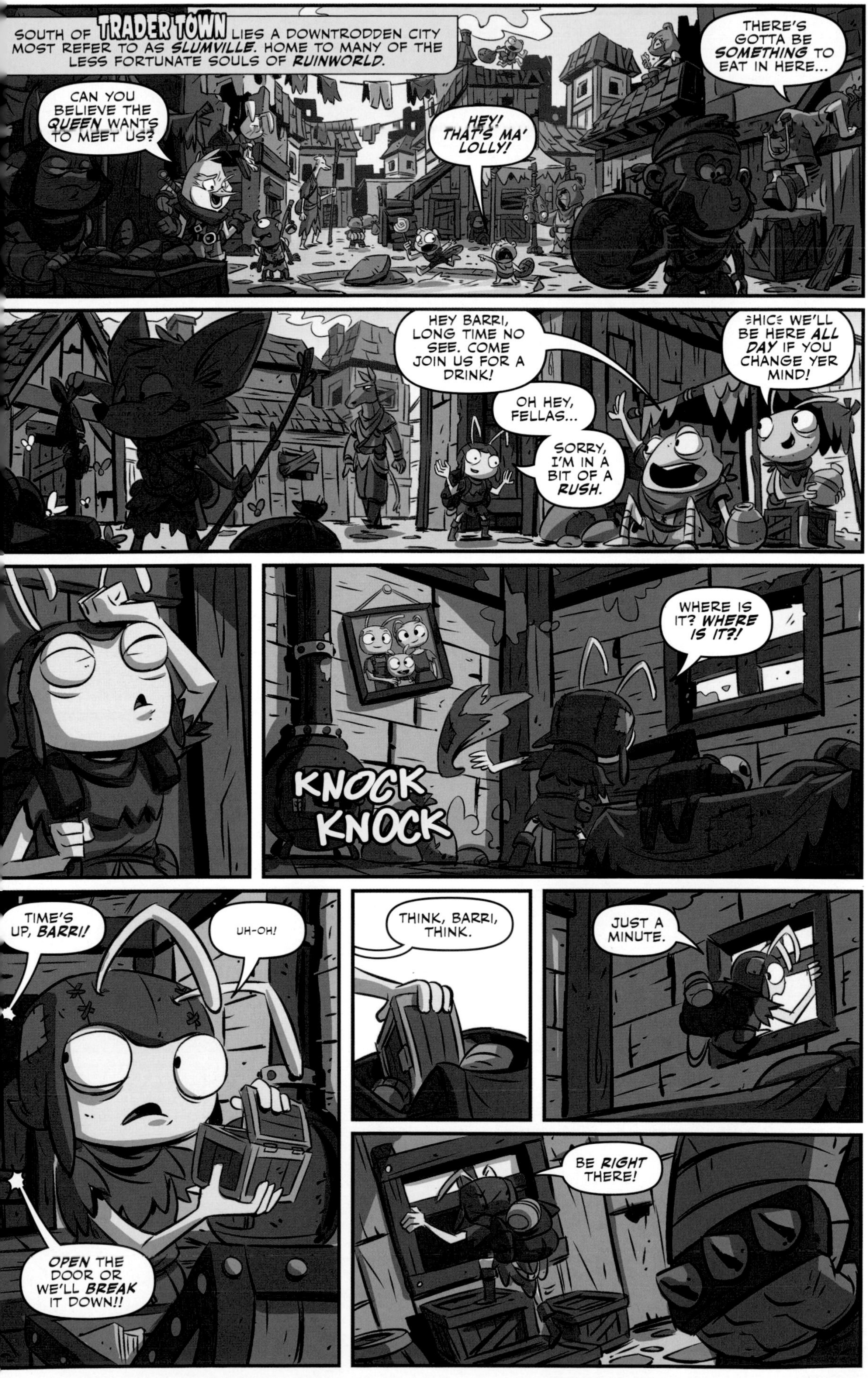
SOUTH OF TRADER TOWN LIES A DOWNTRODDEN CITY MOST REFER TO AS SLUMVILLE. HOME TO MANY OF THE LESS FORTUNATE SOULS OF RUINWORLD.
CAN YOU BELIEVE THE QUEEN WANTS TO MEET US?
HEY! THAT'S MA' LOLLY!
THERE'S GOTTA BE SOMETHING TO EAT IN HERE...
HEY BARRI, LONG TIME NO SEE. COME JOIN US FOR A DRINK!
OH HEY, FELLAS...
SORRY, I'M IN A BIT OF A RUSH.
HIC WE'LL BE HERE ALL DAY IF YOU CHANGE YER MIND!
KNOCK KNOCK
WHERE IS IT? WHERE IS IT?!
TIME'S UP, BARRI!
UH-OH!
OPEN THE DOOR OR WE'LL BREAK IT DOWN!!
THINK, BARRI, THINK.
JUST A MINUTE.
BE RIGHT THERE!

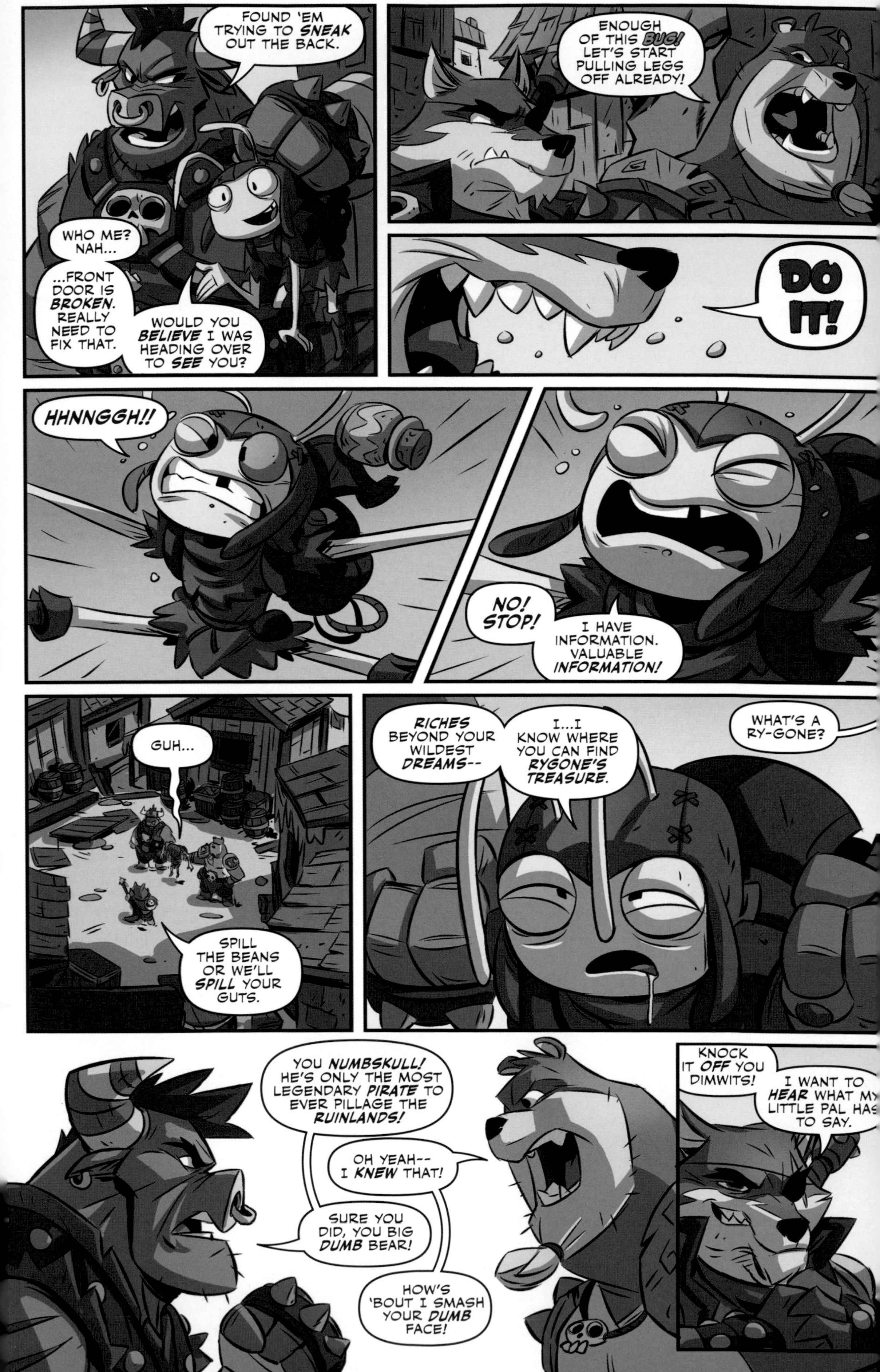

FOUND 'EM TRYING TO SNEAK OUT THE BACK.
WHO ME? NAH...
...FRONT DOOR IS BROKEN. REALLY NEED TO FIX THAT.
WOULD YOU BELIEVE I WAS HEADING OVER TO SEE YOU?
ENOUGH OF THIS BUG! LET'S START PULLING LEGS OFF ALREADY!
DO IT!
HHNNGGH!!
NO! STOP!
I HAVE INFORMATION. VALUABLE INFORMATION!
GUH...
SPILL THE BEANS OR WE'LL SPILL YOUR GUTS.
RICHES BEYOND YOUR WILDEST DREAMS--
I...I KNOW WHERE YOU CAN FIND RYGONE'S TREASURE.
WHAT'S A RY-GONE?
YOU NUMBSKULL! HE'S ONLY THE MOST LEGENDARY PIRATE TO EVER PILLAGE THE RUINLANDS!
OH YEAH-- I KNEW THAT!
SURE YOU DID, YOU BIG DUMB BEAR!
HOW'S 'BOUT I SMASH YOUR DUMB FACE!
KNOCK IT OFF YOU DIMWITS!
I WANT TO HEAR WHAT MY LITTLE PAL HAS TO SAY.

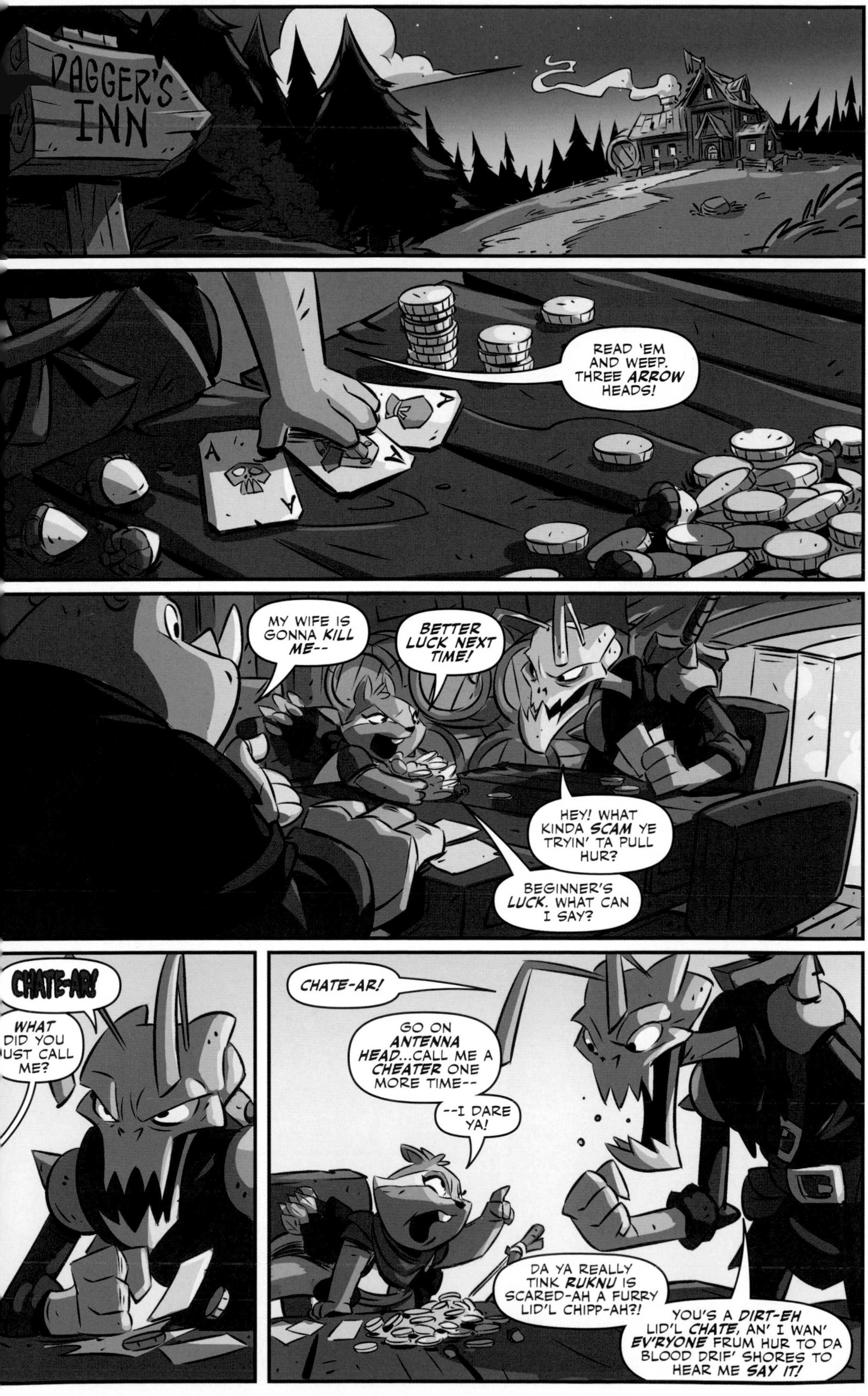
DAGGER'S INN
READ 'EM AND WEEP. THREE ARROW HEADS!
MY WIFE IS GONNA KILL ME--
BETTER LUCK NEXT TIME!
HEY! WHAT KINDA SCAM YE TRYIN' TA PULL HUR?
BEGINNER'S LUCK. WHAT CAN I SAY?
CHATE-AR!
WHAT DID YOU UST CALL ME?
CHATE-AR!
GO ON ANTENNA HEAD...CALL ME A CHEATER ONE MORE TIME--
--I DARE YA!
DA YA REALLY TINK RUKNU IS SCARED-AH A FURRY LID'L CHIPP-AH?!
YOU'S A DIRT-EH LID'L CHATE, AN' I WAN' EV'RYONE FRUM HUR TO DA BLOOD DRIF' SHORES TO HEAR ME SAY IT!

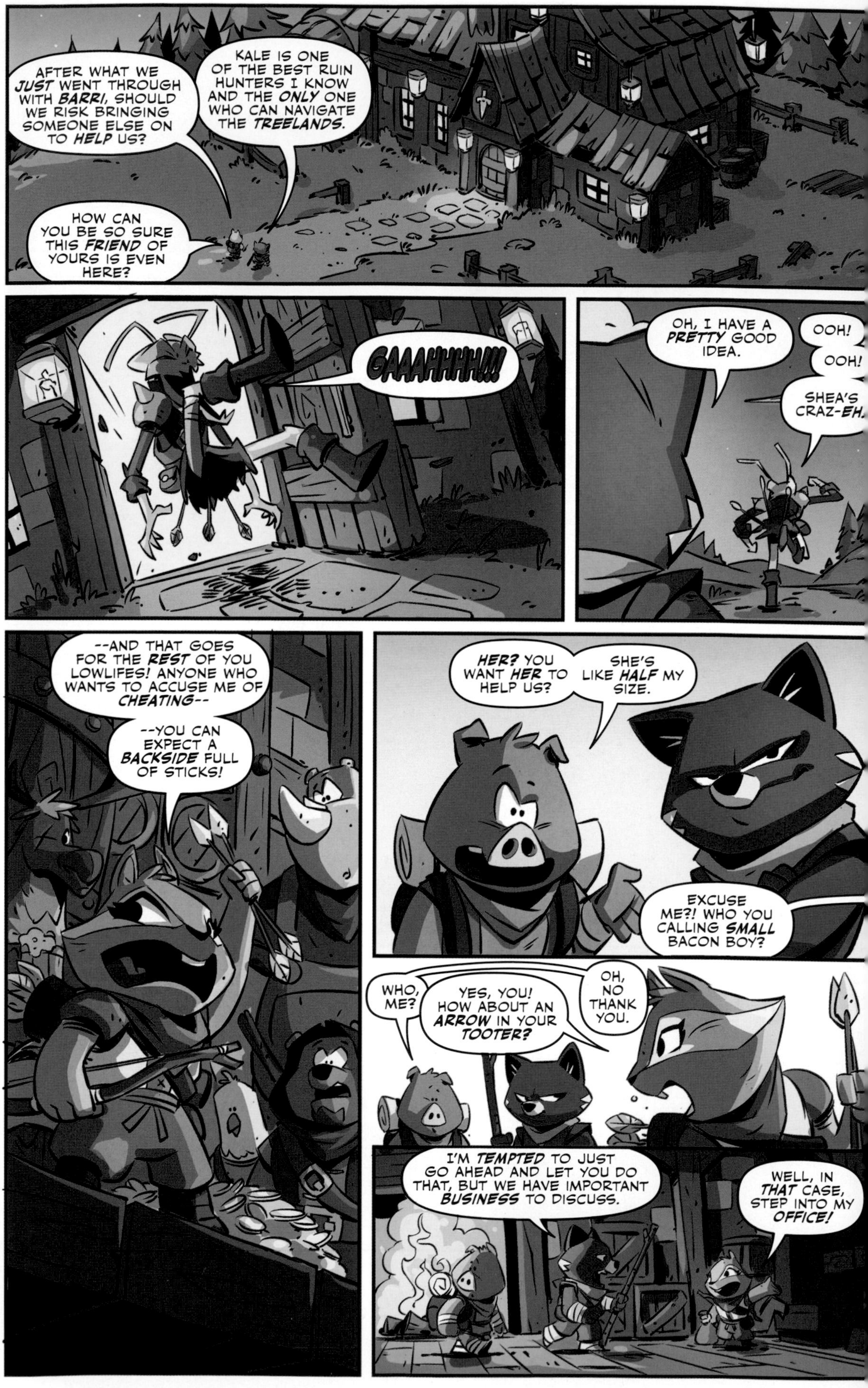
AFTER WHAT WE JUST WENT THROUGH WITH BARRI, SHOULD WE RISK BRINGING SOMEONE ELSE ON TO HELP US?
KALE IS ONE OF THE BEST RUIN HUNTERS I KNOW AND THE ONLY ONE WHO CAN NAVIGATE THE TREELANDS.
HOW CAN YOU BE SO SURE THIS FRIEND OF YOURS IS EVEN HERE?
GAAAHHHH!!!
OH, I HAVE A PRETTY GOOD IDEA.
OOH!
OOH!
SHEA'S CRAZ-EH
--AND THAT GOES FOR THE REST OF YOU LOWLIFES! ANYONE WHO WANTS TO ACCUSE ME OF CHEATING--
--YOU CAN EXPECT A BACKSIDE FULL OF STICKS!
HER? YOU WANT HER TO HELP US?
SHE'S LIKE HALF MY SIZE.
EXCUSE ME?! WHO YOU CALLING SMALL BACON BOY?
WHO, ME?
YES, YOU! HOW ABOUT AN ARROW IN YOUR TOOTER?
OH, NO THANK YOU.
I'M TEMPTED TO JUST GO AHEAD AND LET YOU DO THAT, BUT WE HAVE IMPORTANT BUSINESS TO DISCUSS.
WELL, IN THAT CASE, STEP INTO MY OFFICE!

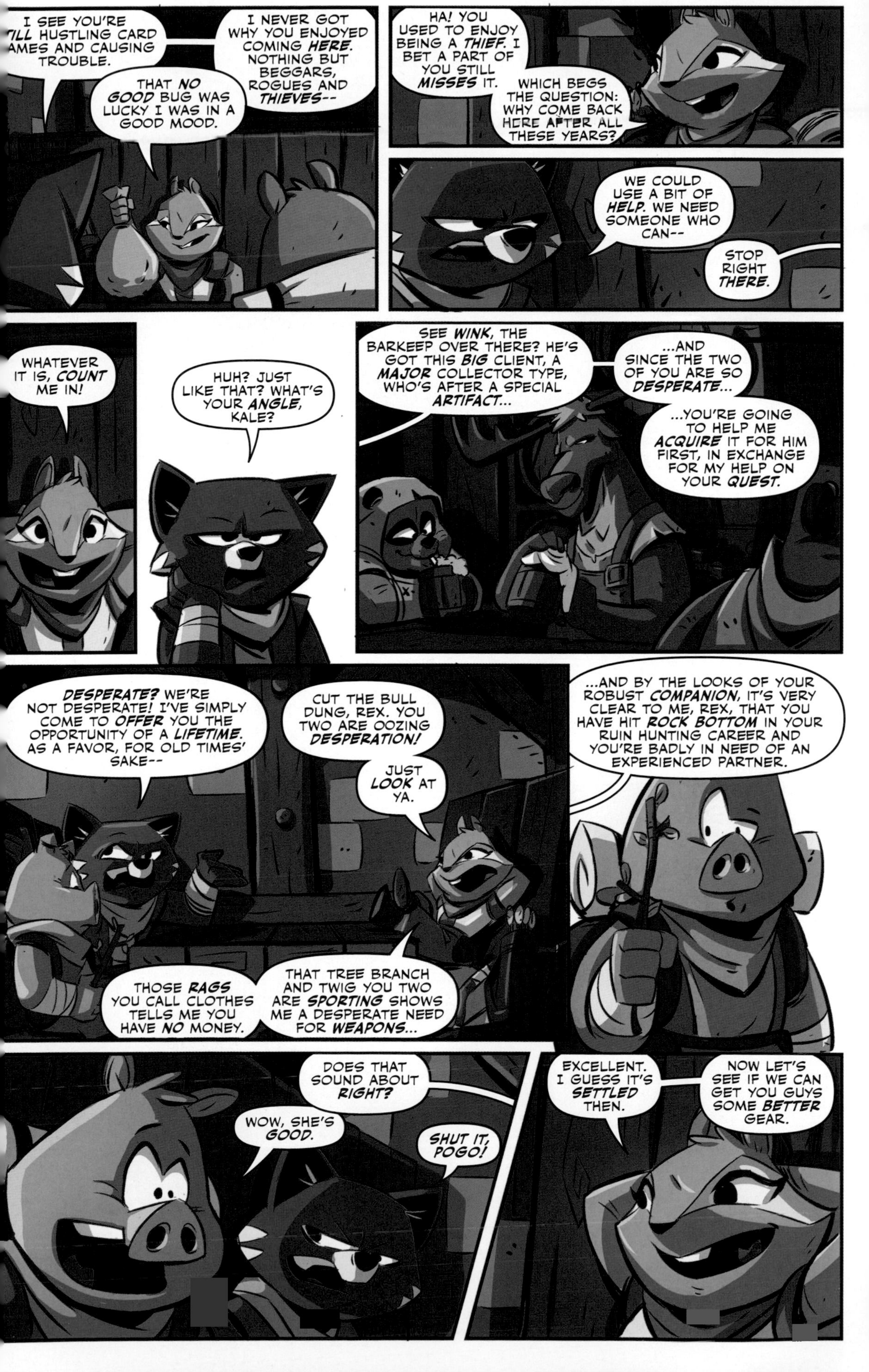
I SEE YOU'RE TILL HUSTLING CARD AMES AND CAUSING TROUBLE.
THAT *NO GOOD* BUG WAS LUCKY I WAS IN A GOOD MOOD.
I NEVER GOT WHY YOU ENJOYED COMING *HERE*. NOTHING BUT BEGGARS, ROGUES AND *THIEVES*--
HA! YOU USED TO ENJOY BEING A *THIEF*. I BET A PART OF YOU STILL *MISSES* IT.
WHICH BEGS THE QUESTION: WHY COME BACK HERE AFTER ALL THESE YEARS?
WE COULD USE A BIT OF *HELP*. WE NEED SOMEONE WHO CAN--
STOP RIGHT *THERE*.
WHATEVER IT IS, *COUNT* ME IN!
HUH? JUST LIKE THAT? WHAT'S YOUR *ANGLE*, KALE?
SEE *WINK*, THE BARKEEP OVER THERE? HE'S GOT THIS *BIG* CLIENT, A *MAJOR* COLLECTOR TYPE, WHO'S AFTER A SPECIAL *ARTIFACT*...
...AND SINCE THE TWO OF YOU ARE SO *DESPERATE*...
...YOU'RE GOING TO HELP ME *ACQUIRE* IT FOR HIM FIRST, IN EXCHANGE FOR MY HELP ON YOUR *QUEST*.
DESPERATE? WE'RE NOT DESPERATE! I'VE SIMPLY COME TO *OFFER* YOU THE OPPORTUNITY OF A *LIFETIME*. AS A FAVOR, FOR OLD TIMES' SAKE--
CUT THE BULL DUNG, REX. YOU TWO ARE OOZING *DESPERATION!*
JUST *LOOK* AT YA.
THOSE *RAGS* YOU CALL CLOTHES TELLS ME YOU HAVE *NO* MONEY.
THAT TREE BRANCH AND TWIG YOU TWO ARE *SPORTING* SHOWS ME A DESPERATE NEED FOR *WEAPONS*...
...AND BY THE LOOKS OF YOUR ROBUST *COMPANION*, IT'S VERY CLEAR TO ME, REX, THAT YOU HAVE HIT *ROCK BOTTOM* IN YOUR RUIN HUNTING CAREER AND YOU'RE BADLY IN NEED OF AN EXPERIENCED PARTNER.
DOES THAT SOUND ABOUT *RIGHT?*
WOW, SHE'S *GOOD*.
SHUT IT, POGO!
EXCELLENT. I GUESS IT'S *SETTLED* THEN.
NOW LET'S SEE IF WE CAN GET YOU GUYS SOME *BETTER* GEAR.

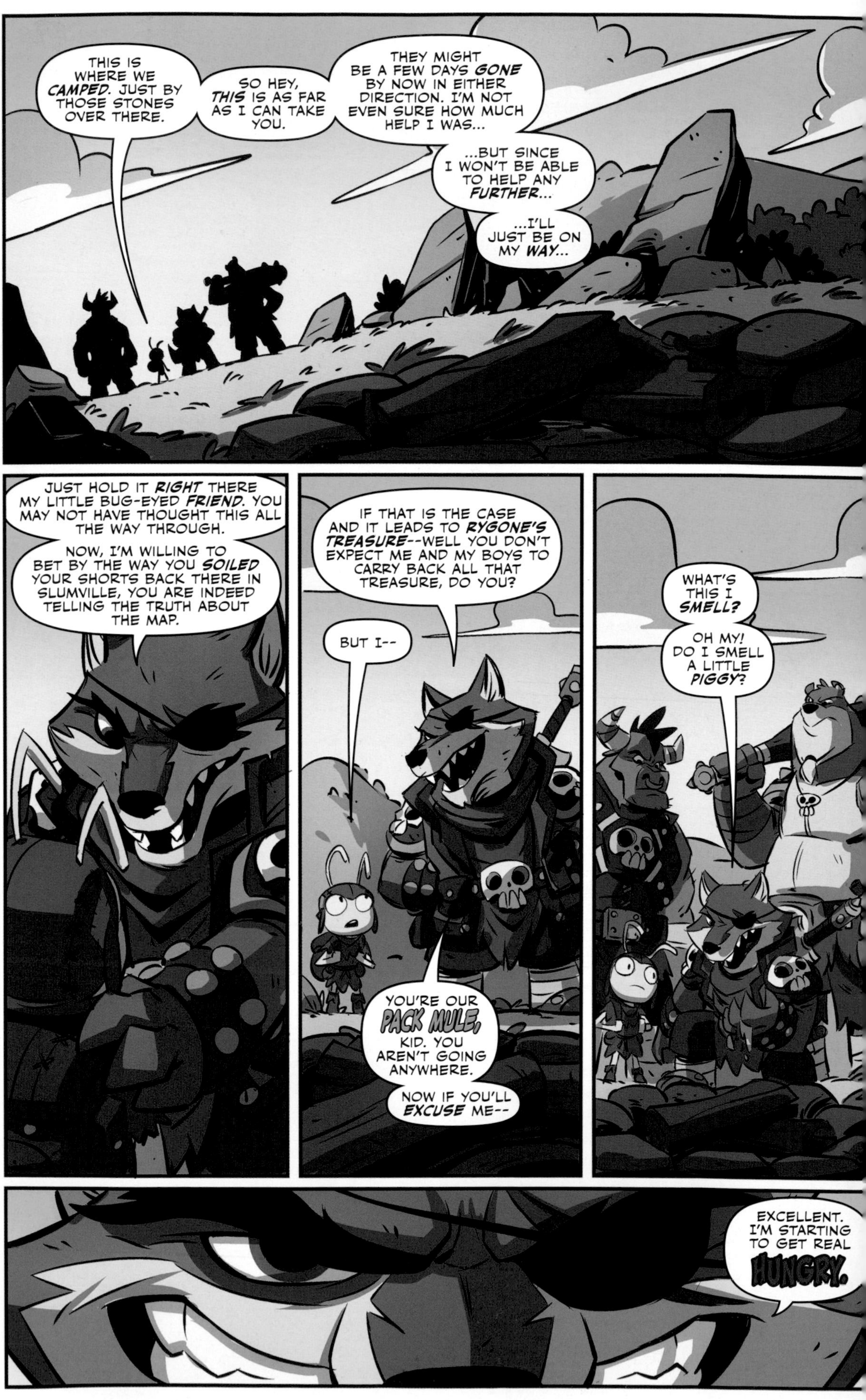
THIS IS WHERE WE CAMPED. JUST BY THOSE STONES OVER THERE.
SO HEY, THIS IS AS FAR AS I CAN TAKE YOU.
THEY MIGHT BE A FEW DAYS GONE BY NOW IN EITHER DIRECTION. I'M NOT EVEN SURE HOW MUCH HELP I WAS...
...BUT SINCE I WON'T BE ABLE TO HELP ANY FURTHER...
...I'LL JUST BE ON MY WAY...
JUST HOLD IT RIGHT THERE MY LITTLE BUG-EYED FRIEND. YOU MAY NOT HAVE THOUGHT THIS ALL THE WAY THROUGH.
NOW, I'M WILLING TO BET BY THE WAY YOU SOILED YOUR SHORTS BACK THERE IN SLUMVILLE, YOU ARE INDEED TELLING THE TRUTH ABOUT THE MAP.
IF THAT IS THE CASE AND IT LEADS TO RYGONE'S TREASURE--WELL YOU DON'T EXPECT ME AND MY BOYS TO CARRY BACK ALL THAT TREASURE, DO YOU?
BUT I--
YOU'RE OUR PACK MULE, KID. YOU AREN'T GOING ANYWHERE.
NOW IF YOU'LL EXCUSE ME--
WHAT'S THIS I SMELL?
OH MY! DO I SMELL A LITTLE PIGGY?
EXCELLENT. I'M STARTING TO GET REAL HUNGRY.

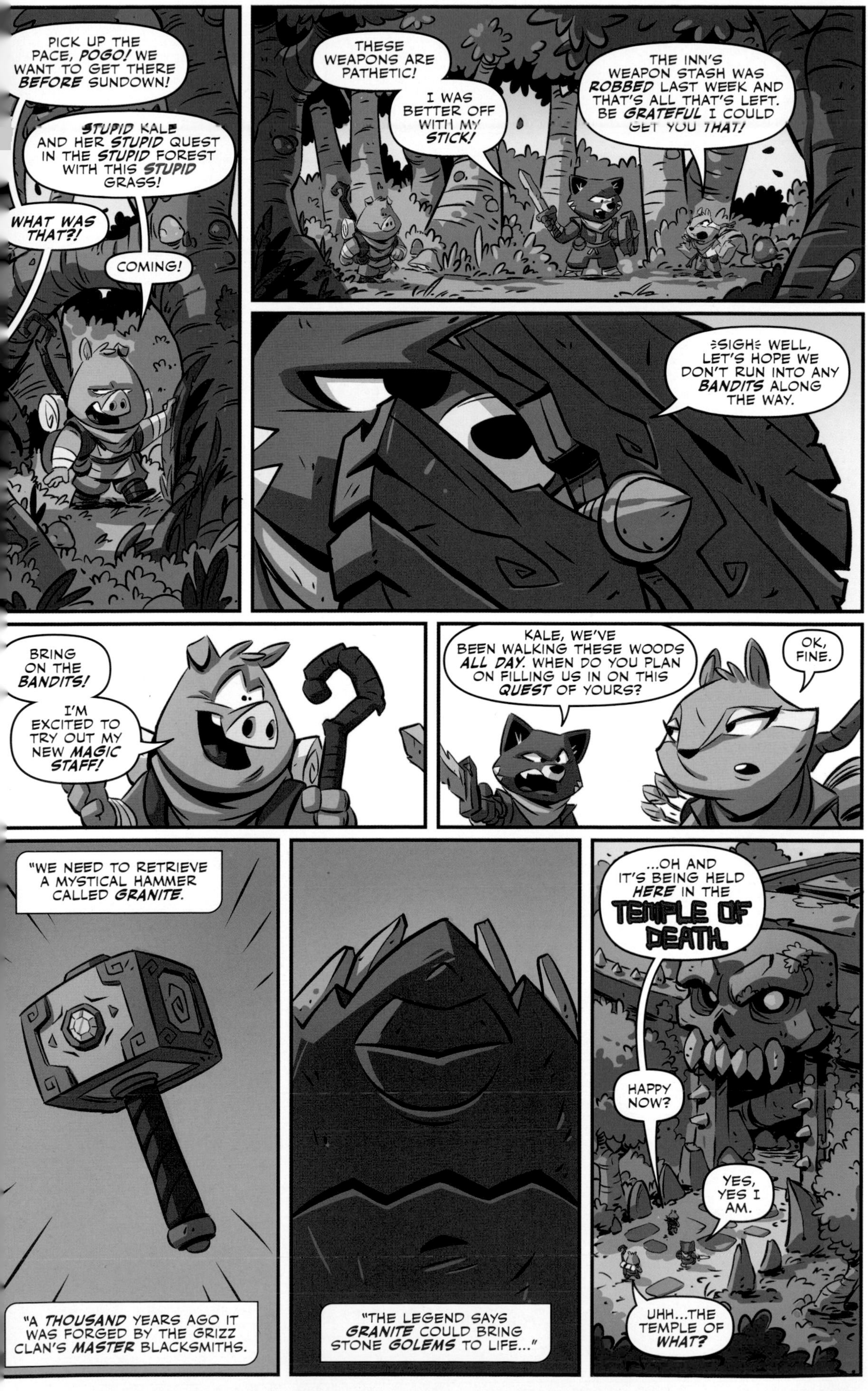
PICK UP THE PACE, *POGO!* WE WANT TO GET THERE *BEFORE* SUNDOWN!
STUPID KALE AND HER *STUPID* QUEST IN THE *STUPID* FOREST WITH THIS *STUPID* GRASS!
WHAT WAS THAT?!
COMING!
THESE WEAPONS ARE PATHETIC!
I WAS BETTER OFF WITH MY *STICK!*
THE INN'S WEAPON STASH WAS *ROBBED* LAST WEEK AND THAT'S ALL THAT'S LEFT. BE *GRATEFUL* I COULD GET YOU *THAT!*
=SIGH= WELL, LET'S HOPE WE DON'T RUN INTO ANY *BANDITS* ALONG THE WAY.
BRING ON THE *BANDITS!*
I'M EXCITED TO TRY OUT MY NEW *MAGIC STAFF!*
KALE, WE'VE BEEN WALKING THESE WOODS *ALL DAY.* WHEN DO YOU PLAN ON FILLING US IN ON THIS *QUEST* OF YOURS?
OK, FINE.
"WE NEED TO RETRIEVE A MYSTICAL HAMMER CALLED *GRANITE*.
"A *THOUSAND* YEARS AGO IT WAS FORGED BY THE GRIZZ CLAN'S *MASTER* BLACKSMITHS.
"THE LEGEND SAYS *GRANITE* COULD BRING STONE *GOLEMS* TO LIFE..."
...OH AND IT'S BEING HELD *HERE* IN THE
TEMPLE OF DEATH.
HAPPY NOW?
YES, YES I AM.
UHH...THE TEMPLE OF *WHAT?*

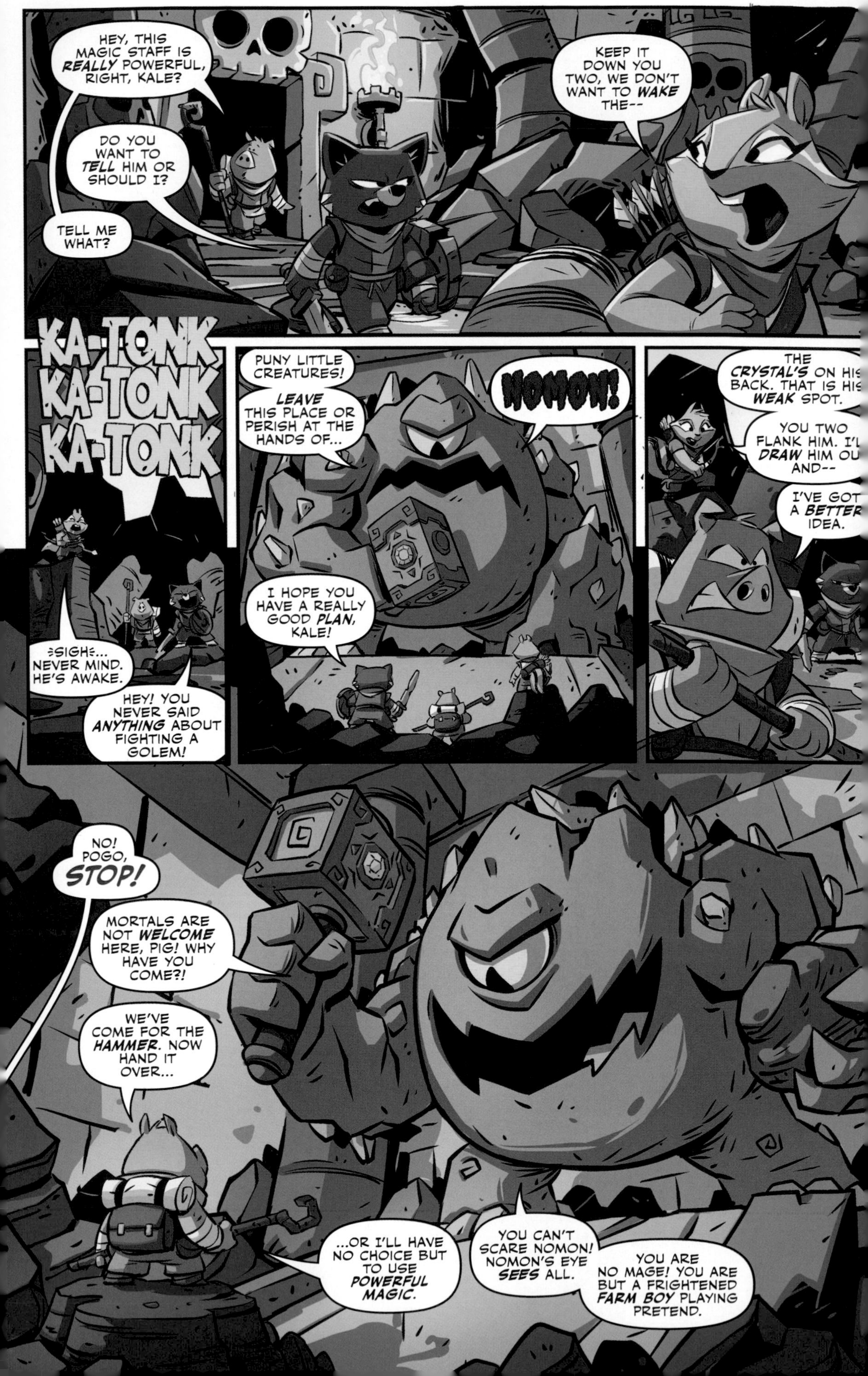
HEY, THIS MAGIC STAFF IS REALLY POWERFUL, RIGHT, KALE?
DO YOU WANT TO TELL HIM OR SHOULD I?
TELL ME WHAT?
KEEP IT DOWN YOU TWO, WE DON'T WANT TO WAKE THE--
KA-TONK KA-TONK KA-TONK
≡SIGH≡... NEVER MIND. HE'S AWAKE.
HEY! YOU NEVER SAID ANYTHING ABOUT FIGHTING A GOLEM!
PUNY LITTLE CREATURES!
LEAVE THIS PLACE OR PERISH AT THE HANDS OF...
NOMON!
I HOPE YOU HAVE A REALLY GOOD PLAN, KALE!
THE CRYSTAL'S ON HIS BACK. THAT IS HIS WEAK SPOT.
YOU TWO FLANK HIM. I'LL DRAW HIM OUT AND--
I'VE GOT A BETTER IDEA.
NO! POGO, STOP!
MORTALS ARE NOT WELCOME HERE, PIG! WHY HAVE YOU COME?!
WE'VE COME FOR THE HAMMER. NOW HAND IT OVER...
...OR I'LL HAVE NO CHOICE BUT TO USE POWERFUL MAGIC.
YOU CAN'T SCARE NOMON! NOMON'S EYE SEES ALL.
YOU ARE NO MAGE! YOU ARE BUT A FRIGHTENED FARM BOY PLAYING PRETEND.

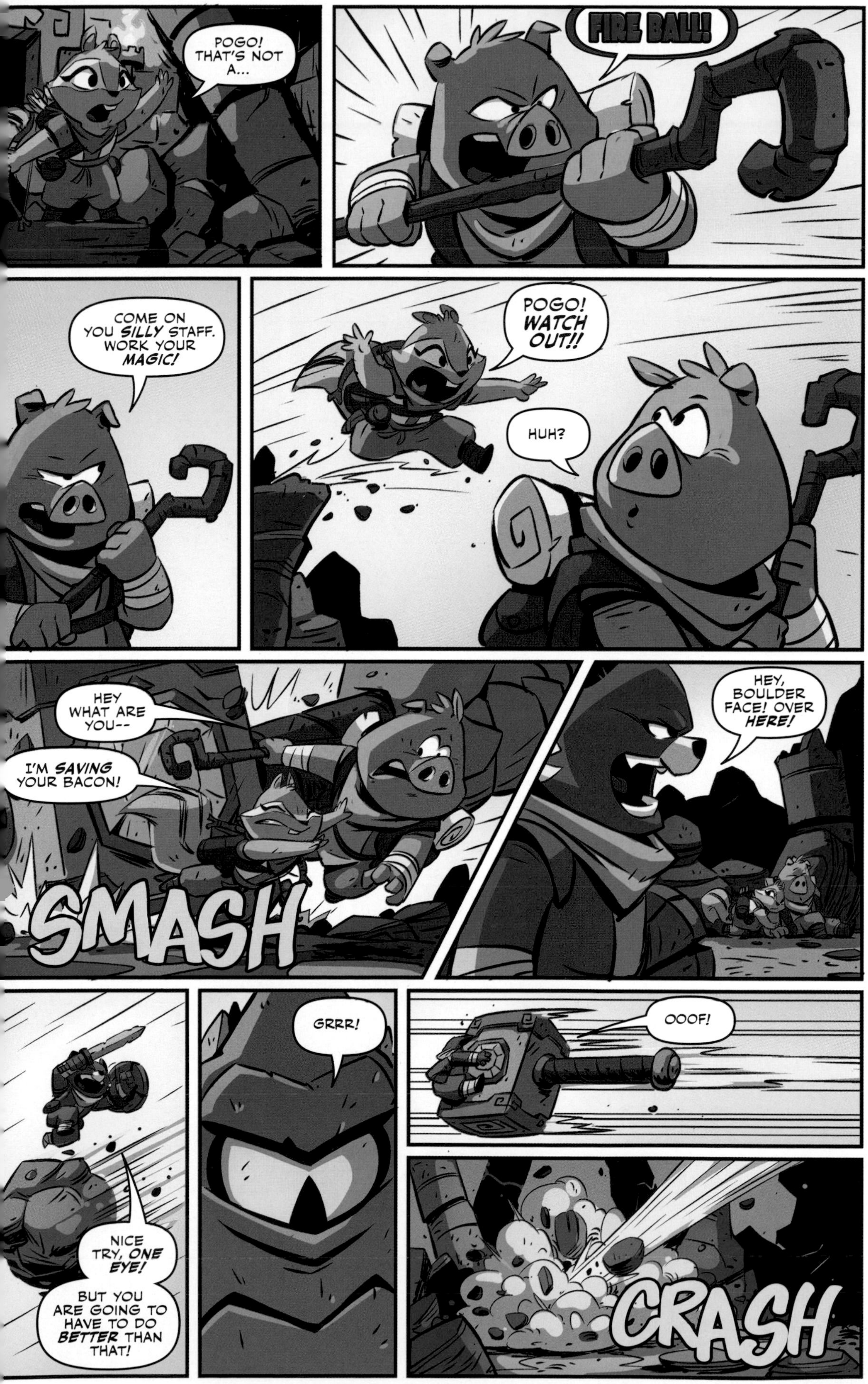

POGO! THAT'S NOT A...
FIRE BALL!
COME ON YOU SILLY STAFF. WORK YOUR MAGIC!
POGO! WATCH OUT!!
HUH?
HEY WHAT ARE YOU--
I'M SAVING YOUR BACON!
SMASH
HEY, BOULDER FACE! OVER HERE!
NICE TRY, ONE EYE!
BUT YOU ARE GOING TO HAVE TO DO BETTER THAN THAT!
GRRR!
OOOF!
CRASH

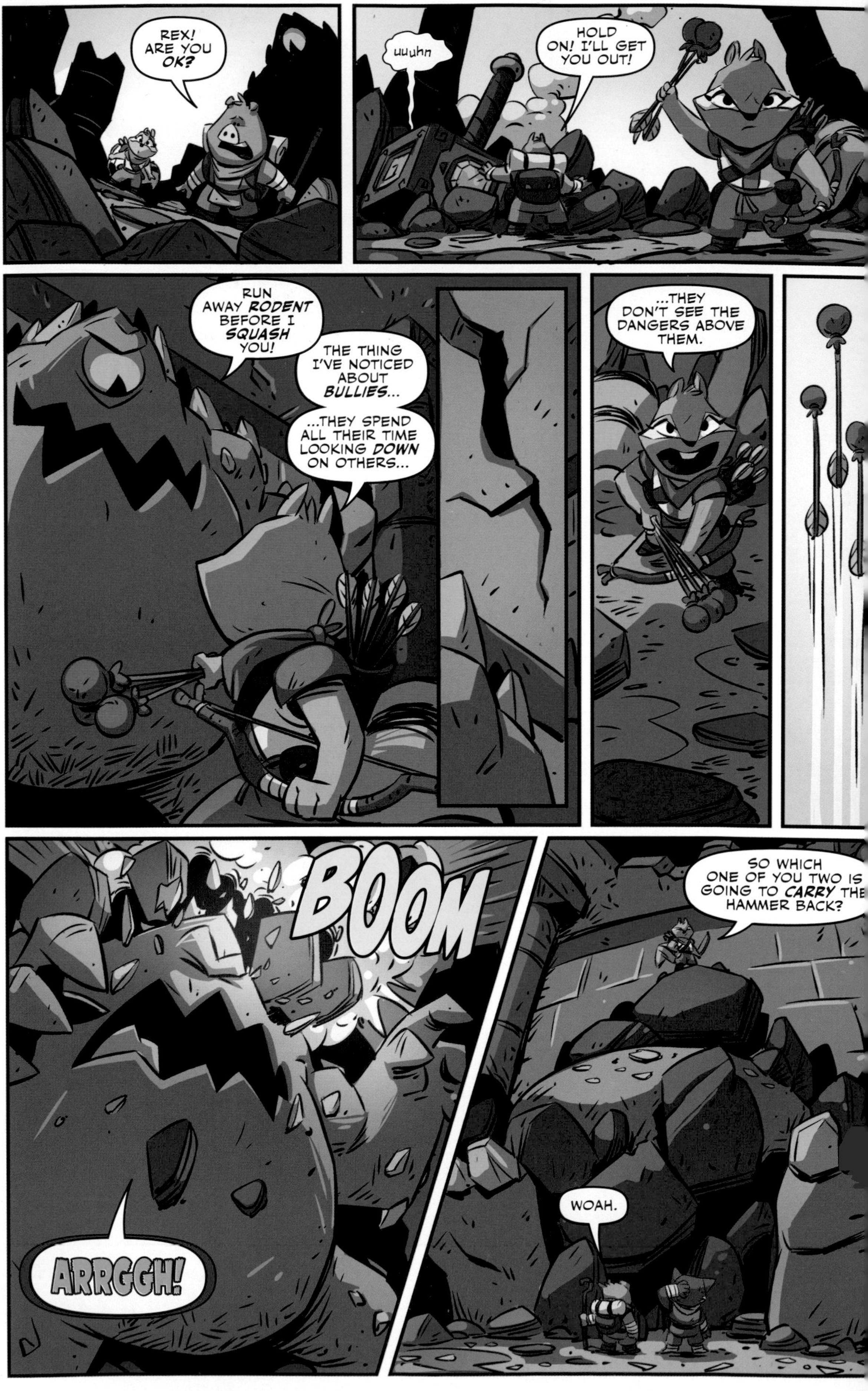
REX! ARE YOU OK?
uuuhn
HOLD ON! I'LL GET YOU OUT!
RUN AWAY RODENT BEFORE I SQUASH YOU!
THE THING I'VE NOTICED ABOUT BULLIES...
...THEY SPEND ALL THEIR TIME LOOKING DOWN ON OTHERS...
...THEY DON'T SEE THE DANGERS ABOVE THEM.
BOOM
ARRGGH!
SO WHICH ONE OF YOU TWO IS GOING TO CARRY THE HAMMER BACK?
WOAH.

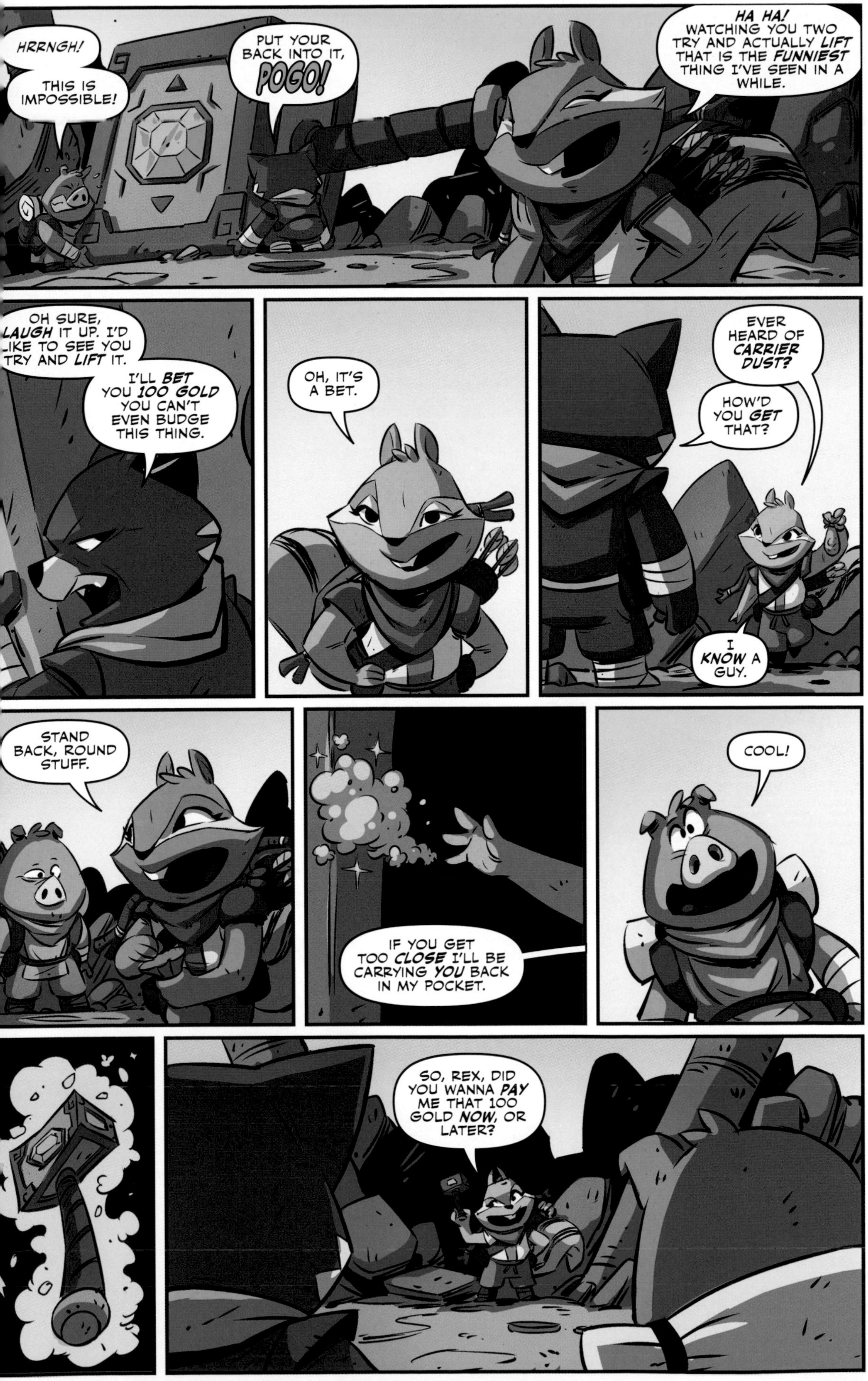
HRRNGH!
THIS IS IMPOSSIBLE!
PUT YOUR BACK INTO IT, POGO!
HA HA! WATCHING YOU TWO TRY AND ACTUALLY LIFT THAT IS THE FUNNIEST THING I'VE SEEN IN A WHILE.
OH SURE, LAUGH IT UP. I'D LIKE TO SEE YOU TRY AND LIFT IT.
I'LL BET YOU 100 GOLD YOU CAN'T EVEN BUDGE THIS THING.
OH, IT'S A BET.
EVER HEARD OF CARRIER DUST?
HOW'D YOU GET THAT?
I KNOW A GUY.
STAND BACK, ROUND STUFF.
IF YOU GET TOO CLOSE I'LL BE CARRYING YOU BACK IN MY POCKET.
COOL!
SO, REX, DID YOU WANNA PAY ME THAT 100 GOLD NOW, OR LATER?

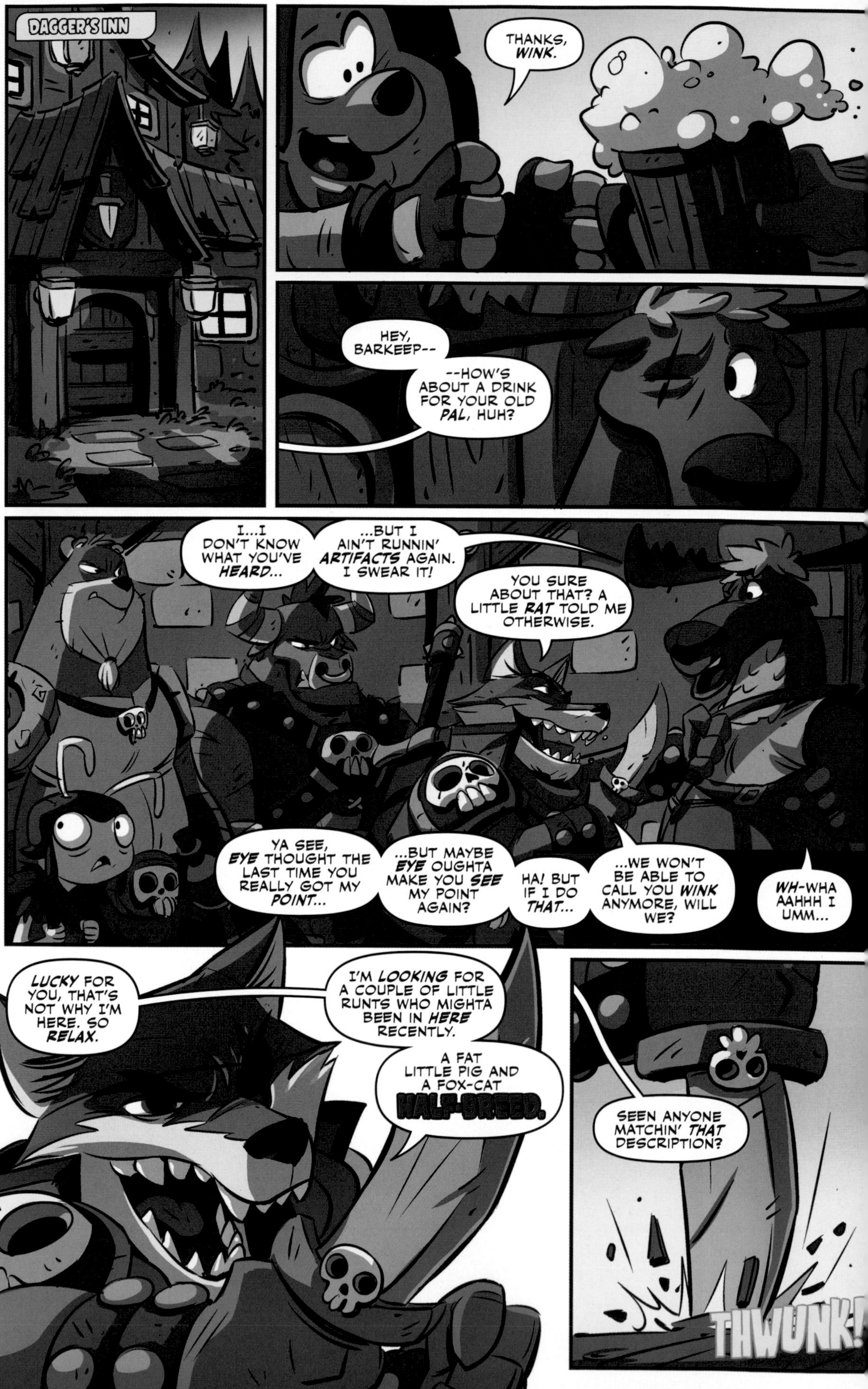
DAGGER'S INN
THANKS, WINK.
HEY, BARKEEP--
--HOW'S ABOUT A DRINK FOR YOUR OLD PAL, HUH?
I...I DON'T KNOW WHAT YOU'VE HEARD...
...BUT I AIN'T RUNNIN' ARTIFACTS AGAIN. I SWEAR IT!
YOU SURE ABOUT THAT? A LITTLE RAT TOLD ME OTHERWISE.
YA SEE, EYE THOUGHT THE LAST TIME YOU REALLY GOT MY POINT...
...BUT MAYBE EYE OUGHTA MAKE YOU SEE MY POINT AGAIN?
HA! BUT IF I DO THAT...
...WE WON'T BE ABLE TO CALL YOU WINK ANYMORE, WILL WE?
WH-WHA AAHHH I UMM...
LUCKY FOR YOU, THAT'S NOT WHY I'M HERE. SO RELAX.
I'M LOOKING FOR A COUPLE OF LITTLE RUNTS WHO MIGHTA BEEN IN HERE RECENTLY.
A FAT LITTLE PIG AND A FOX-CAT HALF-BREED.
SEEN ANYONE MATCHIN' THAT DESCRIPTION?
THWUNK!

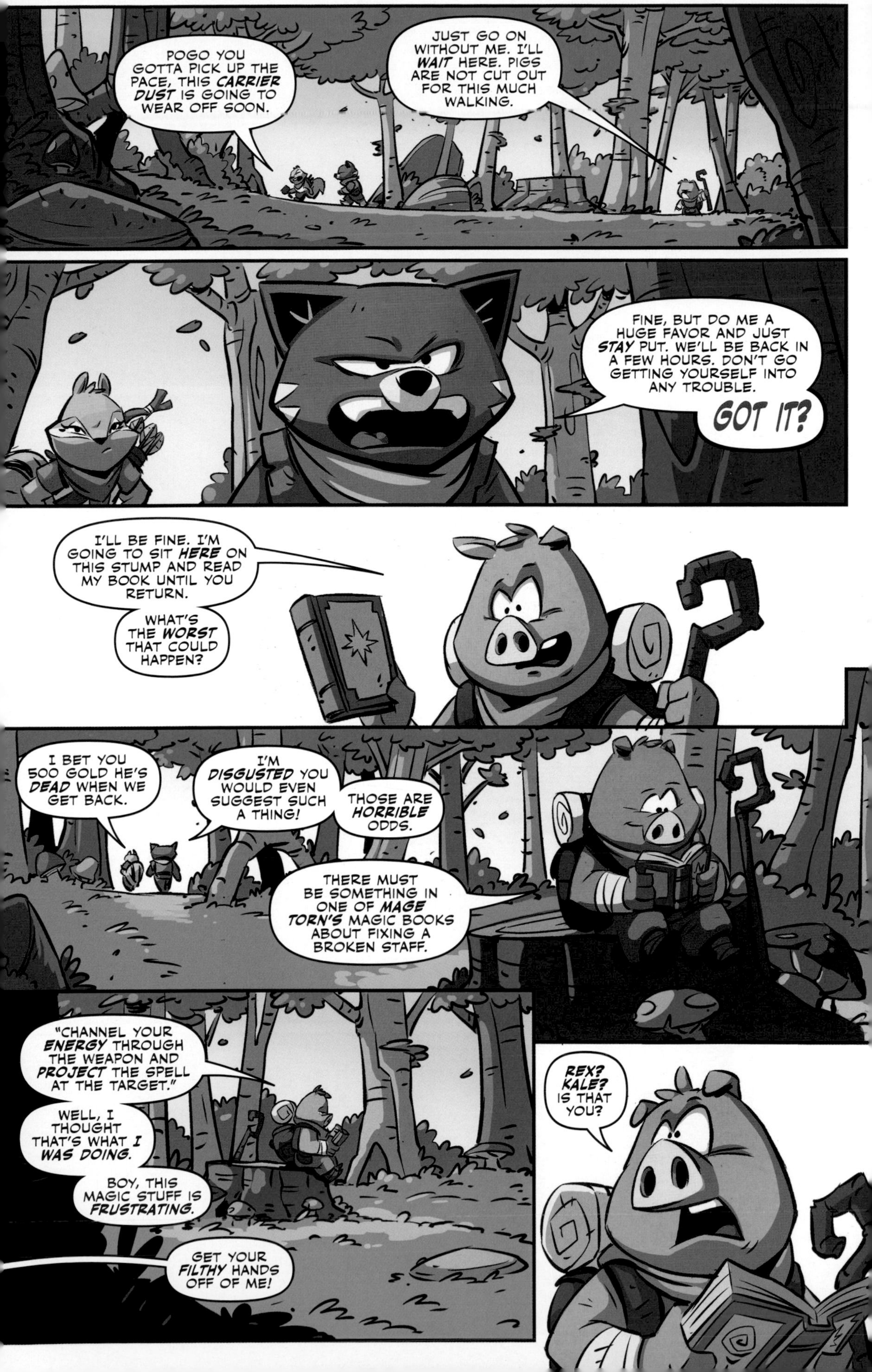
POGO YOU GOTTA PICK UP THE PACE, THIS CARRIER DUST IS GOING TO WEAR OFF SOON.
JUST GO ON WITHOUT ME. I'LL WAIT HERE. PIGS ARE NOT CUT OUT FOR THIS MUCH WALKING.
FINE, BUT DO ME A HUGE FAVOR AND JUST STAY PUT. WE'LL BE BACK IN A FEW HOURS. DON'T GO GETTING YOURSELF INTO ANY TROUBLE.
GOT IT?
I'LL BE FINE. I'M GOING TO SIT HERE ON THIS STUMP AND READ MY BOOK UNTIL YOU RETURN.
WHAT'S THE WORST THAT COULD HAPPEN?
I BET YOU 500 GOLD HE'S DEAD WHEN WE GET BACK.
I'M DISGUSTED YOU WOULD EVEN SUGGEST SUCH A THING!
THOSE ARE HORRIBLE ODDS.
THERE MUST BE SOMETHING IN ONE OF MAGE TORN'S MAGIC BOOKS ABOUT FIXING A BROKEN STAFF.
"CHANNEL YOUR ENERGY THROUGH THE WEAPON AND PROJECT THE SPELL AT THE TARGET."
WELL, I THOUGHT THAT'S WHAT I WAS DOING.
BOY, THIS MAGIC STUFF IS FRUSTRATING.
GET YOUR FILTHY HANDS OFF OF ME!
REX? KALE? IS THAT YOU?

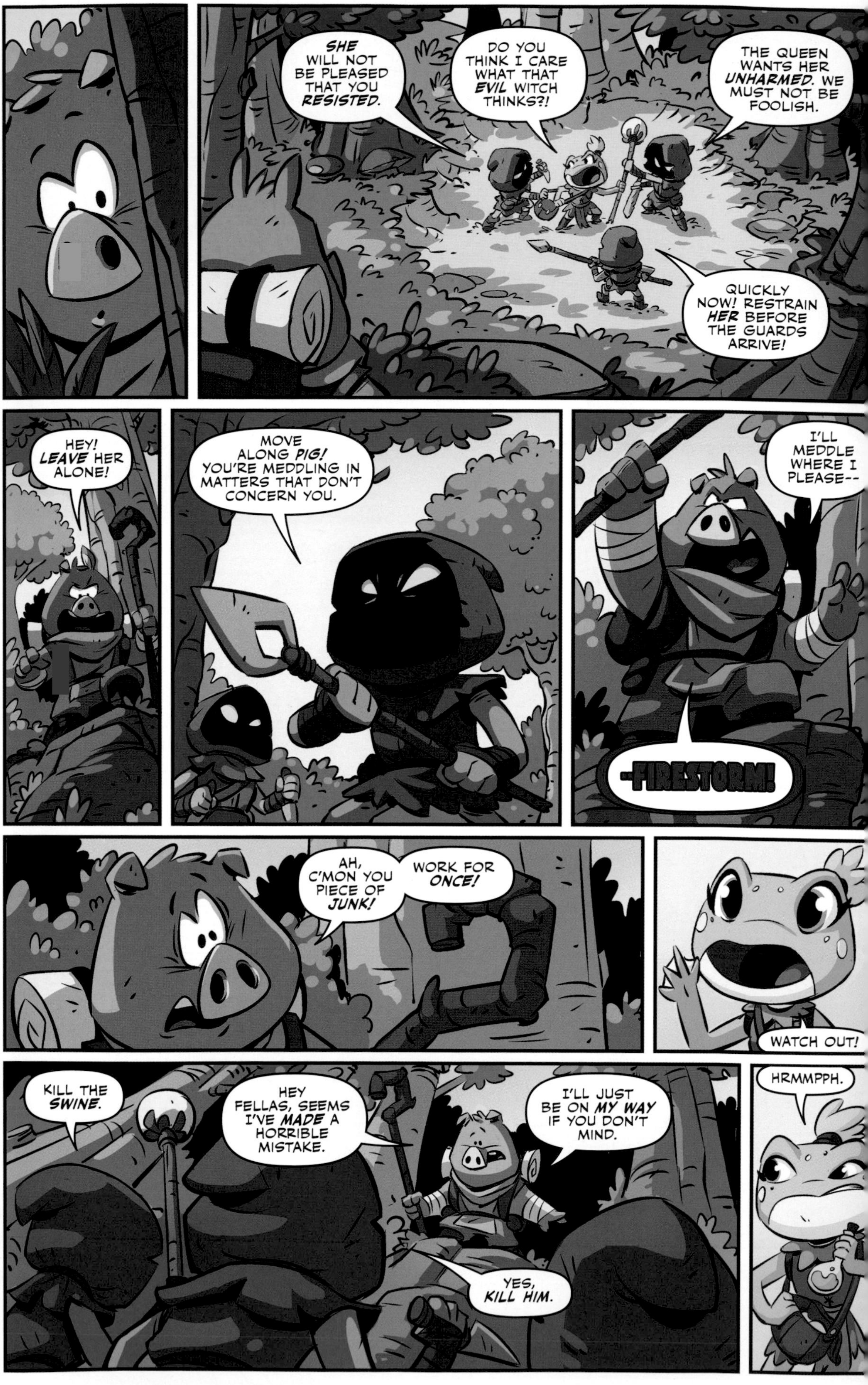
SHE WILL NOT BE PLEASED THAT YOU RESISTED.
DO YOU THINK I CARE WHAT THAT EVIL WITCH THINKS?!
THE QUEEN WANTS HER UNHARMED. WE MUST NOT BE FOOLISH.
QUICKLY NOW! RESTRAIN HER BEFORE THE GUARDS ARRIVE!
HEY! LEAVE HER ALONE!
MOVE ALONG PIG! YOU'RE MEDDLING IN MATTERS THAT DON'T CONCERN YOU.
I'LL MEDDLE WHERE I PLEASE--
--FIRESTORM!
AH, C'MON YOU PIECE OF JUNK!
WORK FOR ONCE!
WATCH OUT!
KILL THE SWINE.
HEY FELLAS, SEEMS I'VE MADE A HORRIBLE MISTAKE.
I'LL JUST BE ON MY WAY IF YOU DON'T MIND.
YES, KILL HIM.
HRMMPPH.

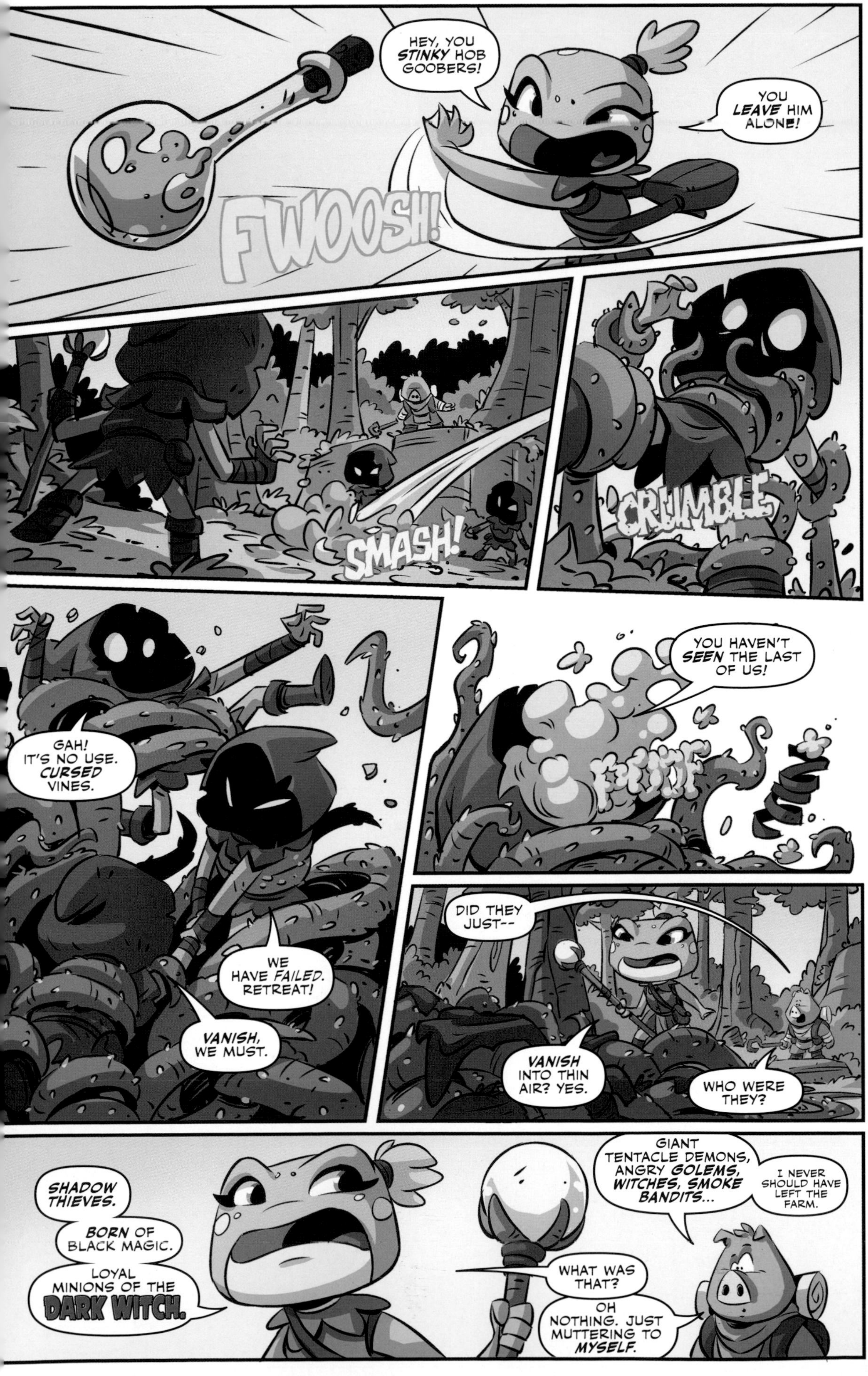
HEY, YOU STINKY HOB GOOBERS!
YOU LEAVE HIM ALONE!
FWOOSH!
SMASH!
CRUMBLE
GAH! IT'S NO USE. CURSED VINES.
WE HAVE FAILED. RETREAT!
VANISH, WE MUST.
YOU HAVEN'T SEEN THE LAST OF US!
POOF
DID THEY JUST--
VANISH INTO THIN AIR? YES.
WHO WERE THEY?
SHADOW THIEVES.
BORN OF BLACK MAGIC.
LOYAL MINIONS OF THE DARK WITCH.
GIANT TENTACLE DEMONS, ANGRY GOLEMS, WITCHES, SMOKE BANDITS...
I NEVER SHOULD HAVE LEFT THE FARM.
WHAT WAS THAT?
OH NOTHING. JUST MUTTERING TO MYSELF.

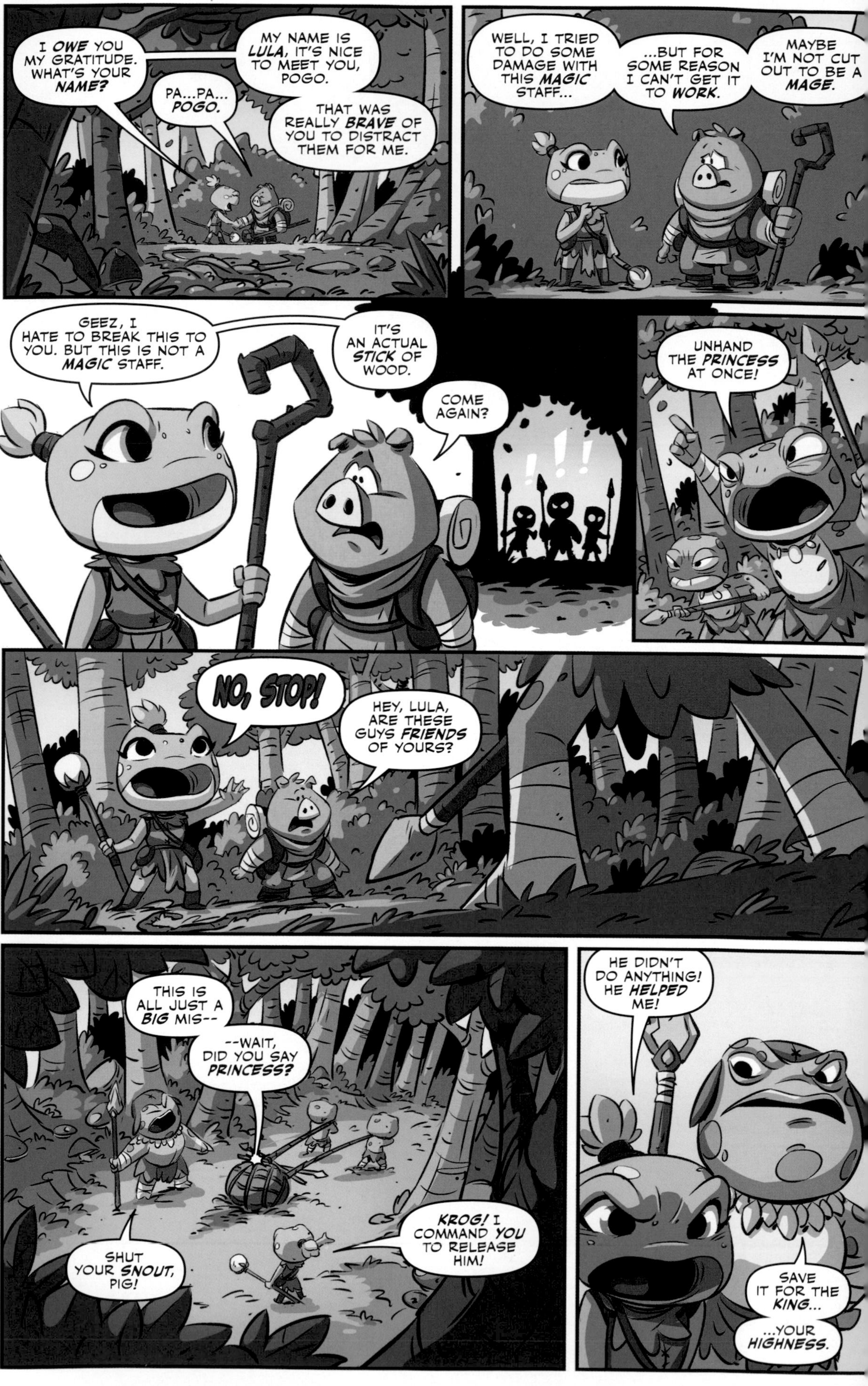
I OWE YOU MY GRATITUDE. WHAT'S YOUR NAME?
PA...PA... POGO.
MY NAME IS LULA, IT'S NICE TO MEET YOU, POGO.
THAT WAS REALLY BRAVE OF YOU TO DISTRACT THEM FOR ME.
WELL, I TRIED TO DO SOME DAMAGE WITH THIS MAGIC STAFF...
...BUT FOR SOME REASON I CAN'T GET IT TO WORK.
MAYBE I'M NOT CUT OUT TO BE A MAGE.
GEEZ, I HATE TO BREAK THIS TO YOU. BUT THIS IS NOT A MAGIC STAFF.
IT'S AN ACTUAL STICK OF WOOD.
COME AGAIN?
! ! !
UNHAND THE PRINCESS AT ONCE!
NO, STOP!
HEY, LULA, ARE THESE GUYS FRIENDS OF YOURS?
THIS IS ALL JUST A BIG MIS--
--WAIT, DID YOU SAY PRINCESS?
SHUT YOUR SNOUT, PIG!
KROG! I COMMAND YOU TO RELEASE HIM!
HE DIDN'T DO ANYTHING! HE HELPED ME!
SAVE IT FOR THE KING...
...YOUR HIGHNESS.

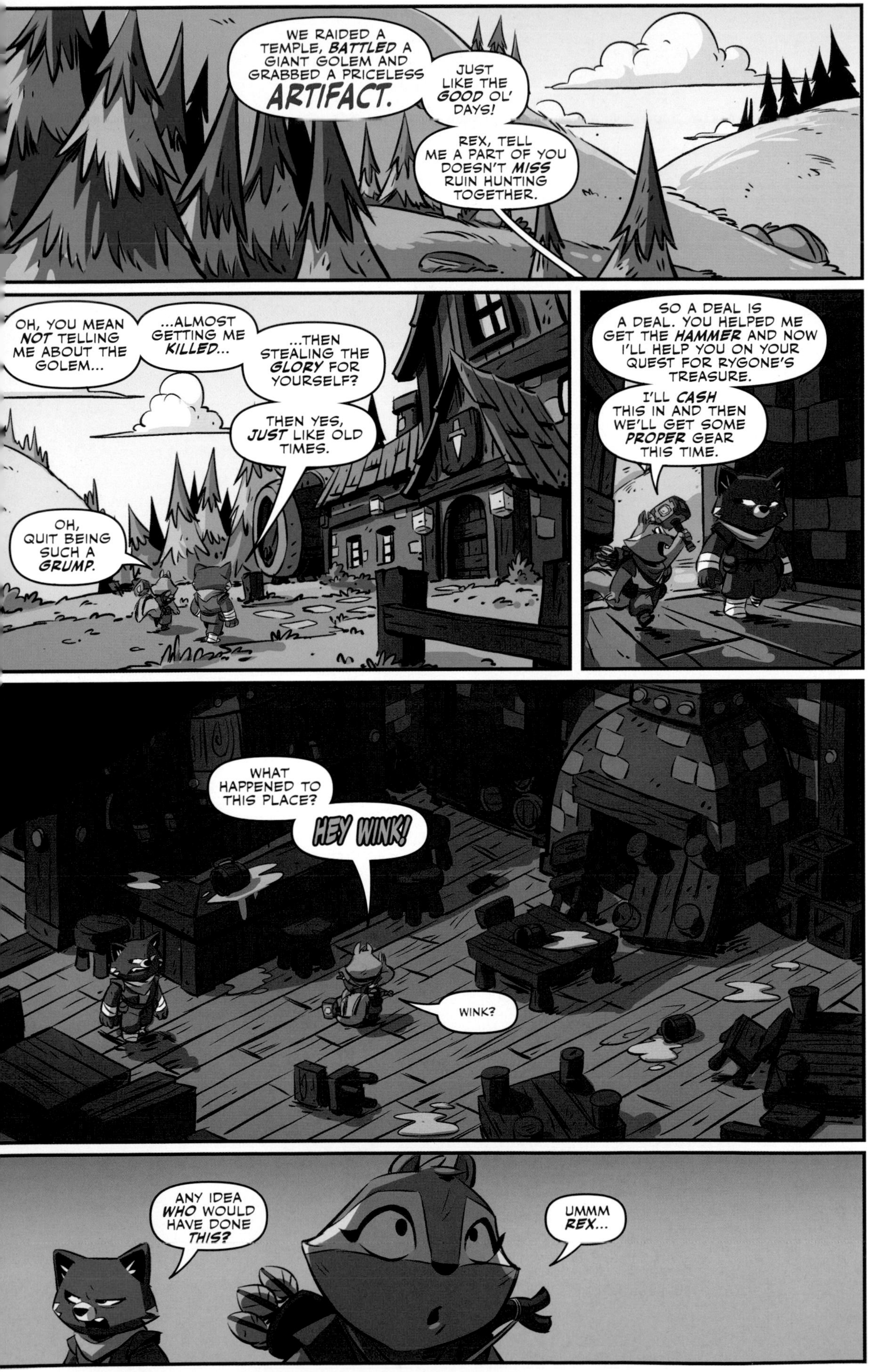

WE RAIDED A TEMPLE, BATTLED A GIANT GOLEM AND GRABBED A PRICELESS ARTIFACT.
JUST LIKE THE GOOD OL' DAYS!
REX, TELL ME A PART OF YOU DOESN'T MISS RUIN HUNTING TOGETHER.
OH, YOU MEAN NOT TELLING ME ABOUT THE GOLEM...
...ALMOST GETTING ME KILLED...
...THEN STEALING THE GLORY FOR YOURSELF?
THEN YES, JUST LIKE OLD TIMES.
OH, QUIT BEING SUCH A GRUMP.
SO A DEAL IS A DEAL. YOU HELPED ME GET THE HAMMER AND NOW I'LL HELP YOU ON YOUR QUEST FOR RYGONE'S TREASURE.
I'LL CASH THIS IN AND THEN WE'LL GET SOME PROPER GEAR THIS TIME.
WHAT HAPPENED TO THIS PLACE?
HEY WINK!
WINK?
ANY IDEA WHO WOULD HAVE DONE THIS?
UMMM REX...

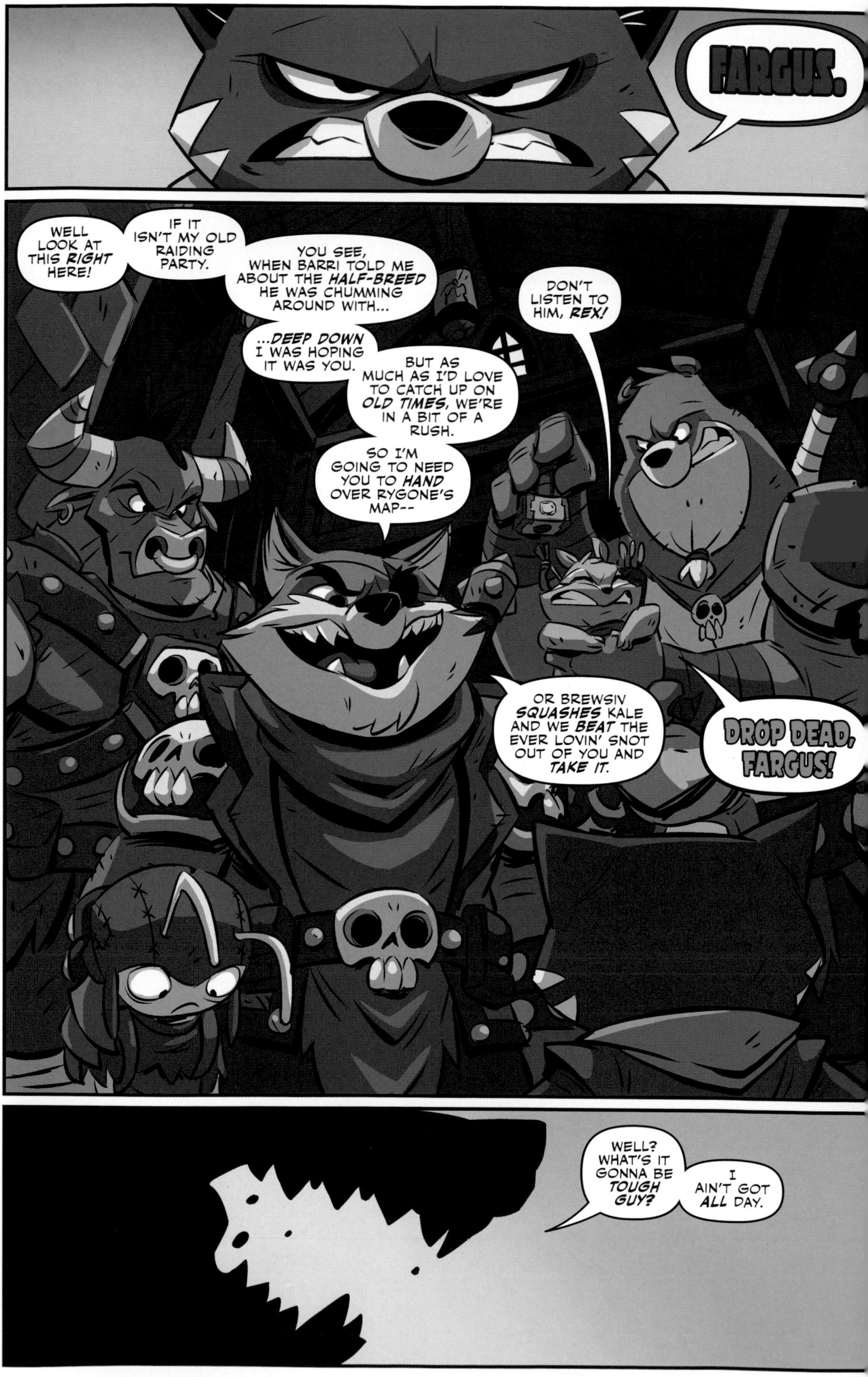
FARGUS.
WELL LOOK AT THIS RIGHT HERE!
IF IT ISN'T MY OLD RAIDING PARTY.
YOU SEE, WHEN BARRI TOLD ME ABOUT THE HALF-BREED HE WAS CHUMMING AROUND WITH...
...DEEP DOWN I WAS HOPING IT WAS YOU.
BUT AS MUCH AS I'D LOVE TO CATCH UP ON OLD TIMES, WE'RE IN A BIT OF A RUSH.
SO I'M GOING TO NEED YOU TO HAND OVER RYGONE'S MAP--
DON'T LISTEN TO HIM, REX!
OR BREWSIV SQUASHES KALE AND WE BEAT THE EVER LOVIN' SNOT OUT OF YOU AND TAKE IT.
DROP DEAD, FARGUS!
WELL? WHAT'S IT GONNA BE TOUGH GUY?
I AIN'T GOT ALL DAY.

BOOM

ISSUE 3 COVER BY DEREK LAUFMAN

CHAPTER 3

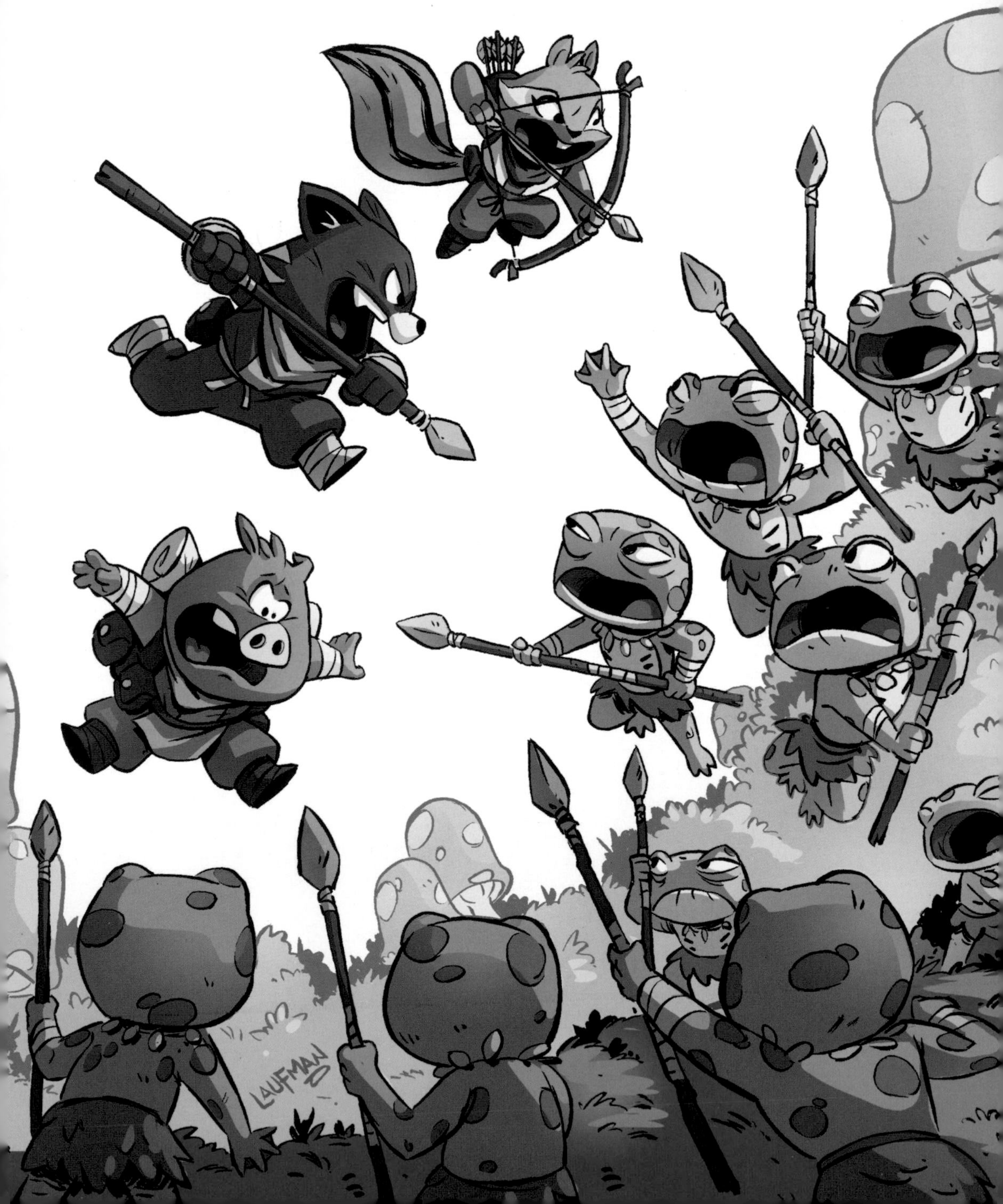
LAUFMAN

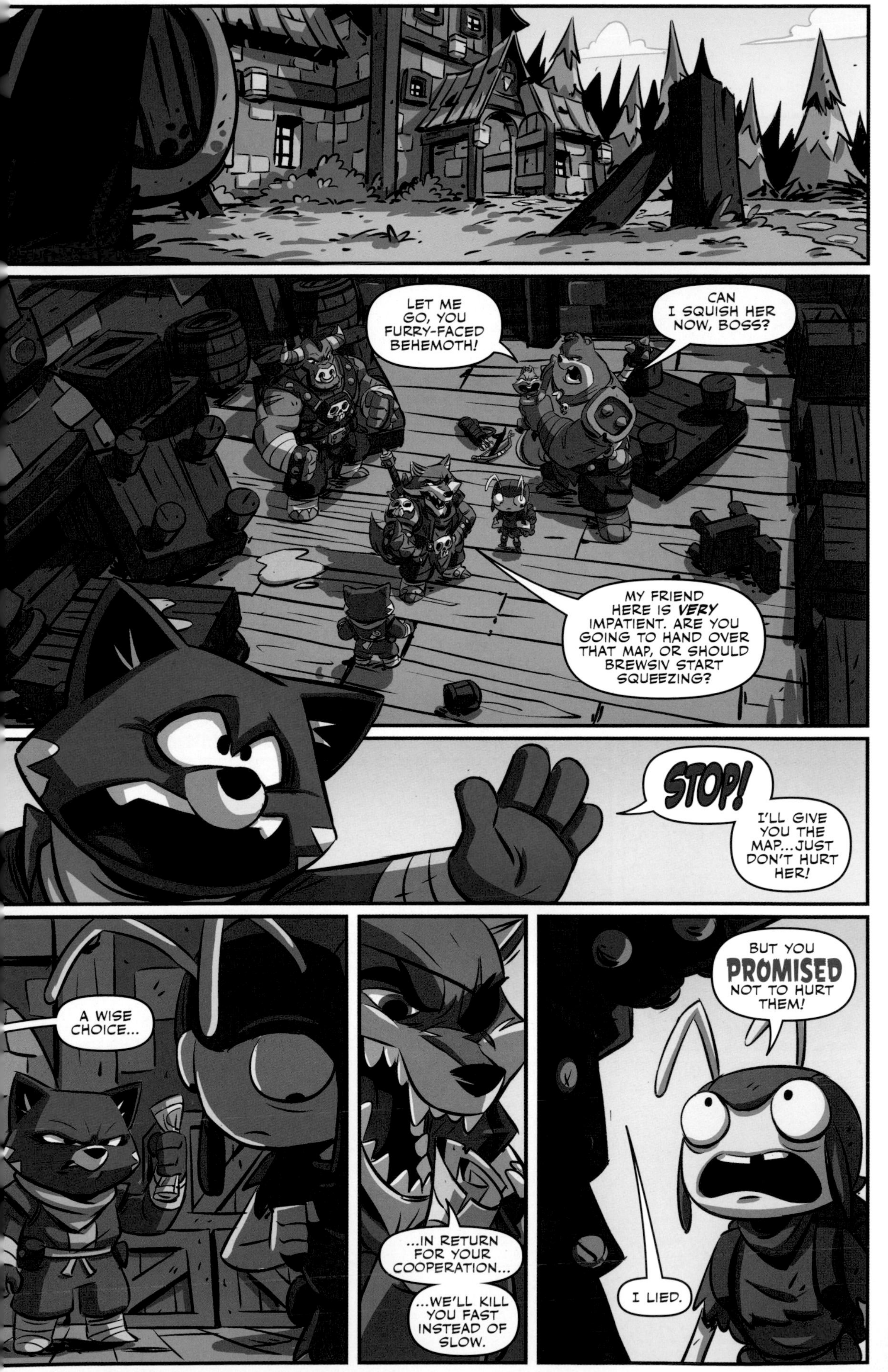

LET ME GO, YOU FURRY-FACED BEHEMOTH!
CAN I SQUISH HER NOW, BOSS?
MY FRIEND HERE IS VERY IMPATIENT. ARE YOU GOING TO HAND OVER THAT MAP, OR SHOULD BREWSIV START SQUEEZING?
STOP!
I'LL GIVE YOU THE MAP...JUST DON'T HURT HER!
A WISE CHOICE...
...IN RETURN FOR YOUR COOPERATION...
...WE'LL KILL YOU FAST INSTEAD OF SLOW.
BUT YOU PROMISED NOT TO HURT THEM!
I LIED.

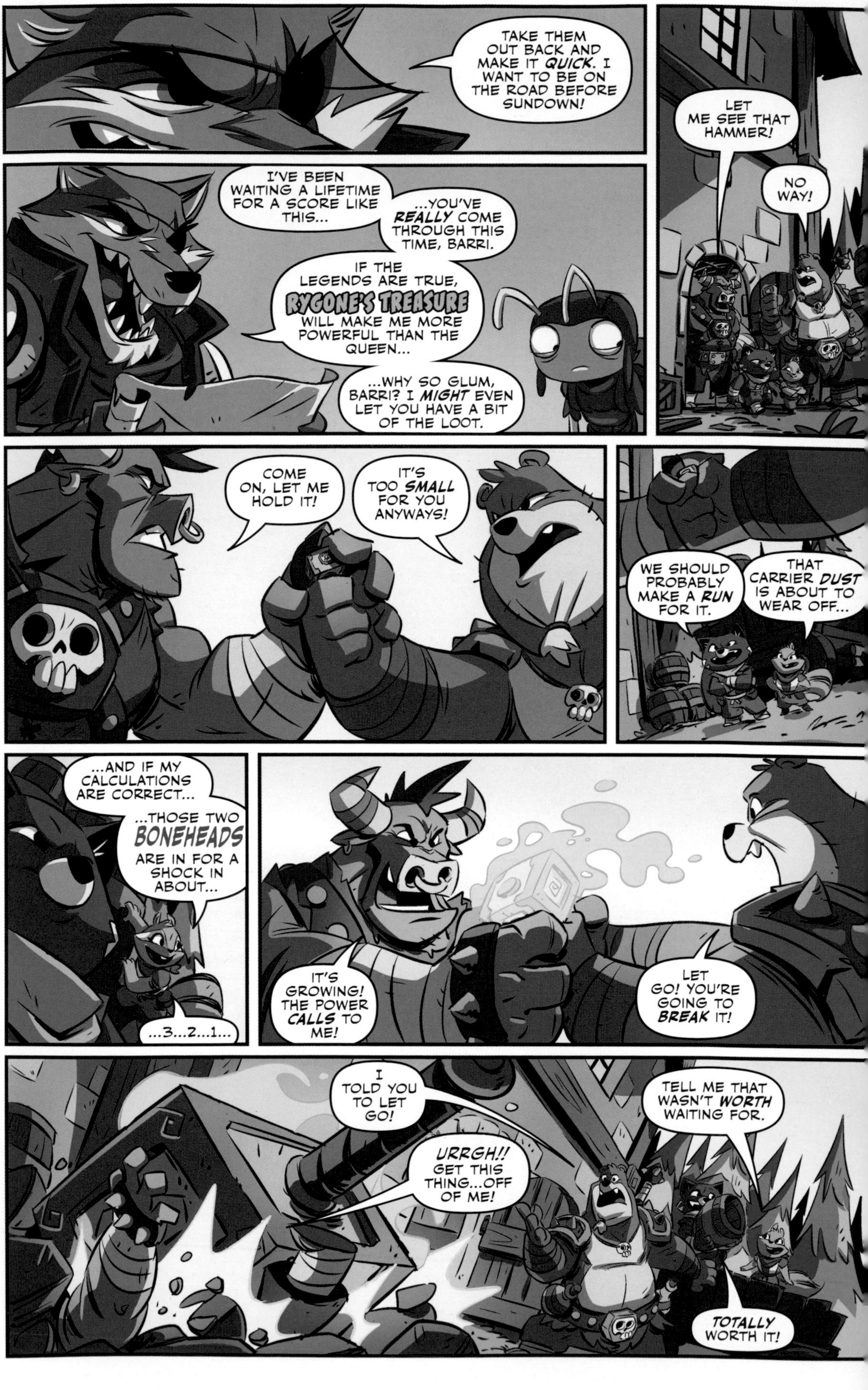
TAKE THEM OUT BACK AND MAKE IT QUICK. I WANT TO BE ON THE ROAD BEFORE SUNDOWN!
I'VE BEEN WAITING A LIFETIME FOR A SCORE LIKE THIS...
...YOU'VE REALLY COME THROUGH THIS TIME, BARRI.
IF THE LEGENDS ARE TRUE, RYGONE'S TREASURE WILL MAKE ME MORE POWERFUL THAN THE QUEEN...
...WHY SO GLUM, BARRI? I MIGHT EVEN LET YOU HAVE A BIT OF THE LOOT.
LET ME SEE THAT HAMMER!
NO WAY!
COME ON, LET ME HOLD IT!
IT'S TOO SMALL FOR YOU ANYWAYS!
WE SHOULD PROBABLY MAKE A RUN FOR IT.
THAT CARRIER DUST IS ABOUT TO WEAR OFF...
...AND IF MY CALCULATIONS ARE CORRECT...
...THOSE TWO BONEHEADS ARE IN FOR A SHOCK IN ABOUT...
...3...2...1...
IT'S GROWING! THE POWER CALLS TO ME!
LET GO! YOU'RE GOING TO BREAK IT!
I TOLD YOU TO LET GO!
URRGH!! GET THIS THING...OFF OF ME!
TELL ME THAT WASN'T WORTH WAITING FOR.
TOTALLY WORTH IT!

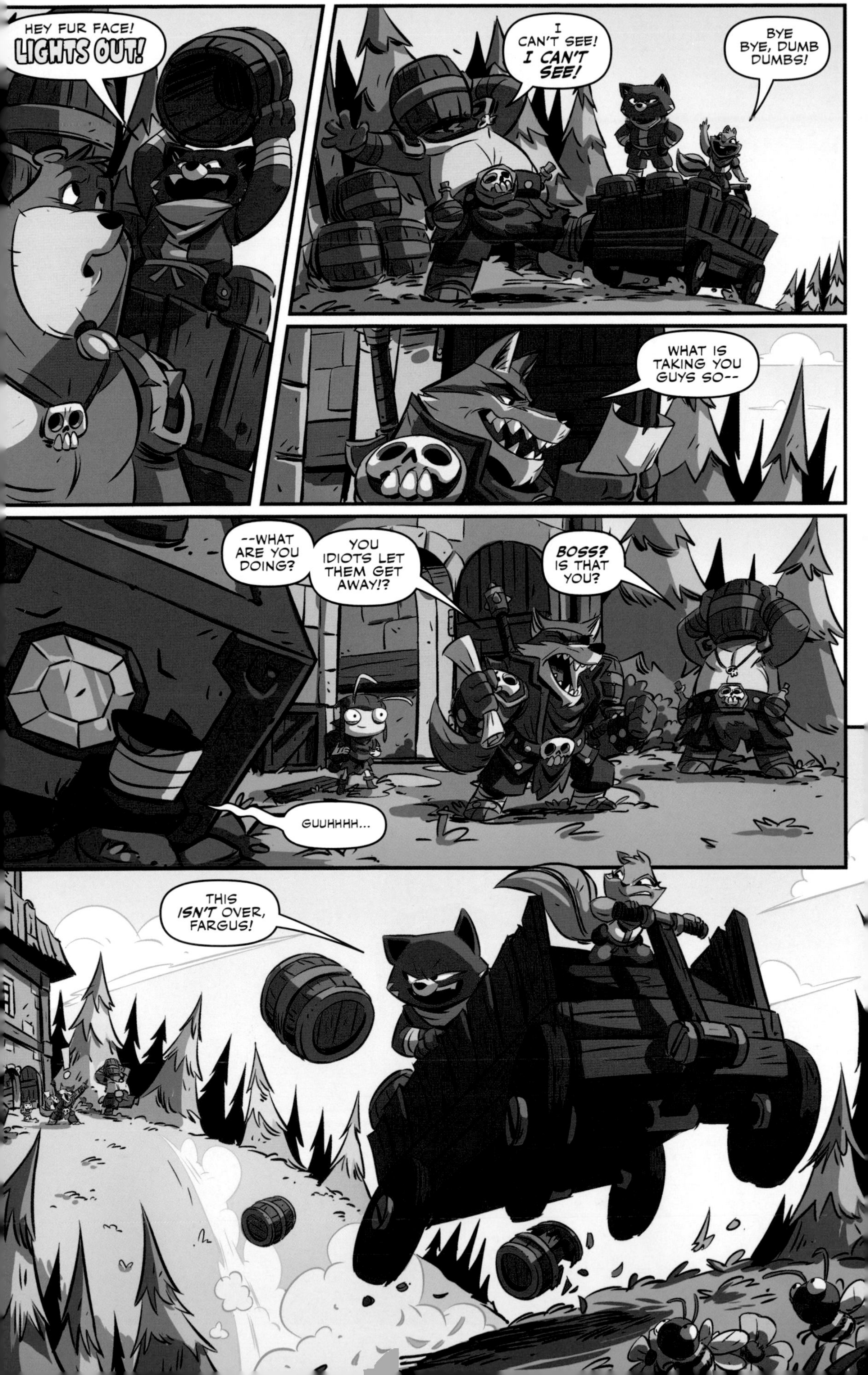
HEY FUR FACE!
LIGHTS OUT!
I CAN'T SEE! I CAN'T SEE!
BYE BYE, DUMB DUMBS!
WHAT IS TAKING YOU GUYS SO--
--WHAT ARE YOU DOING?
YOU IDIOTS LET THEM GET AWAY!?
BOSS? IS THAT YOU?
GUUHHHH...
THIS ISN'T OVER, FARGUS!

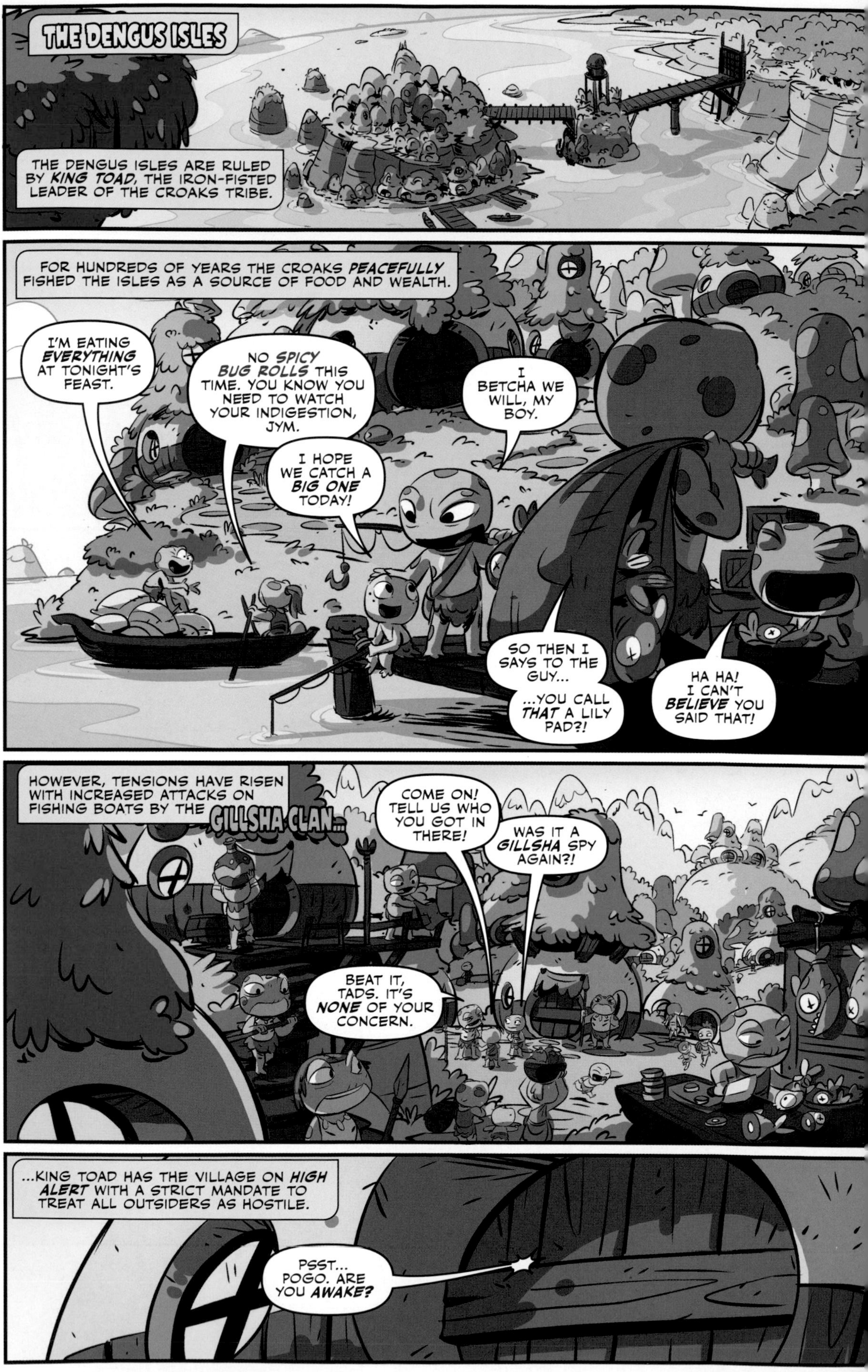
THE DENGUS ISLES
THE DENGUS ISLES ARE RULED BY KING TOAD, THE IRON-FISTED LEADER OF THE CROAKS TRIBE.
FOR HUNDREDS OF YEARS THE CROAKS PEACEFULLY FISHED THE ISLES AS A SOURCE OF FOOD AND WEALTH.
I'M EATING EVERYTHING AT TONIGHT'S FEAST.
NO SPICY BUG ROLLS THIS TIME. YOU KNOW YOU NEED TO WATCH YOUR INDIGESTION, JYM.
I HOPE WE CATCH A BIG ONE TODAY!
I BETCHA WE WILL, MY BOY.
SO THEN I SAYS TO THE GUY...
...YOU CALL THAT A LILY PAD?!
HA HA! I CAN'T BELIEVE YOU SAID THAT!
HOWEVER, TENSIONS HAVE RISEN WITH INCREASED ATTACKS ON FISHING BOATS BY THE GILLSHA CLAN...
COME ON! TELL US WHO YOU GOT IN THERE!
WAS IT A GILLSHA SPY AGAIN?!
BEAT IT, TADS. IT'S NONE OF YOUR CONCERN.
...KING TOAD HAS THE VILLAGE ON HIGH ALERT WITH A STRICT MANDATE TO TREAT ALL OUTSIDERS AS HOSTILE.
PSST... POGO. ARE YOU AWAKE?

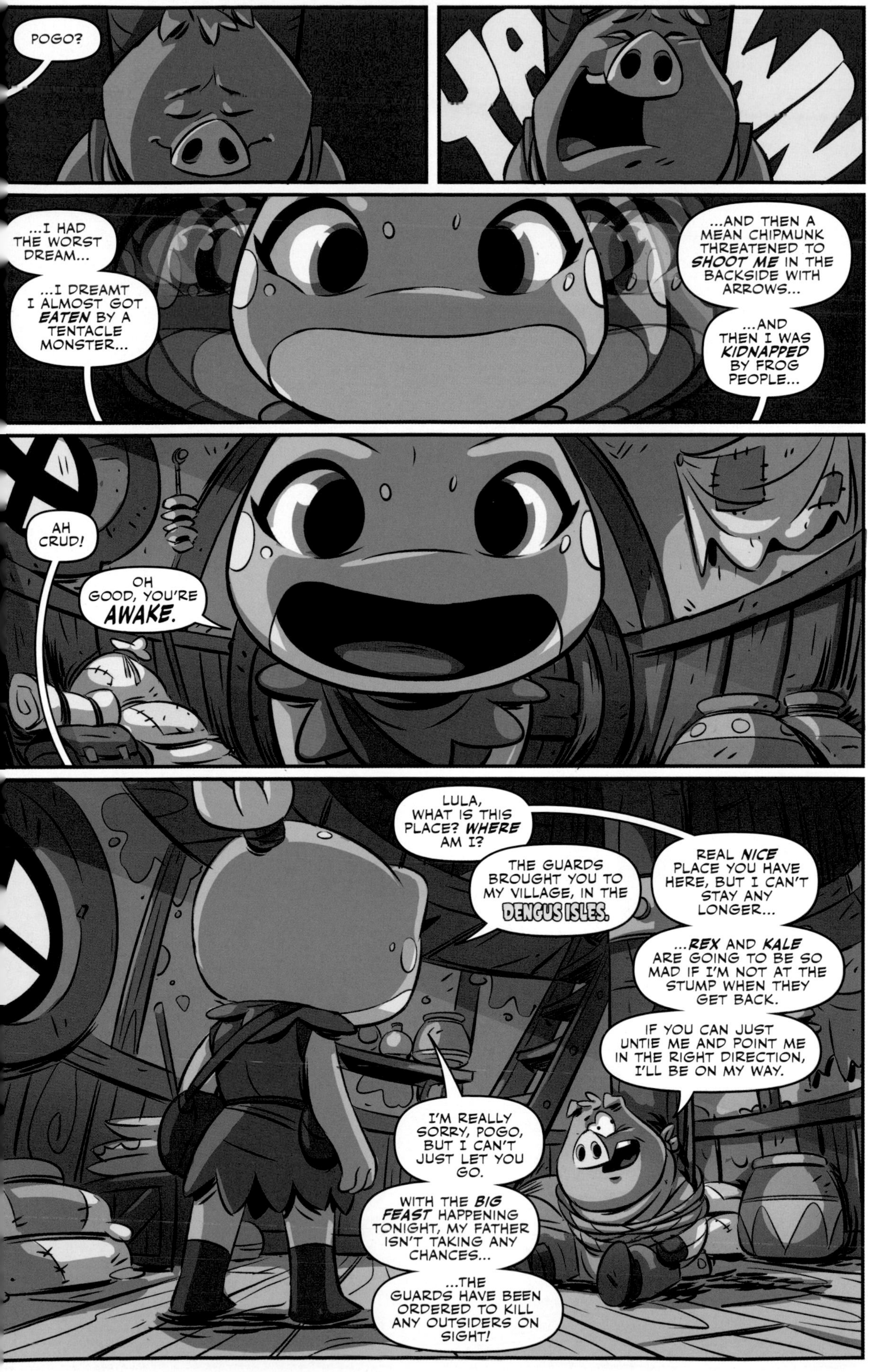
POGO?
...I HAD THE WORST DREAM...
...I DREAMT I ALMOST GOT EATEN BY A TENTACLE MONSTER...
...AND THEN A MEAN CHIPMUNK THREATENED TO SHOOT ME IN THE BACKSIDE WITH ARROWS...
...AND THEN I WAS KIDNAPPED BY FROG PEOPLE...
AH CRUD!
OH GOOD, YOU'RE AWAKE.
LULA, WHAT IS THIS PLACE? WHERE AM I?
THE GUARDS BROUGHT YOU TO MY VILLAGE, IN THE DENGUS ISLES.
REAL NICE PLACE YOU HAVE HERE, BUT I CAN'T STAY ANY LONGER...
...REX AND KALE ARE GOING TO BE SO MAD IF I'M NOT AT THE STUMP WHEN THEY GET BACK.
IF YOU CAN JUST UNTIE ME AND POINT ME IN THE RIGHT DIRECTION, I'LL BE ON MY WAY.
I'M REALLY SORRY, POGO, BUT I CAN'T JUST LET YOU GO.
WITH THE BIG FEAST HAPPENING TONIGHT, MY FATHER ISN'T TAKING ANY CHANCES...
...THE GUARDS HAVE BEEN ORDERED TO KILL ANY OUTSIDERS ON SIGHT!

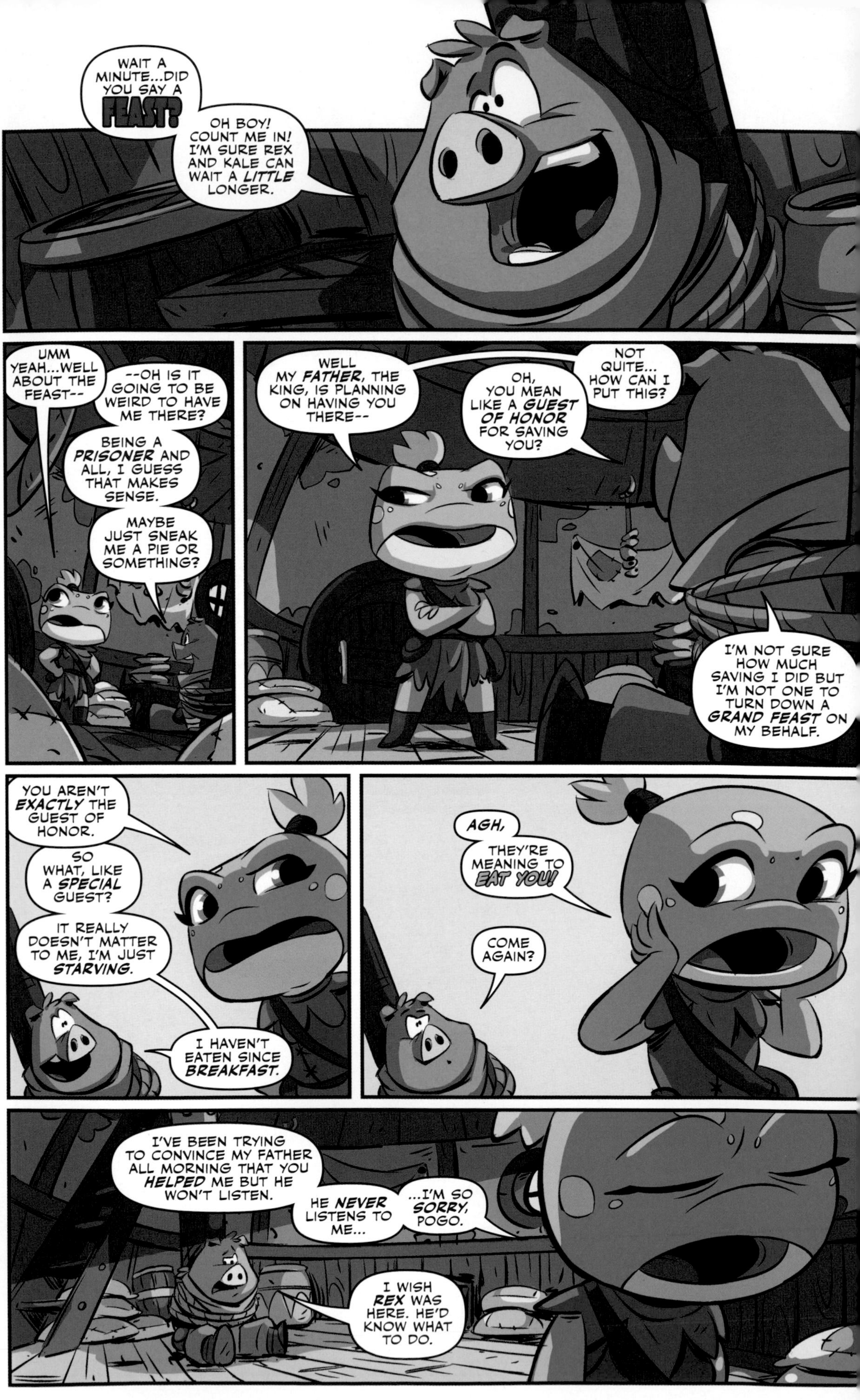

WAIT A MINUTE...DID YOU SAY A FEAST?
OH BOY! COUNT ME IN! I'M SURE REX AND KALE CAN WAIT A LITTLE LONGER.
UMM YEAH...WELL ABOUT THE FEAST--
--OH IS IT GOING TO BE WEIRD TO HAVE ME THERE?
BEING A PRISONER AND ALL, I GUESS THAT MAKES SENSE.
MAYBE JUST SNEAK ME A PIE OR SOMETHING?
WELL MY FATHER, THE KING, IS PLANNING ON HAVING YOU THERE--
NOT QUITE... HOW CAN I PUT THIS?
OH, YOU MEAN LIKE A GUEST OF HONOR FOR SAVING YOU?
I'M NOT SURE HOW MUCH SAVING I DID BUT I'M NOT ONE TO TURN DOWN A GRAND FEAST ON MY BEHALF.
YOU AREN'T EXACTLY THE GUEST OF HONOR.
SO WHAT, LIKE A SPECIAL GUEST?
IT REALLY DOESN'T MATTER TO ME, I'M JUST STARVING.
I HAVEN'T EATEN SINCE BREAKFAST.
AGH,
THEY'RE MEANING TO EAT YOU!
COME AGAIN?
I'VE BEEN TRYING TO CONVINCE MY FATHER ALL MORNING THAT YOU HELPED ME BUT HE WON'T LISTEN.
HE NEVER LISTENS TO ME...
...I'M SO SORRY, POGO.
I WISH REX WAS HERE. HE'D KNOW WHAT TO DO.

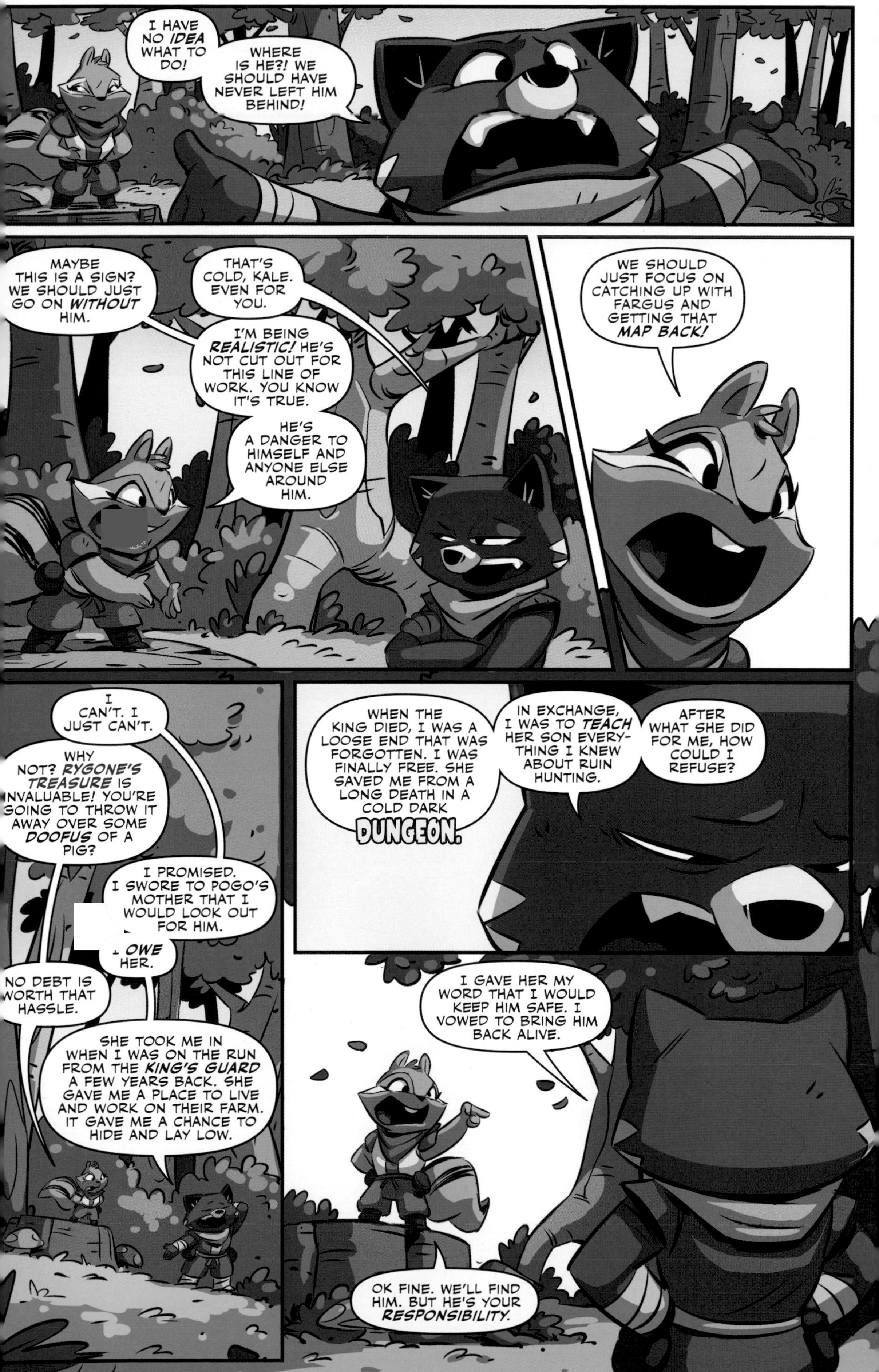
I HAVE NO IDEA WHAT TO DO!
WHERE IS HE?! WE SHOULD HAVE NEVER LEFT HIM BEHIND!
MAYBE THIS IS A SIGN? WE SHOULD JUST GO ON WITHOUT HIM.
THAT'S COLD, KALE. EVEN FOR YOU.
I'M BEING REALISTIC! HE'S NOT CUT OUT FOR THIS LINE OF WORK. YOU KNOW IT'S TRUE.
HE'S A DANGER TO HIMSELF AND ANYONE ELSE AROUND HIM.
WE SHOULD JUST FOCUS ON CATCHING UP WITH FARGUS AND GETTING THAT MAP BACK!
I CAN'T. I JUST CAN'T.
WHY NOT? RYGONE'S TREASURE IS INVALUABLE! YOU'RE GOING TO THROW IT AWAY OVER SOME DOOFUS OF A PIG?
I PROMISED. I SWORE TO POGO'S MOTHER THAT I WOULD LOOK OUT FOR HIM.
I OWE HER.
NO DEBT IS WORTH THAT HASSLE.
SHE TOOK ME IN WHEN I WAS ON THE RUN FROM THE KING'S GUARD A FEW YEARS BACK. SHE GAVE ME A PLACE TO LIVE AND WORK ON THEIR FARM. IT GAVE ME A CHANCE TO HIDE AND LAY LOW.
WHEN THE KING DIED, I WAS A LOOSE END THAT WAS FORGOTTEN. I WAS FINALLY FREE. SHE SAVED ME FROM A LONG DEATH IN A COLD DARK DUNGEON.
IN EXCHANGE, I WAS TO TEACH HER SON EVERYTHING I KNEW ABOUT RUIN HUNTING.
AFTER WHAT SHE DID FOR ME, HOW COULD I REFUSE?
I GAVE HER MY WORD THAT I WOULD KEEP HIM SAFE. I VOWED TO BRING HIM BACK ALIVE.
OK FINE. WE'LL FIND HIM. BUT HE'S YOUR RESPONSIBILITY.

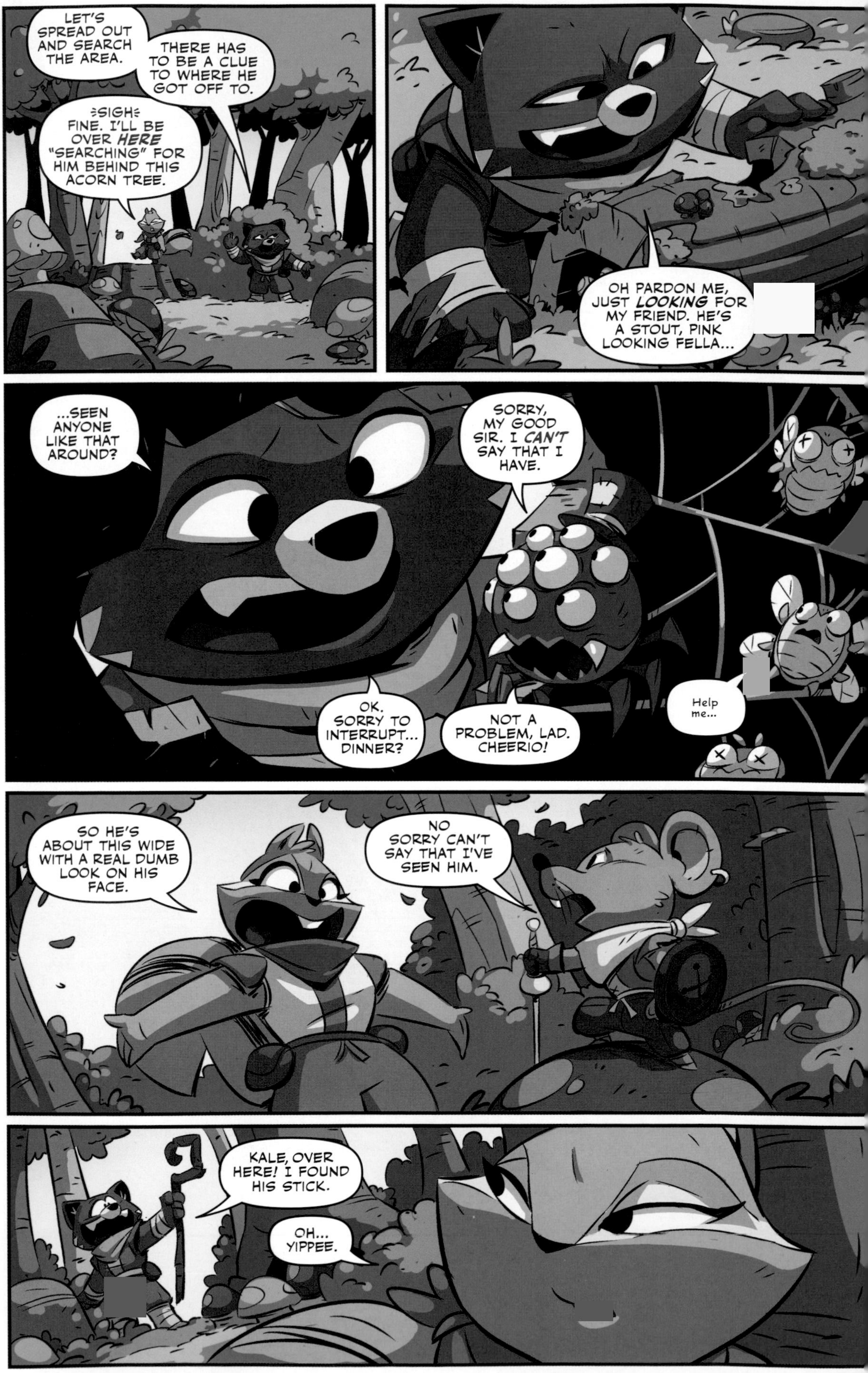
LET'S SPREAD OUT AND SEARCH THE AREA.
THERE HAS TO BE A CLUE TO WHERE HE GOT OFF TO.
≈SIGH≈ FINE. I'LL BE OVER *HERE* "SEARCHING" FOR HIM BEHIND THIS ACORN TREE.
OH PARDON ME, JUST *LOOKING* FOR MY FRIEND. HE'S A STOUT, PINK LOOKING FELLA...
...SEEN ANYONE LIKE THAT AROUND?
SORRY, MY GOOD SIR. I *CAN'T* SAY THAT I HAVE.
OK. SORRY TO INTERRUPT... DINNER?
NOT A PROBLEM, LAD. CHEERIO!
Help me...
SO HE'S ABOUT THIS WIDE WITH A REAL DUMB LOOK ON HIS FACE.
NO SORRY CAN'T SAY THAT I'VE SEEN HIM.
KALE, OVER HERE! I FOUND HIS STICK.
OH... YIPPEE.

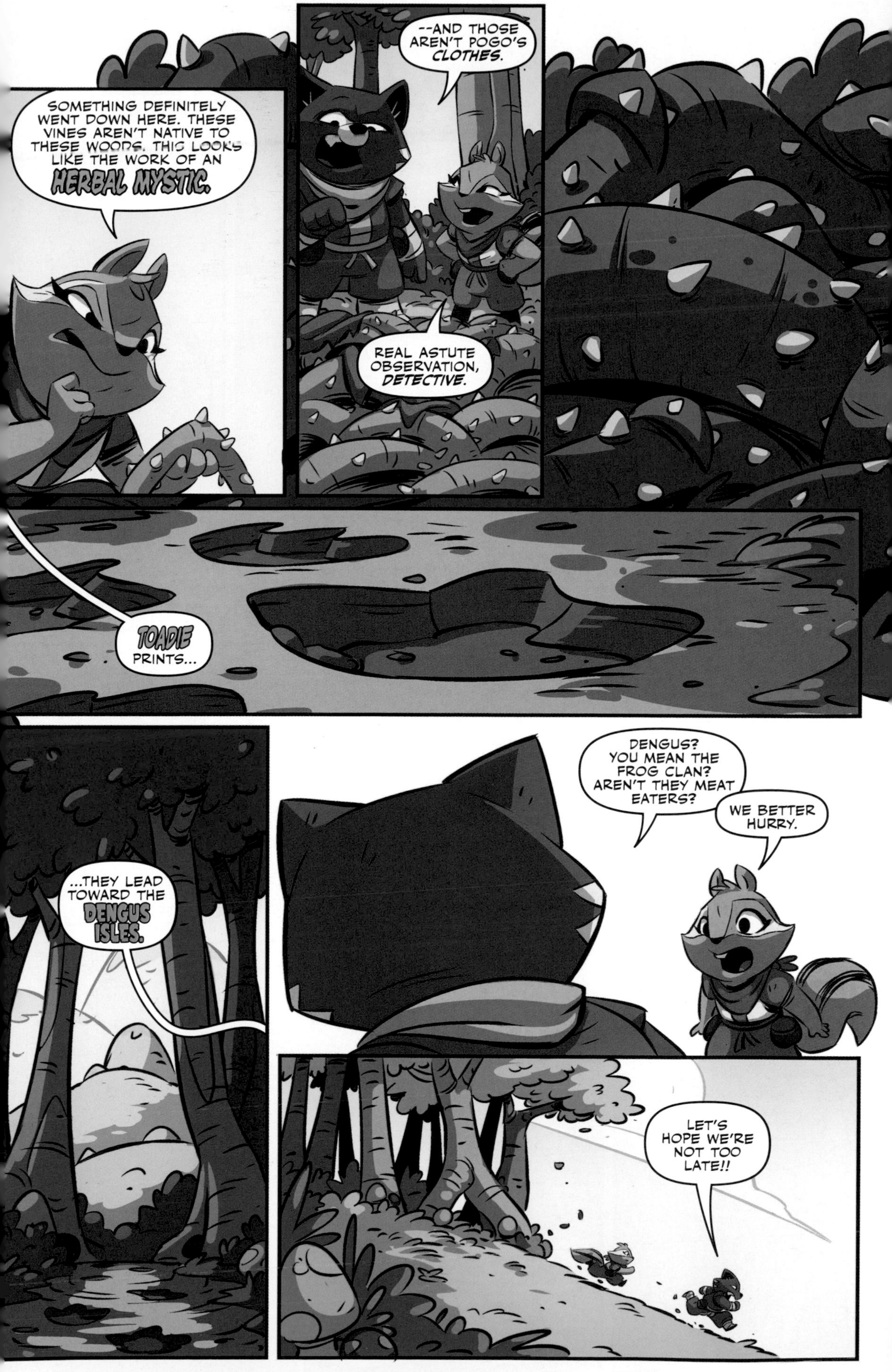
SOMETHING DEFINITELY WENT DOWN HERE. THESE VINES AREN'T NATIVE TO THESE WOODS. THIS LOOKS LIKE THE WORK OF AN HERBAL MYSTIC.
--AND THOSE AREN'T POGO'S CLOTHES.
REAL ASTUTE OBSERVATION, DETECTIVE.
TOADIE PRINTS...
...THEY LEAD TOWARD THE DENGUS ISLES.
DENGUS? YOU MEAN THE FROG CLAN? AREN'T THEY MEAT EATERS?
WE BETTER HURRY.
LET'S HOPE WE'RE NOT TOO LATE!!

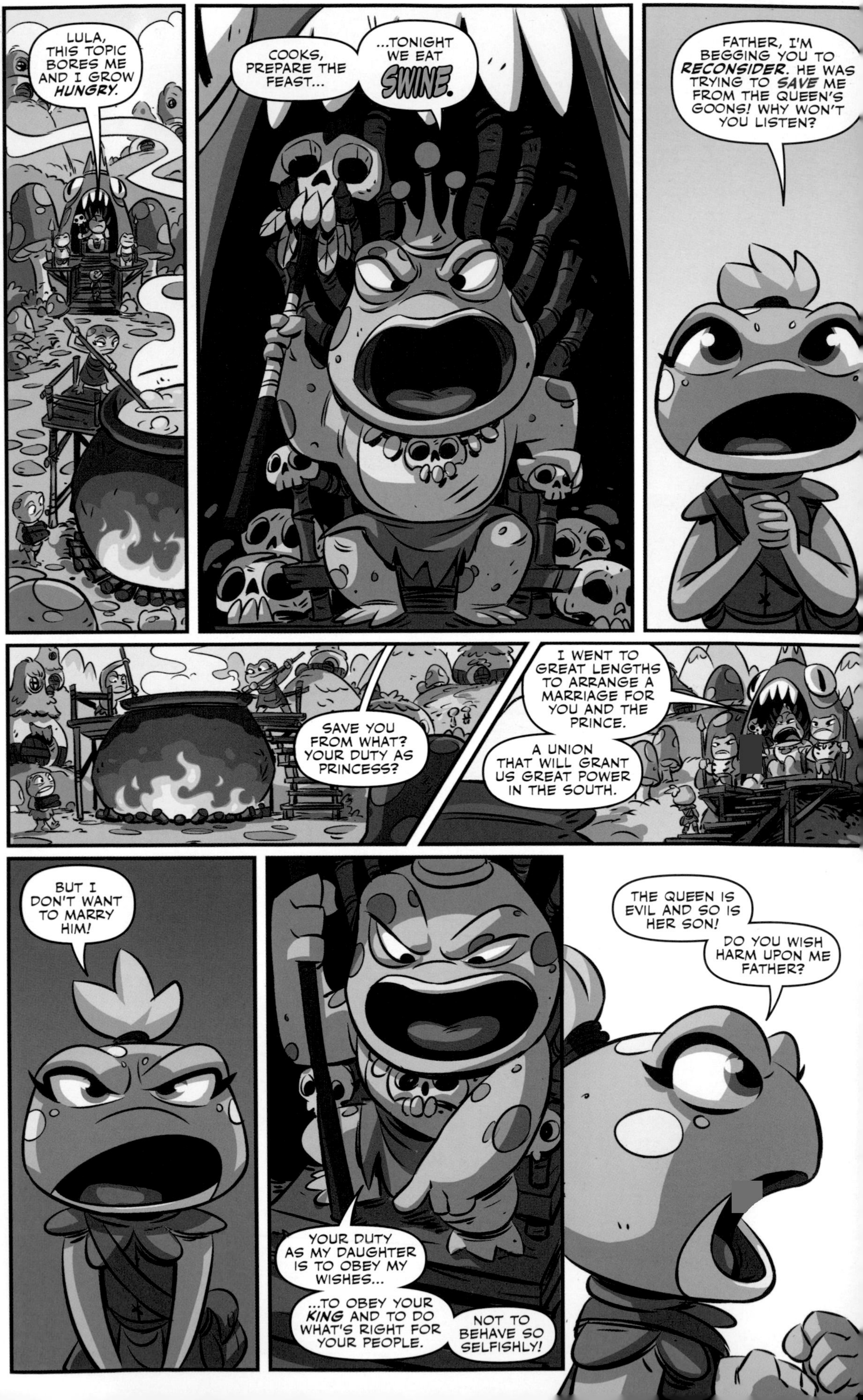

LULA, THIS TOPIC BORES ME AND I GROW *HUNGRY*.
COOKS, PREPARE THE FEAST...
...TONIGHT WE EAT
SWINE.
FATHER, I'M BEGGING YOU TO *RECONSIDER*. HE WAS TRYING TO *SAVE* ME FROM THE QUEEN'S GOONS! WHY WON'T YOU LISTEN?
SAVE YOU FROM WHAT? YOUR DUTY AS PRINCESS?
I WENT TO GREAT LENGTHS TO ARRANGE A MARRIAGE FOR YOU AND THE PRINCE.
A UNION THAT WILL GRANT US GREAT POWER IN THE SOUTH.
BUT I DON'T WANT TO MARRY HIM!
YOUR DUTY AS MY DAUGHTER IS TO OBEY MY WISHES...
...TO OBEY YOUR *KING* AND TO DO WHAT'S RIGHT FOR YOUR PEOPLE.
NOT TO BEHAVE SO SELFISHLY!
THE QUEEN IS EVIL AND SO IS HER SON!
DO YOU WISH HARM UPON ME FATHER?

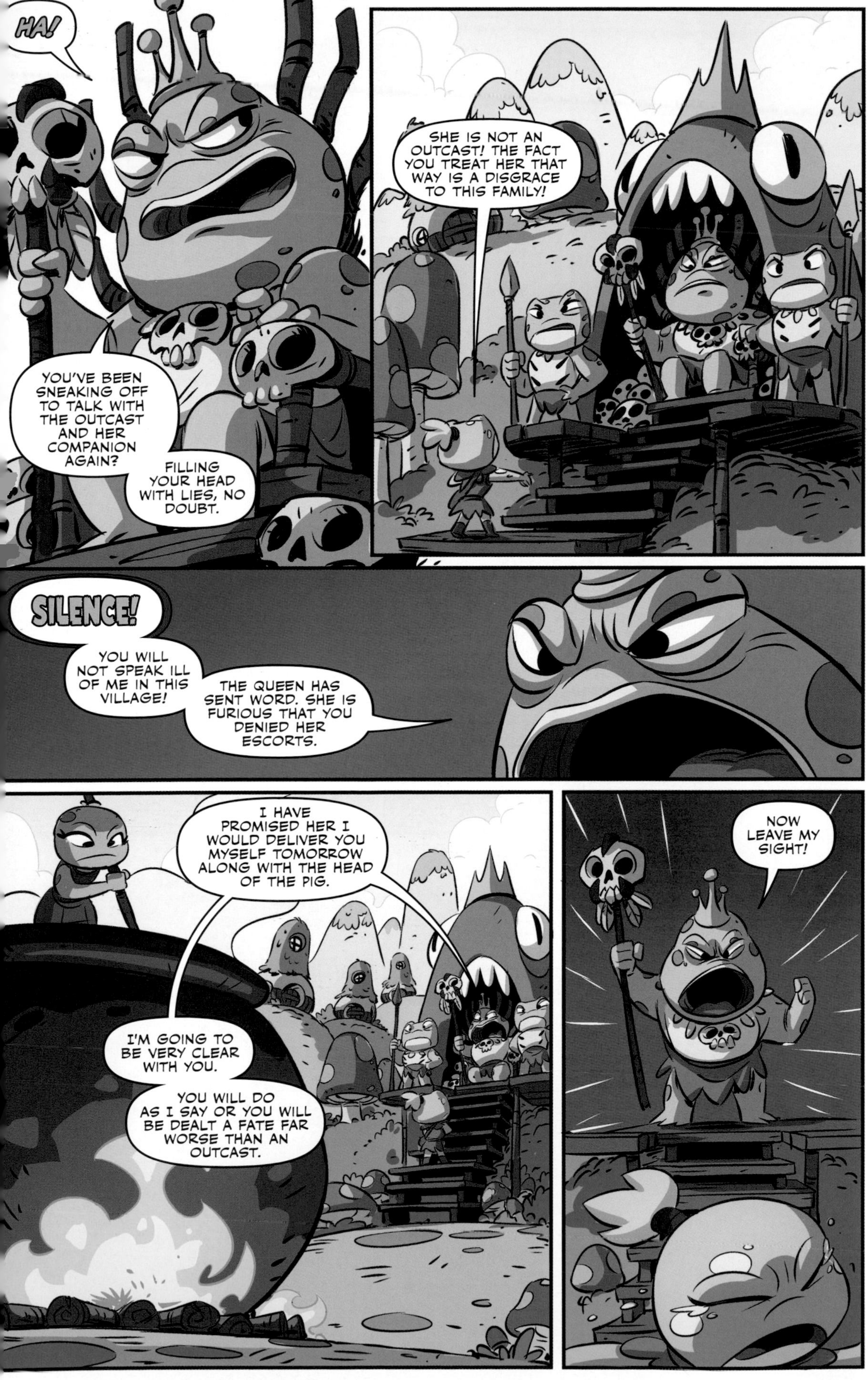
HA!
YOU'VE BEEN SNEAKING OFF TO TALK WITH THE OUTCAST AND HER COMPANION AGAIN?
FILLING YOUR HEAD WITH LIES, NO DOUBT.
SHE IS NOT AN OUTCAST! THE FACT YOU TREAT HER THAT WAY IS A DISGRACE TO THIS FAMILY!
SILENCE!
YOU WILL NOT SPEAK ILL OF ME IN THIS VILLAGE!
THE QUEEN HAS SENT WORD. SHE IS FURIOUS THAT YOU DENIED HER ESCORTS.
I HAVE PROMISED HER I WOULD DELIVER YOU MYSELF TOMORROW ALONG WITH THE HEAD OF THE PIG.
I'M GOING TO BE VERY CLEAR WITH YOU.
YOU WILL DO AS I SAY OR YOU WILL BE DEALT A FATE FAR WORSE THAN AN OUTCAST.
NOW LEAVE MY SIGHT!

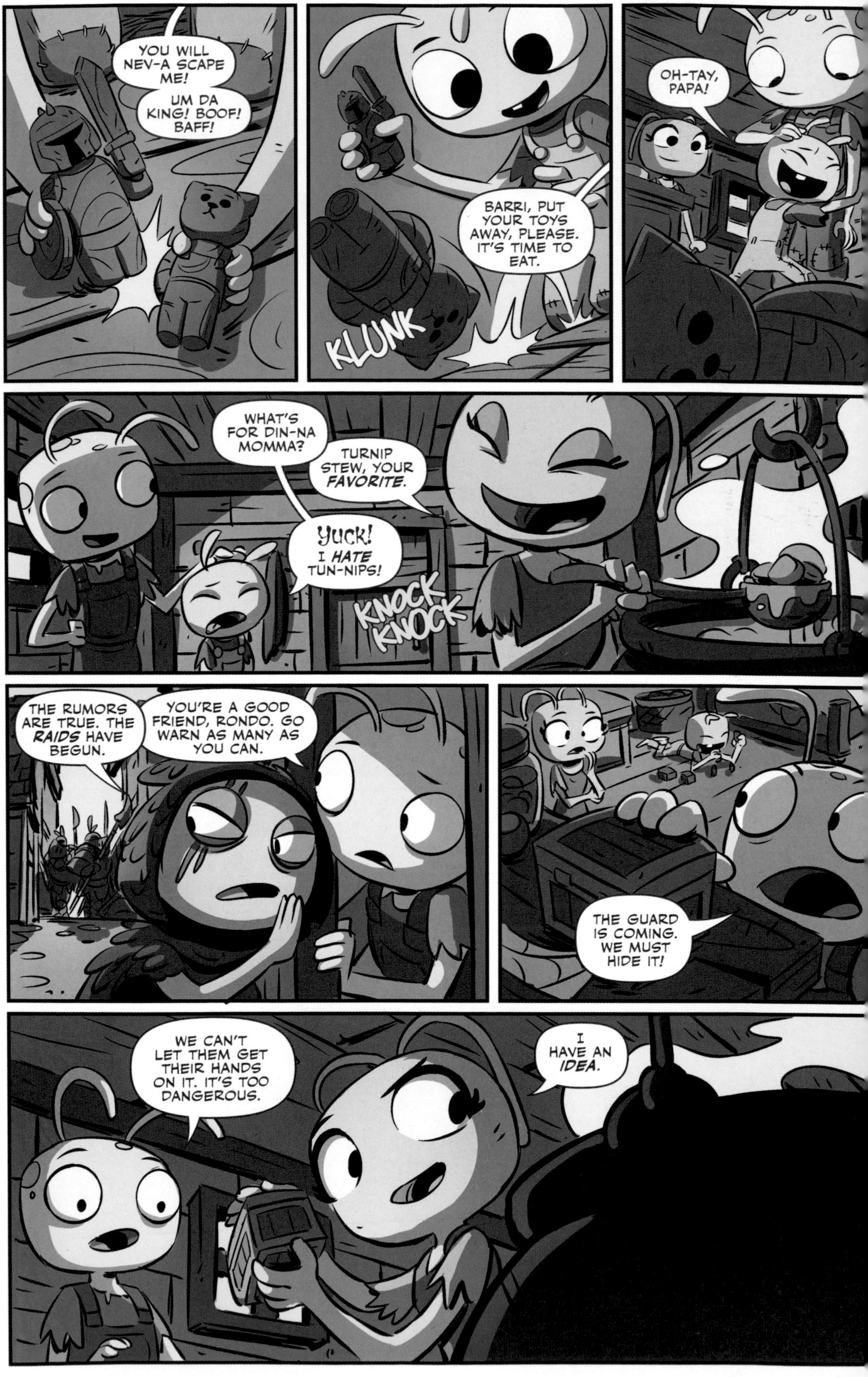
YOU WILL NEV-A SCAPE ME!
UM DA KING! BOOF! BAFF!
BARRI, PUT YOUR TOYS AWAY, PLEASE. IT'S TIME TO EAT.
KLUNK
OH-TAY, PAPA!
WHAT'S FOR DIN-NA MOMMA?
TURNIP STEW, YOUR FAVORITE.
YUCK! I HATE TUN-NIPS!
KNOCK KNOCK
THE RUMORS ARE TRUE. THE RAIDS HAVE BEGUN.
YOU'RE A GOOD FRIEND, RONDO. GO WARN AS MANY AS YOU CAN.
THE GUARD IS COMING. WE MUST HIDE IT!
WE CAN'T LET THEM GET THEIR HANDS ON IT. IT'S TOO DANGEROUS.
I HAVE AN IDEA.

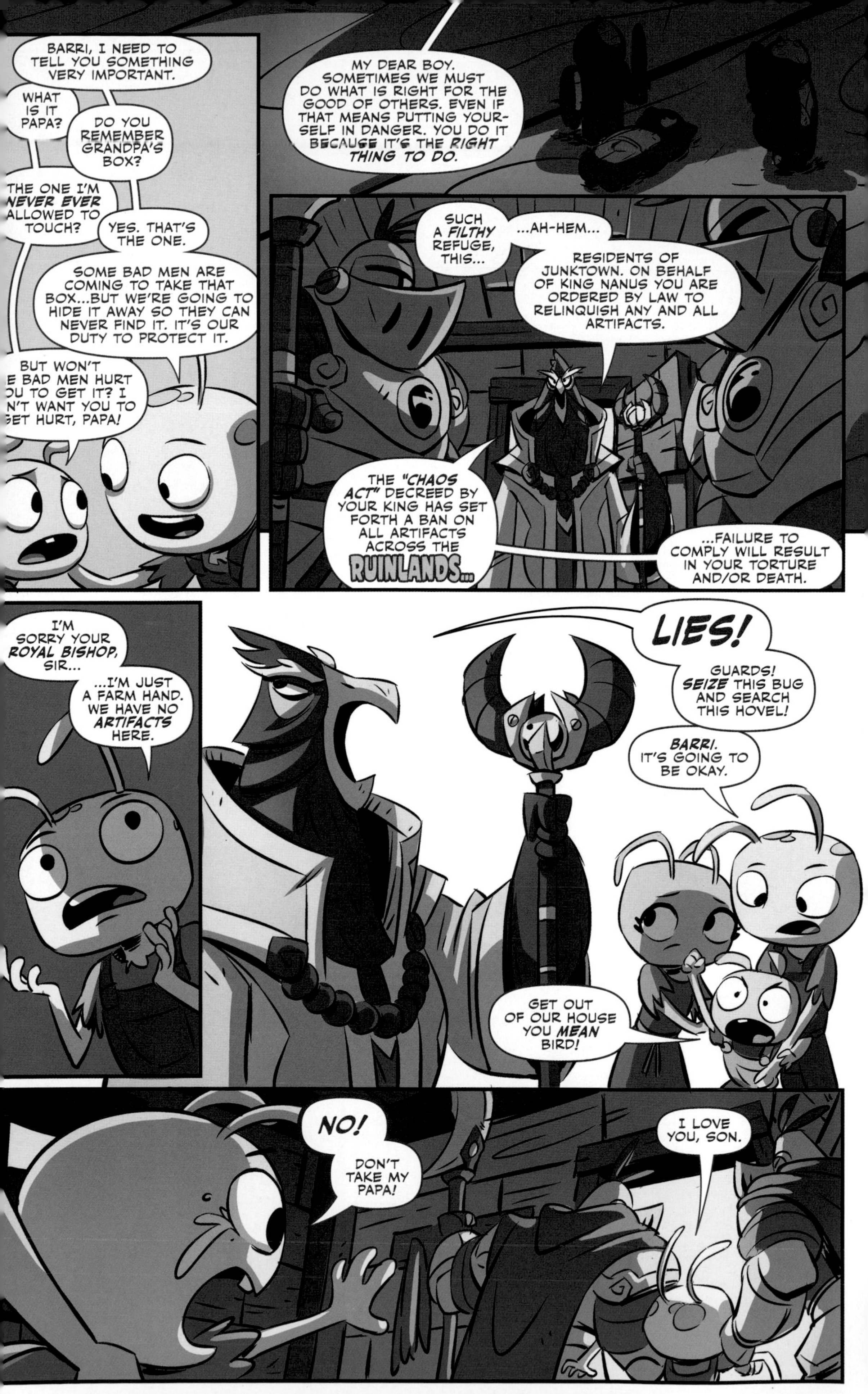

MY DEAR BOY. SOMETIMES WE MUST DO WHAT IS RIGHT FOR THE GOOD OF OTHERS. EVEN IF THAT MEANS PUTTING YOURSELF IN DANGER. YOU DO IT BECAUSE IT'S THE RIGHT THING TO DO.
BARRI, I NEED TO TELL YOU SOMETHING VERY IMPORTANT.
WHAT IS IT PAPA?
DO YOU REMEMBER GRANDPA'S BOX?
THE ONE I'M NEVER EVER ALLOWED TO TOUCH?
YES. THAT'S THE ONE.
SOME BAD MEN ARE COMING TO TAKE THAT BOX...BUT WE'RE GOING TO HIDE IT AWAY SO THEY CAN NEVER FIND IT. IT'S OUR DUTY TO PROTECT IT.
BUT WON'T E BAD MEN HURT OU TO GET IT? I N'T WANT YOU TO ET HURT, PAPA!
SUCH A FILTHY REFUGE, THIS...
...AH-HEM...
RESIDENTS OF JUNKTOWN. ON BEHALF OF KING NANUS YOU ARE ORDERED BY LAW TO RELINQUISH ANY AND ALL ARTIFACTS.
THE "CHAOS ACT" DECREED BY YOUR KING HAS SET FORTH A BAN ON ALL ARTIFACTS ACROSS THE RUINLANDS...
...FAILURE TO COMPLY WILL RESULT IN YOUR TORTURE AND/OR DEATH.
I'M SORRY YOUR ROYAL BISHOP, SIR...
...I'M JUST A FARM HAND. WE HAVE NO ARTIFACTS HERE.
LIES!
GUARDS! SEIZE THIS BUG AND SEARCH THIS HOVEL!
BARRI. IT'S GOING TO BE OKAY.
GET OUT OF OUR HOUSE YOU MEAN BIRD!
NO!
DON'T TAKE MY PAPA!
I LOVE YOU, SON.

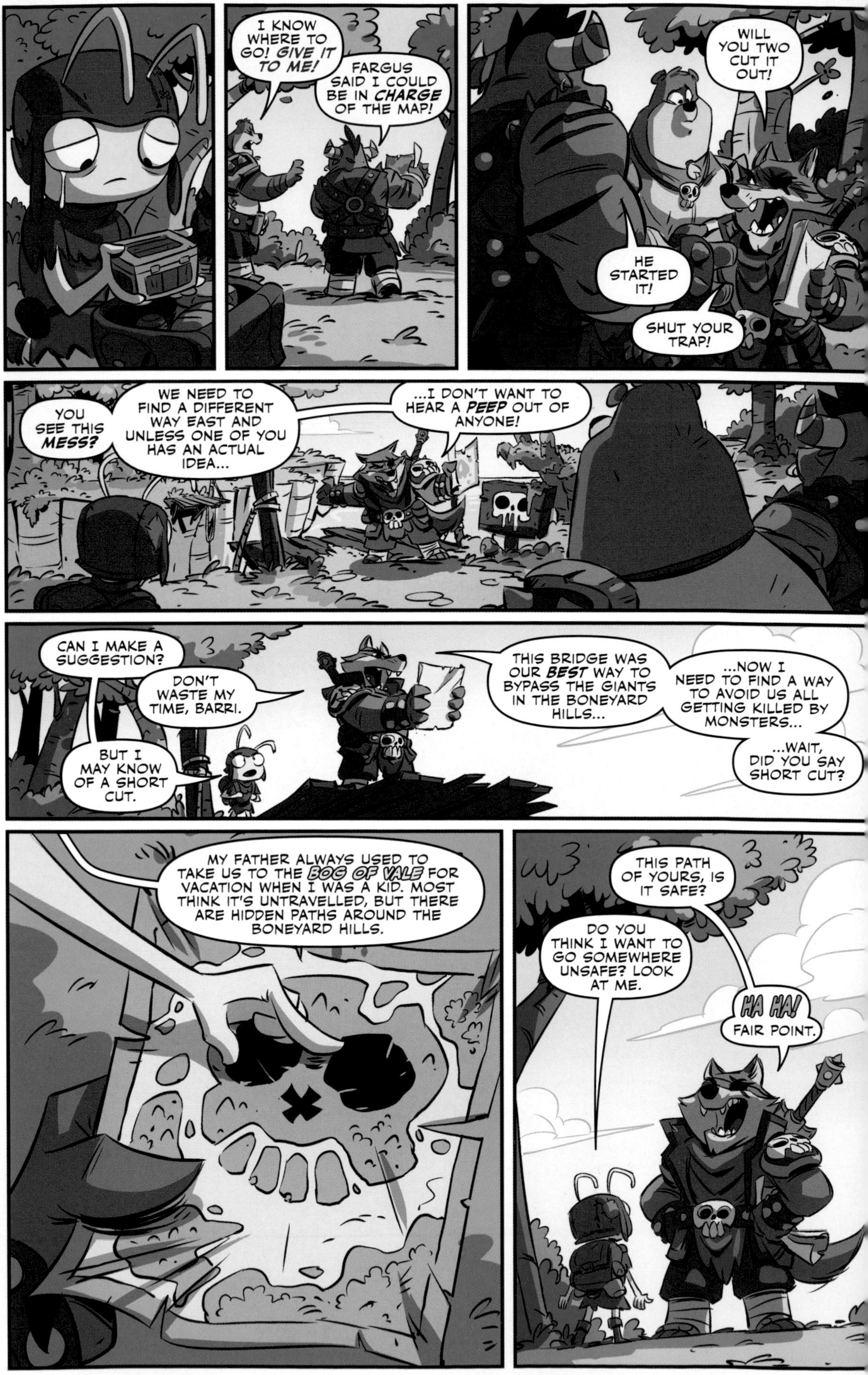
I KNOW WHERE TO GO! GIVE IT TO ME!
FARGUS SAID I COULD BE IN CHARGE OF THE MAP!
WILL YOU TWO CUT IT OUT!
HE STARTED IT!
SHUT YOUR TRAP!
YOU SEE THIS MESS?
WE NEED TO FIND A DIFFERENT WAY EAST AND UNLESS ONE OF YOU HAS AN ACTUAL IDEA...
...I DON'T WANT TO HEAR A PEEP OUT OF ANYONE!
CAN I MAKE A SUGGESTION?
DON'T WASTE MY TIME, BARRI.
BUT I MAY KNOW OF A SHORT CUT.
THIS BRIDGE WAS OUR BEST WAY TO BYPASS THE GIANTS IN THE BONEYARD HILLS...
...NOW I NEED TO FIND A WAY TO AVOID US ALL GETTING KILLED BY MONSTERS...
...WAIT, DID YOU SAY SHORT CUT?
MY FATHER ALWAYS USED TO TAKE US TO THE BOG OF VALE FOR VACATION WHEN I WAS A KID. MOST THINK IT'S UNTRAVELLED, BUT THERE ARE HIDDEN PATHS AROUND THE BONEYARD HILLS.
THIS PATH OF YOURS, IS IT SAFE?
DO YOU THINK I WANT TO GO SOMEWHERE UNSAFE? LOOK AT ME.
HA HA! FAIR POINT.

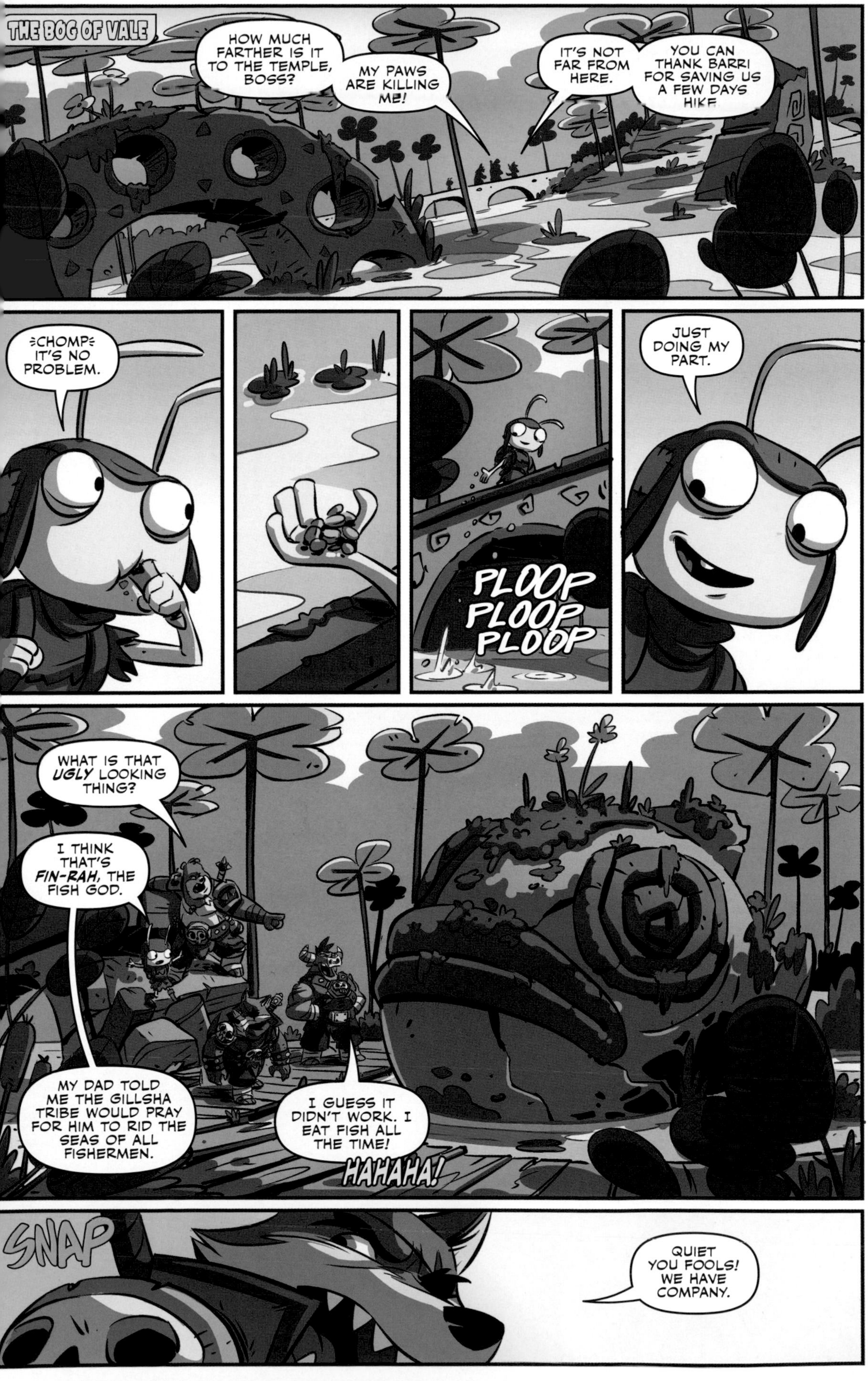
THE BOG OF VALE
HOW MUCH FARTHER IS IT TO THE TEMPLE, BOSS?
MY PAWS ARE KILLING ME!
IT'S NOT FAR FROM HERE.
YOU CAN THANK BARRI FOR SAVING US A FEW DAYS HIKE.
CHOMP IT'S NO PROBLEM.
PLOOP PLOOP PLOOP
JUST DOING MY PART.
WHAT IS THAT UGLY LOOKING THING?
I THINK THAT'S FIN-RAH, THE FISH GOD.
MY DAD TOLD ME THE GILLSHA TRIBE WOULD PRAY FOR HIM TO RID THE SEAS OF ALL FISHERMEN.
I GUESS IT DIDN'T WORK. I EAT FISH ALL THE TIME!
HAHAHA!
SNAP
QUIET YOU FOOLS! WE HAVE COMPANY.

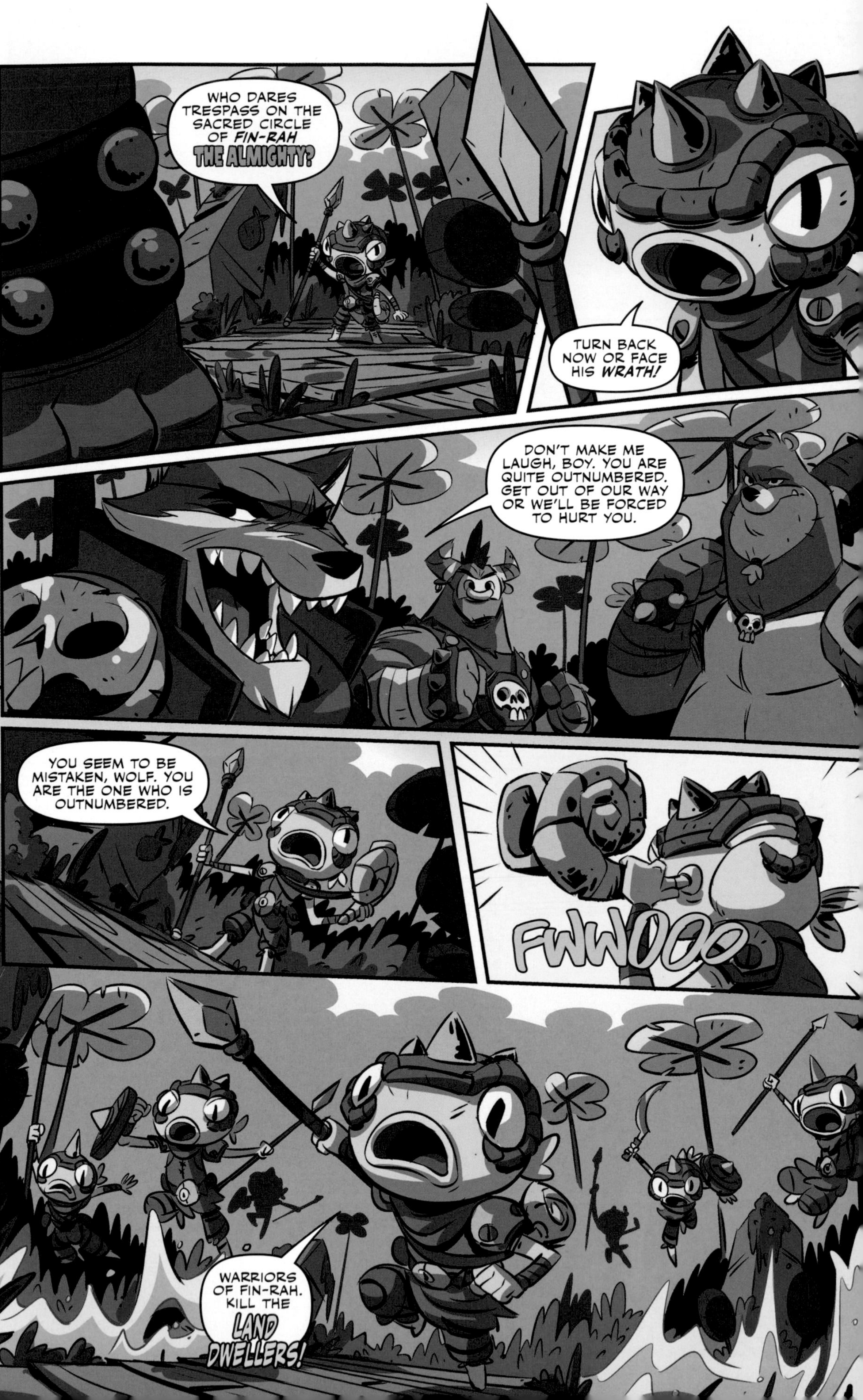
WHO DARES TRESPASS ON THE SACRED CIRCLE OF FIN-RAH THE ALMIGHTY?
TURN BACK NOW OR FACE HIS WRATH!
DON'T MAKE ME LAUGH, BOY. YOU ARE QUITE OUTNUMBERED. GET OUT OF OUR WAY OR WE'LL BE FORCED TO HURT YOU.
YOU SEEM TO BE MISTAKEN, WOLF. YOU ARE THE ONE WHO IS OUTNUMBERED.
FWWOOO
WARRIORS OF FIN-RAH. KILL THE LAND DWELLERS!

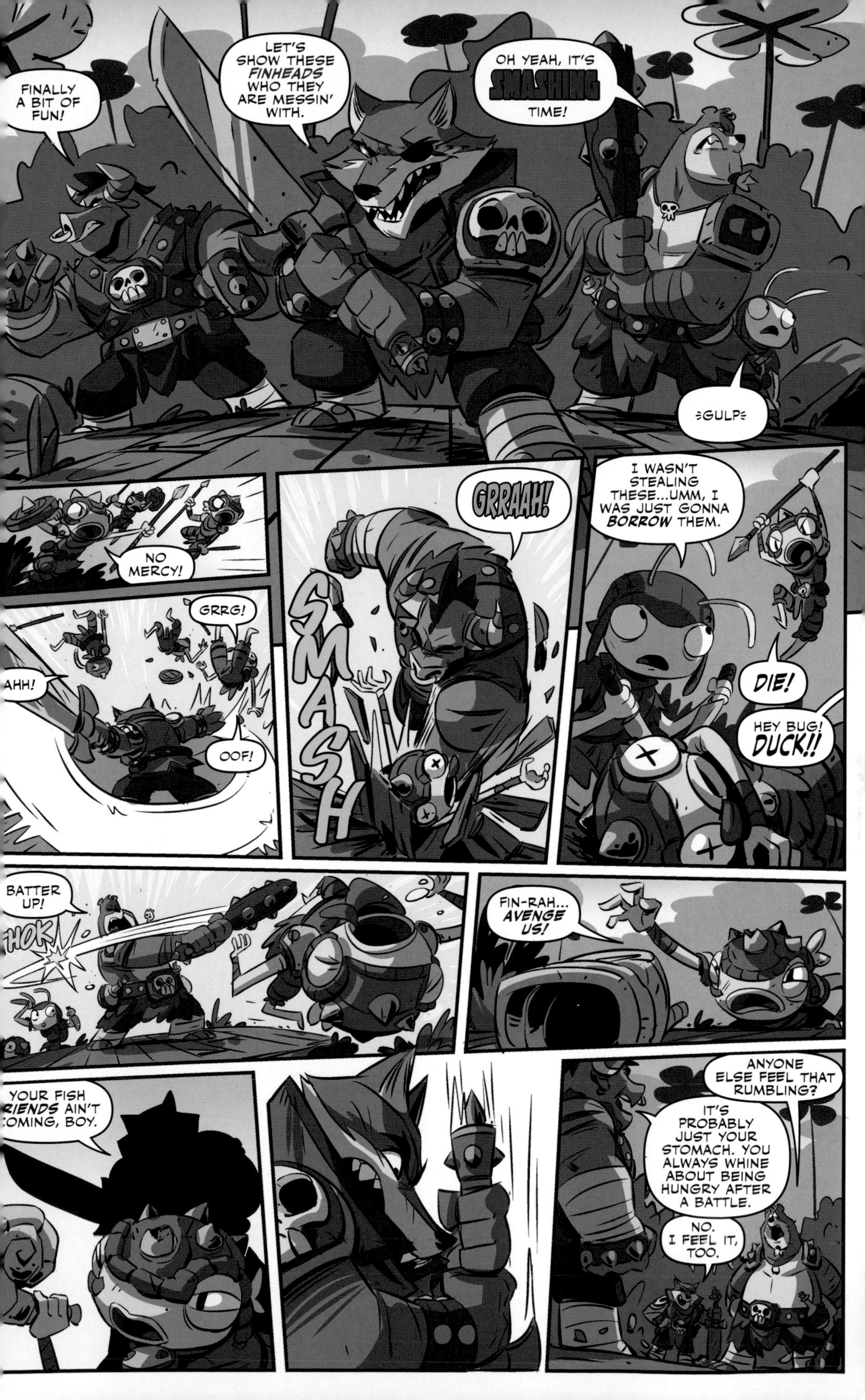
FINALLY A BIT OF FUN!
LET'S SHOW THESE FINHEADS WHO THEY ARE MESSIN' WITH.
OH YEAH, IT'S SMASHING TIME!
GULP
NO MERCY!
GRRAAH!
SMASH
I WASN'T STEALING THESE...UMM, I WAS JUST GONNA BORROW THEM.
GRRG!
AHH!
OOF!
DIE!
HEY BUG! DUCK!!
BATTER UP!
THOK
FIN-RAH... AVENGE US!
YOUR FISH FRIENDS AIN'T COMING, BOY.
ANYONE ELSE FEEL THAT RUMBLING?
IT'S PROBABLY JUST YOUR STOMACH. YOU ALWAYS WHINE ABOUT BEING HUNGRY AFTER A BATTLE.
NO. I FEEL IT, TOO.

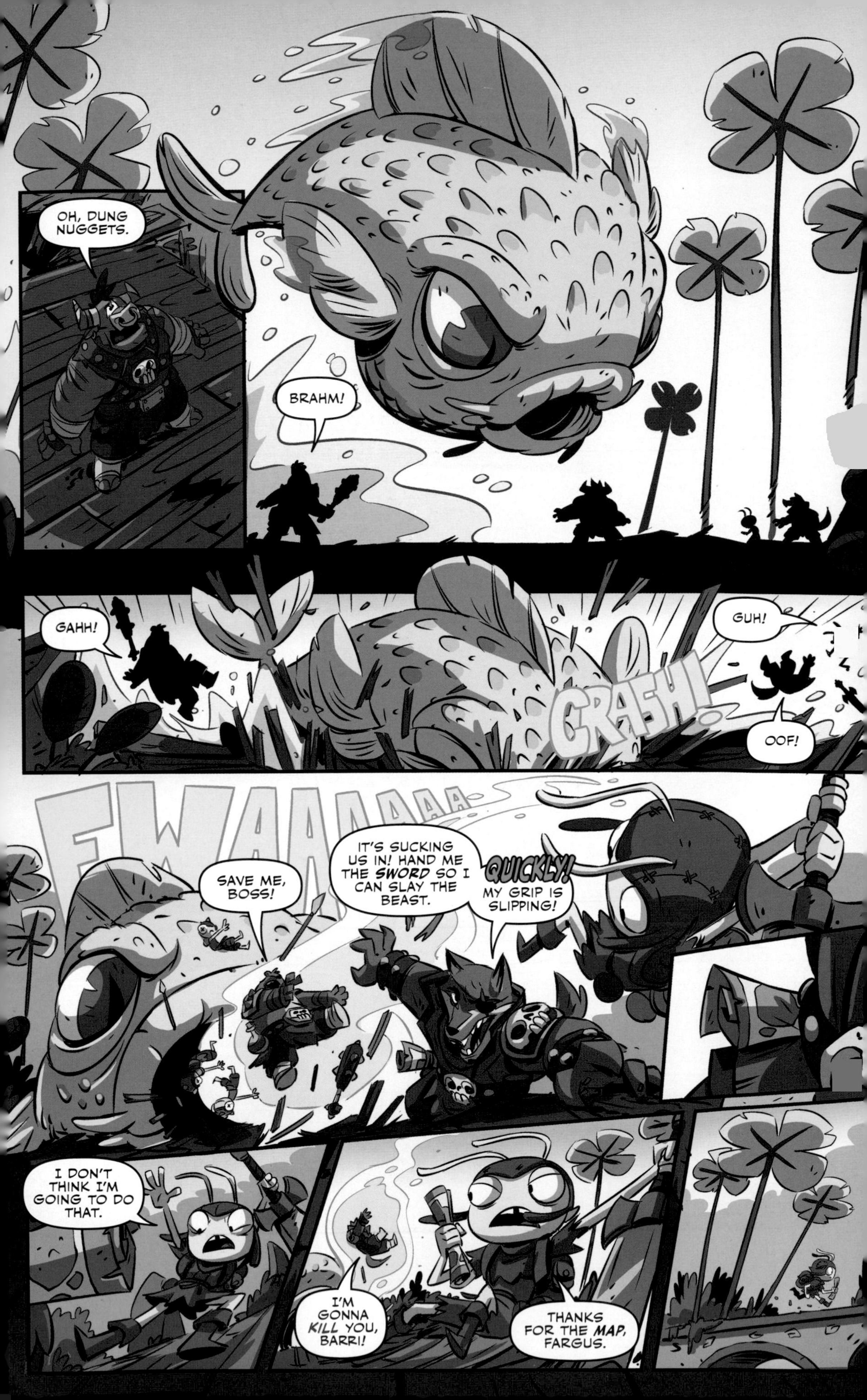
OH, DUNG NUGGETS.
BRAHM!
GAHH!
GUH!
CRASH!
OOF!
FWAAAAAA
SAVE ME, BOSS!
IT'S SUCKING US IN! HAND ME THE SWORD SO I CAN SLAY THE BEAST.
QUICKLY! MY GRIP IS SLIPPING!
I DON'T THINK I'M GOING TO DO THAT.
I'M GONNA KILL YOU, BARRI!
THANKS FOR THE MAP, FARGUS.

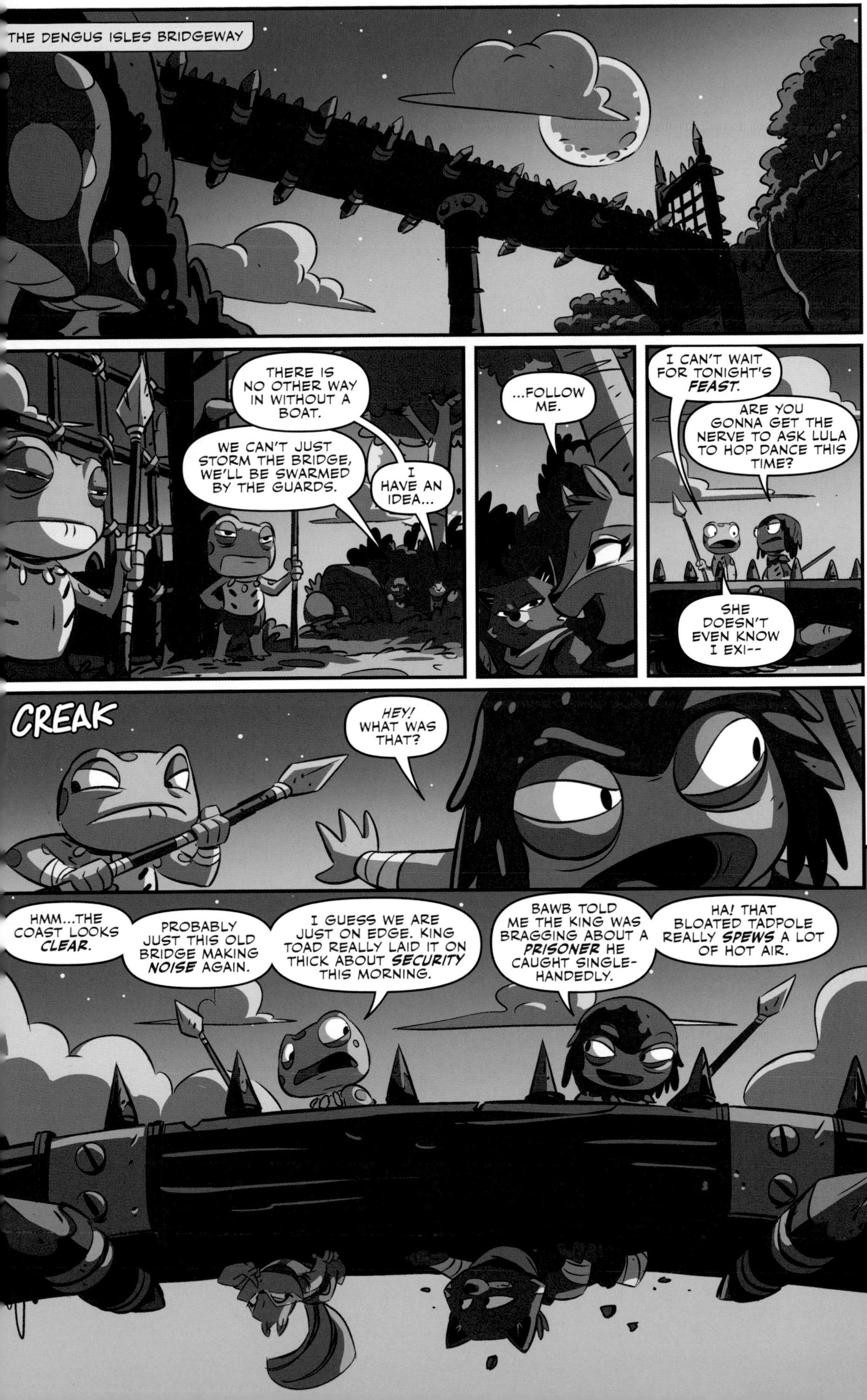
THE DENGUS ISLES BRIDGEWAY
THERE IS NO OTHER WAY IN WITHOUT A BOAT.
WE CAN'T JUST STORM THE BRIDGE, WE'LL BE SWARMED BY THE GUARDS.
I HAVE AN IDEA...
...FOLLOW ME.
I CAN'T WAIT FOR TONIGHT'S *FEAST.*
ARE YOU GONNA GET THE NERVE TO ASK LULA TO HOP DANCE THIS TIME?
SHE DOESN'T EVEN KNOW I EXI--
CREAK
HEY! WHAT WAS THAT?
HMM...THE COAST LOOKS *CLEAR*.
PROBABLY JUST THIS OLD BRIDGE MAKING *NOISE* AGAIN.
I GUESS WE ARE JUST ON EDGE. KING TOAD REALLY LAID IT ON THICK ABOUT *SECURITY* THIS MORNING.
BAWB TOLD ME THE KING WAS BRAGGING ABOUT A *PRISONER* HE CAUGHT SINGLE-HANDEDLY.
HA! THAT BLOATED TADPOLE REALLY *SPEWS* A LOT OF HOT AIR.

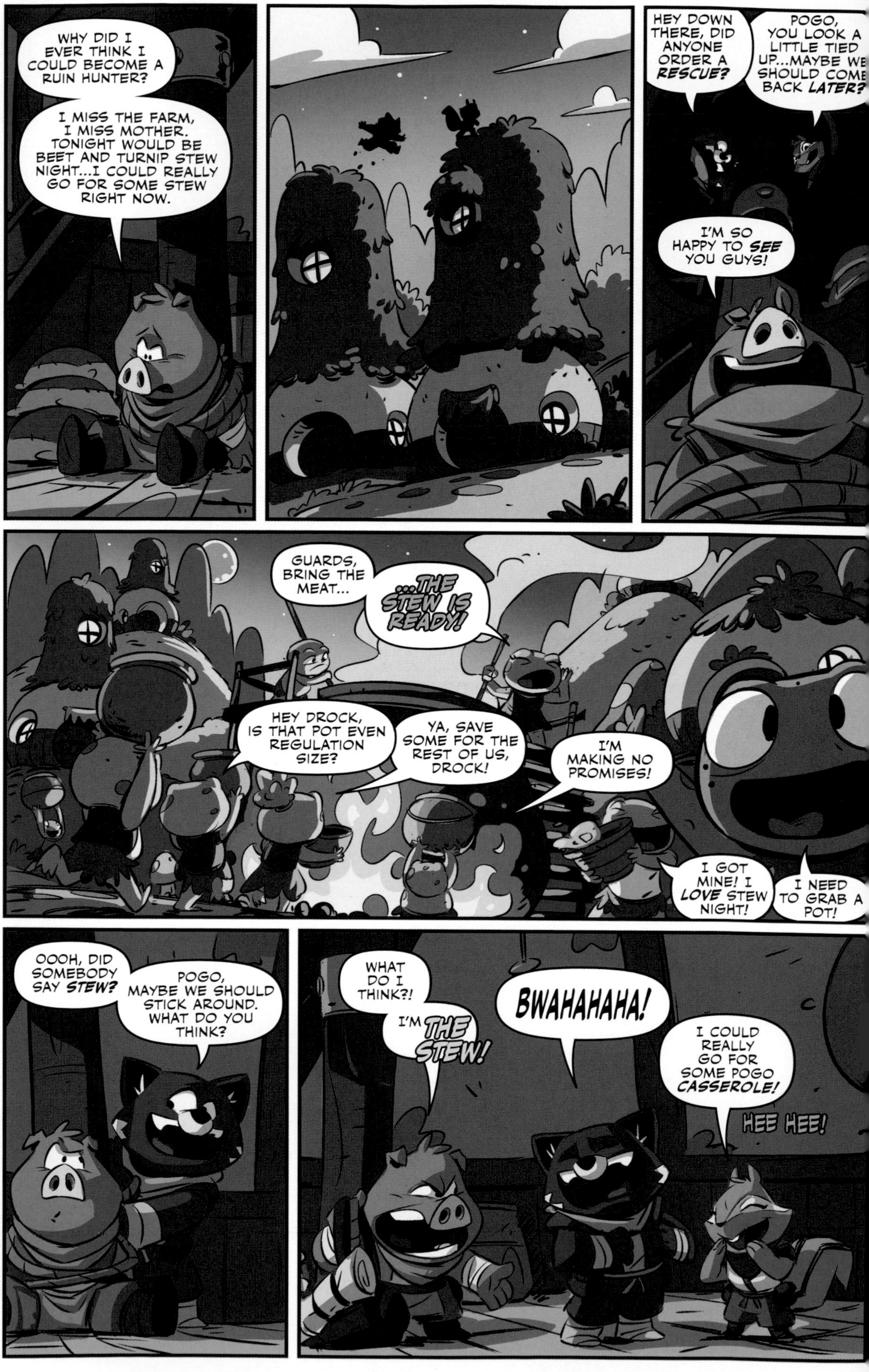
WHY DID I EVER THINK I COULD BECOME A RUIN HUNTER?
I MISS THE FARM, I MISS MOTHER. TONIGHT WOULD BE BEET AND TURNIP STEW NIGHT...I COULD REALLY GO FOR SOME STEW RIGHT NOW.
HEY DOWN THERE, DID ANYONE ORDER A RESCUE?
POGO, YOU LOOK A LITTLE TIED UP...MAYBE WE SHOULD COME BACK LATER?
I'M SO HAPPY TO SEE YOU GUYS!
GUARDS, BRING THE MEAT...
...THE STEW IS READY!
HEY DROCK, IS THAT POT EVEN REGULATION SIZE?
YA, SAVE SOME FOR THE REST OF US, DROCK!
I'M MAKING NO PROMISES!
I GOT MINE! I LOVE STEW NIGHT!
I NEED TO GRAB A POT!
OOOH, DID SOMEBODY SAY STEW?
POGO, MAYBE WE SHOULD STICK AROUND. WHAT DO YOU THINK?
WHAT DO I THINK?!
I'M THE STEW!
BWAHAHAHA!
I COULD REALLY GO FOR SOME POGO CASSEROLE!
HEE HEE!

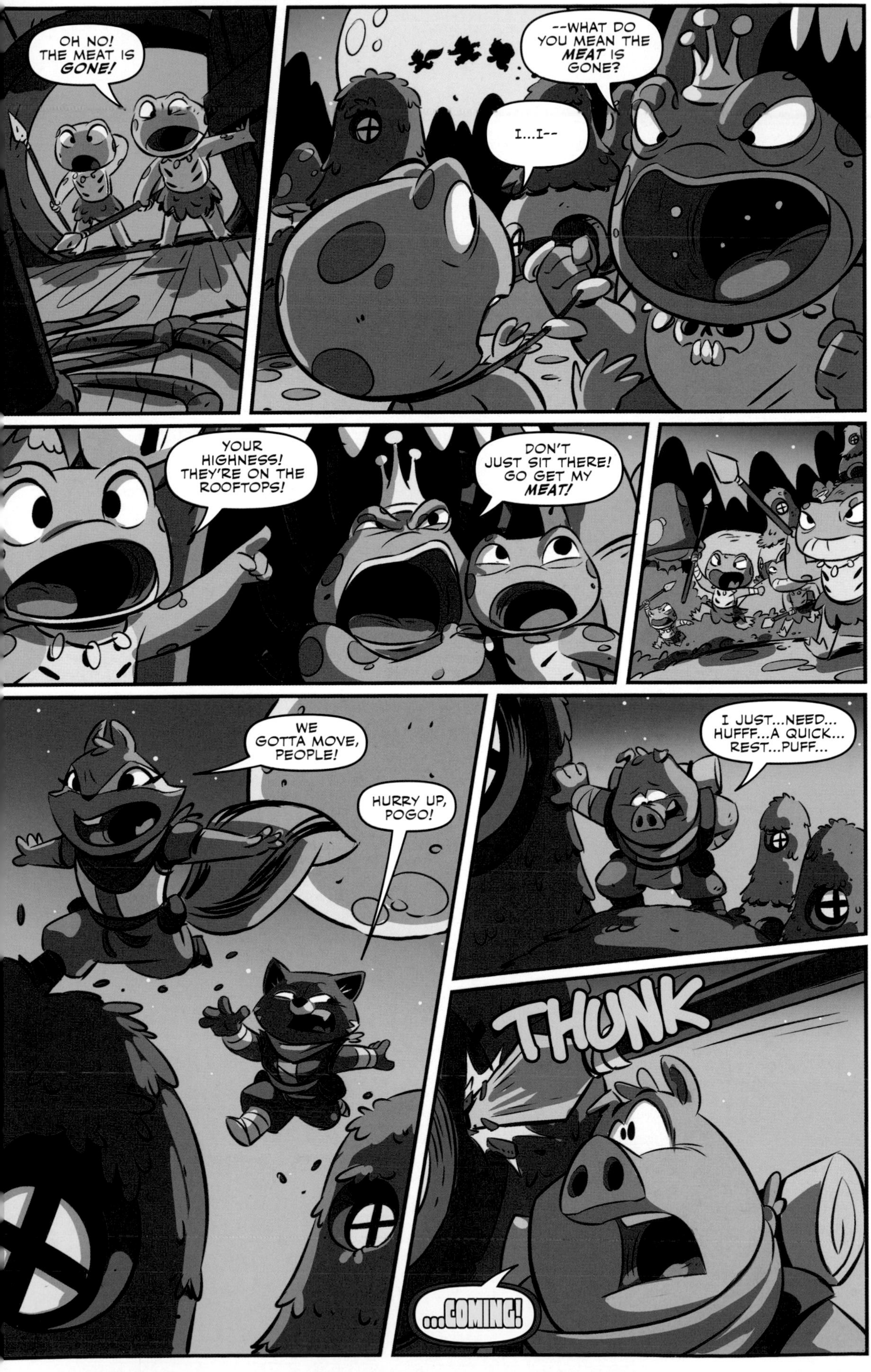
OH NO! THE MEAT IS GONE!
--WHAT DO YOU MEAN THE MEAT IS GONE?
I...I--
YOUR HIGHNESS! THEY'RE ON THE ROOFTOPS!
DON'T JUST SIT THERE! GO GET MY MEAT!
WE GOTTA MOVE, PEOPLE!
HURRY UP, POGO!
I JUST...NEED... HUFFF...A QUICK... REST...PUFF...
THUNK
...COMING!

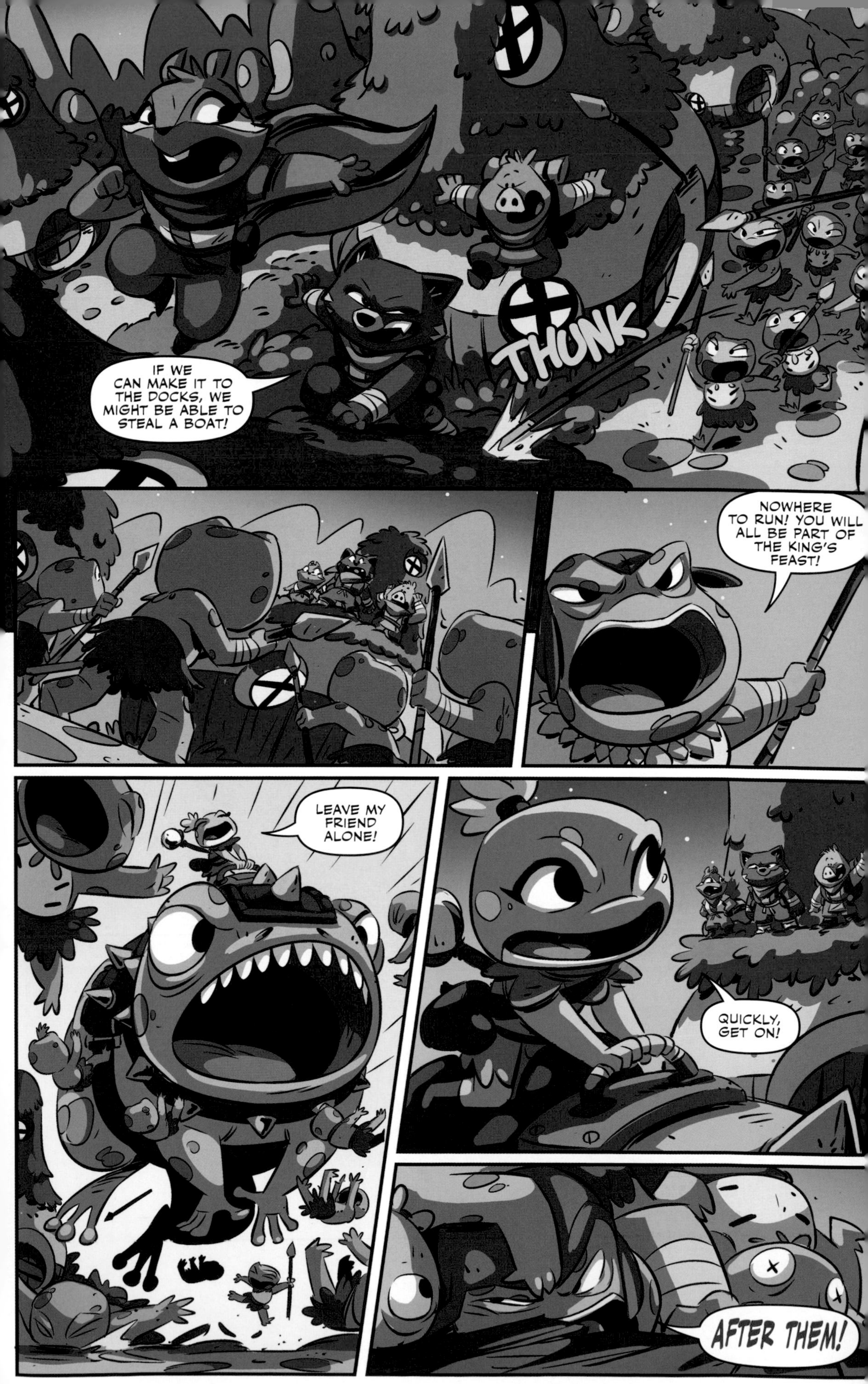
IF WE CAN MAKE IT TO THE DOCKS, WE MIGHT BE ABLE TO STEAL A BOAT!
THUNK
NOWHERE TO RUN! YOU WILL ALL BE PART OF THE KING'S FEAST!
LEAVE MY FRIEND ALONE!
QUICKLY, GET ON!
AFTER THEM!

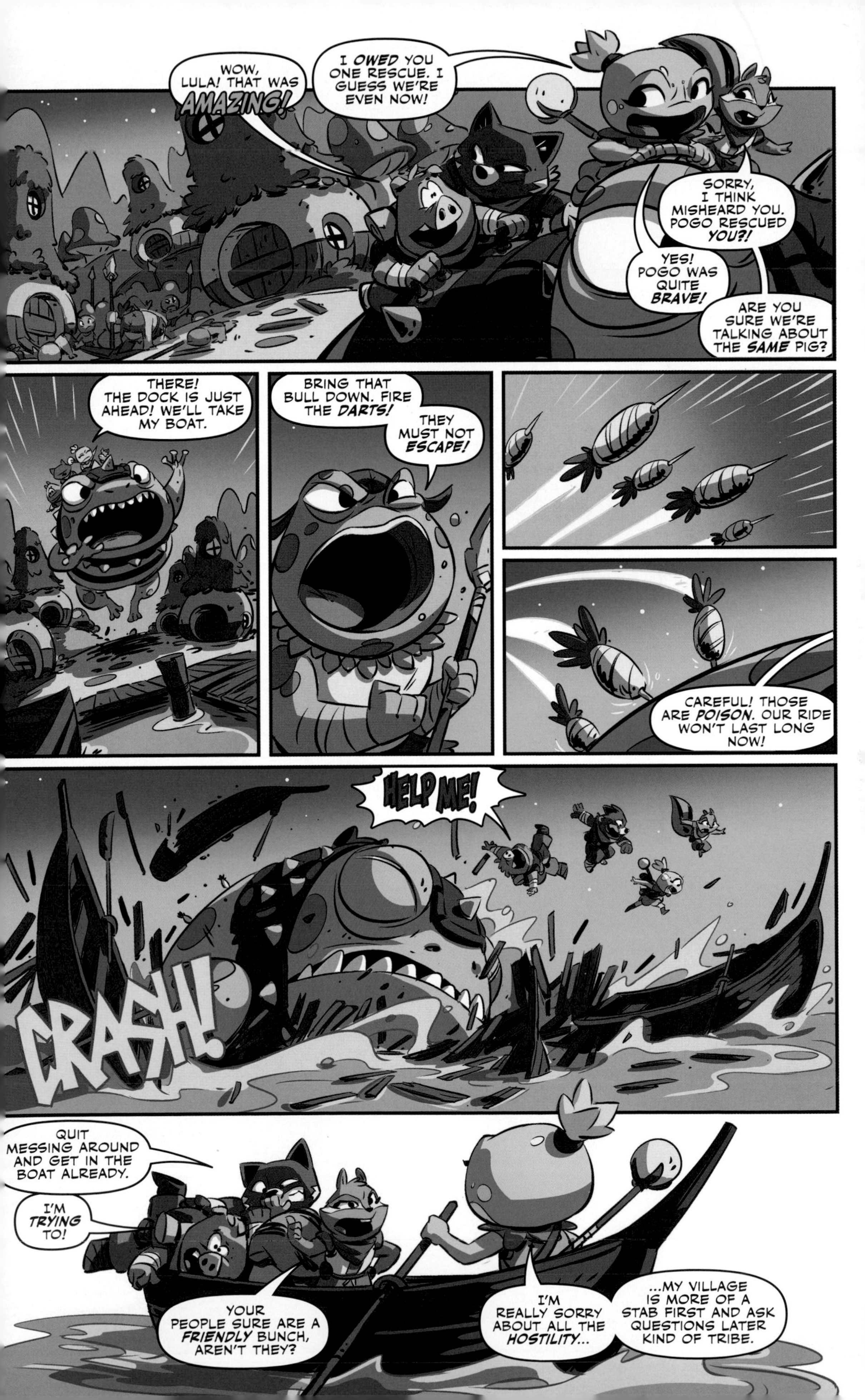
WOW, LULA! THAT WAS AMAZING!
I OWED YOU ONE RESCUE. I GUESS WE'RE EVEN NOW!
SORRY, I THINK MISHEARD YOU. POGO RESCUED YOU?!
YES! POGO WAS QUITE BRAVE!
ARE YOU SURE WE'RE TALKING ABOUT THE SAME PIG?
THERE! THE DOCK IS JUST AHEAD! WE'LL TAKE MY BOAT.
BRING THAT BULL DOWN. FIRE THE DARTS!
THEY MUST NOT ESCAPE!
CAREFUL! THOSE ARE POISON. OUR RIDE WON'T LAST LONG NOW!
HELP ME!
CRASH!
QUIT MESSING AROUND AND GET IN THE BOAT ALREADY.
I'M TRYING TO!
YOUR PEOPLE SURE ARE A FRIENDLY BUNCH, AREN'T THEY?
I'M REALLY SORRY ABOUT ALL THE HOSTILITY...
...MY VILLAGE IS MORE OF A STAB FIRST AND ASK QUESTIONS LATER KIND OF TRIBE.

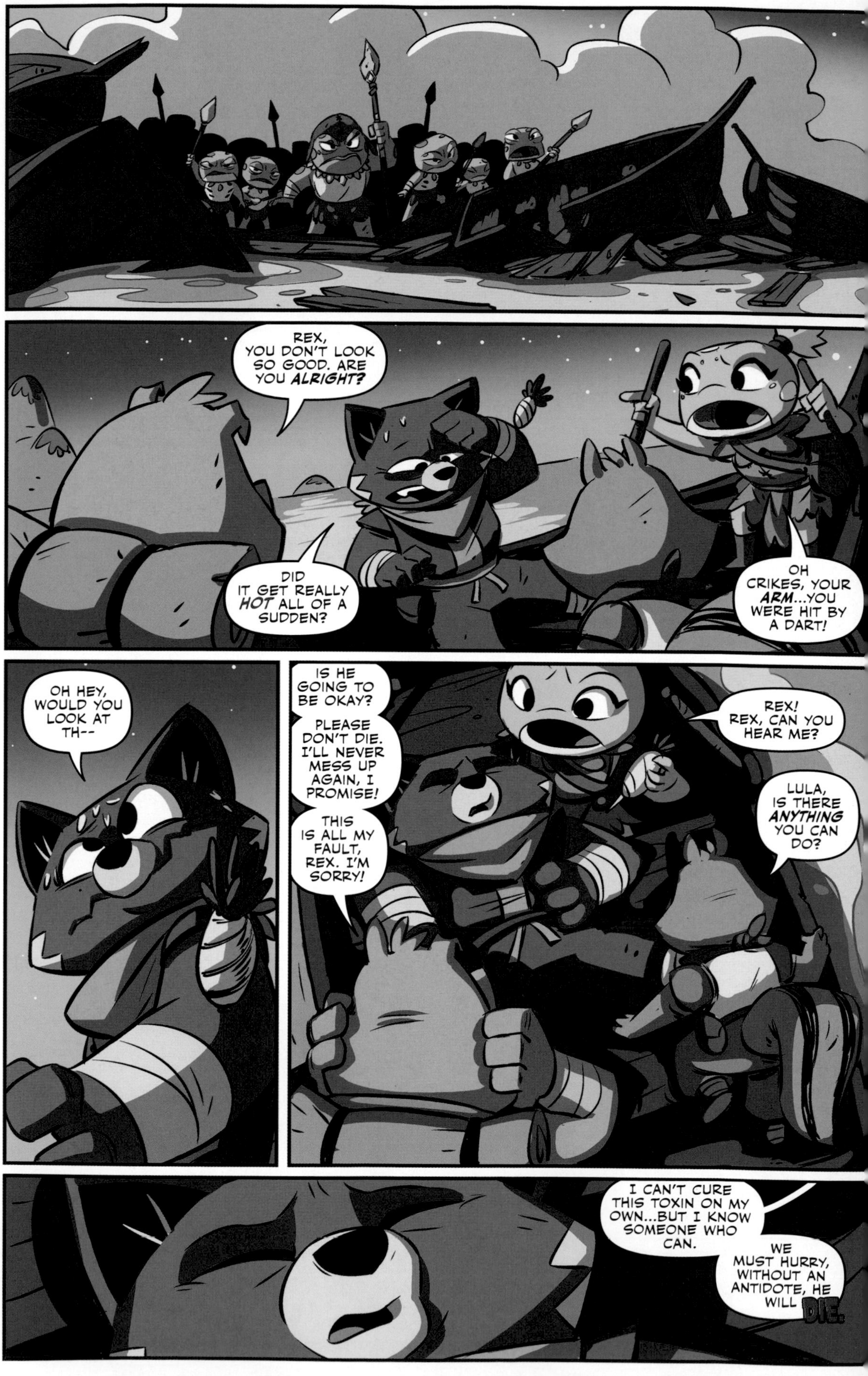
REX, YOU DON'T LOOK SO GOOD. ARE YOU ALRIGHT?
DID IT GET REALLY HOT ALL OF A SUDDEN?
OH CRIKES, YOUR ARM...YOU WERE HIT BY A DART!
OH HEY, WOULD YOU LOOK AT TH--
IS HE GOING TO BE OKAY?
PLEASE DON'T DIE. I'LL NEVER MESS UP AGAIN, I PROMISE!
THIS IS ALL MY FAULT, REX. I'M SORRY!
REX! REX, CAN YOU HEAR ME?
LULA, IS THERE ANYTHING YOU CAN DO?
I CAN'T CURE THIS TOXIN ON MY OWN...BUT I KNOW SOMEONE WHO CAN.
WE MUST HURRY, WITHOUT AN ANTIDOTE, HE WILL DIE.

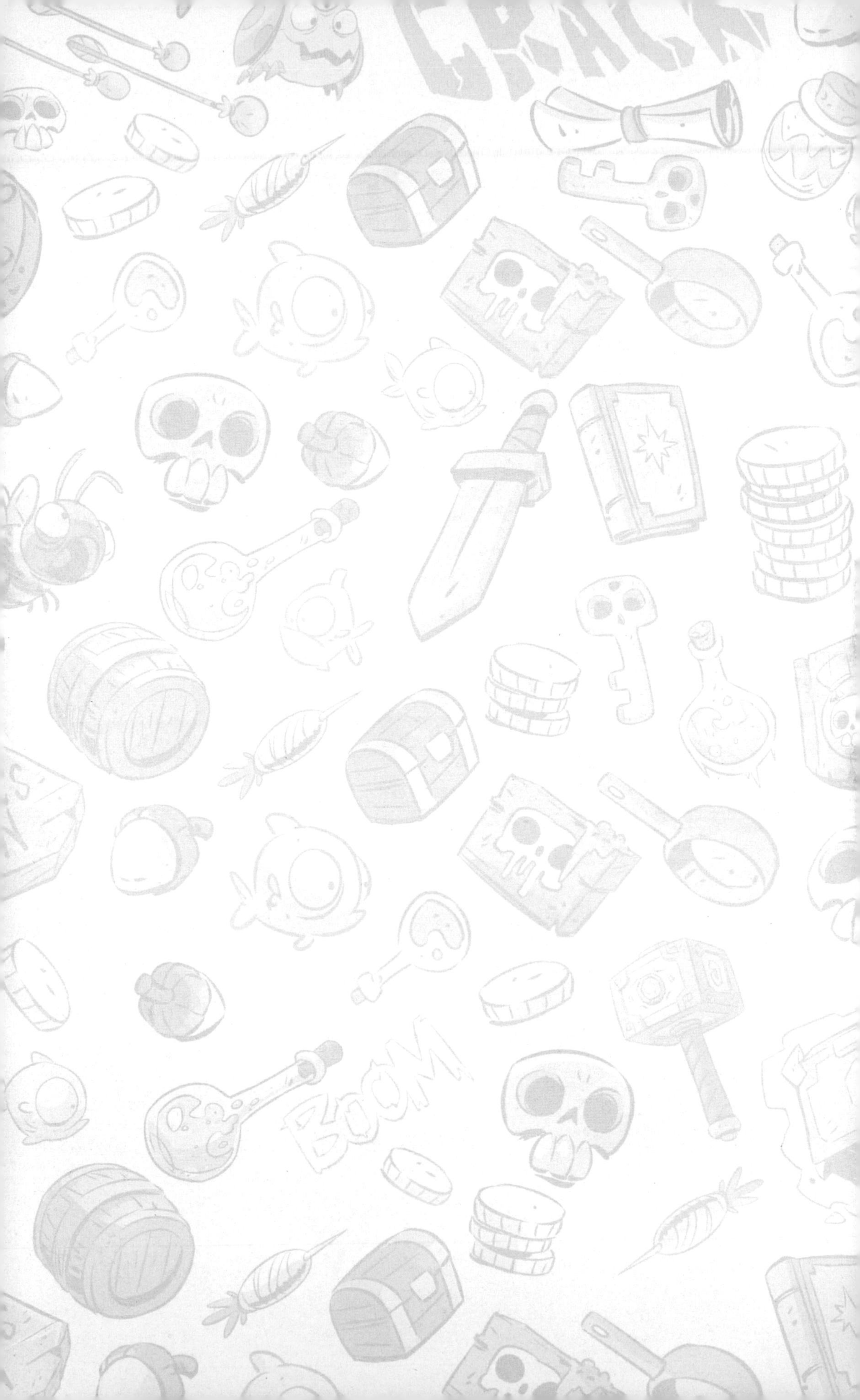
BOOM

ISSUE 4 COVER BY DEREK LAUFMAN

CHAPTER 4

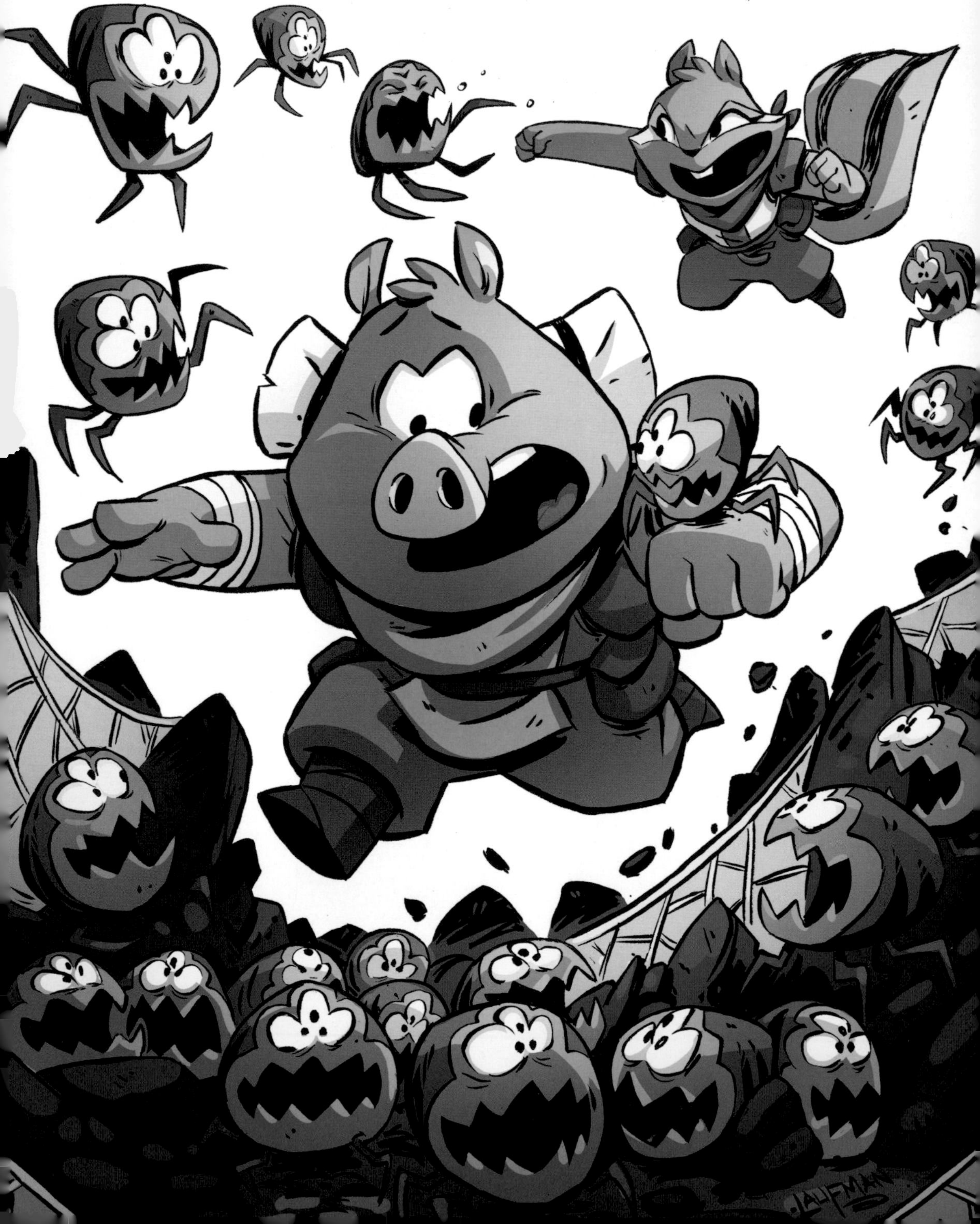

LAUFMAN

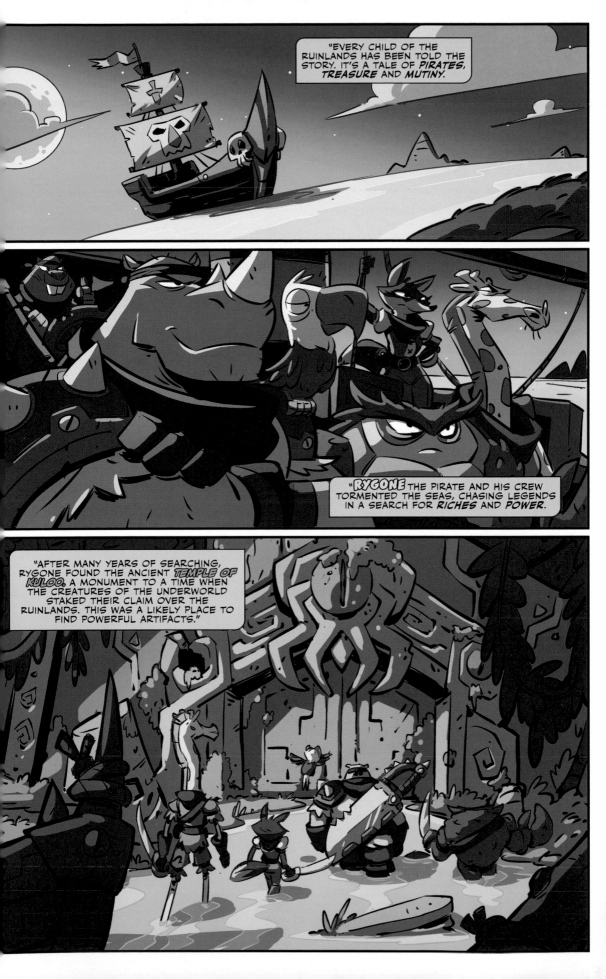

"EVERY CHILD OF THE RUINLANDS HAS BEEN TOLD THE STORY. IT'S A TALE OF *PIRATES*, *TREASURE* AND *MUTINY*.

"*RYGONE* THE PIRATE AND HIS CREW TORMENTED THE SEAS, CHASING LEGENDS IN A SEARCH FOR *RICHES* AND *POWER*.

"AFTER MANY YEARS OF SEARCHING, RYGONE FOUND THE ANCIENT *TEMPLE OF KULOO*, A MONUMENT TO A TIME WHEN THE CREATURES OF THE UNDERWORLD STAKED THEIR CLAIM OVER THE RUINLANDS. THIS WAS A LIKELY PLACE TO FIND POWERFUL ARTIFACTS."

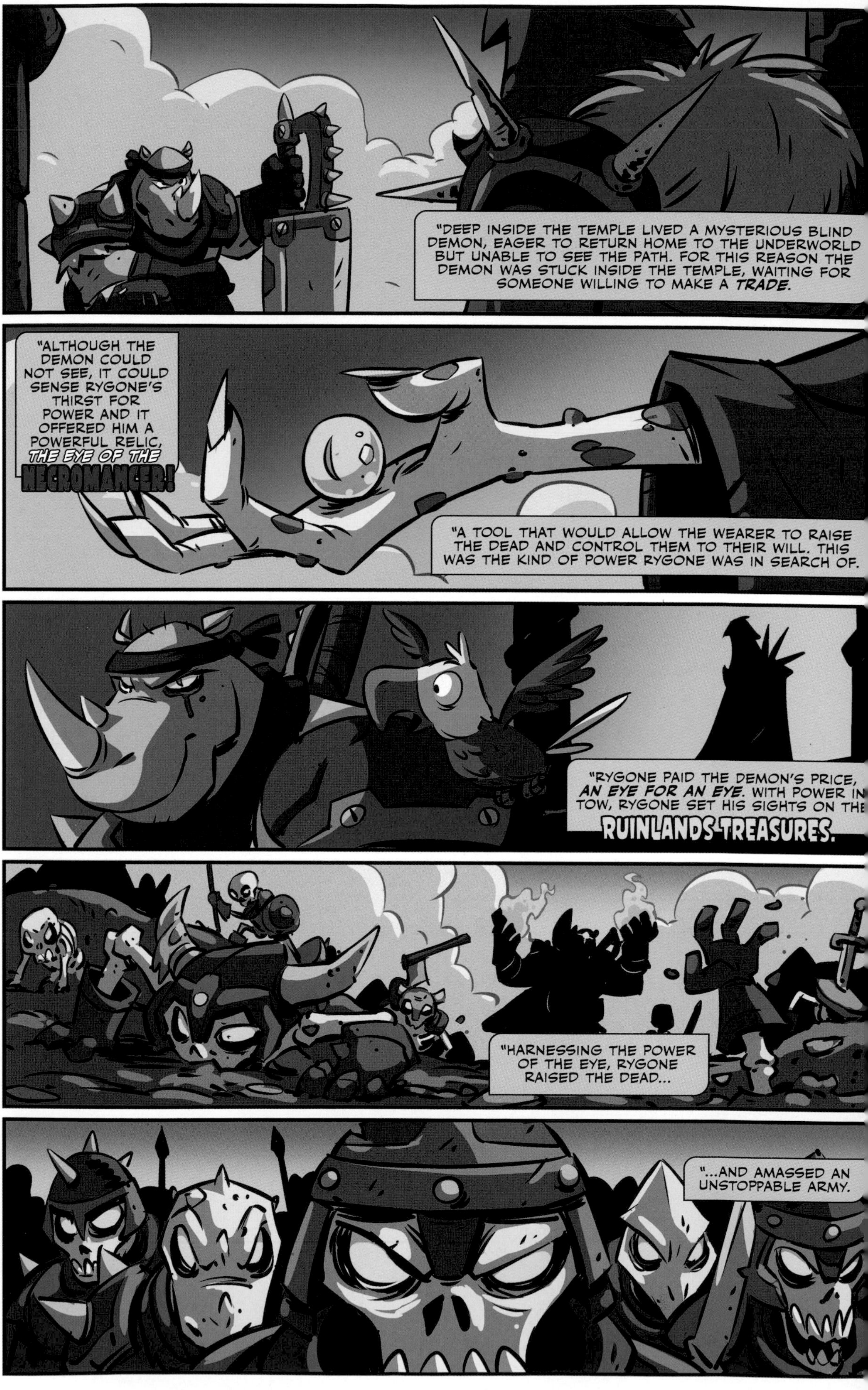
"DEEP INSIDE THE TEMPLE LIVED A MYSTERIOUS BLIND DEMON, EAGER TO RETURN HOME TO THE UNDERWORLD BUT UNABLE TO SEE THE PATH. FOR THIS REASON THE DEMON WAS STUCK INSIDE THE TEMPLE, WAITING FOR SOMEONE WILLING TO MAKE A *TRADE*.
"ALTHOUGH THE DEMON COULD NOT SEE, IT COULD SENSE RYGONE'S THIRST FOR POWER AND IT OFFERED HIM A POWERFUL RELIC, *THE EYE OF THE* NECROMANCER!
"A TOOL THAT WOULD ALLOW THE WEARER TO RAISE THE DEAD AND CONTROL THEM TO THEIR WILL. THIS WAS THE KIND OF POWER RYGONE WAS IN SEARCH OF.
"RYGONE PAID THE DEMON'S PRICE, ***AN EYE FOR AN EYE***. WITH POWER IN TOW, RYGONE SET HIS SIGHTS ON THE RUINLANDS TREASURES.
"HARNESSING THE POWER OF THE EYE, RYGONE RAISED THE DEAD...
"...AND AMASSED AN UNSTOPPABLE ARMY.

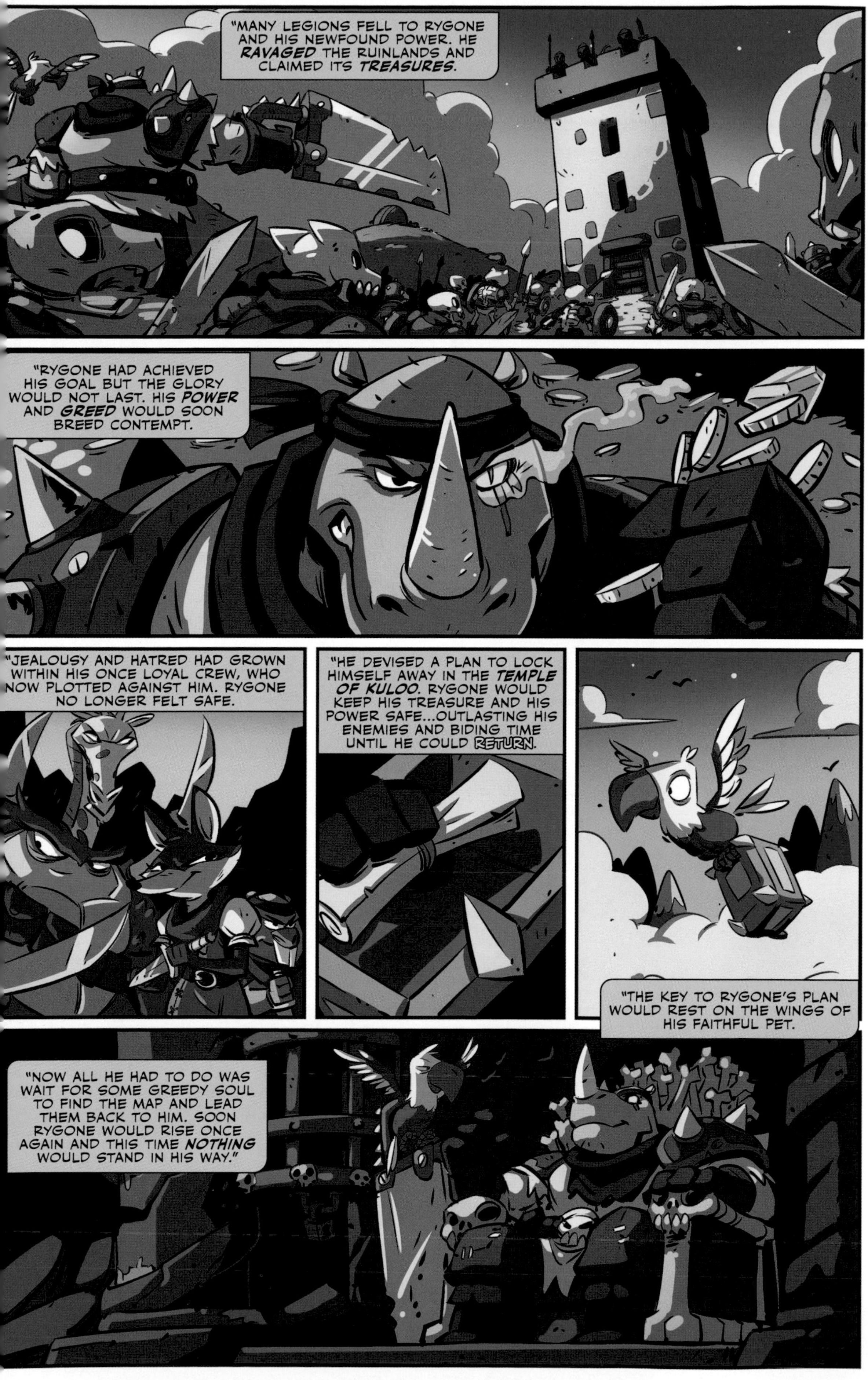
"MANY LEGIONS FELL TO RYGONE AND HIS NEWFOUND POWER. HE RAVAGED THE RUINLANDS AND CLAIMED ITS TREASURES.
"RYGONE HAD ACHIEVED HIS GOAL BUT THE GLORY WOULD NOT LAST. HIS POWER AND GREED WOULD SOON BREED CONTEMPT.
"JEALOUSY AND HATRED HAD GROWN WITHIN HIS ONCE LOYAL CREW, WHO NOW PLOTTED AGAINST HIM. RYGONE NO LONGER FELT SAFE.
"HE DEVISED A PLAN TO LOCK HIMSELF AWAY IN THE TEMPLE OF KULOO. RYGONE WOULD KEEP HIS TREASURE AND HIS POWER SAFE...OUTLASTING HIS ENEMIES AND BIDING TIME UNTIL HE COULD RETURN.
"THE KEY TO RYGONE'S PLAN WOULD REST ON THE WINGS OF HIS FAITHFUL PET.
"NOW ALL HE HAD TO DO WAS WAIT FOR SOME GREEDY SOUL TO FIND THE MAP AND LEAD THEM BACK TO HIM. SOON RYGONE WOULD RISE ONCE AGAIN AND THIS TIME NOTHING WOULD STAND IN HIS WAY."

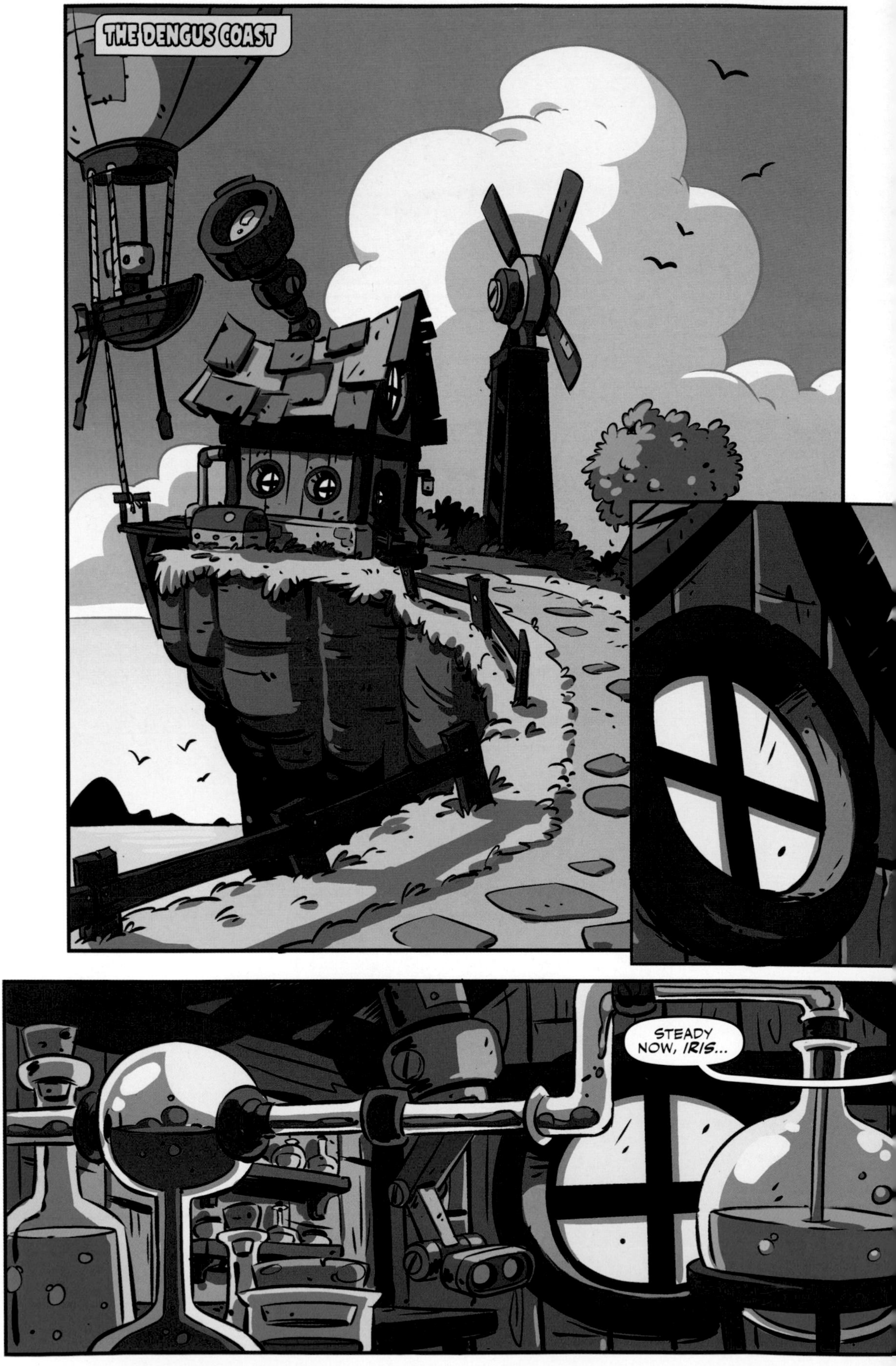
THE DENGUS COAST
STEADY NOW, IRIS...

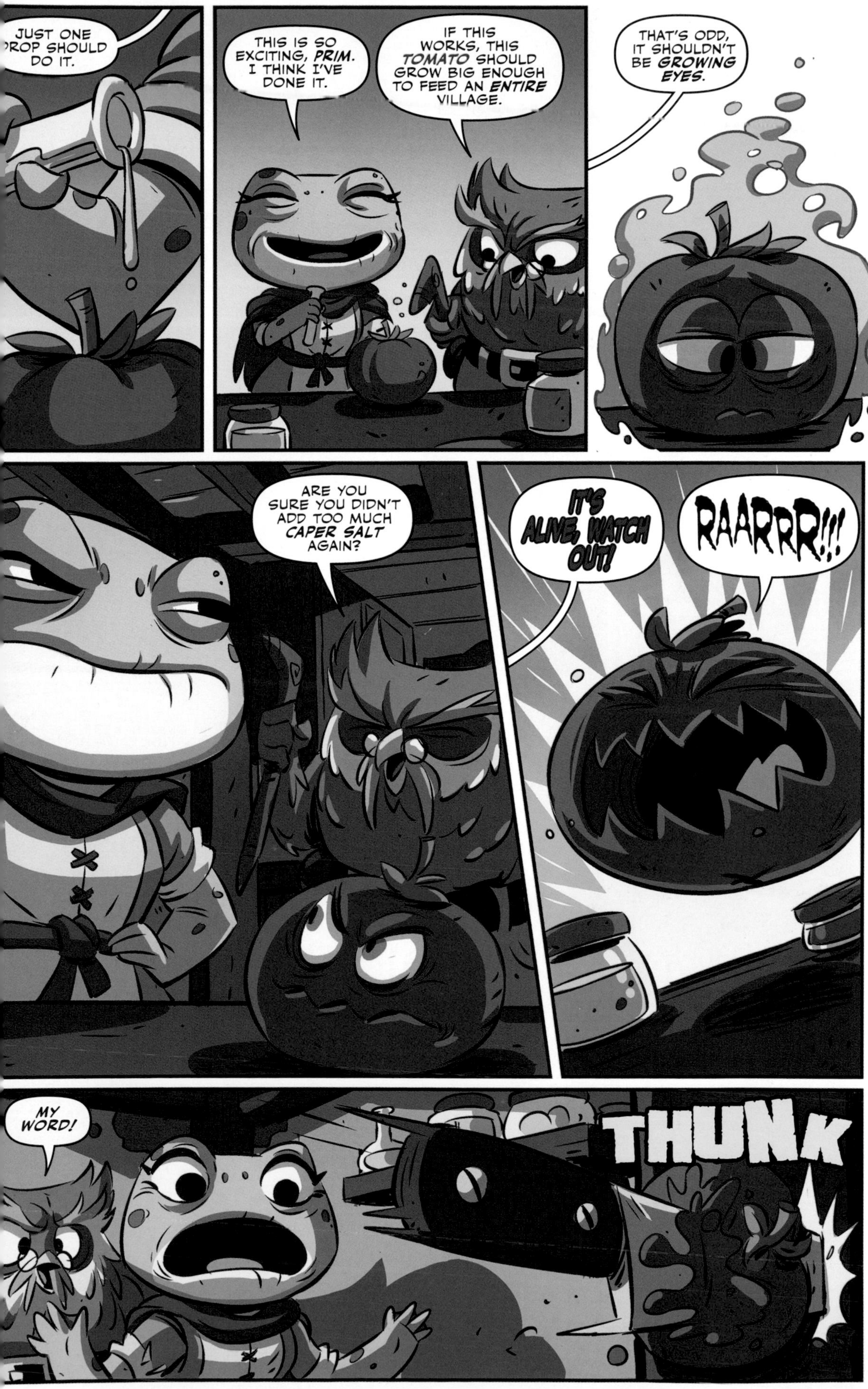
JUST ONE DROP SHOULD DO IT.
THIS IS SO EXCITING, PRIM. I THINK I'VE DONE IT.
IF THIS WORKS, THIS TOMATO SHOULD GROW BIG ENOUGH TO FEED AN ENTIRE VILLAGE.
THAT'S ODD, IT SHOULDN'T BE GROWING EYES.
ARE YOU SURE YOU DIDN'T ADD TOO MUCH CAPER SALT AGAIN?
IT'S ALIVE, WATCH OUT!
RAARRR!!!
MY WORD!
THUNK

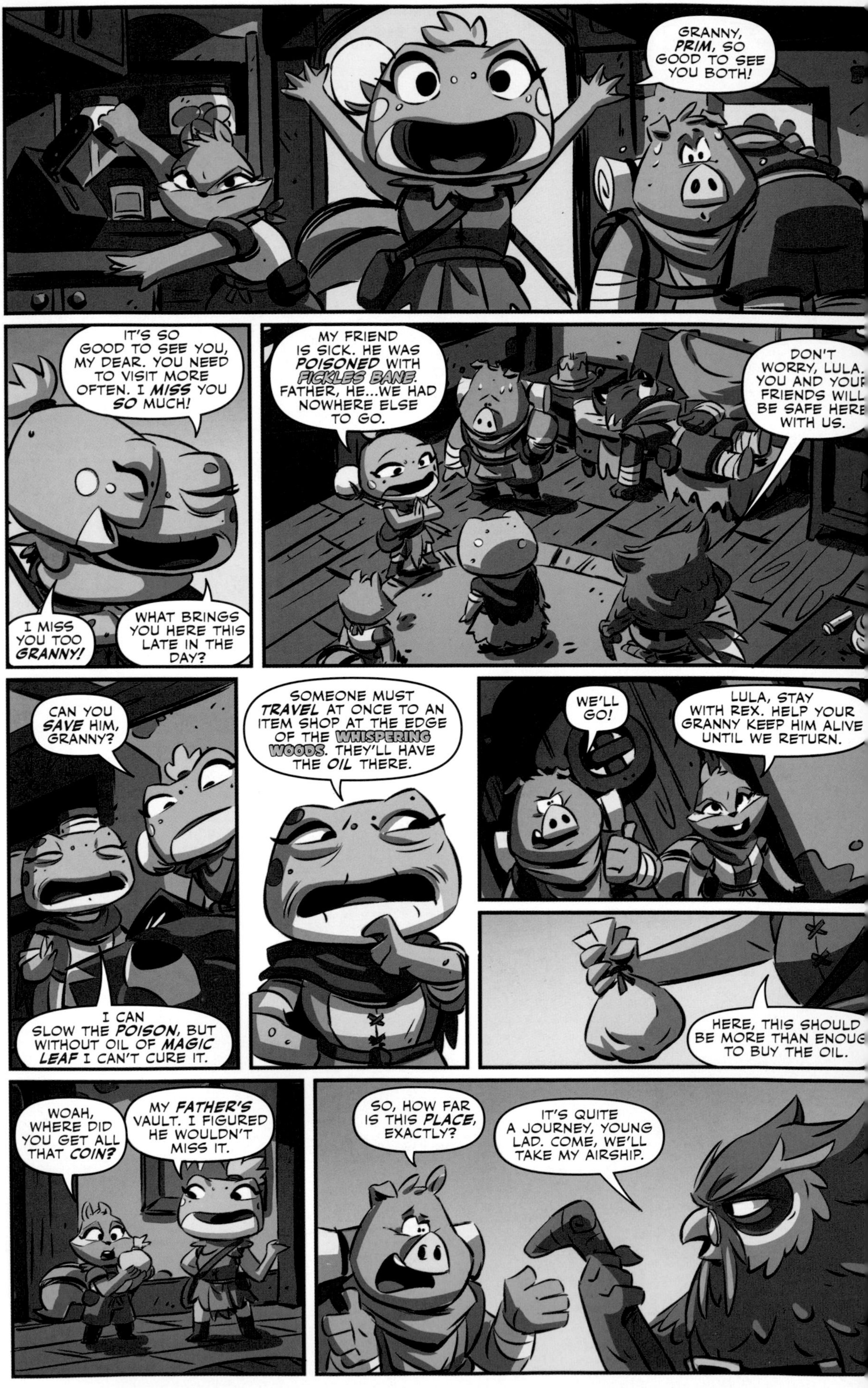
GRANNY, PRIM, SO GOOD TO SEE YOU BOTH!
IT'S SO GOOD TO SEE YOU, MY DEAR. YOU NEED TO VISIT MORE OFTEN. I MISS YOU SO MUCH!
I MISS YOU TOO GRANNY!
WHAT BRINGS YOU HERE THIS LATE IN THE DAY?
MY FRIEND IS SICK. HE WAS POISONED WITH FICKLES BANE. FATHER, HE...WE HAD NOWHERE ELSE TO GO.
DON'T WORRY, LULA. YOU AND YOUR FRIENDS WILL BE SAFE HERE WITH US.
CAN YOU SAVE HIM, GRANNY?
I CAN SLOW THE POISON, BUT WITHOUT OIL OF MAGIC LEAF I CAN'T CURE IT.
SOMEONE MUST TRAVEL AT ONCE TO AN ITEM SHOP AT THE EDGE OF THE WHISPERING WOODS. THEY'LL HAVE THE OIL THERE.
WE'LL GO!
LULA, STAY WITH REX. HELP YOUR GRANNY KEEP HIM ALIVE UNTIL WE RETURN.
HERE, THIS SHOULD BE MORE THAN ENOUG TO BUY THE OIL.
WOAH, WHERE DID YOU GET ALL THAT COIN?
MY FATHER'S VAULT. I FIGURED HE WOULDN'T MISS IT.
SO, HOW FAR IS THIS PLACE, EXACTLY?
IT'S QUITE A JOURNEY, YOUNG LAD. COME, WE'LL TAKE MY AIRSHIP.

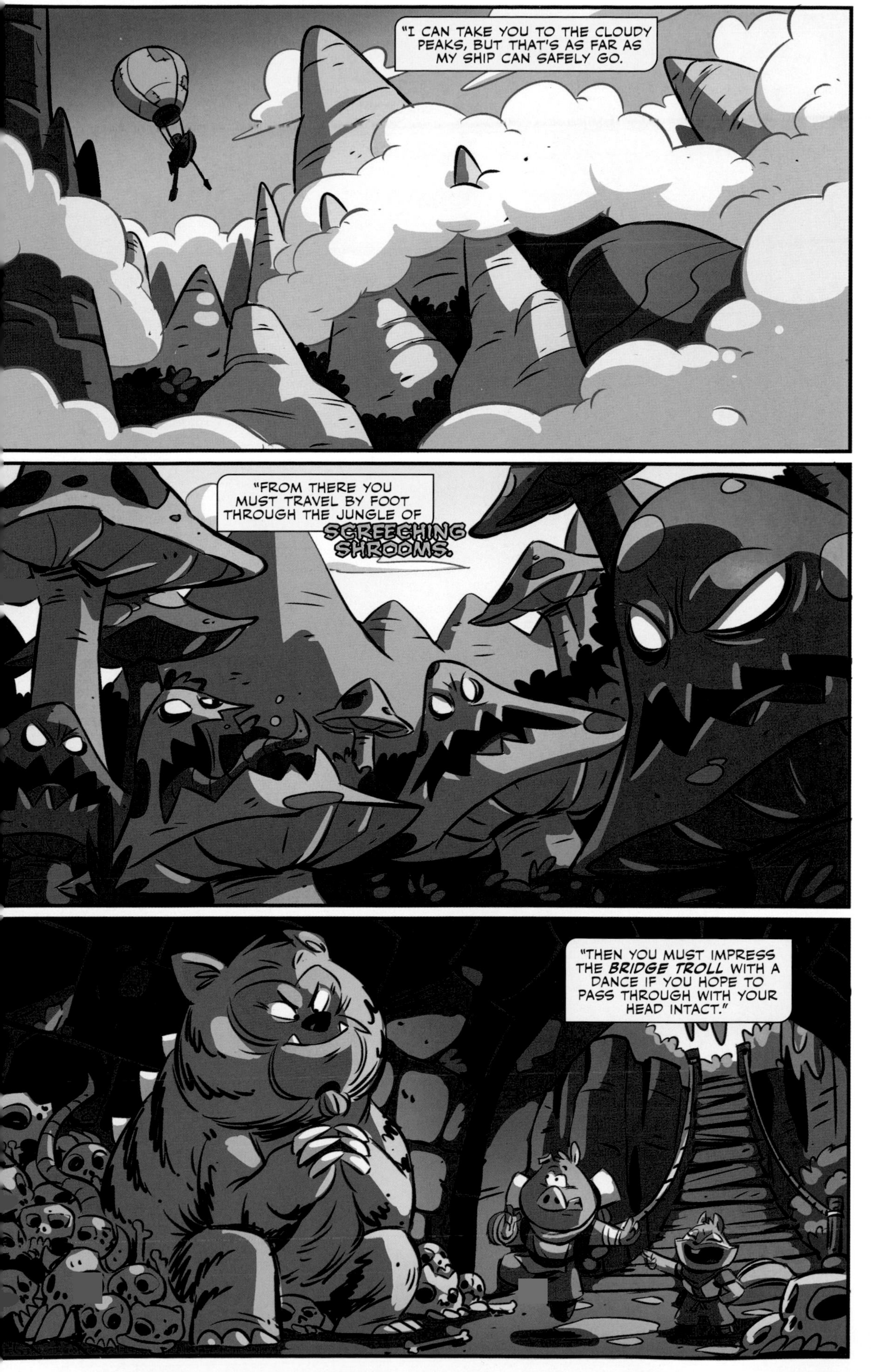
"I CAN TAKE YOU TO THE CLOUDY PEAKS, BUT THAT'S AS FAR AS MY SHIP CAN SAFELY GO.
"FROM THERE YOU MUST TRAVEL BY FOOT THROUGH THE JUNGLE OF
SCREECHING SHROOMS.
"THEN YOU MUST IMPRESS THE *BRIDGE TROLL* WITH A DANCE IF YOU HOPE TO PASS THROUGH WITH YOUR HEAD INTACT."

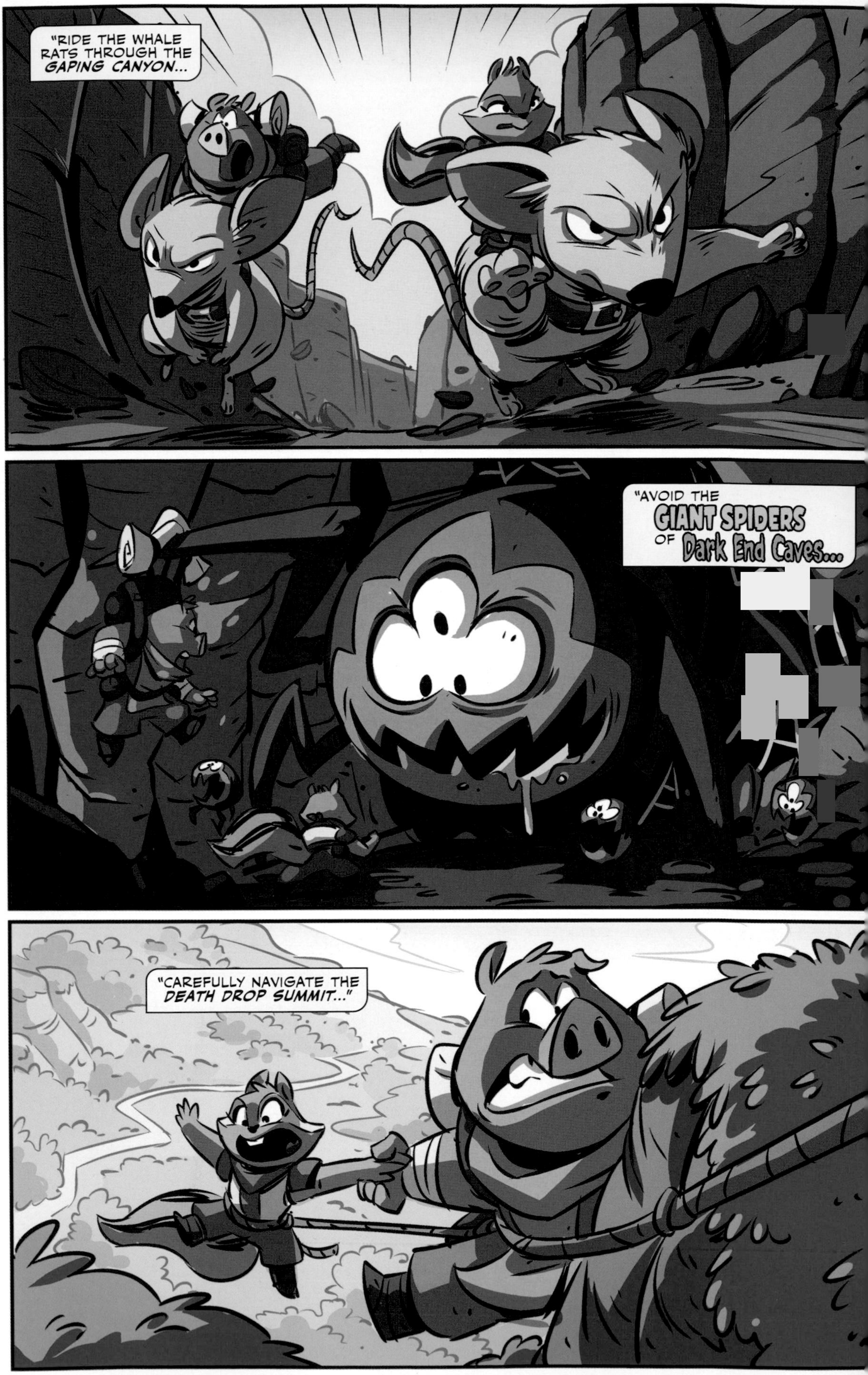
"RIDE THE WHALE RATS THROUGH THE GAPING CANYON...
"AVOID THE GIANT SPIDERS OF Dark End Caves...
"CAREFULLY NAVIGATE THE DEATH DROP SUMMIT..."

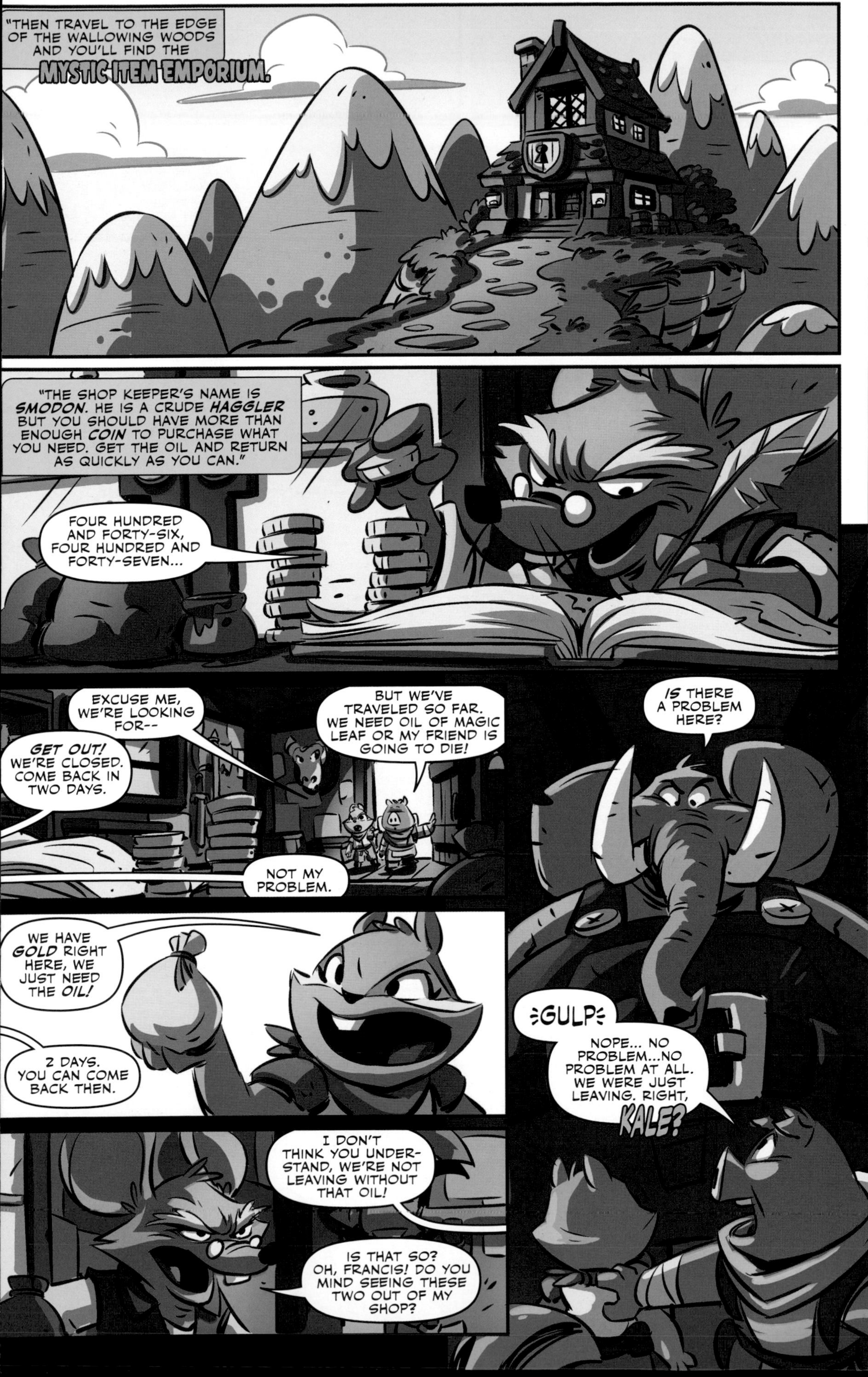
"THEN TRAVEL TO THE EDGE OF THE WALLOWING WOODS AND YOU'LL FIND THE
MYSTIC ITEM EMPORIUM.
"THE SHOP KEEPER'S NAME IS SMODON. HE IS A CRUDE HAGGLER BUT YOU SHOULD HAVE MORE THAN ENOUGH COIN TO PURCHASE WHAT YOU NEED. GET THE OIL AND RETURN AS QUICKLY AS YOU CAN."
FOUR HUNDRED AND FORTY-SIX, FOUR HUNDRED AND FORTY-SEVEN...
EXCUSE ME, WE'RE LOOKING FOR--
GET OUT! WE'RE CLOSED. COME BACK IN TWO DAYS.
BUT WE'VE TRAVELED SO FAR. WE NEED OIL OF MAGIC LEAF OR MY FRIEND IS GOING TO DIE!
NOT MY PROBLEM.
WE HAVE GOLD RIGHT HERE, WE JUST NEED THE OIL!
2 DAYS. YOU CAN COME BACK THEN.
I DON'T THINK YOU UNDER-STAND, WE'RE NOT LEAVING WITHOUT THAT OIL!
IS THAT SO? OH, FRANCIS! DO YOU MIND SEEING THESE TWO OUT OF MY SHOP?
IS THERE A PROBLEM HERE?
GULP
NOPE... NO PROBLEM...NO PROBLEM AT ALL. WE WERE JUST LEAVING. RIGHT, KALE?

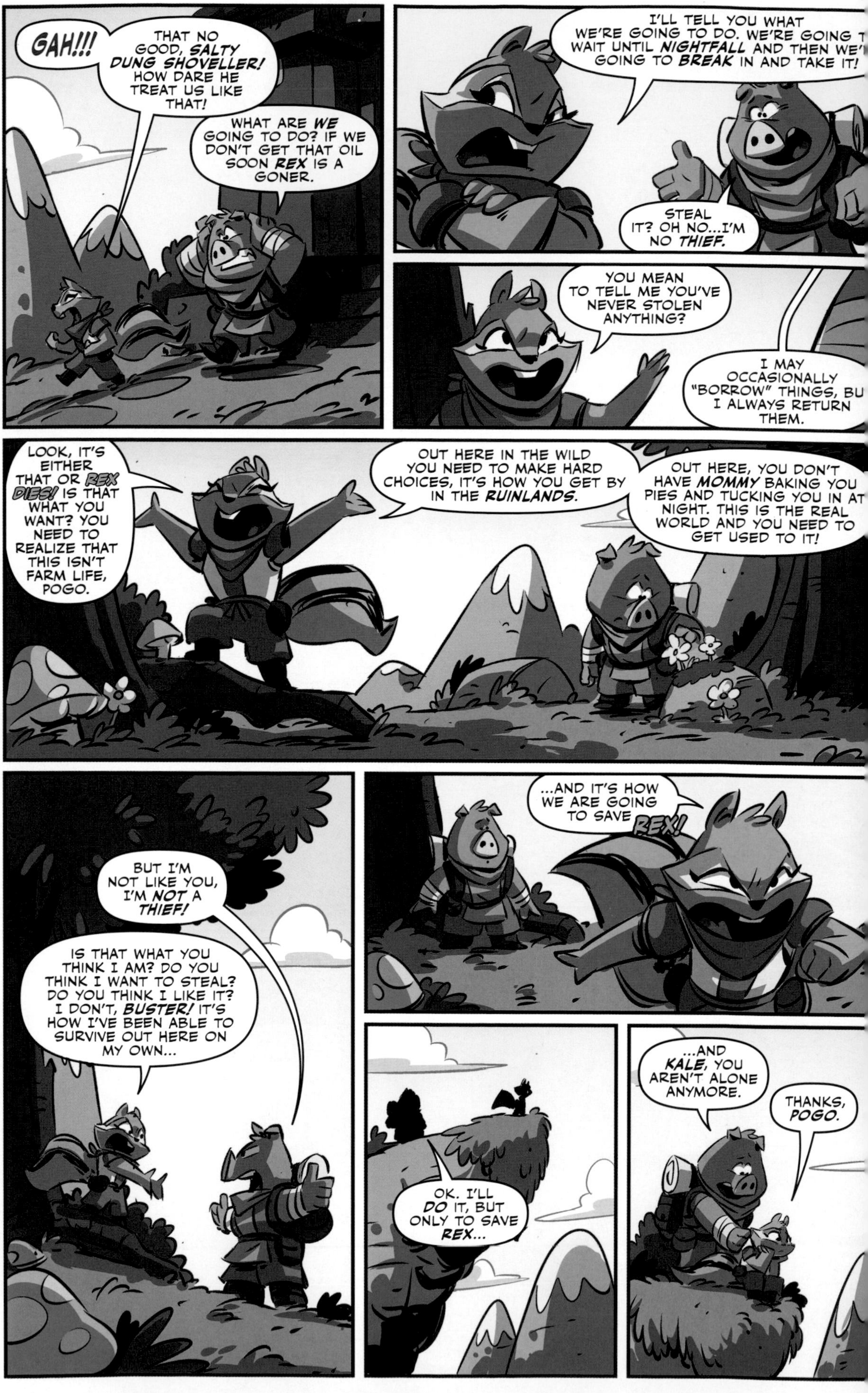
GAH!!!
THAT NO GOOD, SALTY DUNG SHOVELLER! HOW DARE HE TREAT US LIKE THAT!
WHAT ARE WE GOING TO DO? IF WE DON'T GET THAT OIL SOON REX IS A GONER.
I'LL TELL YOU WHAT WE'RE GOING TO DO. WE'RE GOING T WAIT UNTIL NIGHTFALL AND THEN WE' GOING TO BREAK IN AND TAKE IT!
STEAL IT? OH NO...I'M NO THIEF.
YOU MEAN TO TELL ME YOU'VE NEVER STOLEN ANYTHING?
I MAY OCCASIONALLY "BORROW" THINGS, BU I ALWAYS RETURN THEM.
LOOK, IT'S EITHER THAT OR REX DIES! IS THAT WHAT YOU WANT? YOU NEED TO REALIZE THAT THIS ISN'T FARM LIFE, POGO.
OUT HERE IN THE WILD YOU NEED TO MAKE HARD CHOICES, IT'S HOW YOU GET BY IN THE RUINLANDS.
OUT HERE, YOU DON'T HAVE MOMMY BAKING YOU PIES AND TUCKING YOU IN AT NIGHT. THIS IS THE REAL WORLD AND YOU NEED TO GET USED TO IT!
BUT I'M NOT LIKE YOU, I'M NOT A THIEF!
IS THAT WHAT YOU THINK I AM? DO YOU THINK I WANT TO STEAL? DO YOU THINK I LIKE IT? I DON'T, BUSTER! IT'S HOW I'VE BEEN ABLE TO SURVIVE OUT HERE ON MY OWN...
...AND IT'S HOW WE ARE GOING TO SAVE REX!
OK. I'LL DO IT, BUT ONLY TO SAVE REX...
...AND KALE, YOU AREN'T ALONE ANYMORE.
THANKS, POGO.

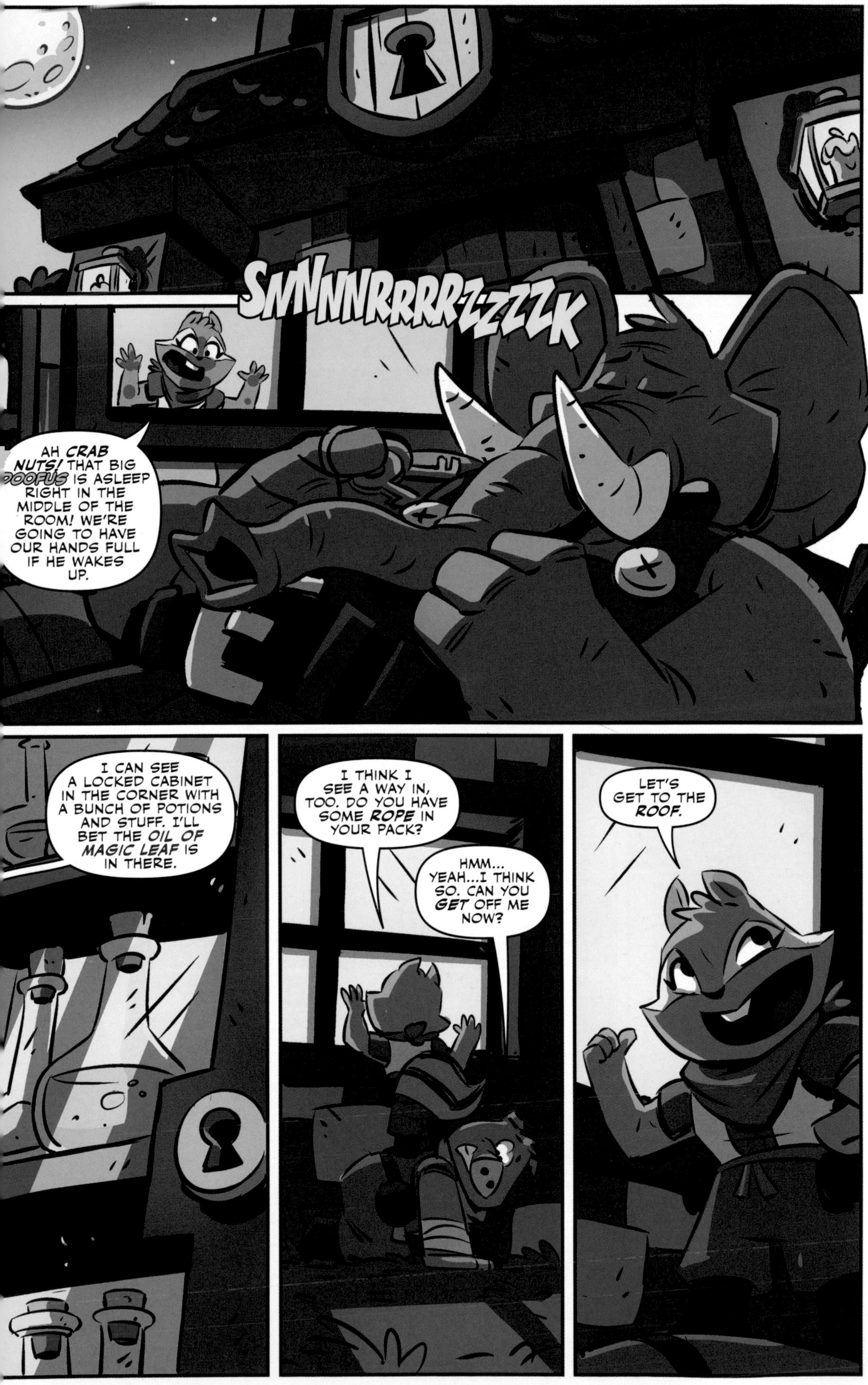
SNNNNRRRRZZZZK
AH CRAB NUTS! THAT BIG DOOFUS IS ASLEEP RIGHT IN THE MIDDLE OF THE ROOM! WE'RE GOING TO HAVE OUR HANDS FULL IF HE WAKES UP.
I CAN SEE A LOCKED CABINET IN THE CORNER WITH A BUNCH OF POTIONS AND STUFF. I'LL BET THE OIL OF MAGIC LEAF IS IN THERE.
I THINK I SEE A WAY IN, TOO. DO YOU HAVE SOME ROPE IN YOUR PACK?
HMM... YEAH...I THINK SO. CAN YOU GET OFF ME NOW?
LET'S GET TO THE ROOF.

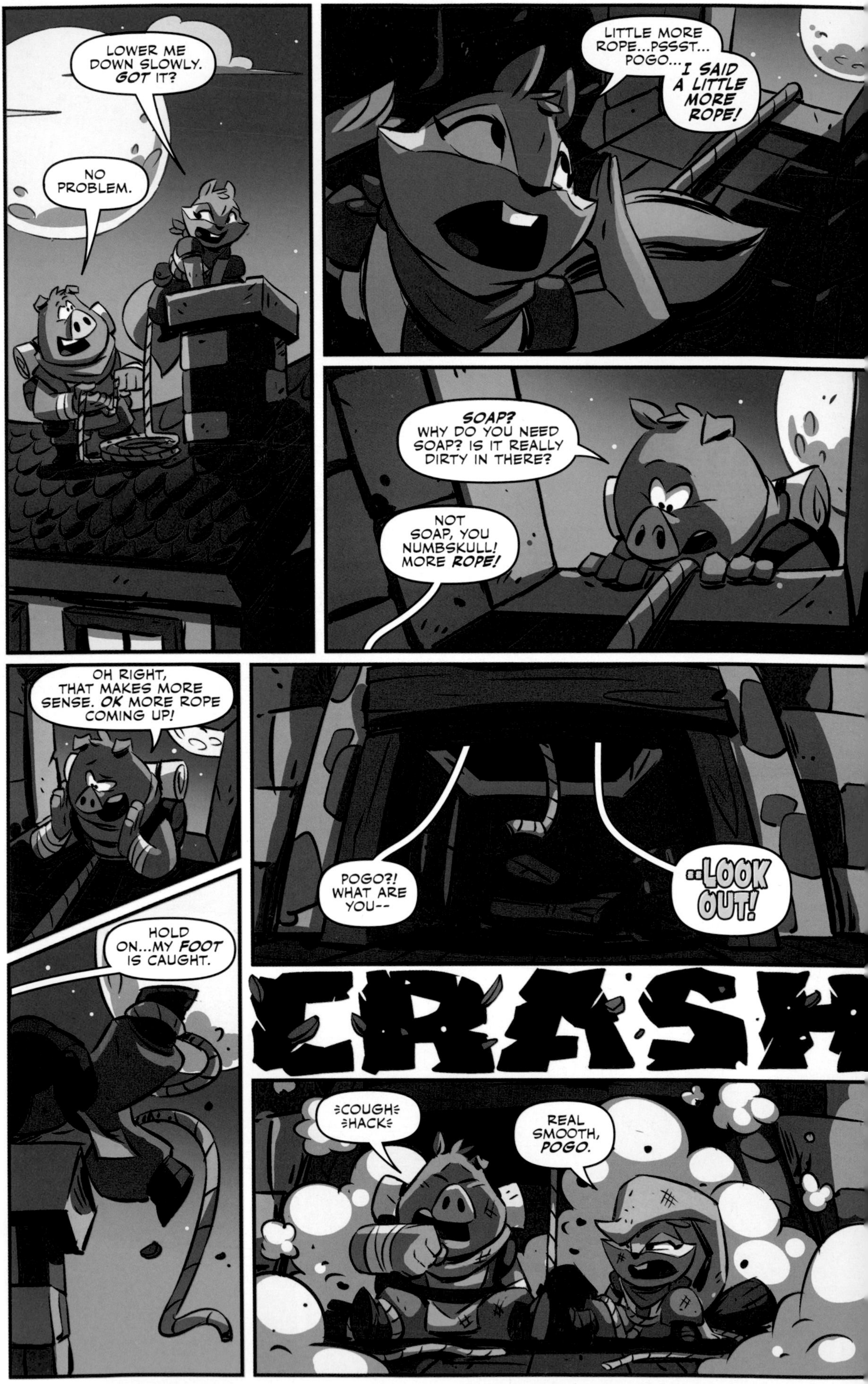
LOWER ME DOWN SLOWLY. GOT IT?
NO PROBLEM.
LITTLE MORE ROPE...PSSST... POGO... I SAID A LITTLE MORE ROPE!
SOAP? WHY DO YOU NEED SOAP? IS IT REALLY DIRTY IN THERE?
NOT SOAP, YOU NUMBSKULL! MORE ROPE!
OH RIGHT, THAT MAKES MORE SENSE. OK MORE ROPE COMING UP!
HOLD ON...MY FOOT IS CAUGHT.
POGO?! WHAT ARE YOU--
--LOOK OUT!
CRASH
COUGH HACK
REAL SMOOTH, POGO.

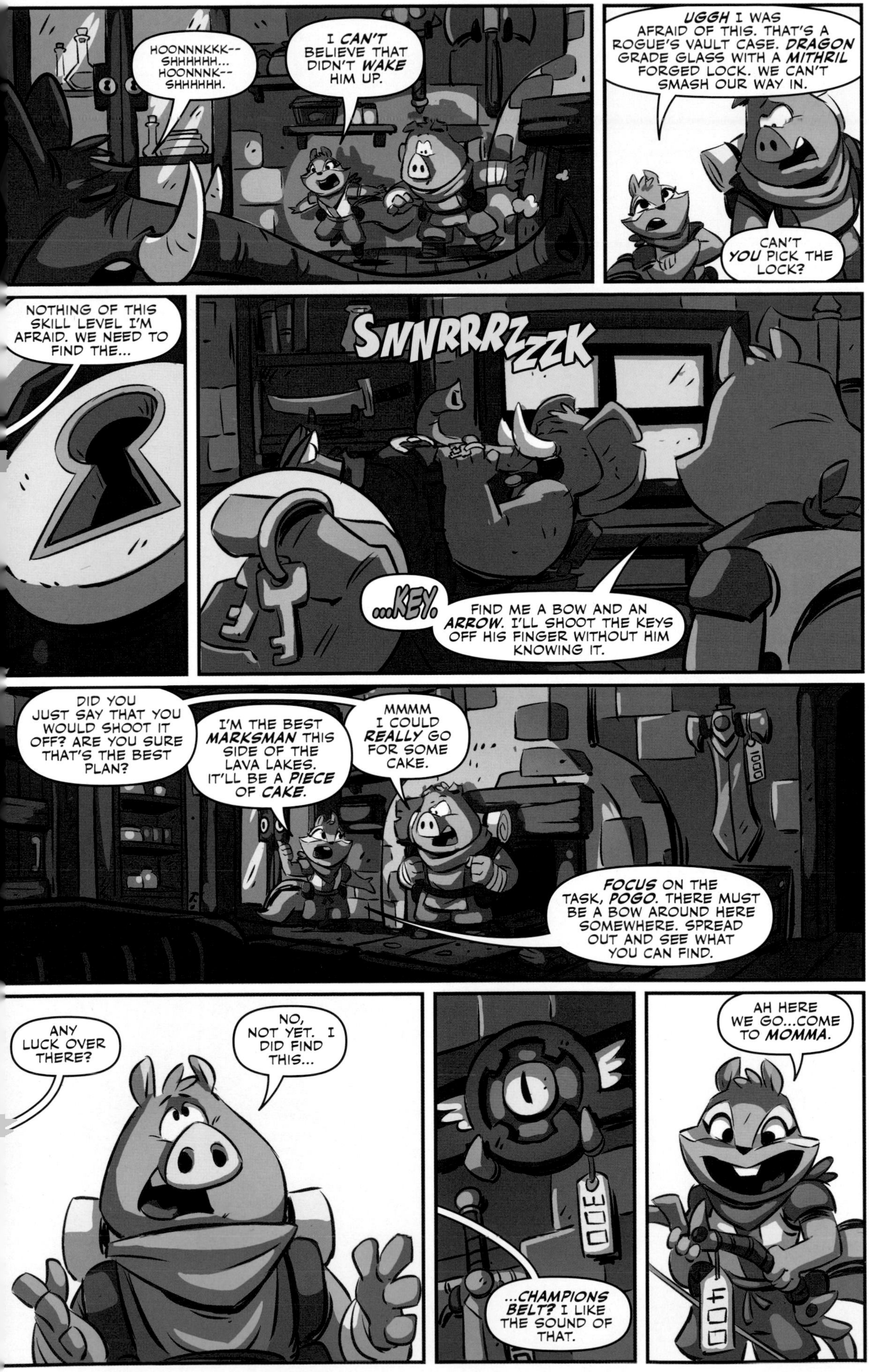
HOONNNKKK--
SHHHHHH...
HOONNNK--
SHHHHHH.
I CAN'T BELIEVE THAT DIDN'T WAKE HIM UP.
UGGH I WAS AFRAID OF THIS. THAT'S A ROGUE'S VAULT CASE. DRAGON GRADE GLASS WITH A MITHRIL FORGED LOCK. WE CAN'T SMASH OUR WAY IN.
CAN'T YOU PICK THE LOCK?
NOTHING OF THIS SKILL LEVEL I'M AFRAID. WE NEED TO FIND THE...
SNNRRRRZZZK
...KEY.
FIND ME A BOW AND AN ARROW. I'LL SHOOT THE KEYS OFF HIS FINGER WITHOUT HIM KNOWING IT.
DID YOU JUST SAY THAT YOU WOULD SHOOT IT OFF? ARE YOU SURE THAT'S THE BEST PLAN?
I'M THE BEST MARKSMAN THIS SIDE OF THE LAVA LAKES. IT'LL BE A PIECE OF CAKE.
MMMM I COULD REALLY GO FOR SOME CAKE.
1000
FOCUS ON THE TASK, POGO. THERE MUST BE A BOW AROUND HERE SOMEWHERE. SPREAD OUT AND SEE WHAT YOU CAN FIND.
ANY LUCK OVER THERE?
NO, NOT YET. I DID FIND THIS...
300
...CHAMPIONS BELT? I LIKE THE SOUND OF THAT.
AH HERE WE GO...COME TO MOMMA.
400

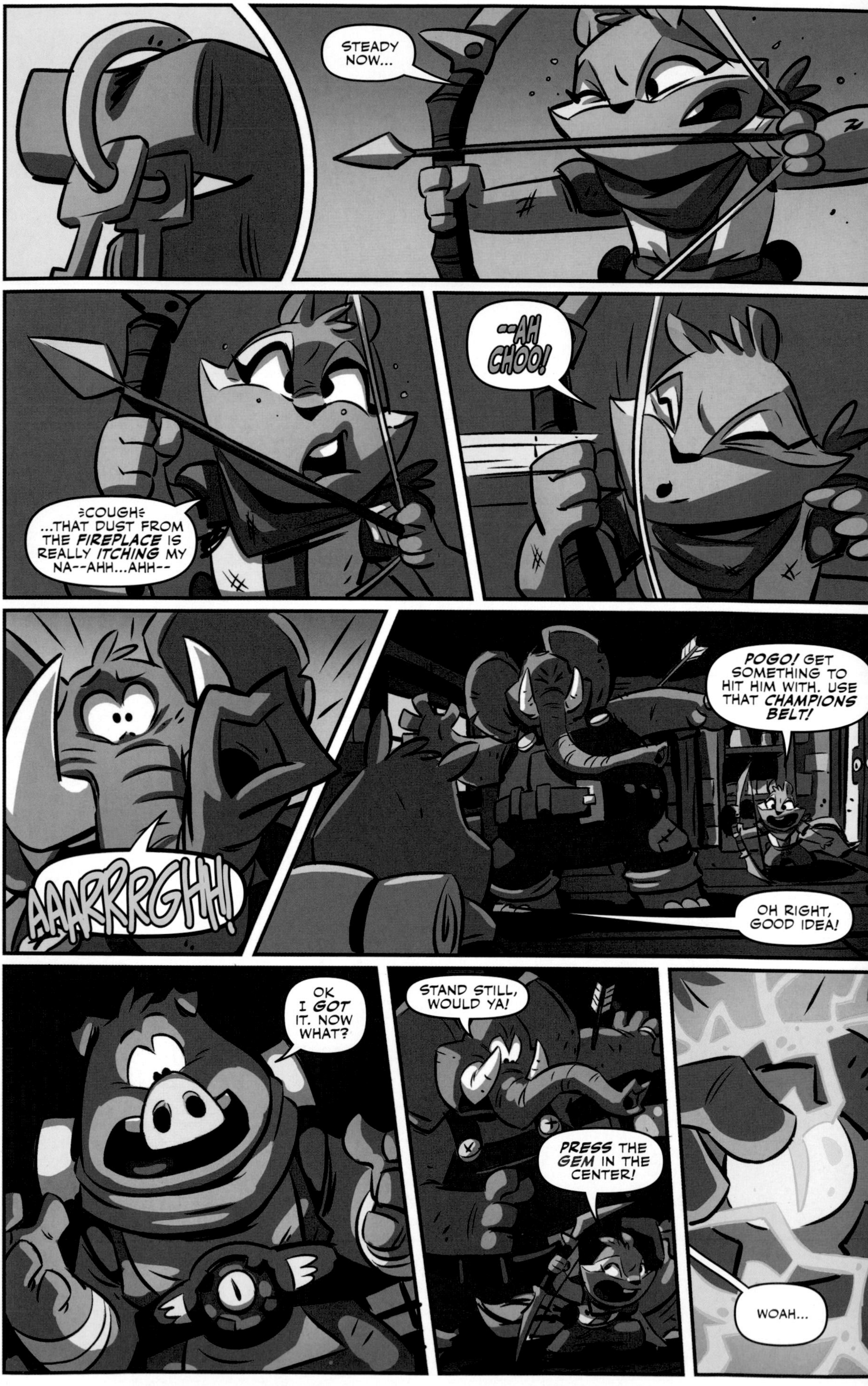
STEADY NOW...
≈COUGH≈ ...THAT DUST FROM THE *FIREPLACE* IS REALLY *ITCHING* MY NA--AHH...AHH--
--AH CHOO!
AAARRRGHH!
POGO! GET SOMETHING TO HIT HIM WITH. USE THAT *CHAMPIONS BELT!*
OH RIGHT, GOOD IDEA!
OK I *GOT* IT. NOW WHAT?
STAND STILL, WOULD YA!
PRESS THE *GEM* IN THE CENTER!
WOAH...

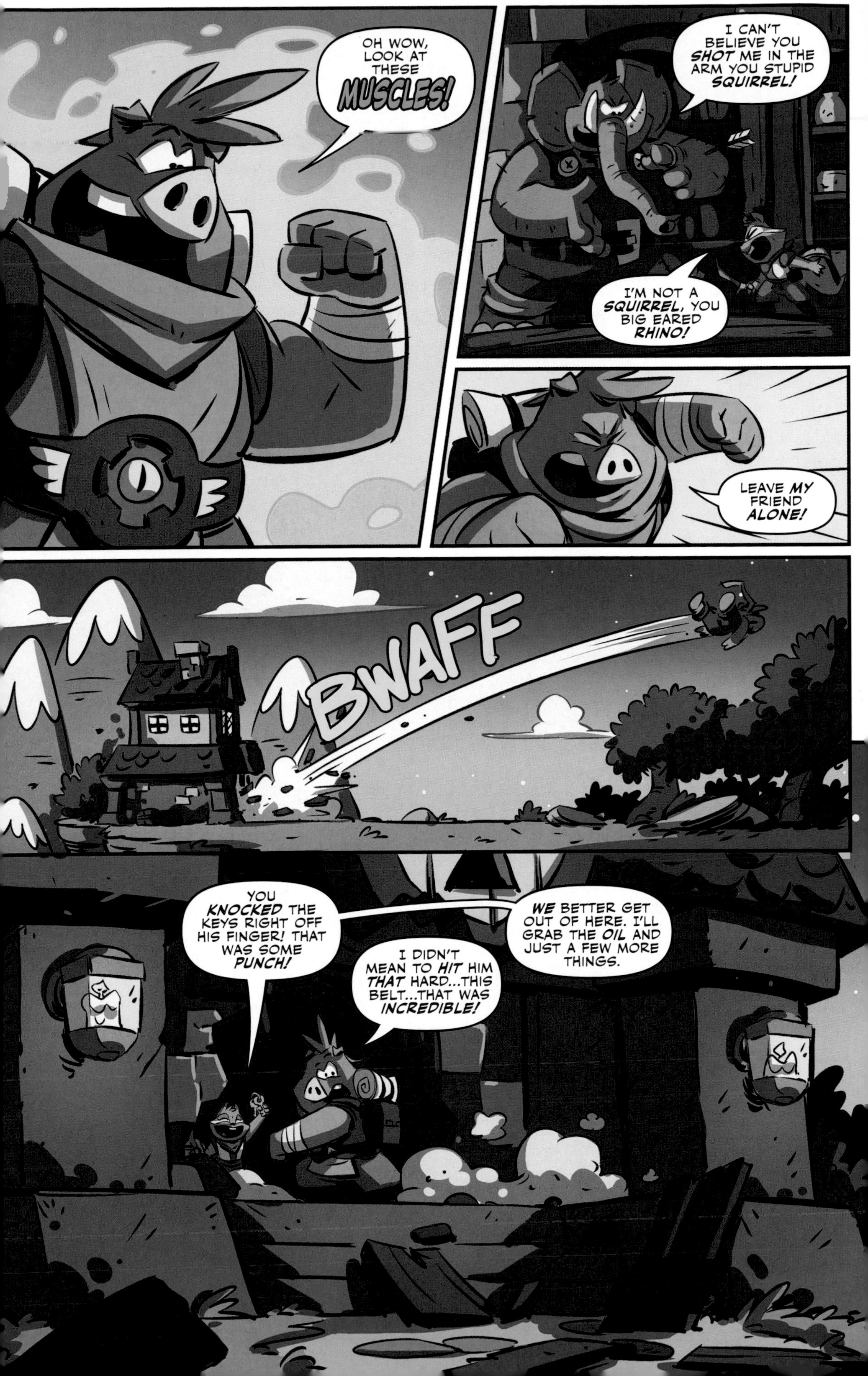
OH WOW, LOOK AT THESE MUSCLES!
I CAN'T BELIEVE YOU SHOT ME IN THE ARM YOU STUPID SQUIRREL!
I'M NOT A SQUIRREL, YOU BIG EARED RHINO!
LEAVE MY FRIEND ALONE!
BWAFF
YOU KNOCKED THE KEYS RIGHT OFF HIS FINGER! THAT WAS SOME PUNCH!
I DIDN'T MEAN TO HIT HIM THAT HARD...THIS BELT...THAT WAS INCREDIBLE!
WE BETTER GET OUT OF HERE. I'LL GRAB THE OIL AND JUST A FEW MORE THINGS.

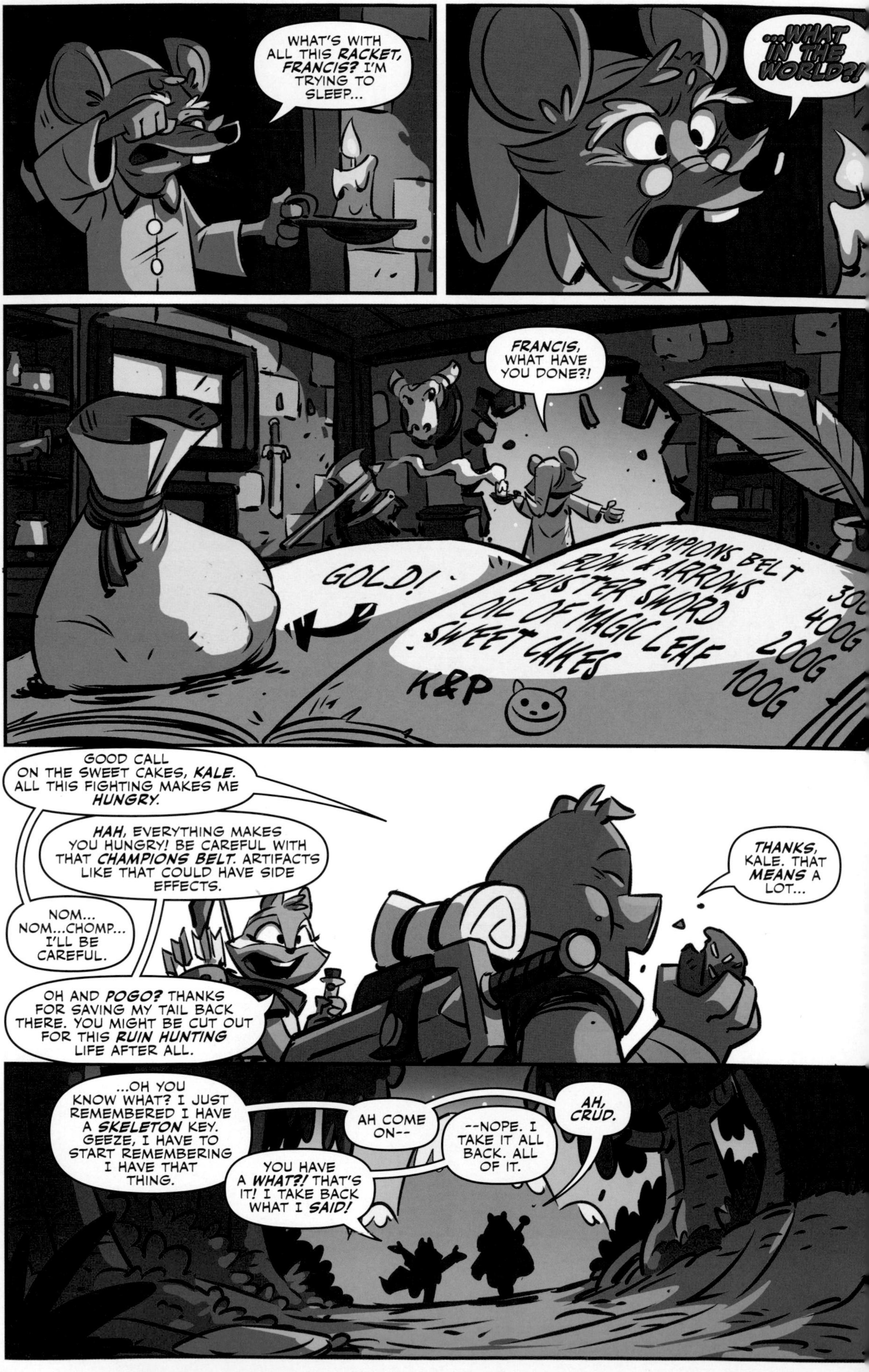
WHAT'S WITH ALL THIS RACKET, FRANCIS? I'M TRYING TO SLEEP...
...WHAT IN THE WORLD?!
FRANCIS, WHAT HAVE YOU DONE?!
GOLD!
CHAMPIONS BELT 300G
BOW & ARROWS 400G
BUSTER SWORD
OIL OF MAGIC LEAF 200G
SWEET CAKES 100G
K&P
GOOD CALL ON THE SWEET CAKES, KALE. ALL THIS FIGHTING MAKES ME HUNGRY.
HAH, EVERYTHING MAKES YOU HUNGRY! BE CAREFUL WITH THAT CHAMPIONS BELT. ARTIFACTS LIKE THAT COULD HAVE SIDE EFFECTS.
NOM... NOM...CHOMP... I'LL BE CAREFUL.
OH AND POGO? THANKS FOR SAVING MY TAIL BACK THERE. YOU MIGHT BE CUT OUT FOR THIS RUIN HUNTING LIFE AFTER ALL.
THANKS, KALE. THAT MEANS A LOT...
...OH YOU KNOW WHAT? I JUST REMEMBERED I HAVE A SKELETON KEY. GEEZE, I HAVE TO START REMEMBERING I HAVE THAT THING.
YOU HAVE A WHAT?! THAT'S IT! I TAKE BACK WHAT I SAID!
AH COME ON--
--NOPE. I TAKE IT ALL BACK. ALL OF IT.
AH, CRUD.

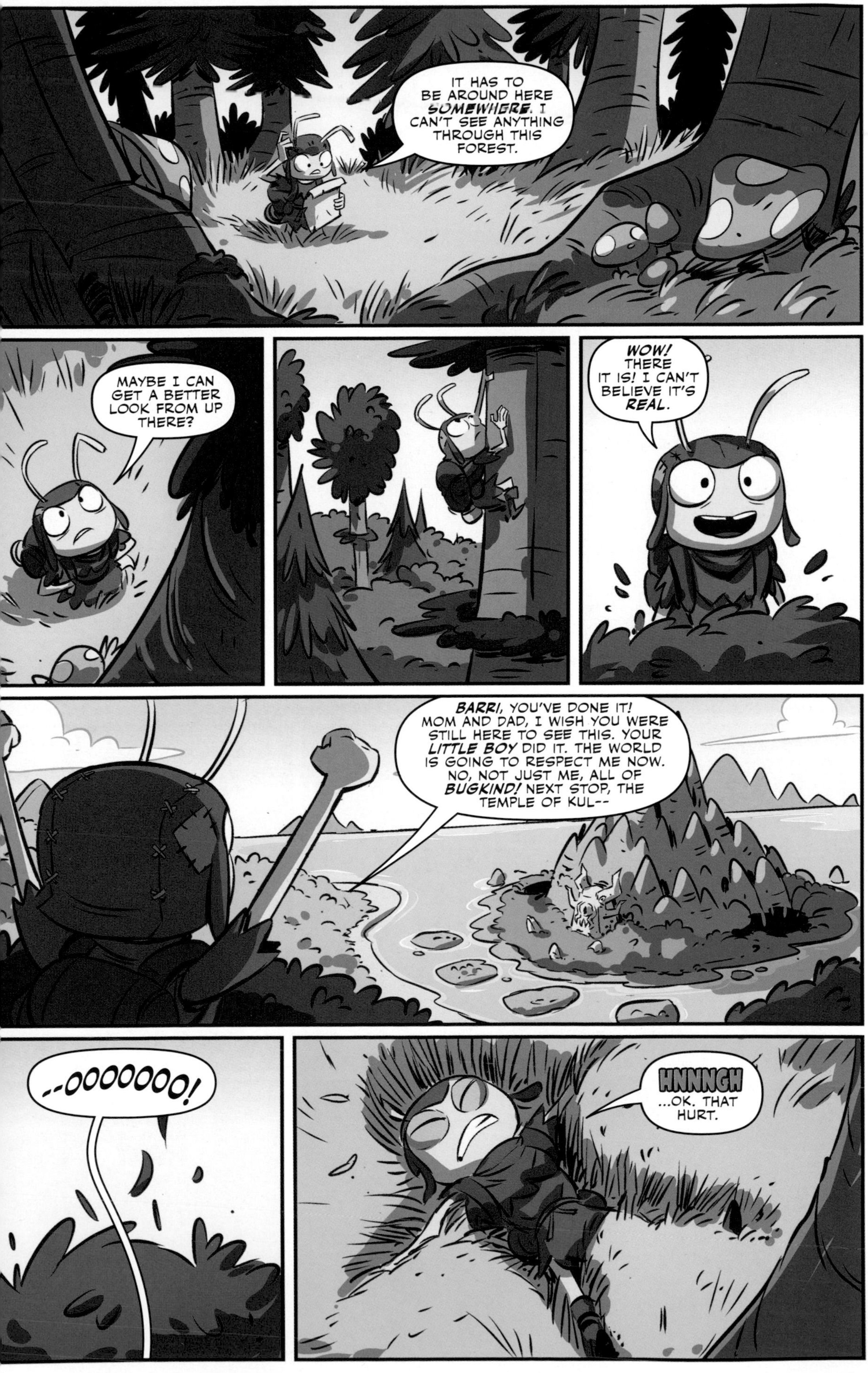

IT HAS TO BE AROUND HERE SOMEWHERE. I CAN'T SEE ANYTHING THROUGH THIS FOREST.
MAYBE I CAN GET A BETTER LOOK FROM UP THERE?
WOW! THERE IT IS! I CAN'T BELIEVE IT'S REAL.
BARRI, YOU'VE DONE IT! MOM AND DAD, I WISH YOU WERE STILL HERE TO SEE THIS. YOUR LITTLE BOY DID IT. THE WORLD IS GOING TO RESPECT ME NOW. NO, NOT JUST ME, ALL OF BUGKIND! NEXT STOP, THE TEMPLE OF KUL--
--OOOOOOO!
HNNNGH
...OK. THAT HURT.

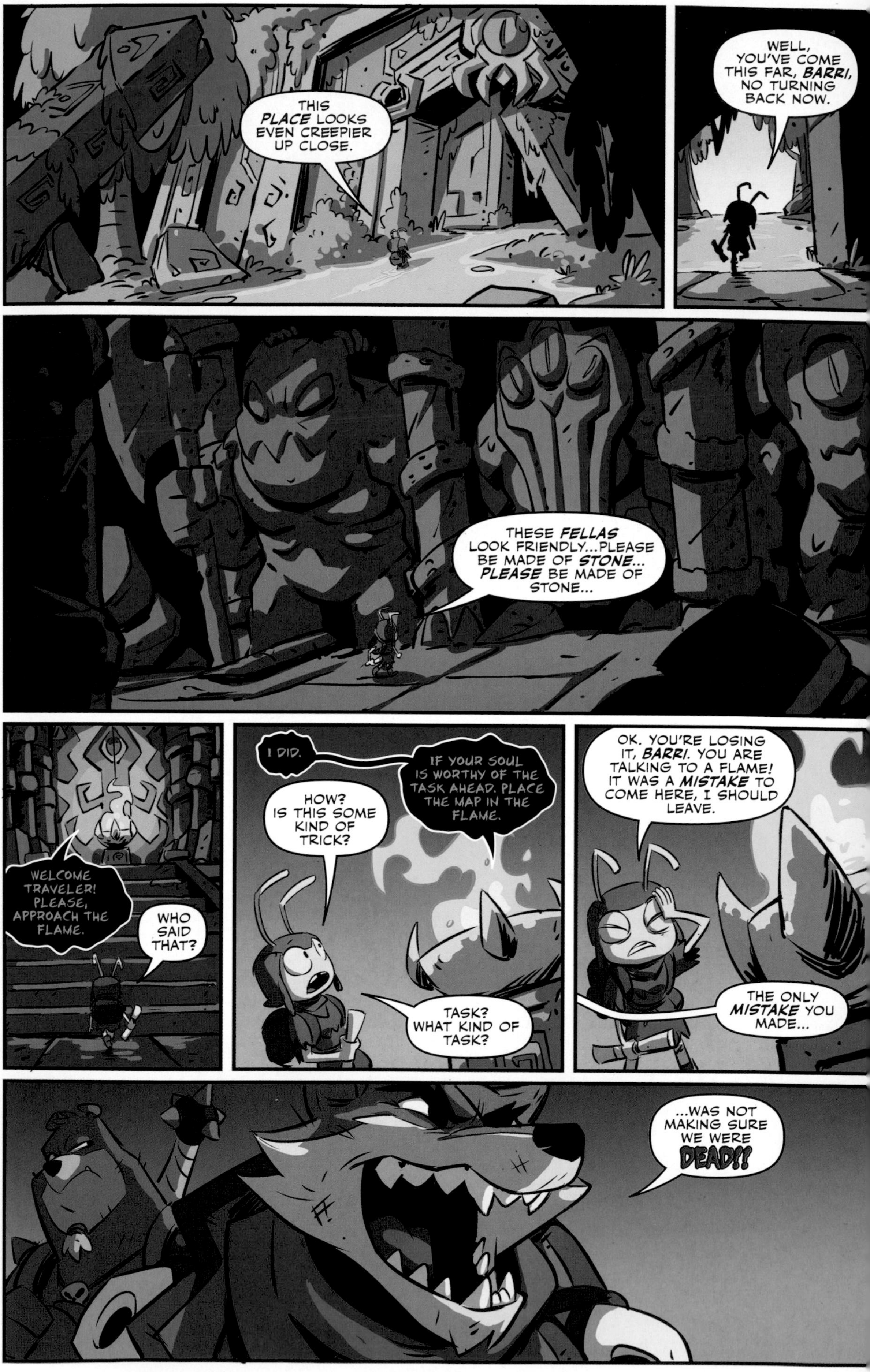
THIS PLACE LOOKS EVEN CREEPIER UP CLOSE.
WELL, YOU'VE COME THIS FAR, BARRI, NO TURNING BACK NOW.
THESE FELLAS LOOK FRIENDLY...PLEASE BE MADE OF STONE... PLEASE BE MADE OF STONE...
WELCOME TRAVELER! PLEASE, APPROACH THE FLAME.
WHO SAID THAT?
I DID.
HOW? IS THIS SOME KIND OF TRICK?
IF YOUR SOUL IS WORTHY OF THE TASK AHEAD. PLACE THE MAP IN THE FLAME.
TASK? WHAT KIND OF TASK?
OK. YOU'RE LOSING IT, BARRI. YOU ARE TALKING TO A FLAME! IT WAS A MISTAKE TO COME HERE, I SHOULD LEAVE.
THE ONLY MISTAKE YOU MADE...
...WAS NOT MAKING SURE WE WERE DEAD!!

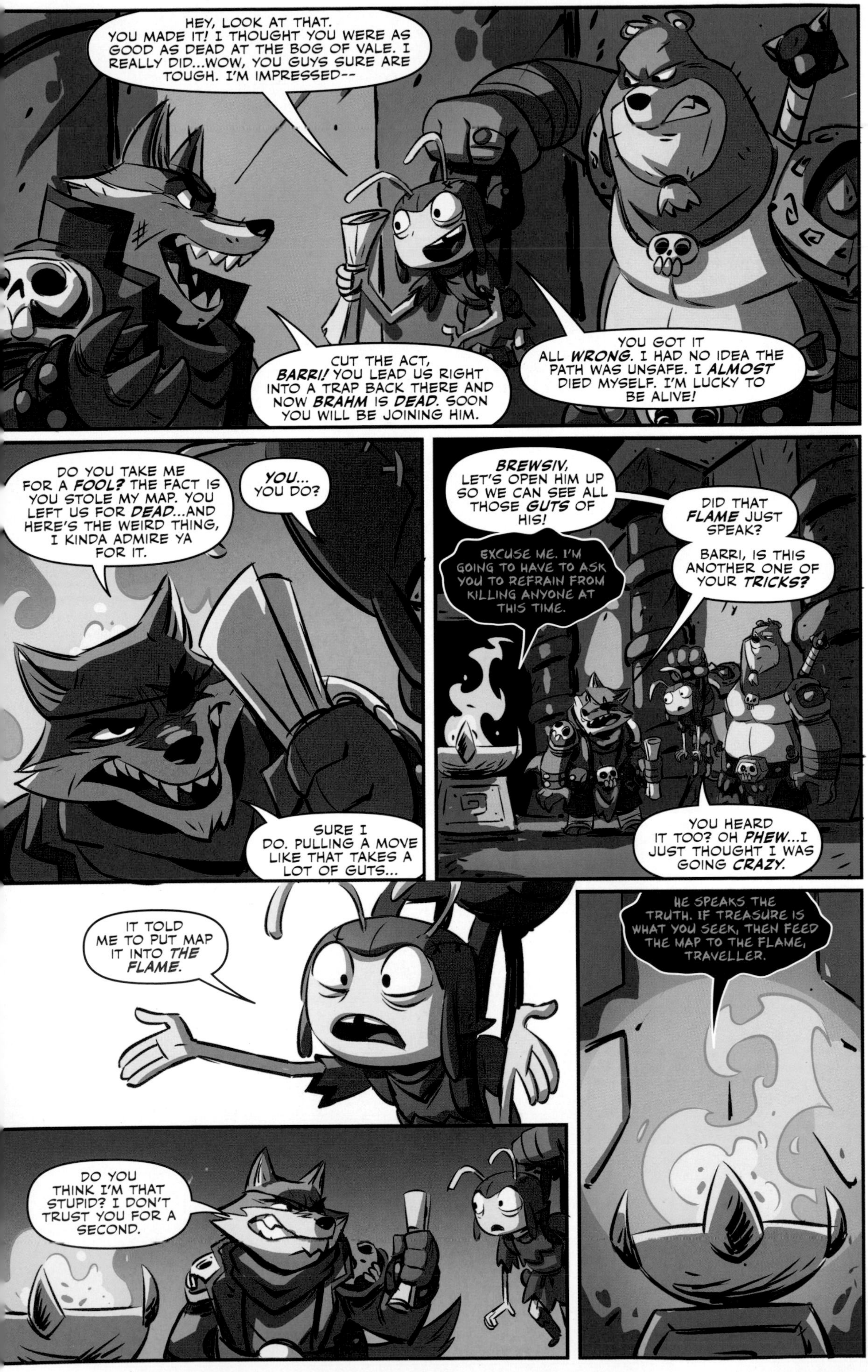
HEY, LOOK AT THAT. YOU MADE IT! I THOUGHT YOU WERE AS GOOD AS DEAD AT THE BOG OF VALE. I REALLY DID...WOW, YOU GUYS SURE ARE TOUGH. I'M IMPRESSED--
CUT THE ACT, BARRI! YOU LEAD US RIGHT INTO A TRAP BACK THERE AND NOW BRAHM IS DEAD. SOON YOU WILL BE JOINING HIM.
YOU GOT IT ALL WRONG. I HAD NO IDEA THE PATH WAS UNSAFE. I ALMOST DIED MYSELF. I'M LUCKY TO BE ALIVE!
DO YOU TAKE ME FOR A FOOL? THE FACT IS YOU STOLE MY MAP. YOU LEFT US FOR DEAD...AND HERE'S THE WEIRD THING, I KINDA ADMIRE YA FOR IT.
YOU... YOU DO?
SURE I DO. PULLING A MOVE LIKE THAT TAKES A LOT OF GUTS...
BREWSIV, LET'S OPEN HIM UP SO WE CAN SEE ALL THOSE GUTS OF HIS!
EXCUSE ME. I'M GOING TO HAVE TO ASK YOU TO REFRAIN FROM KILLING ANYONE AT THIS TIME.
DID THAT FLAME JUST SPEAK?
BARRI, IS THIS ANOTHER ONE OF YOUR TRICKS?
YOU HEARD IT TOO? OH PHEW...I JUST THOUGHT I WAS GOING CRAZY.
IT TOLD ME TO PUT MAP IT INTO THE FLAME.
HE SPEAKS THE TRUTH. IF TREASURE IS WHAT YOU SEEK, THEN FEED THE MAP TO THE FLAME, TRAVELLER.
DO YOU THINK I'M THAT STUPID? I DON'T TRUST YOU FOR A SECOND.

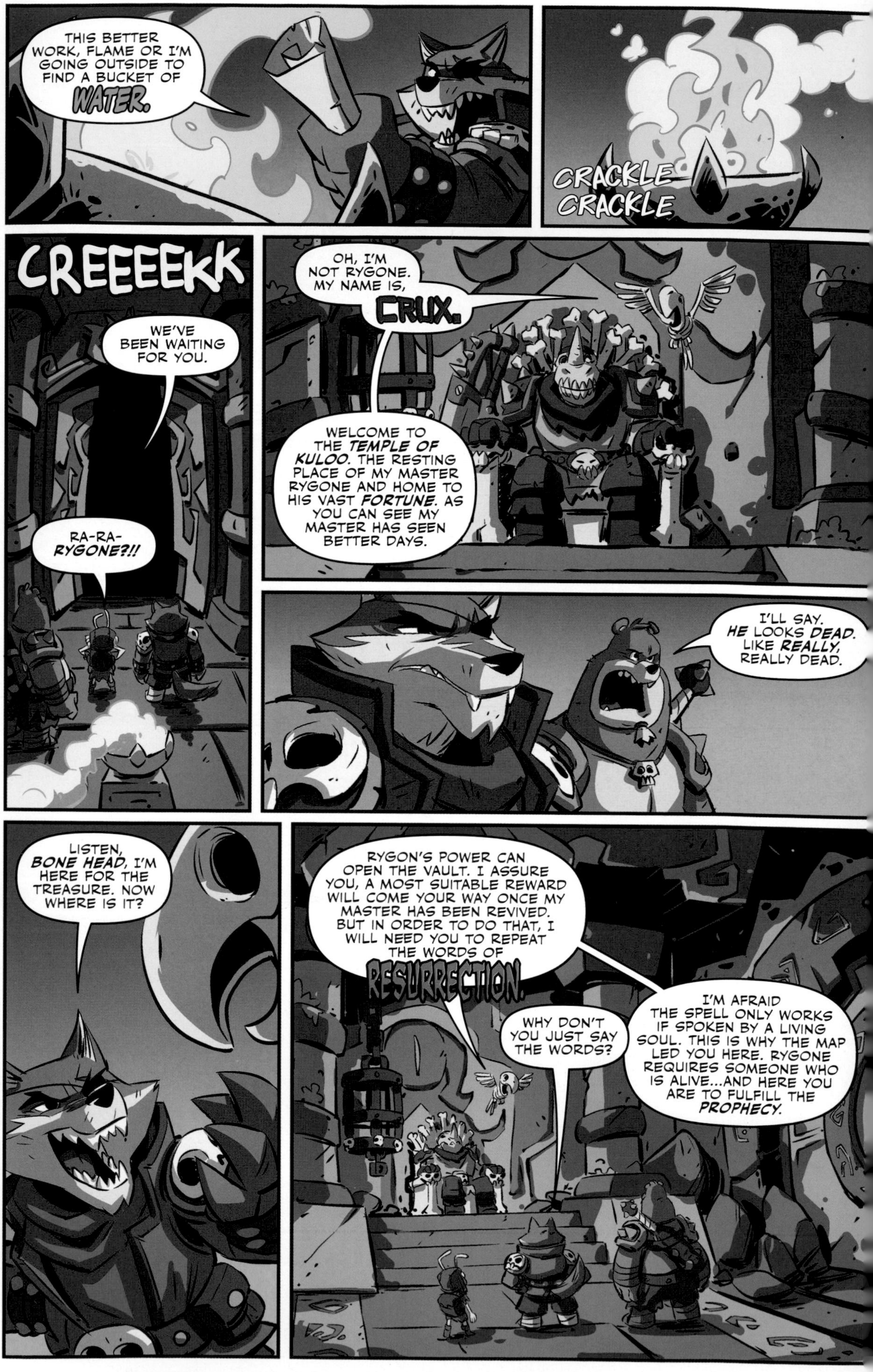
THIS BETTER WORK, FLAME OR I'M GOING OUTSIDE TO FIND A BUCKET OF WATER.
CRACKLE CRACKLE
CREEEEEKK
WE'VE BEEN WAITING FOR YOU.
RA-RA- RYGONE?!!
OH, I'M NOT RYGONE. MY NAME IS, CRUX.
WELCOME TO THE TEMPLE OF KULOO. THE RESTING PLACE OF MY MASTER RYGONE AND HOME TO HIS VAST FORTUNE. AS YOU CAN SEE MY MASTER HAS SEEN BETTER DAYS.
I'LL SAY. HE LOOKS DEAD. LIKE REALLY, REALLY DEAD.
LISTEN, BONE HEAD, I'M HERE FOR THE TREASURE. NOW WHERE IS IT?
RYGON'S POWER CAN OPEN THE VAULT. I ASSURE YOU, A MOST SUITABLE REWARD WILL COME YOUR WAY ONCE MY MASTER HAS BEEN REVIVED. BUT IN ORDER TO DO THAT, I WILL NEED YOU TO REPEAT THE WORDS OF RESURRECTION.
WHY DON'T YOU JUST SAY THE WORDS?
I'M AFRAID THE SPELL ONLY WORKS IF SPOKEN BY A LIVING SOUL. THIS IS WHY THE MAP LED YOU HERE. RYGONE REQUIRES SOMEONE WHO IS ALIVE...AND HERE YOU ARE TO FULFILL THE PROPHECY.

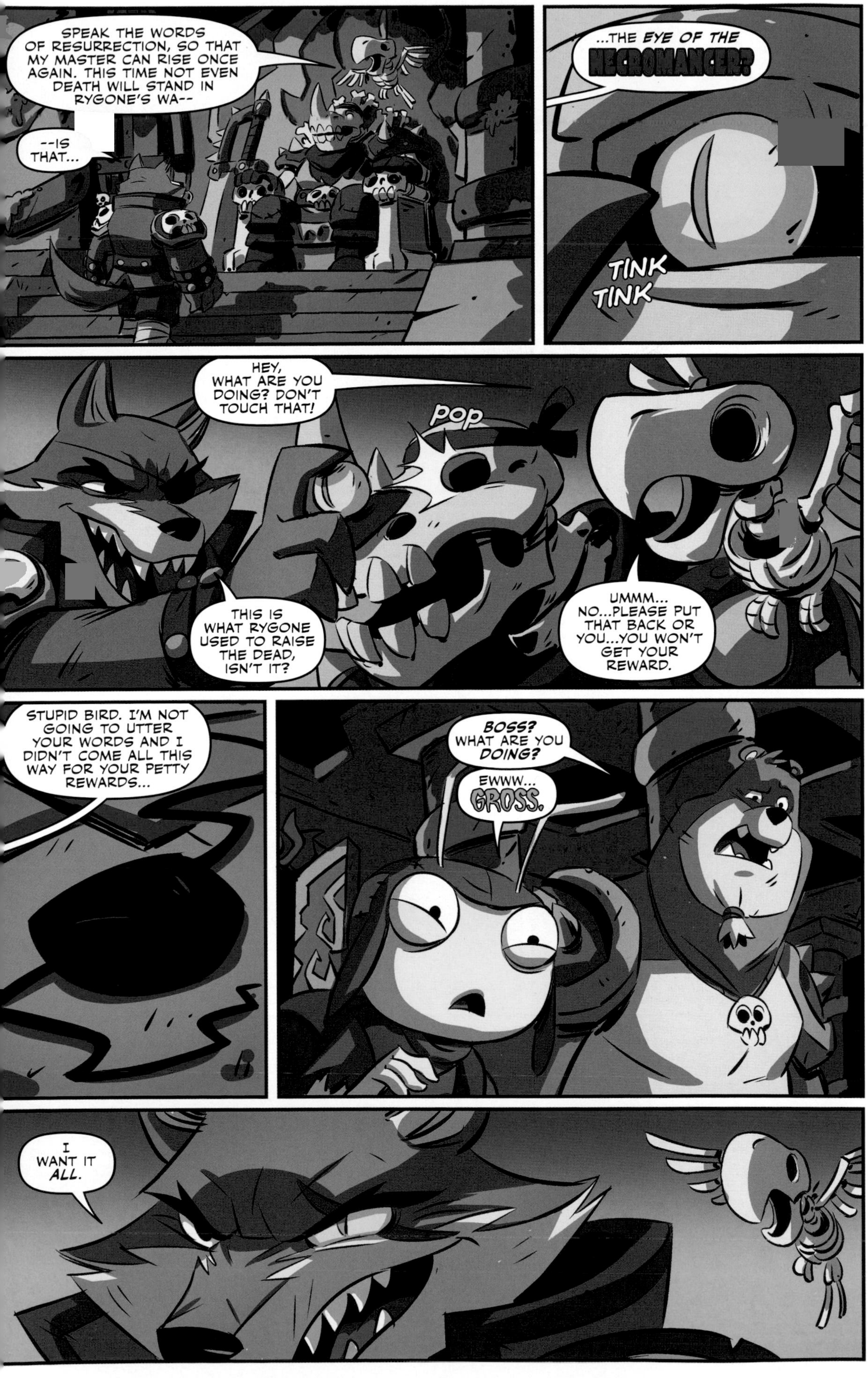
SPEAK THE WORDS OF RESURRECTION, SO THAT MY MASTER CAN RISE ONCE AGAIN. THIS TIME NOT EVEN DEATH WILL STAND IN RYGONE'S WA--
--IS THAT...
...THE EYE OF THE NECROMANCER?
TINK TINK
HEY, WHAT ARE YOU DOING? DON'T TOUCH THAT!
POP
THIS IS WHAT RYGONE USED TO RAISE THE DEAD, ISN'T IT?
UMMM... NO...PLEASE PUT THAT BACK OR YOU...YOU WON'T GET YOUR REWARD.
STUPID BIRD. I'M NOT GOING TO UTTER YOUR WORDS AND I DIDN'T COME ALL THIS WAY FOR YOUR PETTY REWARDS...
BOSS? WHAT ARE YOU DOING?
EWWW... GROSS.
I WANT IT ALL.

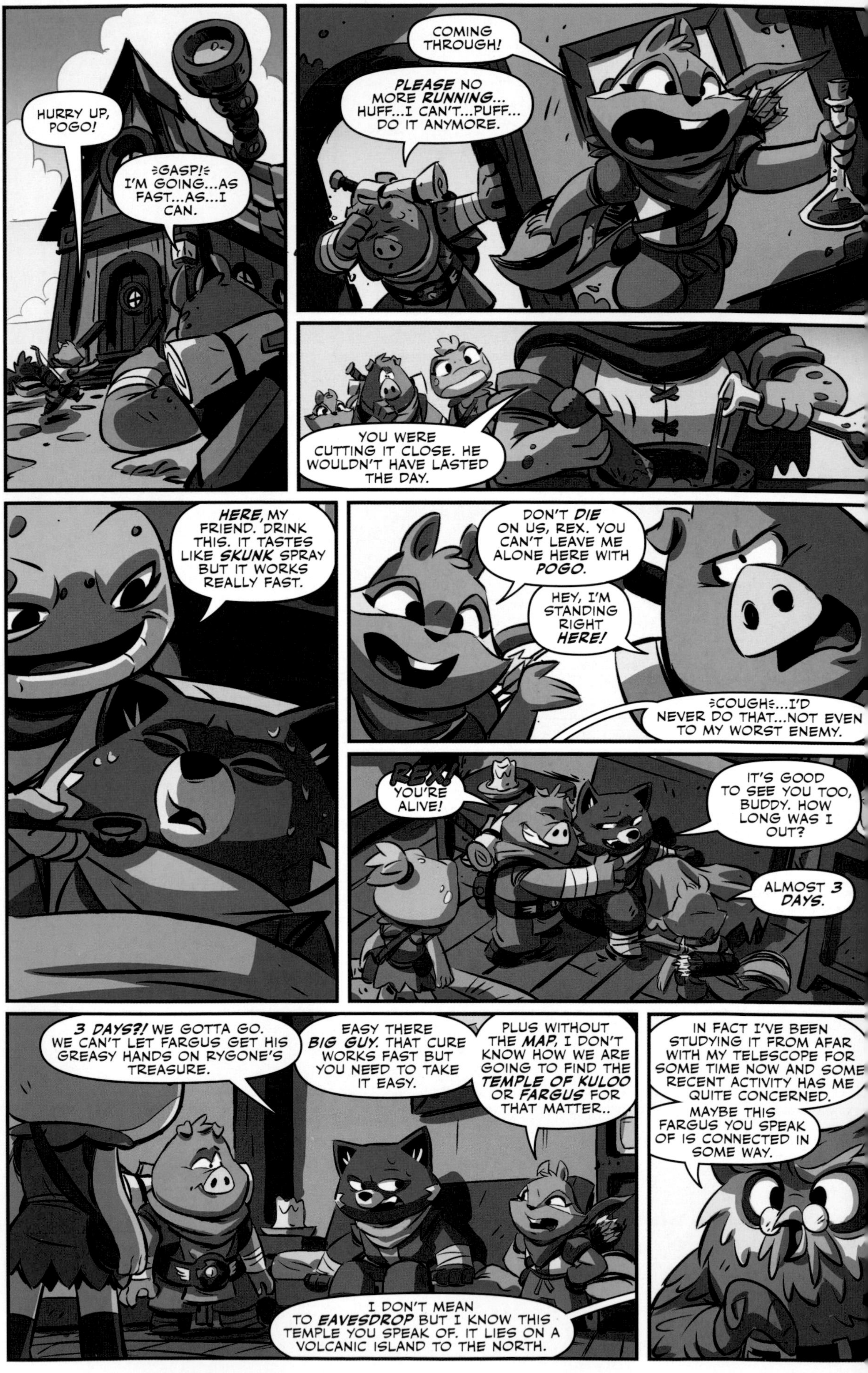
HURRY UP, POGO!
≑GASP!≑ I'M GOING...AS FAST...AS...I CAN.
COMING THROUGH!
PLEASE NO MORE RUNNING... HUFF...I CAN'T...PUFF... DO IT ANYMORE.
YOU WERE CUTTING IT CLOSE. HE WOULDN'T HAVE LASTED THE DAY.
HERE, MY FRIEND. DRINK THIS. IT TASTES LIKE SKUNK SPRAY BUT IT WORKS REALLY FAST.
DON'T DIE ON US, REX. YOU CAN'T LEAVE ME ALONE HERE WITH POGO.
HEY, I'M STANDING RIGHT HERE!
≑COUGH≑...I'D NEVER DO THAT...NOT EVEN TO MY WORST ENEMY.
REX! YOU'RE ALIVE!
IT'S GOOD TO SEE YOU TOO, BUDDY. HOW LONG WAS I OUT?
ALMOST 3 DAYS.
3 DAYS?! WE GOTTA GO. WE CAN'T LET FARGUS GET HIS GREASY HANDS ON RYGONE'S TREASURE.
EASY THERE BIG GUY. THAT CURE WORKS FAST BUT YOU NEED TO TAKE IT EASY.
PLUS WITHOUT THE MAP, I DON'T KNOW HOW WE ARE GOING TO FIND THE TEMPLE OF KULOO OR FARGUS FOR THAT MATTER..
I DON'T MEAN TO EAVESDROP BUT I KNOW THIS TEMPLE YOU SPEAK OF. IT LIES ON A VOLCANIC ISLAND TO THE NORTH.
IN FACT I'VE BEEN STUDYING IT FROM AFAR WITH MY TELESCOPE FOR SOME TIME NOW AND SOME RECENT ACTIVITY HAS ME QUITE CONCERNED.
MAYBE THIS FARGUS YOU SPEAK OF IS CONNECTED IN SOME WAY.

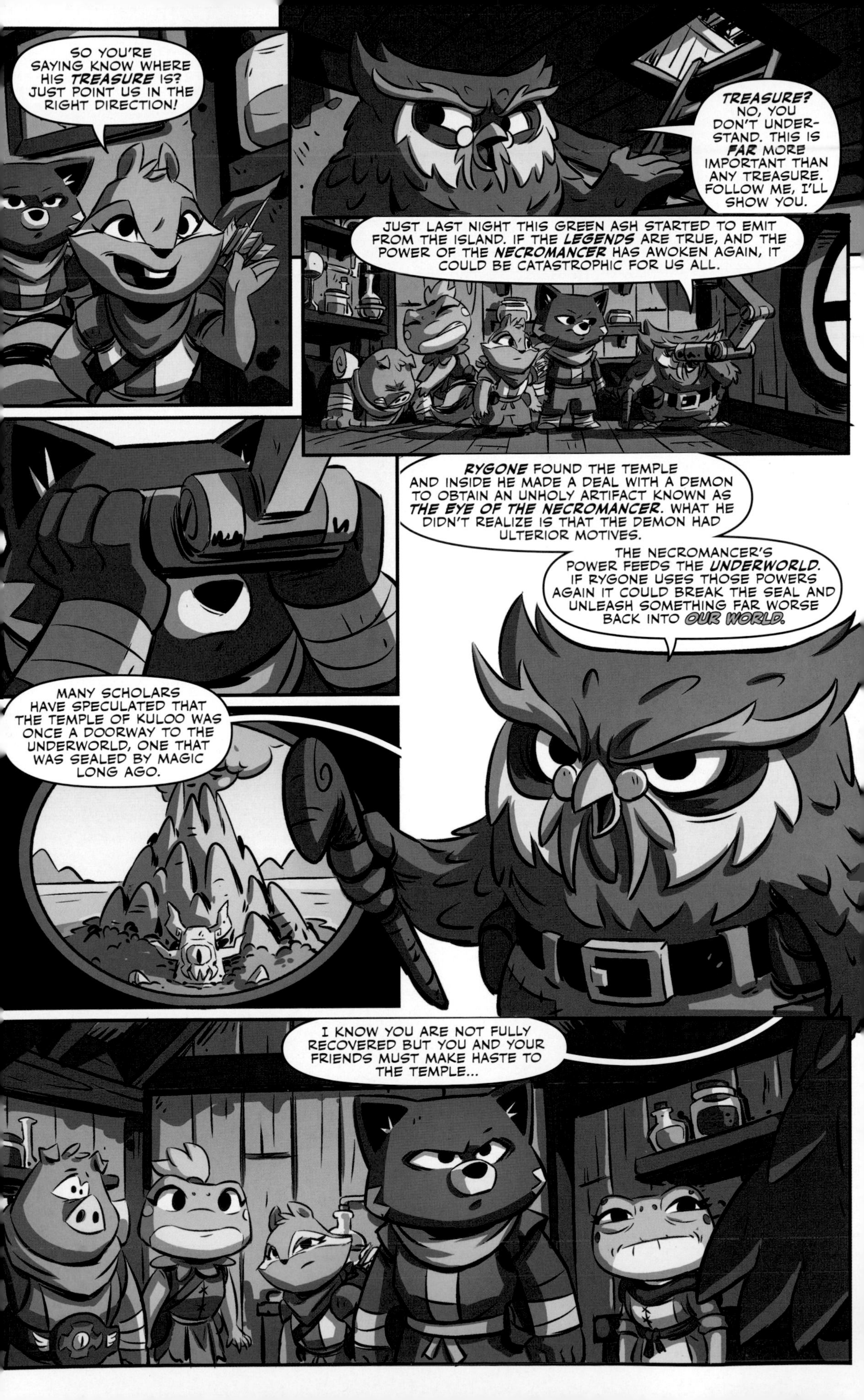
SO YOU'RE SAYING KNOW WHERE HIS TREASURE IS? JUST POINT US IN THE RIGHT DIRECTION!
TREASURE? NO, YOU DON'T UNDERSTAND. THIS IS FAR MORE IMPORTANT THAN ANY TREASURE. FOLLOW ME, I'LL SHOW YOU.
JUST LAST NIGHT THIS GREEN ASH STARTED TO EMIT FROM THE ISLAND. IF THE LEGENDS ARE TRUE, AND THE POWER OF THE NECROMANCER HAS AWOKEN AGAIN, IT COULD BE CATASTROPHIC FOR US ALL.
RYGONE FOUND THE TEMPLE AND INSIDE HE MADE A DEAL WITH A DEMON TO OBTAIN AN UNHOLY ARTIFACT KNOWN AS THE EYE OF THE NECROMANCER. WHAT HE DIDN'T REALIZE IS THAT THE DEMON HAD ULTERIOR MOTIVES.
THE NECROMANCER'S POWER FEEDS THE UNDERWORLD. IF RYGONE USES THOSE POWERS AGAIN IT COULD BREAK THE SEAL AND UNLEASH SOMETHING FAR WORSE BACK INTO OUR WORLD.
MANY SCHOLARS HAVE SPECULATED THAT THE TEMPLE OF KULOO WAS ONCE A DOORWAY TO THE UNDERWORLD, ONE THAT WAS SEALED BY MAGIC LONG AGO.
I KNOW YOU ARE NOT FULLY RECOVERED BUT YOU AND YOUR FRIENDS MUST MAKE HASTE TO THE TEMPLE...

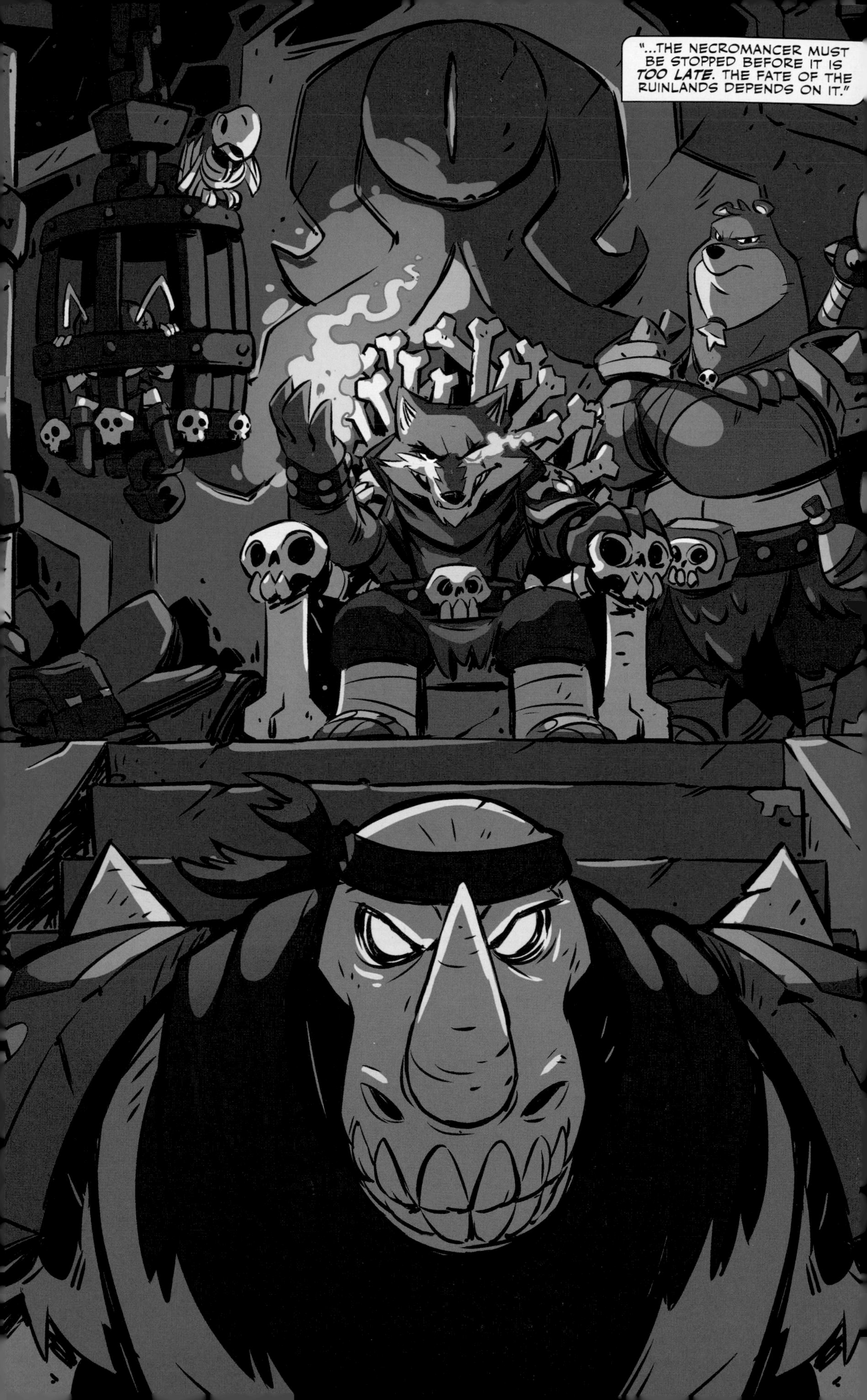
"...THE NECROMANCER MUST BE STOPPED BEFORE IT IS *TOO LATE*. THE FATE OF THE RUINLANDS DEPENDS ON IT."

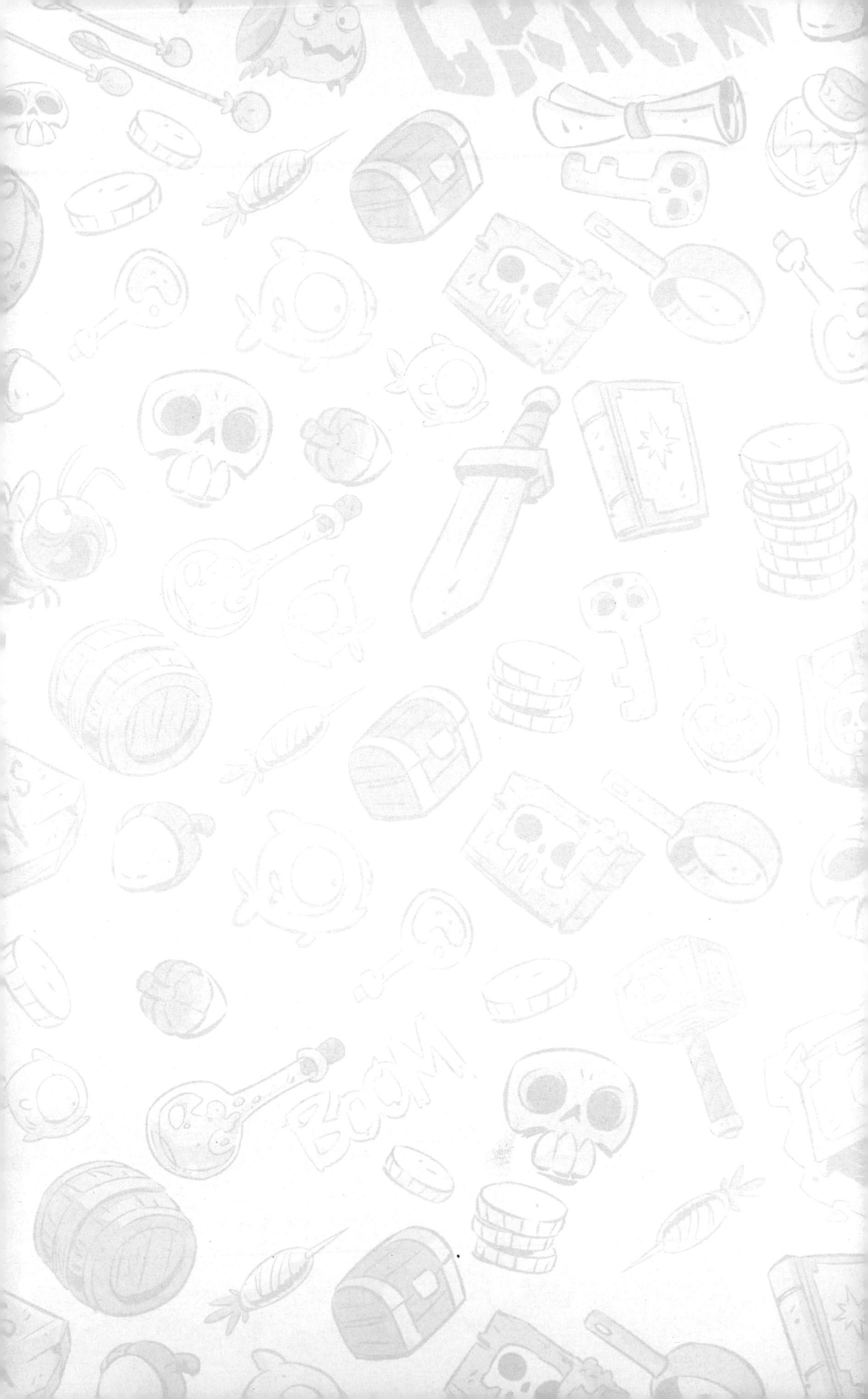
BOOM!

ISSUE 5 COVER BY DEREK LAUFMAN

CHAPTER 5

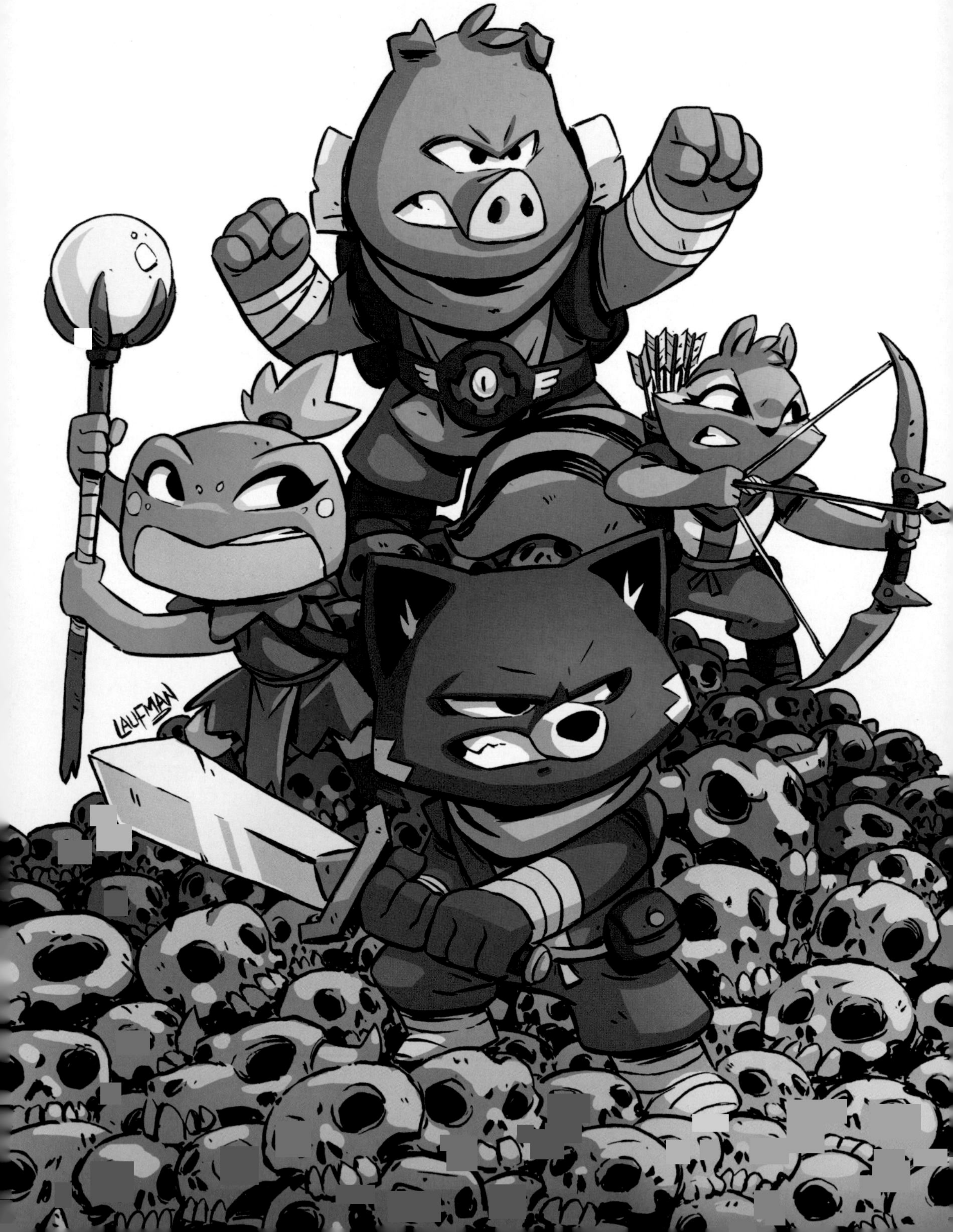
LAUFMAN

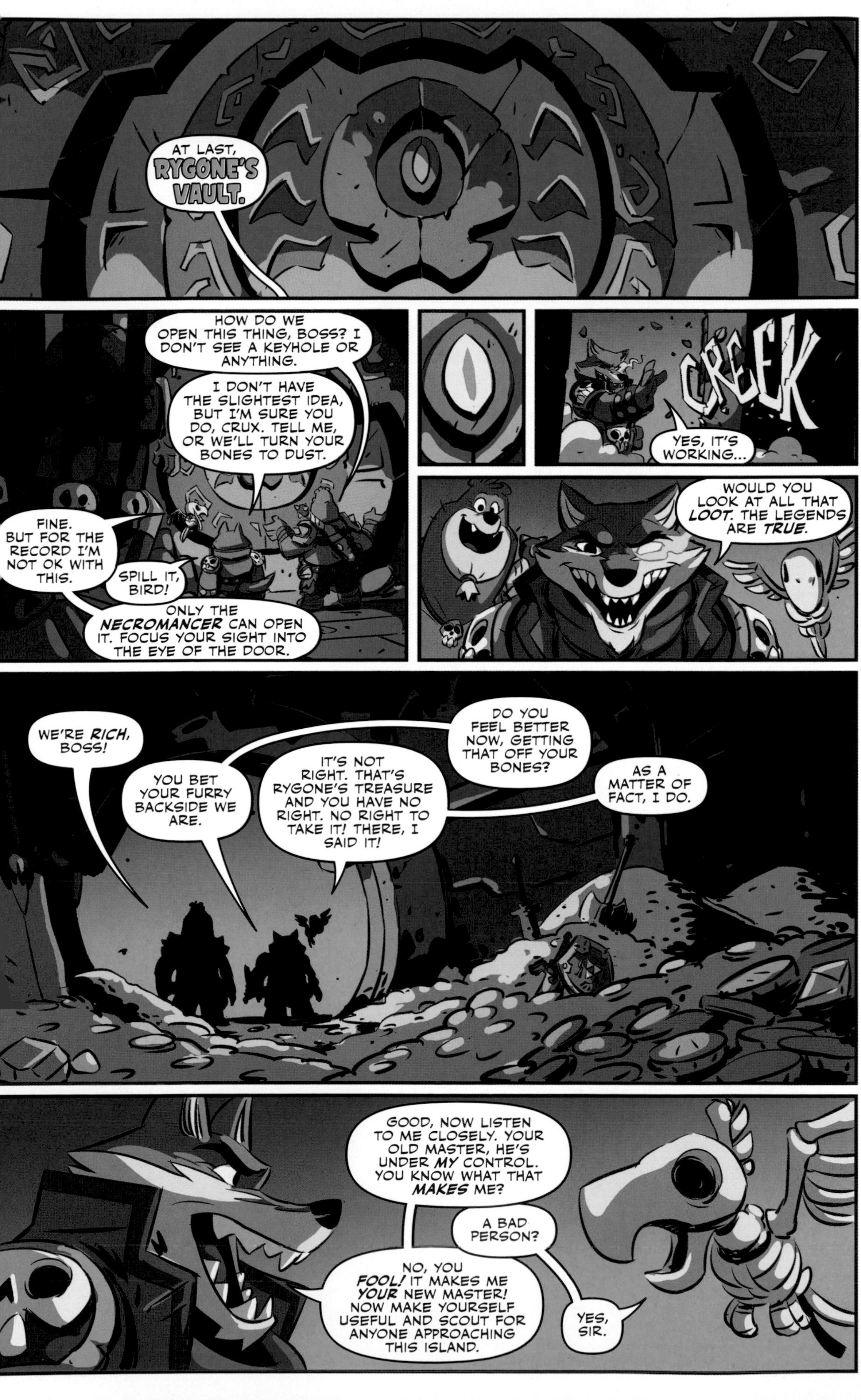
AT LAST, RYGONE'S VAULT.
HOW DO WE OPEN THIS THING, BOSS? I DON'T SEE A KEYHOLE OR ANYTHING.
I DON'T HAVE THE SLIGHTEST IDEA, BUT I'M SURE YOU DO, CRUX. TELL ME, OR WE'LL TURN YOUR BONES TO DUST.
FINE. BUT FOR THE RECORD I'M NOT OK WITH THIS.
SPILL IT, BIRD!
ONLY THE NECROMANCER CAN OPEN IT. FOCUS YOUR SIGHT INTO THE EYE OF THE DOOR.
CREEK
YES, IT'S WORKING...
WOULD YOU LOOK AT ALL THAT LOOT. THE LEGENDS ARE TRUE.
WE'RE RICH, BOSS!
YOU BET YOUR FURRY BACKSIDE WE ARE.
IT'S NOT RIGHT. THAT'S RYGONE'S TREASURE AND YOU HAVE NO RIGHT. NO RIGHT TO TAKE IT! THERE, I SAID IT!
DO YOU FEEL BETTER NOW, GETTING THAT OFF YOUR BONES?
AS A MATTER OF FACT, I DO.
GOOD, NOW LISTEN TO ME CLOSELY. YOUR OLD MASTER, HE'S UNDER MY CONTROL. YOU KNOW WHAT THAT MAKES ME?
A BAD PERSON?
NO, YOU FOOL! IT MAKES ME YOUR NEW MASTER! NOW MAKE YOURSELF USEFUL AND SCOUT FOR ANYONE APPROACHING THIS ISLAND.
YES, SIR.

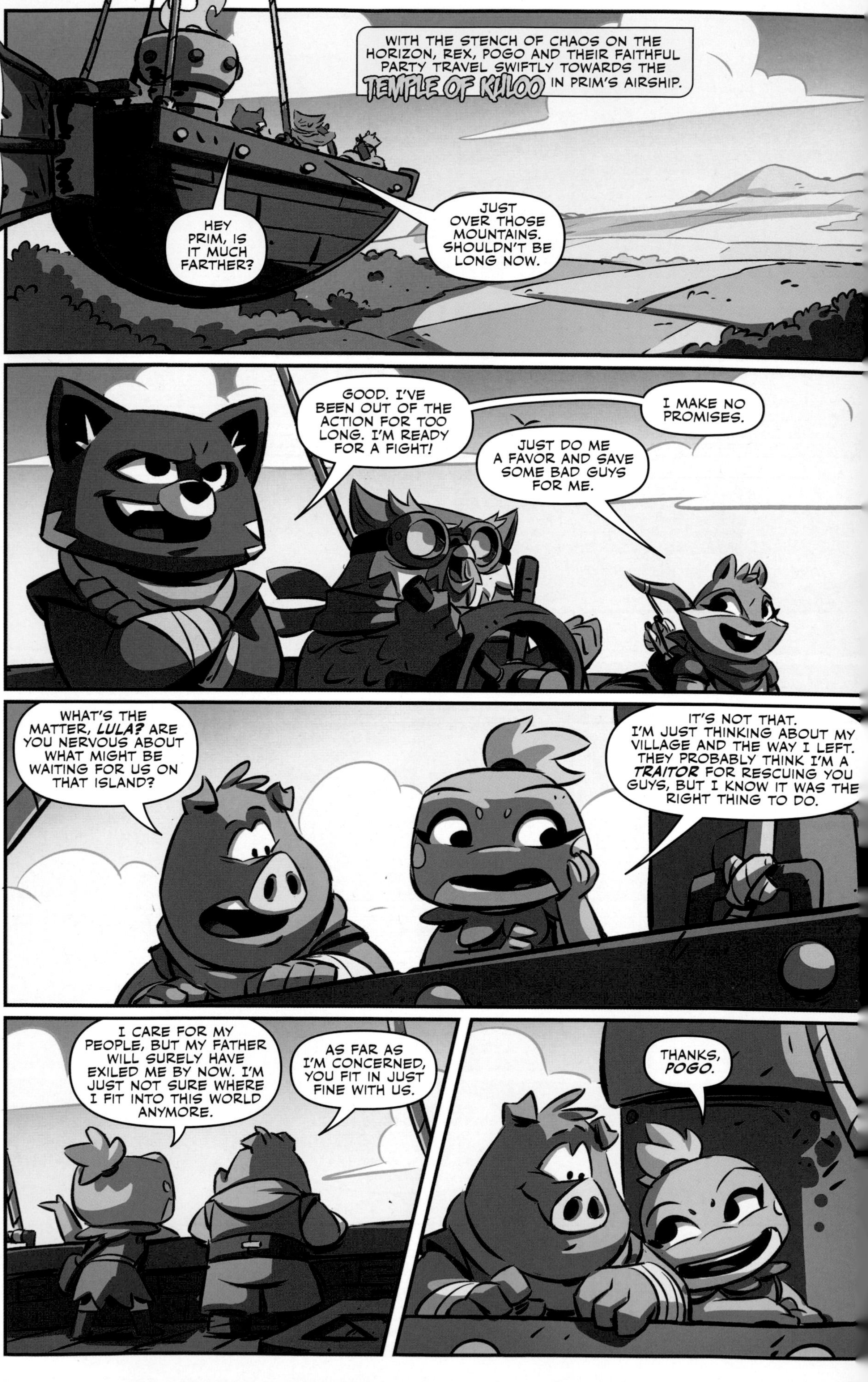
WITH THE STENCH OF CHAOS ON THE HORIZON, REX, POGO AND THEIR FAITHFUL PARTY TRAVEL SWIFTLY TOWARDS THE TEMPLE OF KULOO IN PRIM'S AIRSHIP.
HEY PRIM, IS IT MUCH FARTHER?
JUST OVER THOSE MOUNTAINS. SHOULDN'T BE LONG NOW.
GOOD. I'VE BEEN OUT OF THE ACTION FOR TOO LONG. I'M READY FOR A FIGHT!
JUST DO ME A FAVOR AND SAVE SOME BAD GUYS FOR ME.
I MAKE NO PROMISES.
WHAT'S THE MATTER, LULA? ARE YOU NERVOUS ABOUT WHAT MIGHT BE WAITING FOR US ON THAT ISLAND?
IT'S NOT THAT. I'M JUST THINKING ABOUT MY VILLAGE AND THE WAY I LEFT. THEY PROBABLY THINK I'M A TRAITOR FOR RESCUING YOU GUYS, BUT I KNOW IT WAS THE RIGHT THING TO DO.
I CARE FOR MY PEOPLE, BUT MY FATHER WILL SURELY HAVE EXILED ME BY NOW. I'M JUST NOT SURE WHERE I FIT INTO THIS WORLD ANYMORE.
AS FAR AS I'M CONCERNED, YOU FIT IN JUST FINE WITH US.
THANKS, POGO.

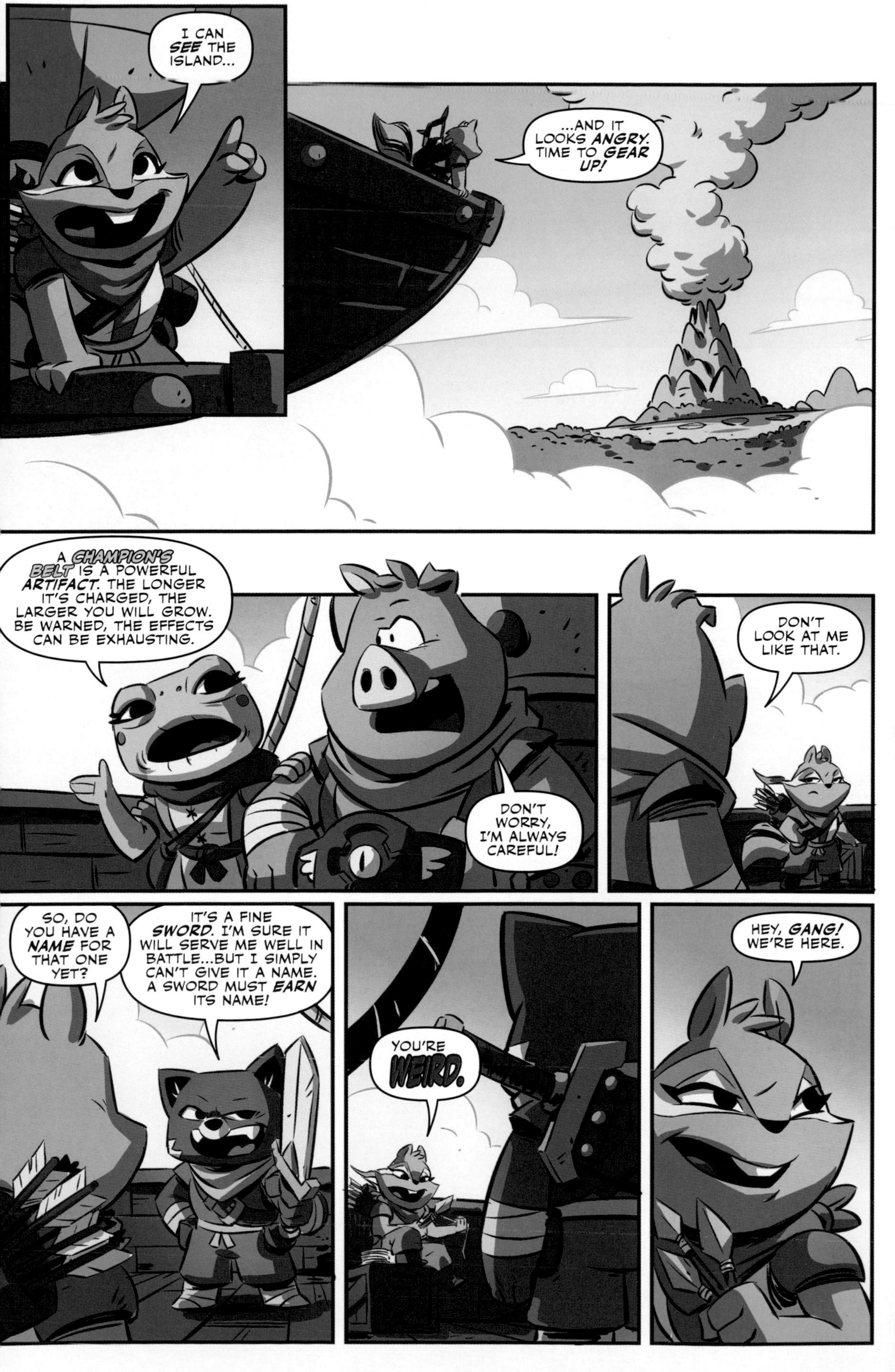
I CAN SEE THE ISLAND...
...AND IT LOOKS ANGRY. TIME TO GEAR UP!
A CHAMPION'S BELT IS A POWERFUL ARTIFACT. THE LONGER IT'S CHARGED, THE LARGER YOU WILL GROW. BE WARNED, THE EFFECTS CAN BE EXHAUSTING.
DON'T WORRY, I'M ALWAYS CAREFUL!
DON'T LOOK AT ME LIKE THAT.
SO, DO YOU HAVE A NAME FOR THAT ONE YET?
IT'S A FINE SWORD. I'M SURE IT WILL SERVE ME WELL IN BATTLE...BUT I SIMPLY CAN'T GIVE IT A NAME. A SWORD MUST EARN ITS NAME!
YOU'RE WEIRD.
HEY, GANG! WE'RE HERE.

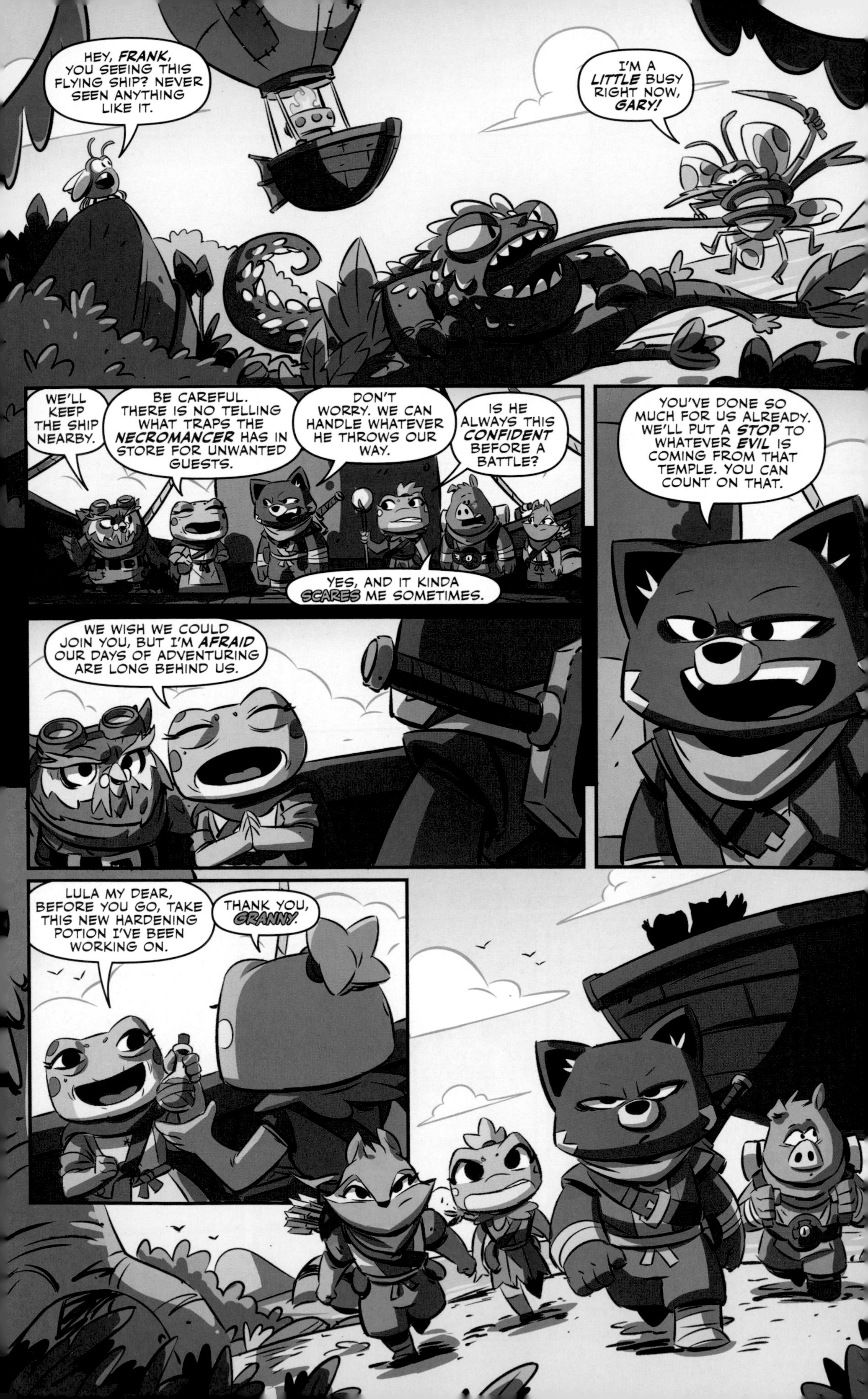
HEY, FRANK, YOU SEEING THIS FLYING SHIP? NEVER SEEN ANYTHING LIKE IT.
I'M A LITTLE BUSY RIGHT NOW, GARY!
WE'LL KEEP THE SHIP NEARBY.
BE CAREFUL. THERE IS NO TELLING WHAT TRAPS THE NECROMANCER HAS IN STORE FOR UNWANTED GUESTS.
DON'T WORRY. WE CAN HANDLE WHATEVER HE THROWS OUR WAY.
IS HE ALWAYS THIS CONFIDENT BEFORE A BATTLE?
YES, AND IT KINDA SCARES ME SOMETIMES.
YOU'VE DONE SO MUCH FOR US ALREADY. WE'LL PUT A STOP TO WHATEVER EVIL IS COMING FROM THAT TEMPLE. YOU CAN COUNT ON THAT.
WE WISH WE COULD JOIN YOU, BUT I'M AFRAID OUR DAYS OF ADVENTURING ARE LONG BEHIND US.
LULA MY DEAR, BEFORE YOU GO, TAKE THIS NEW HARDENING POTION I'VE BEEN WORKING ON.
THANK YOU, GRANNY.

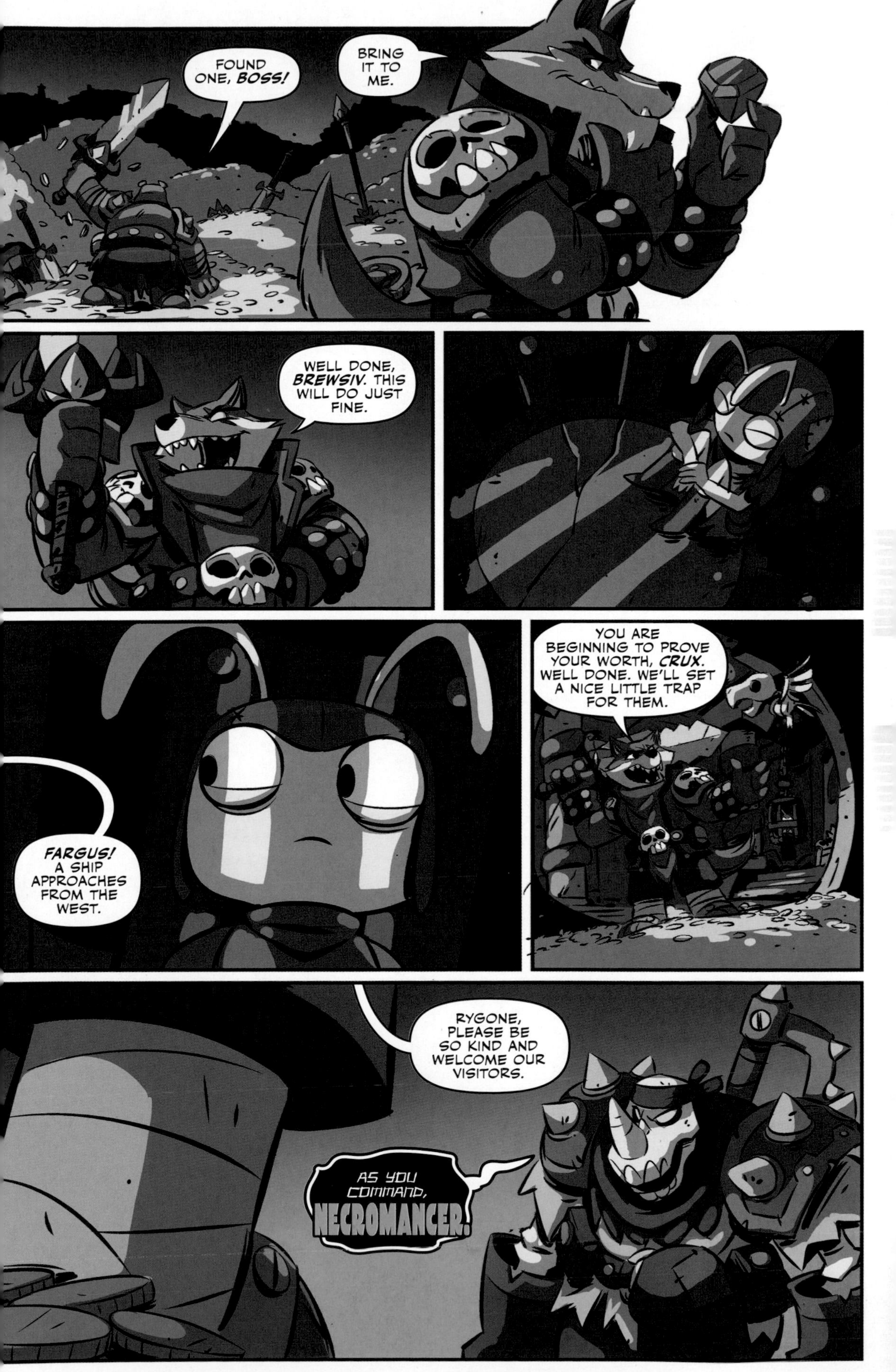
FOUND ONE, BOSS!
BRING IT TO ME.
WELL DONE, BREWSIV. THIS WILL DO JUST FINE.
FARGUS! A SHIP APPROACHES FROM THE WEST.
YOU ARE BEGINNING TO PROVE YOUR WORTH, CRUX. WELL DONE. WE'LL SET A NICE LITTLE TRAP FOR THEM.
RYGONE, PLEASE BE SO KIND AND WELCOME OUR VISITORS.
AS YOU COMMAND, NECROMANCER!

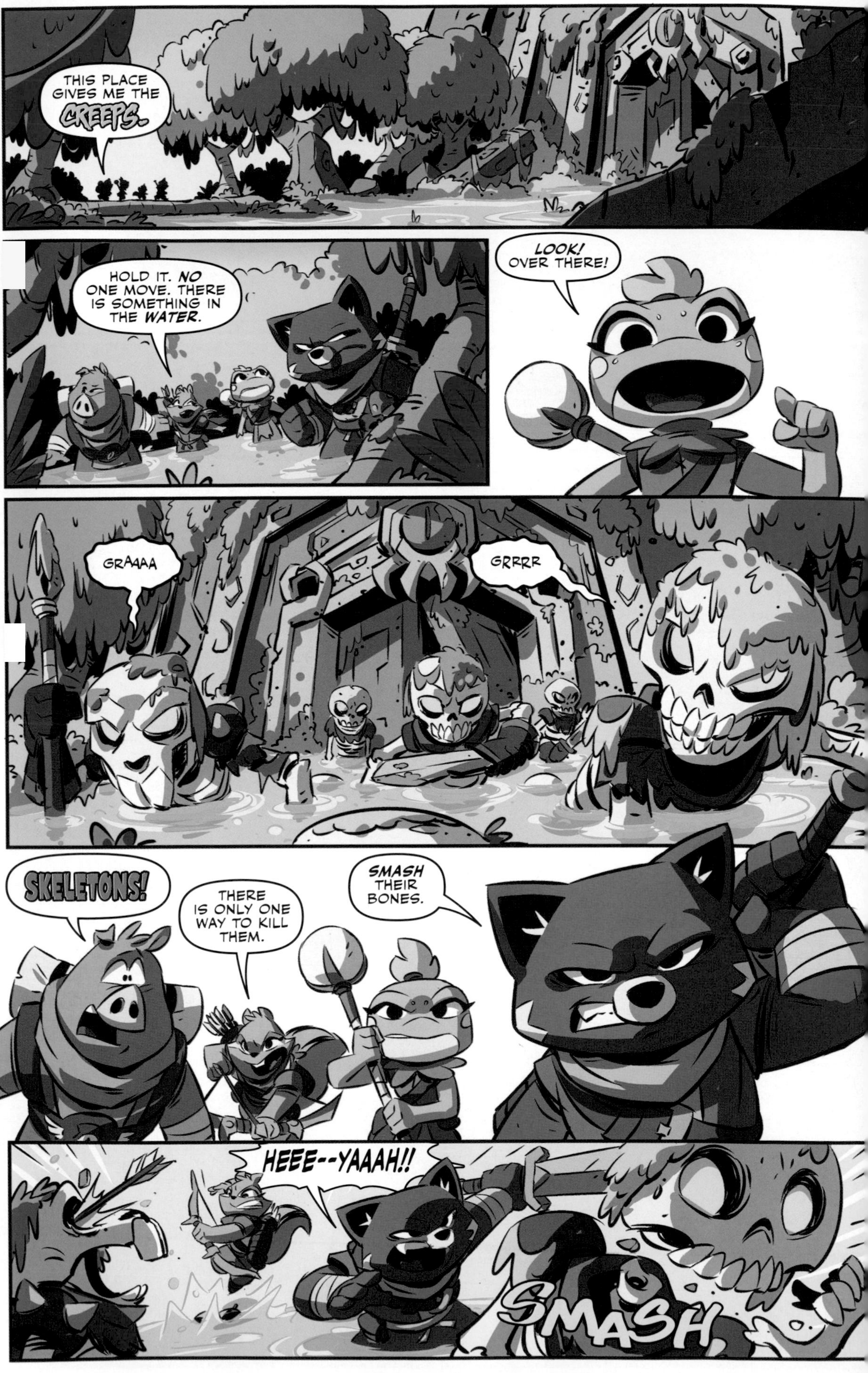
THIS PLACE GIVES ME THE CREEPS.
HOLD IT. NO ONE MOVE. THERE IS SOMETHING IN THE WATER.
LOOK! OVER THERE!
GRAAAA
GRRRR
SKELETONS!
THERE IS ONLY ONE WAY TO KILL THEM.
SMASH THEIR BONES.
HEEE--YAAAH!!
SMASH

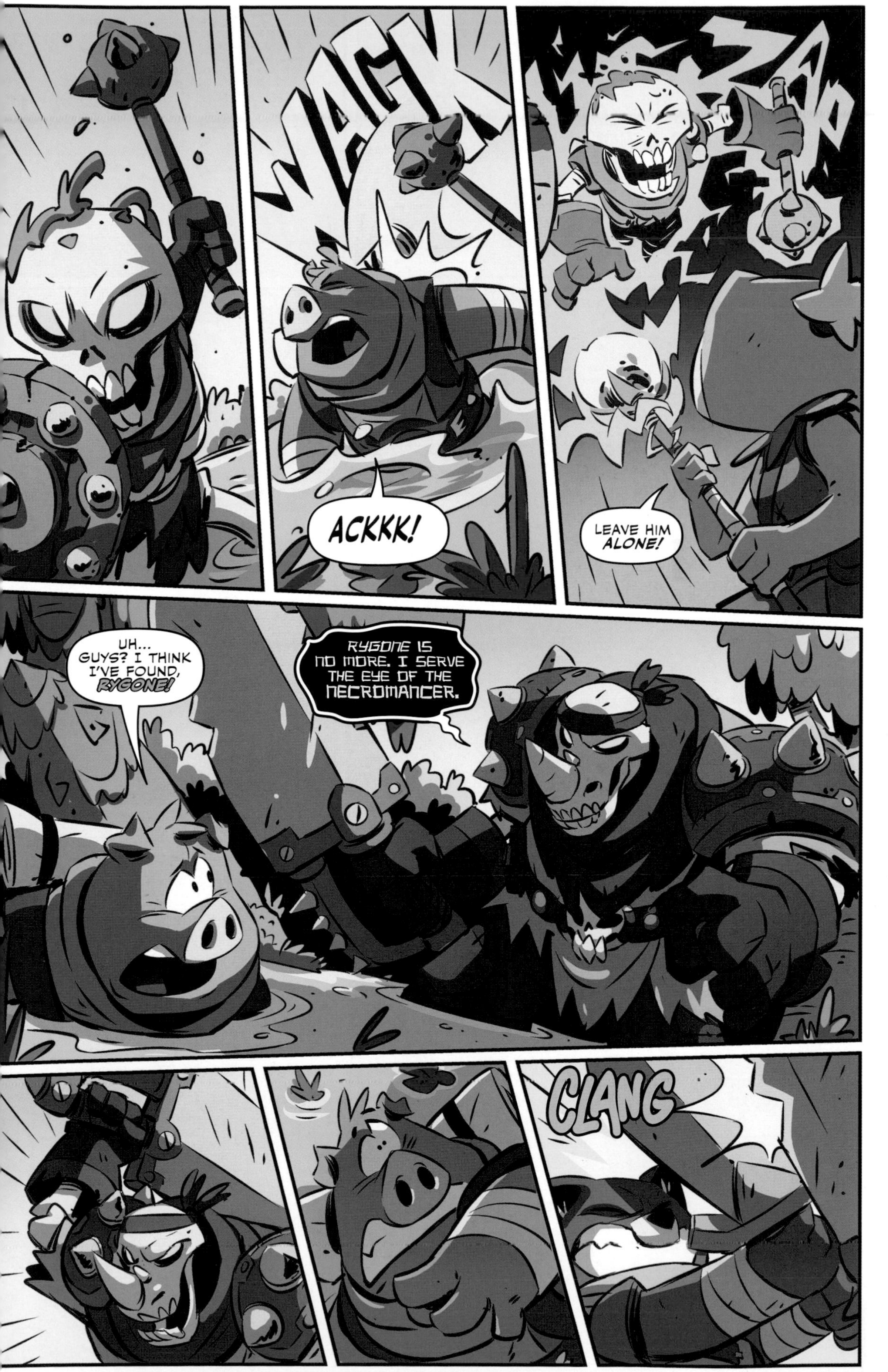

WACK
ACKKK!
ZAP
LEAVE HIM ALONE!
UH... GUYS? I THINK I'VE FOUND, RYGONE!
RYGONE IS NO MORE. I SERVE THE EYE OF THE NECROMANCER.
CLANG

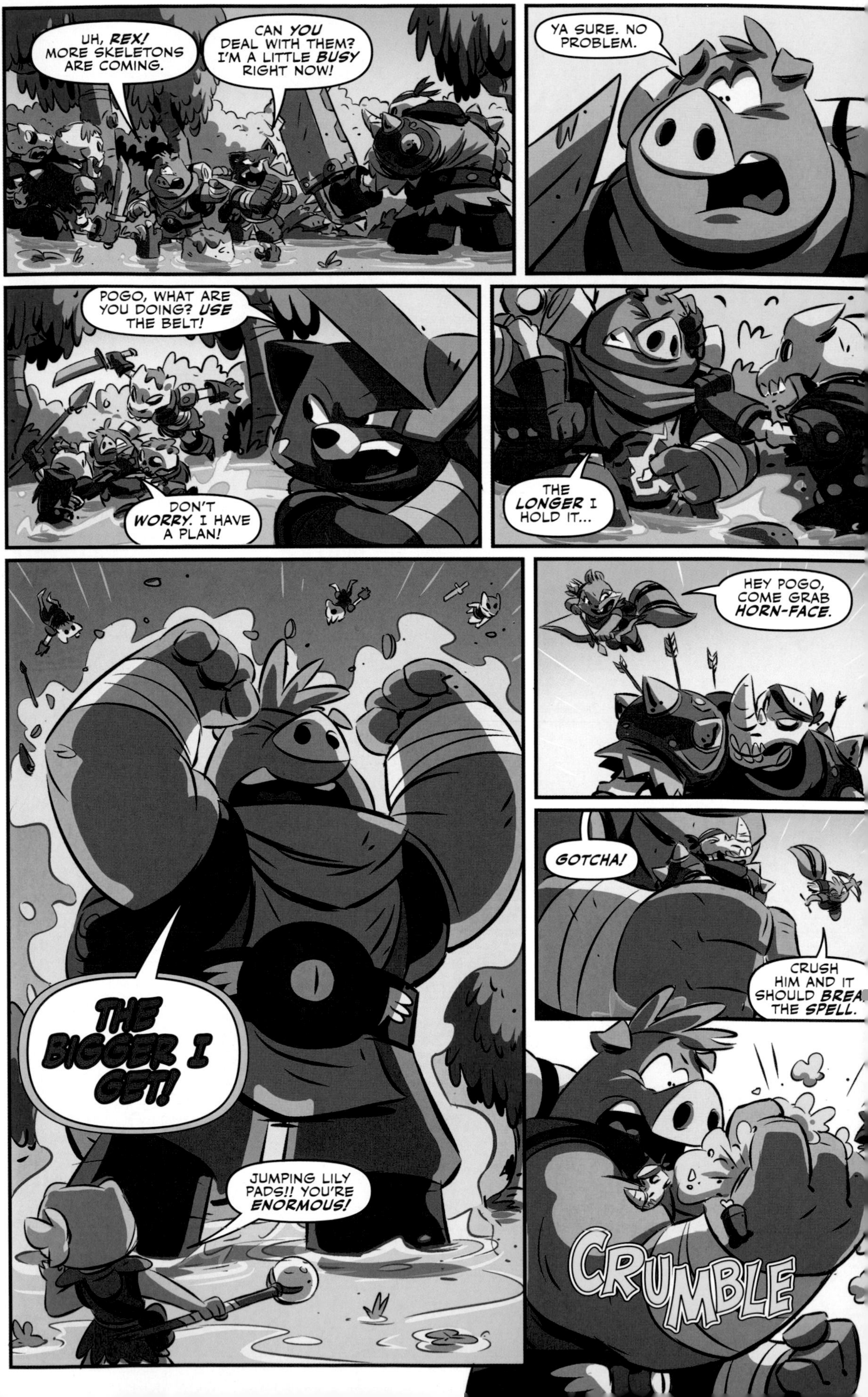
UH, REX! MORE SKELETONS ARE COMING.
CAN YOU DEAL WITH THEM? I'M A LITTLE BUSY RIGHT NOW!
YA SURE. NO PROBLEM.
POGO, WHAT ARE YOU DOING? USE THE BELT!
DON'T WORRY. I HAVE A PLAN!
THE LONGER I HOLD IT...
THE BIGGER I GET!
JUMPING LILY PADS!! YOU'RE ENORMOUS!
HEY POGO, COME GRAB HORN-FACE.
GOTCHA!
CRUSH HIM AND IT SHOULD BREA THE SPELL.
CRUMBLE

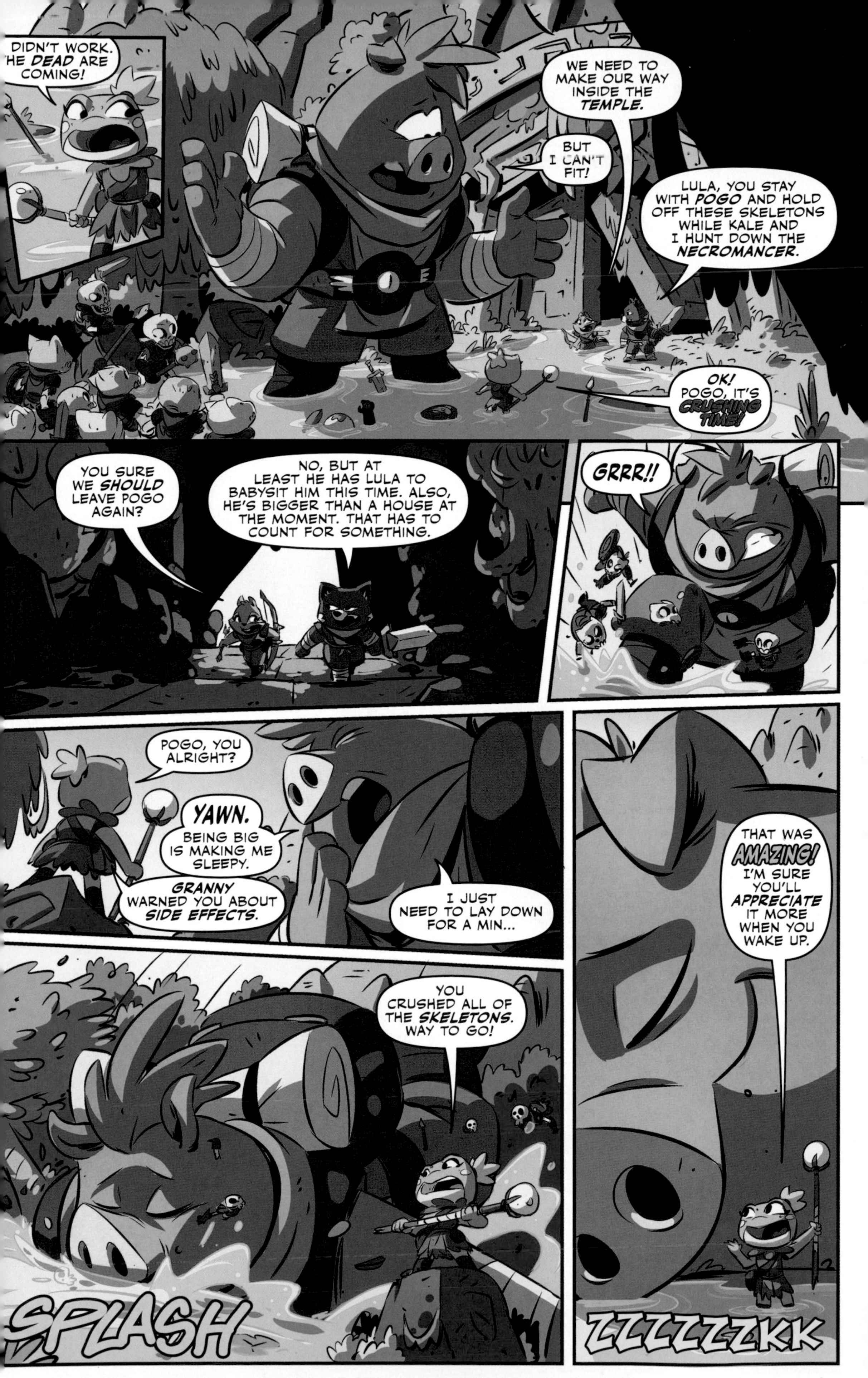

DIDN'T WORK. HE DEAD ARE COMING!
WE NEED TO MAKE OUR WAY INSIDE THE TEMPLE.
BUT I CAN'T FIT!
LULA, YOU STAY WITH POGO AND HOLD OFF THESE SKELETONS WHILE KALE AND I HUNT DOWN THE NECROMANCER.
OK! POGO, IT'S CRUSHING TIME!
YOU SURE WE SHOULD LEAVE POGO AGAIN?
NO, BUT AT LEAST HE HAS LULA TO BABYSIT HIM THIS TIME. ALSO, HE'S BIGGER THAN A HOUSE AT THE MOMENT. THAT HAS TO COUNT FOR SOMETHING.
GRRR!!
POGO, YOU ALRIGHT?
YAWN. BEING BIG IS MAKING ME SLEEPY.
GRANNY WARNED YOU ABOUT SIDE EFFECTS.
I JUST NEED TO LAY DOWN FOR A MIN...
YOU CRUSHED ALL OF THE SKELETONS. WAY TO GO!
SPLASH
THAT WAS AMAZING! I'M SURE YOU'LL APPRECIATE IT MORE WHEN YOU WAKE UP.
ZZZZZZZKK

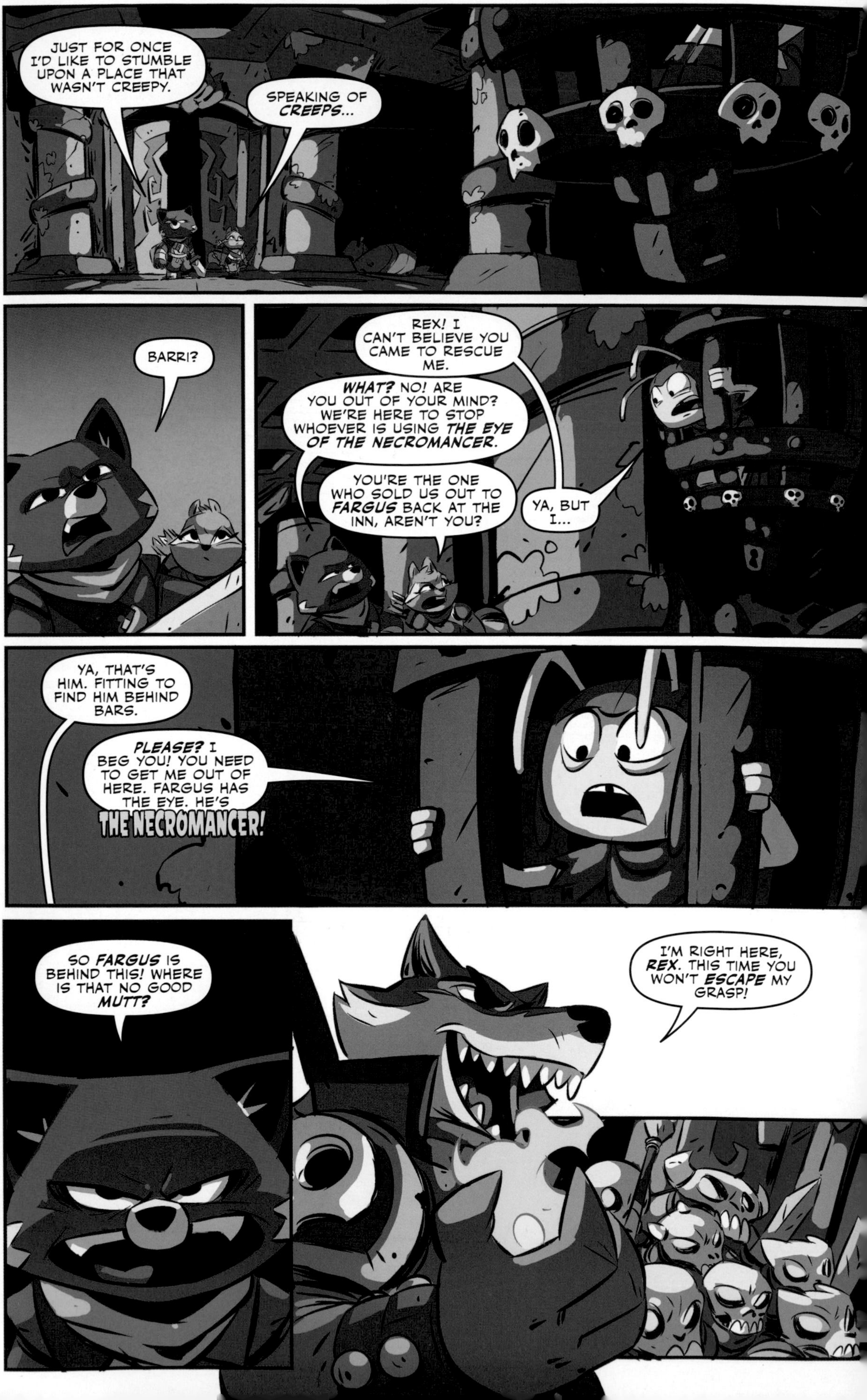
JUST FOR ONCE I'D LIKE TO STUMBLE UPON A PLACE THAT WASN'T CREEPY.
SPEAKING OF *CREEPS*...
BARRI?
REX! I CAN'T BELIEVE YOU CAME TO RESCUE ME.
WHAT? NO! ARE YOU OUT OF YOUR MIND? WE'RE HERE TO STOP WHOEVER IS USING *THE EYE OF THE NECROMANCER*.
YOU'RE THE ONE WHO SOLD US OUT TO *FARGUS* BACK AT THE INN, AREN'T YOU?
YA, BUT I...
YA, THAT'S HIM. FITTING TO FIND HIM BEHIND BARS.
PLEASE? I BEG YOU! YOU NEED TO GET ME OUT OF HERE. FARGUS HAS THE EYE. HE'S THE NECROMANCER!
SO *FARGUS* IS BEHIND THIS! WHERE IS THAT NO GOOD *MUTT?*
I'M RIGHT HERE, *REX*. THIS TIME YOU WON'T *ESCAPE* MY GRASP!

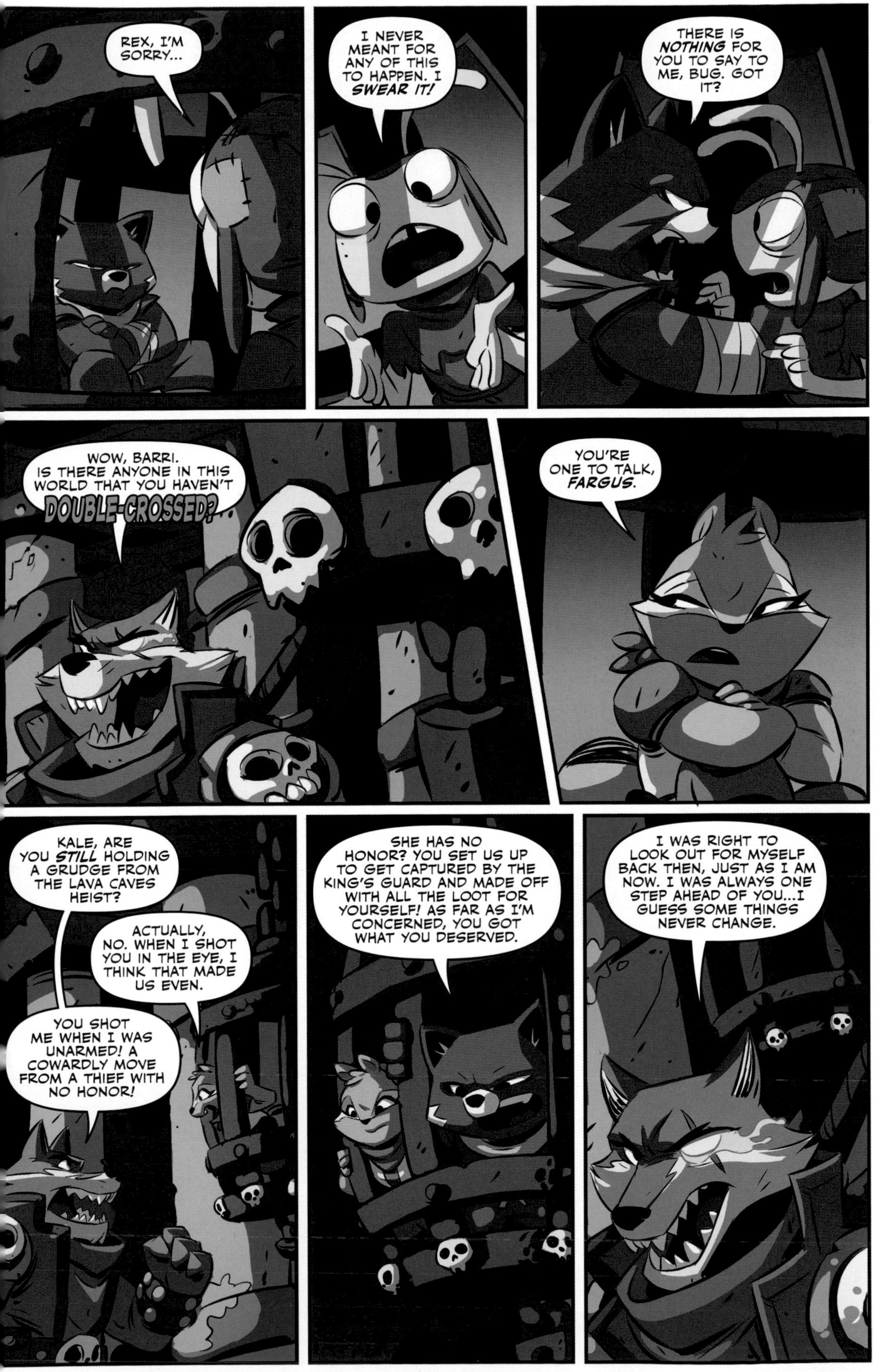
REX, I'M SORRY...
I NEVER MEANT FOR ANY OF THIS TO HAPPEN. I SWEAR IT!
THERE IS NOTHING FOR YOU TO SAY TO ME, BUG. GOT IT?
WOW, BARRI. IS THERE ANYONE IN THIS WORLD THAT YOU HAVEN'T DOUBLE-CROSSED?
YOU'RE ONE TO TALK, FARGUS.
KALE, ARE YOU STILL HOLDING A GRUDGE FROM THE LAVA CAVES HEIST?
ACTUALLY, NO. WHEN I SHOT YOU IN THE EYE, I THINK THAT MADE US EVEN.
YOU SHOT ME WHEN I WAS UNARMED! A COWARDLY MOVE FROM A THIEF WITH NO HONOR!
SHE HAS NO HONOR? YOU SET US UP TO GET CAPTURED BY THE KING'S GUARD AND MADE OFF WITH ALL THE LOOT FOR YOURSELF! AS FAR AS I'M CONCERNED, YOU GOT WHAT YOU DESERVED.
I WAS RIGHT TO LOOK OUT FOR MYSELF BACK THEN, JUST AS I AM NOW. I WAS ALWAYS ONE STEP AHEAD OF YOU...I GUESS SOME THINGS NEVER CHANGE.

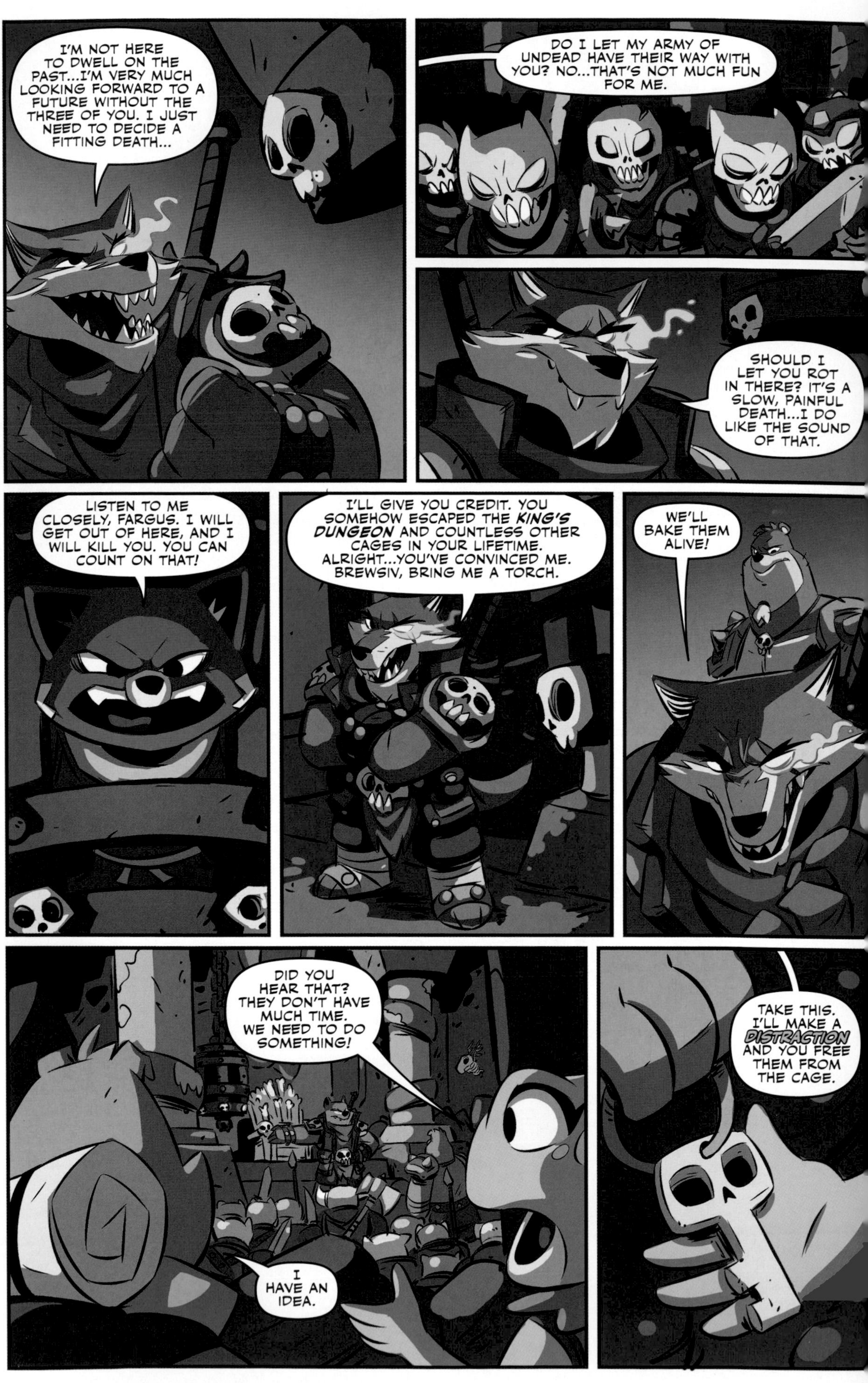

I'M NOT HERE TO DWELL ON THE PAST...I'M VERY MUCH LOOKING FORWARD TO A FUTURE WITHOUT THE THREE OF YOU. I JUST NEED TO DECIDE A FITTING DEATH...
DO I LET MY ARMY OF UNDEAD HAVE THEIR WAY WITH YOU? NO...THAT'S NOT MUCH FUN FOR ME.
SHOULD I LET YOU ROT IN THERE? IT'S A SLOW, PAINFUL DEATH...I DO LIKE THE SOUND OF THAT.
LISTEN TO ME CLOSELY, FARGUS. I WILL GET OUT OF HERE, AND I WILL KILL YOU. YOU CAN COUNT ON THAT!
I'LL GIVE YOU CREDIT. YOU SOMEHOW ESCAPED THE KING'S DUNGEON AND COUNTLESS OTHER CAGES IN YOUR LIFETIME. ALRIGHT...YOU'VE CONVINCED ME. BREWSIV, BRING ME A TORCH.
WE'LL BAKE THEM ALIVE!
DID YOU HEAR THAT? THEY DON'T HAVE MUCH TIME. WE NEED TO DO SOMETHING!
I HAVE AN IDEA.
TAKE THIS. I'LL MAKE A DISTRACTION AND YOU FREE THEM FROM THE CAGE.

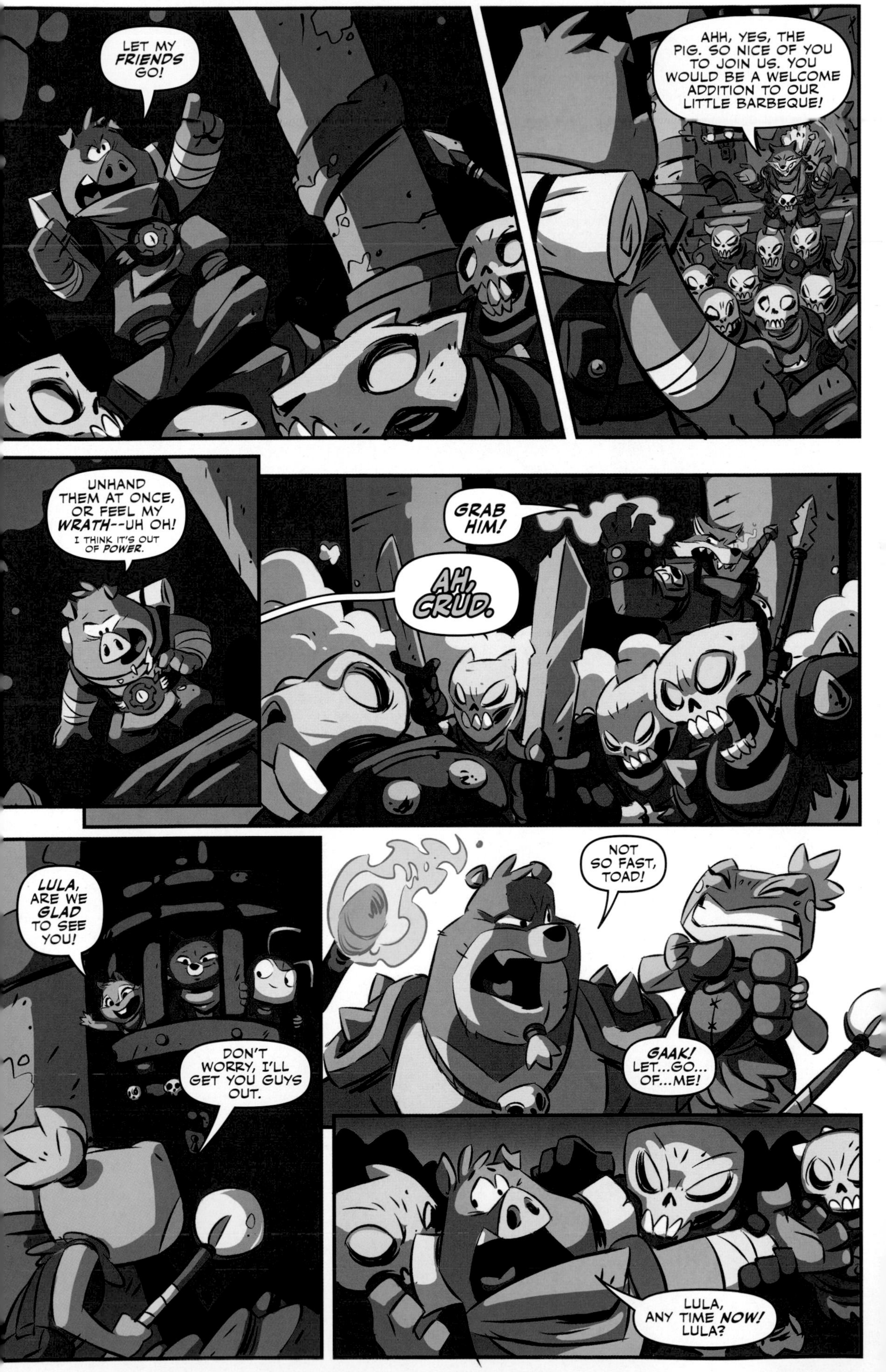
LET MY *FRIENDS* GO!
AHH, YES, THE PIG. SO NICE OF YOU TO JOIN US. YOU WOULD BE A WELCOME ADDITION TO OUR LITTLE BARBEQUE!
UNHAND THEM AT ONCE, OR FEEL MY *WRATH*--UH OH!
I THINK IT'S OUT OF *POWER*.
GRAB HIM!
AH, CRUD.
LULA, ARE WE *GLAD* TO SEE YOU!
DON'T WORRY, I'LL GET YOU GUYS OUT.
NOT SO FAST, TOAD!
GAAK! LET...GO... OF...ME!
LULA, ANY TIME *NOW!* LULA?

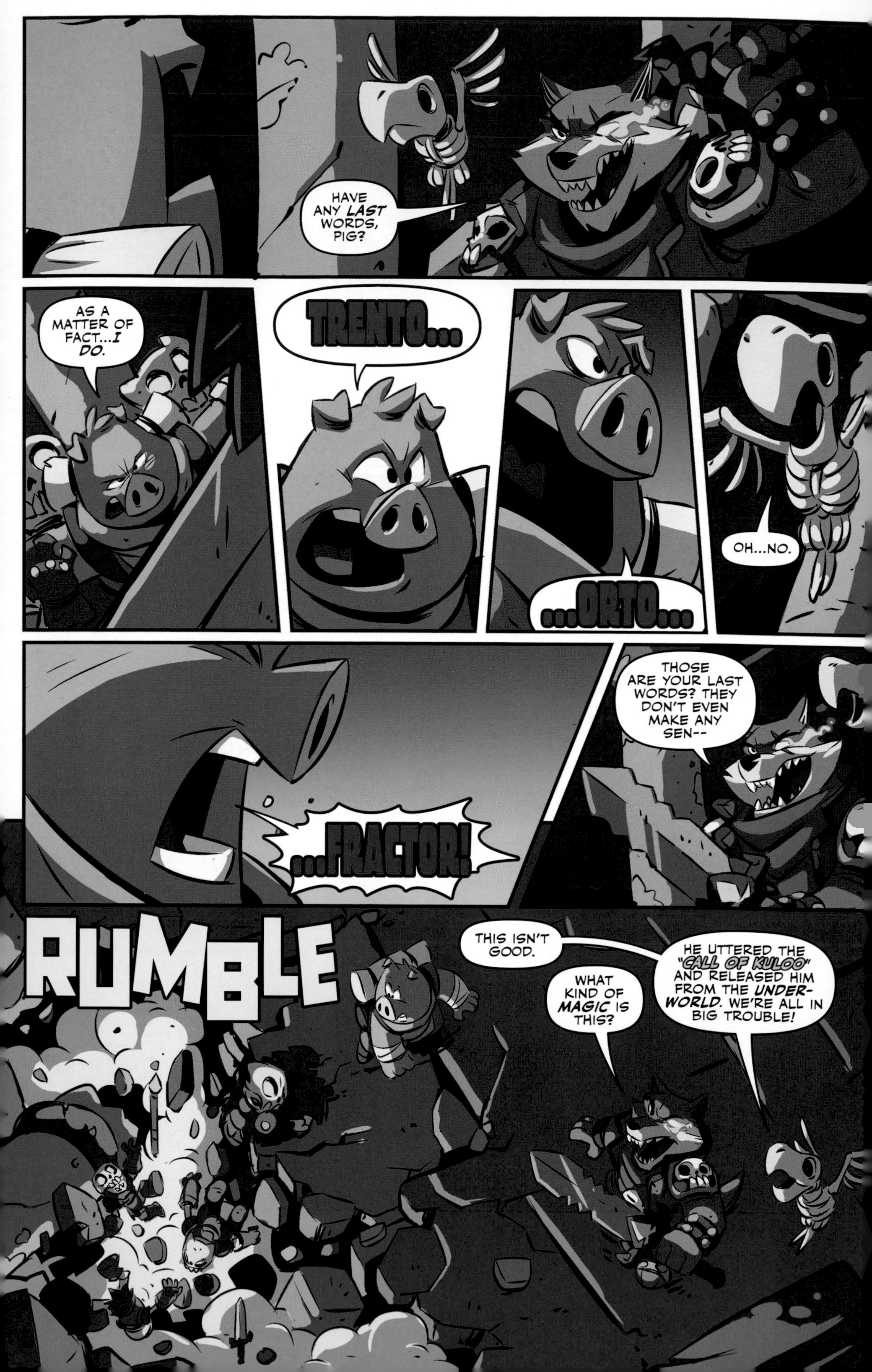
HAVE ANY *LAST* WORDS, PIG?
AS A MATTER OF FACT...*I DO.*
TRENTO...
...ORTO...
OH...NO.
...FRACTOR!
THOSE ARE YOUR LAST WORDS? THEY DON'T EVEN MAKE ANY SEN--
RUMBLE
THIS ISN'T GOOD.
WHAT KIND OF *MAGIC* IS THIS?
HE UTTERED THE "*CALL OF KULOO*" AND RELEASED HIM FROM THE *UNDER-WORLD*. WE'RE ALL IN BIG TROUBLE!

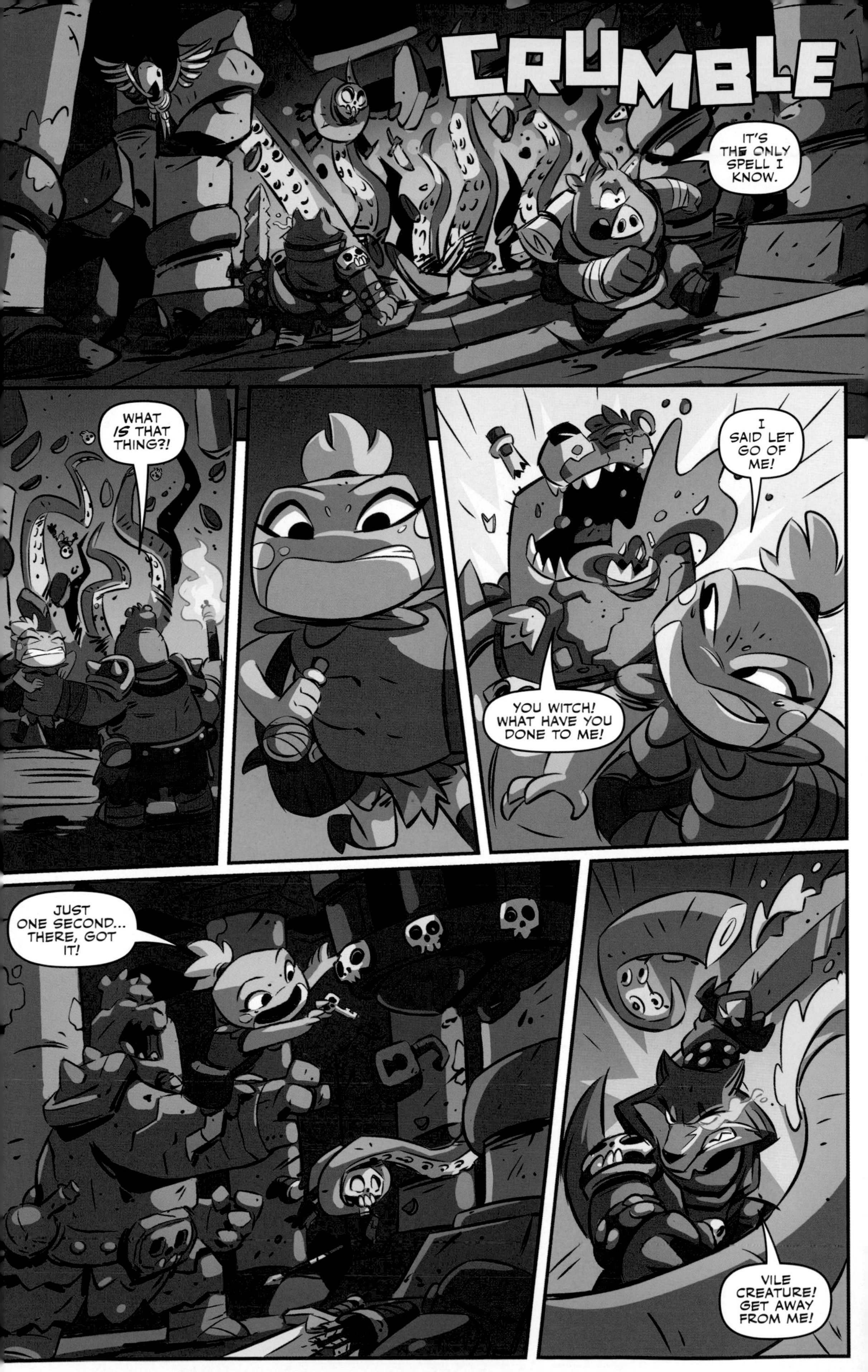
CRUMBLE
IT'S THE ONLY SPELL I KNOW.
WHAT IS THAT THING?!
I SAID LET GO OF ME!
YOU WITCH! WHAT HAVE YOU DONE TO ME!
JUST ONE SECOND... THERE, GOT IT!
VILE CREATURE! GET AWAY FROM ME!

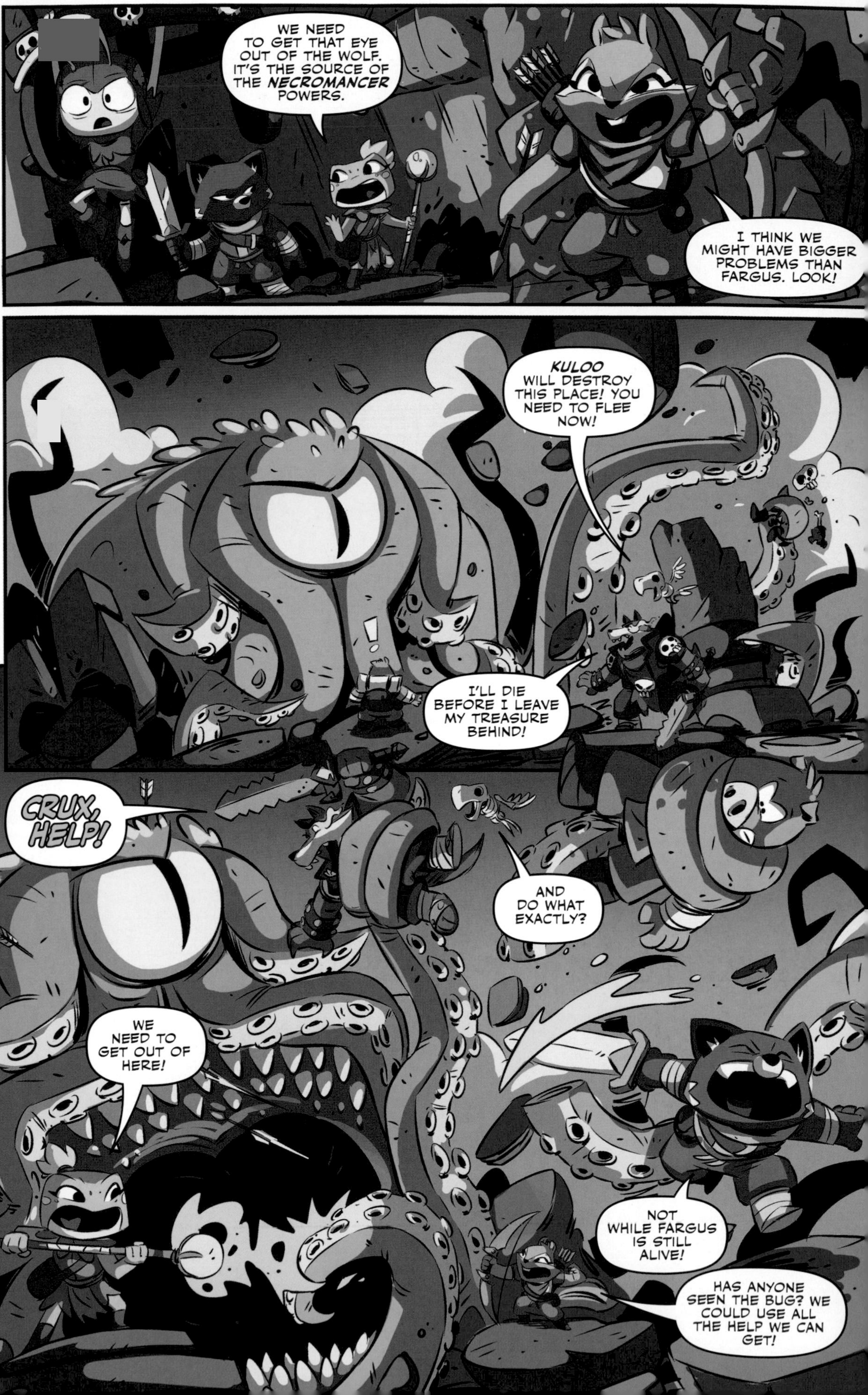

WE NEED TO GET THAT EYE OUT OF THE WOLF. IT'S THE SOURCE OF THE *NECROMANCER* POWERS.
I THINK WE MIGHT HAVE BIGGER PROBLEMS THAN FARGUS. LOOK!
KULOO WILL DESTROY THIS PLACE! YOU NEED TO FLEE NOW!
I'LL DIE BEFORE I LEAVE MY TREASURE BEHIND!
CRUX, HELP!
AND DO WHAT EXACTLY?
WE NEED TO GET OUT OF HERE!
NOT WHILE FARGUS IS STILL ALIVE!
HAS ANYONE SEEN THE BUG? WE COULD USE ALL THE HELP WE CAN GET!

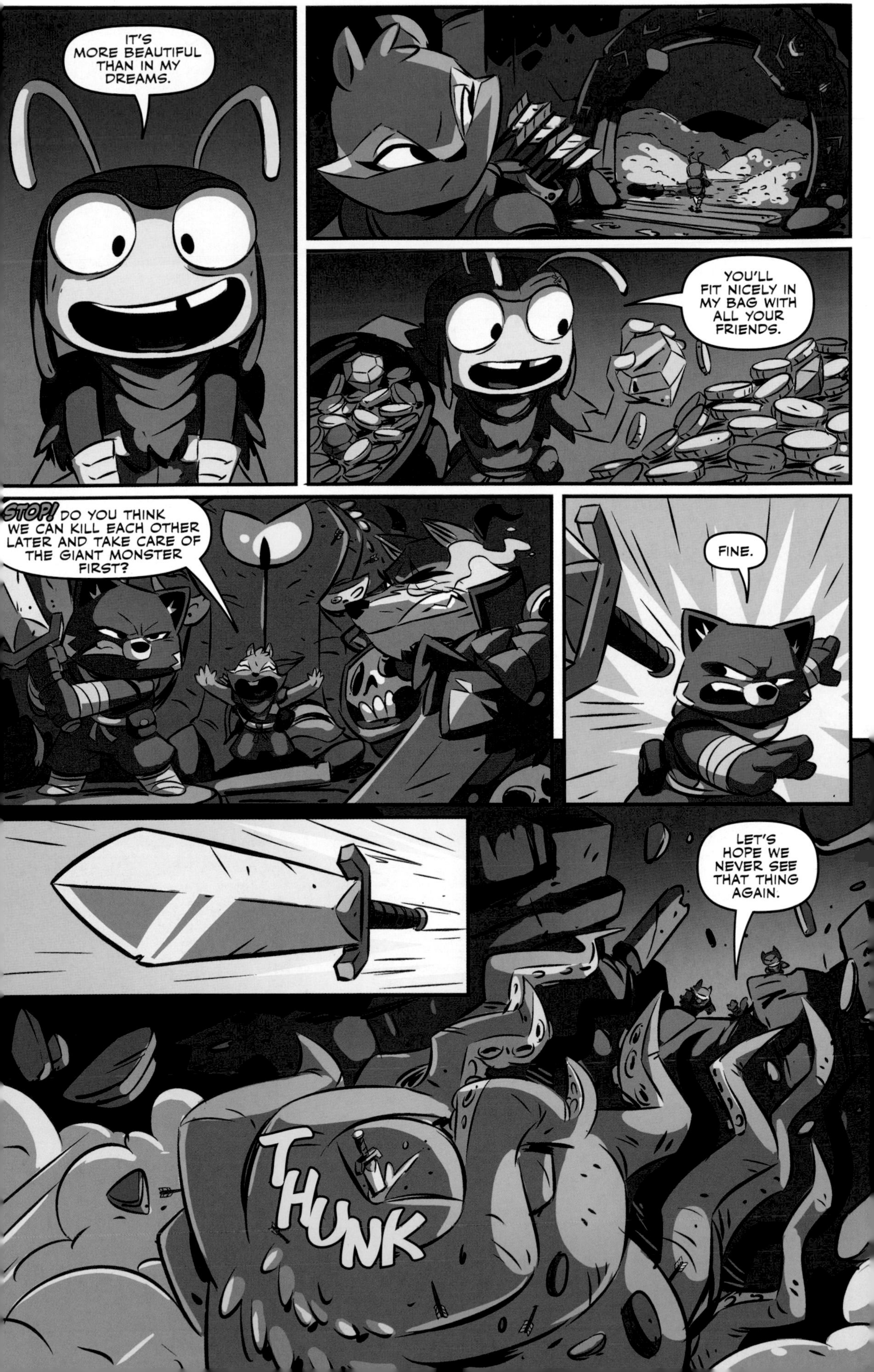

IT'S MORE BEAUTIFUL THAN IN MY DREAMS.
YOU'LL FIT NICELY IN MY BAG WITH ALL YOUR FRIENDS.
STOP! DO YOU THINK WE CAN KILL EACH OTHER LATER AND TAKE CARE OF THE GIANT MONSTER FIRST?
FINE.
LET'S HOPE WE NEVER SEE THAT THING AGAIN.
THUNK

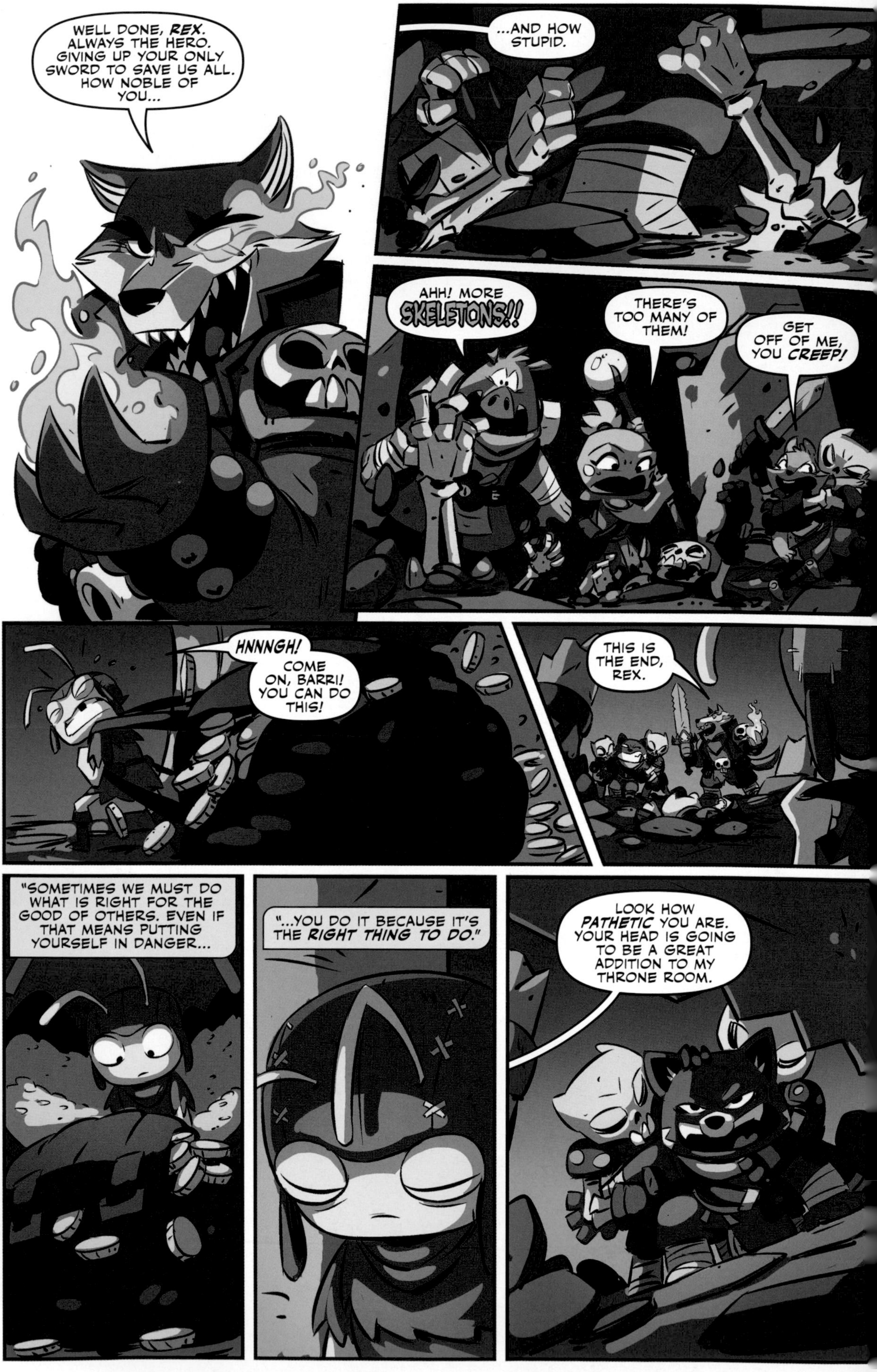
WELL DONE, *REX*. ALWAYS THE HERO. GIVING UP YOUR ONLY SWORD TO SAVE US ALL. HOW NOBLE OF YOU...
...AND HOW STUPID.
AHH! MORE SKELETONS!!
THERE'S TOO MANY OF THEM!
GET OFF OF ME, YOU *CREEP!*
HNNNGH!
COME ON, BARRI! YOU CAN DO THIS!
THIS IS THE END, REX.
"SOMETIMES WE MUST DO WHAT IS RIGHT FOR THE GOOD OF OTHERS. EVEN IF THAT MEANS PUTTING YOURSELF IN DANGER...
"...YOU DO IT BECAUSE IT'S THE *RIGHT THING TO DO*."
LOOK HOW *PATHETIC* YOU ARE. YOUR HEAD IS GOING TO BE A GREAT ADDITION TO MY THRONE ROOM.

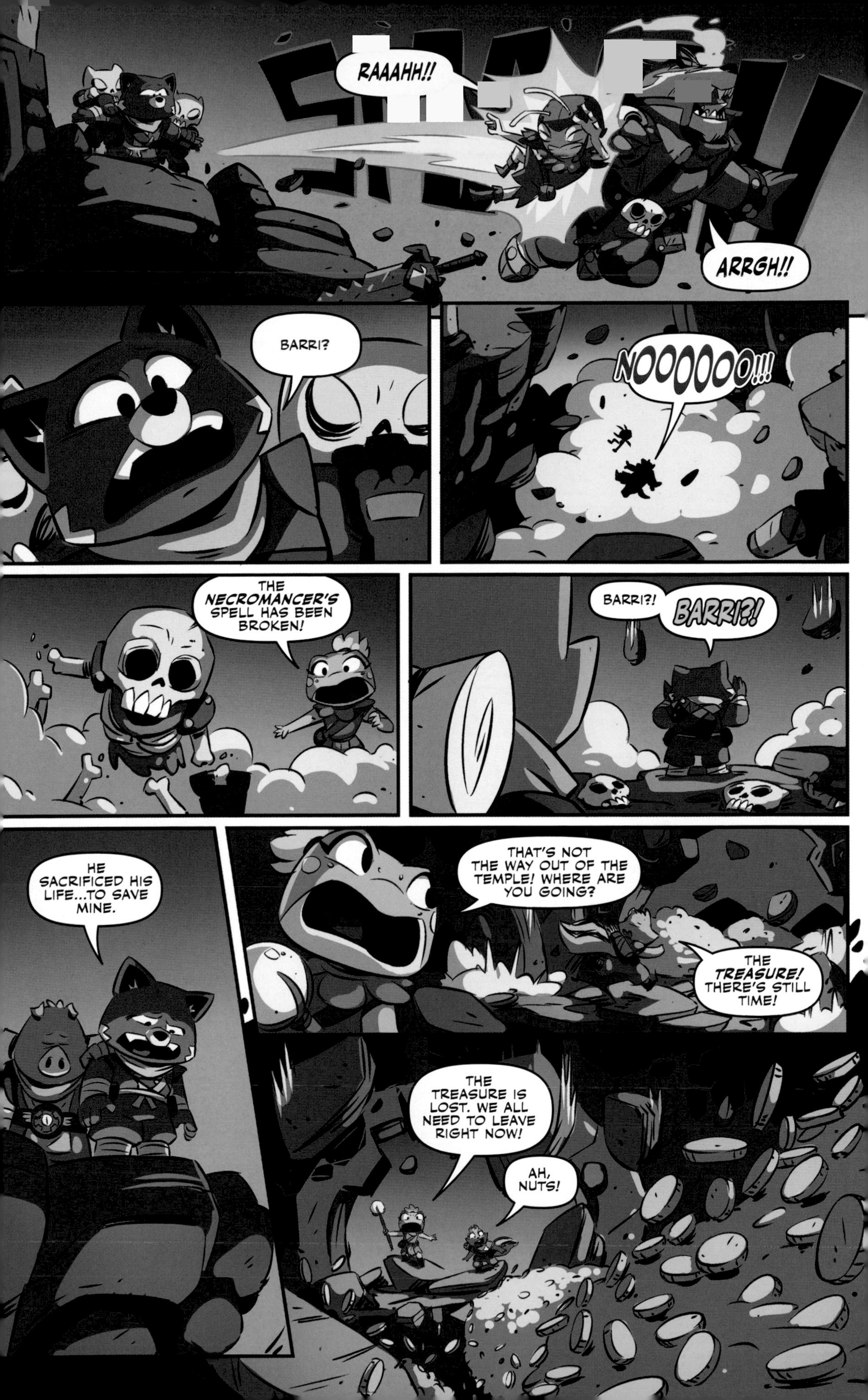
RAAAHH!!
ARRGH!!
BARRI?
NOOOOOO!!!
THE NECROMANCER'S SPELL HAS BEEN BROKEN!
BARRI?!
BARRI?!
HE SACRIFICED HIS LIFE...TO SAVE MINE.
THAT'S NOT THE WAY OUT OF THE TEMPLE! WHERE ARE YOU GOING?
THE TREASURE! THERE'S STILL TIME!
THE TREASURE IS LOST. WE ALL NEED TO LEAVE RIGHT NOW!
AH, NUTS!

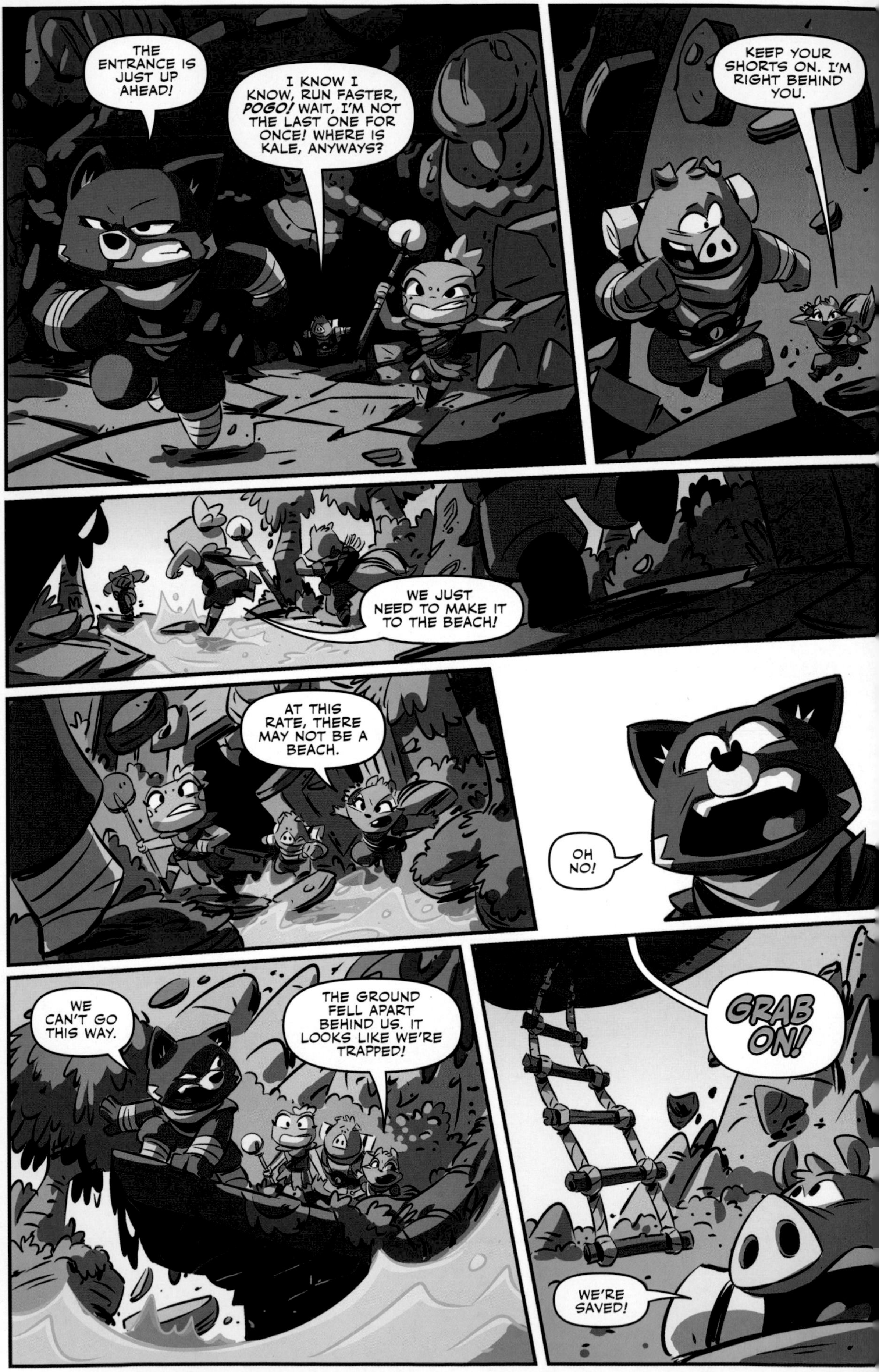
THE ENTRANCE IS JUST UP AHEAD!
I KNOW I KNOW, RUN FASTER, *POGO!* WAIT, I'M NOT THE LAST ONE FOR ONCE! WHERE IS KALE, ANYWAYS?
KEEP YOUR SHORTS ON. I'M RIGHT BEHIND YOU.
WE JUST NEED TO MAKE IT TO THE BEACH!
AT THIS RATE, THERE MAY NOT BE A BEACH.
OH NO!
WE CAN'T GO THIS WAY.
THE GROUND FELL APART BEHIND US. IT LOOKS LIKE WE'RE TRAPPED!
GRAB ON!
WE'RE SAVED!

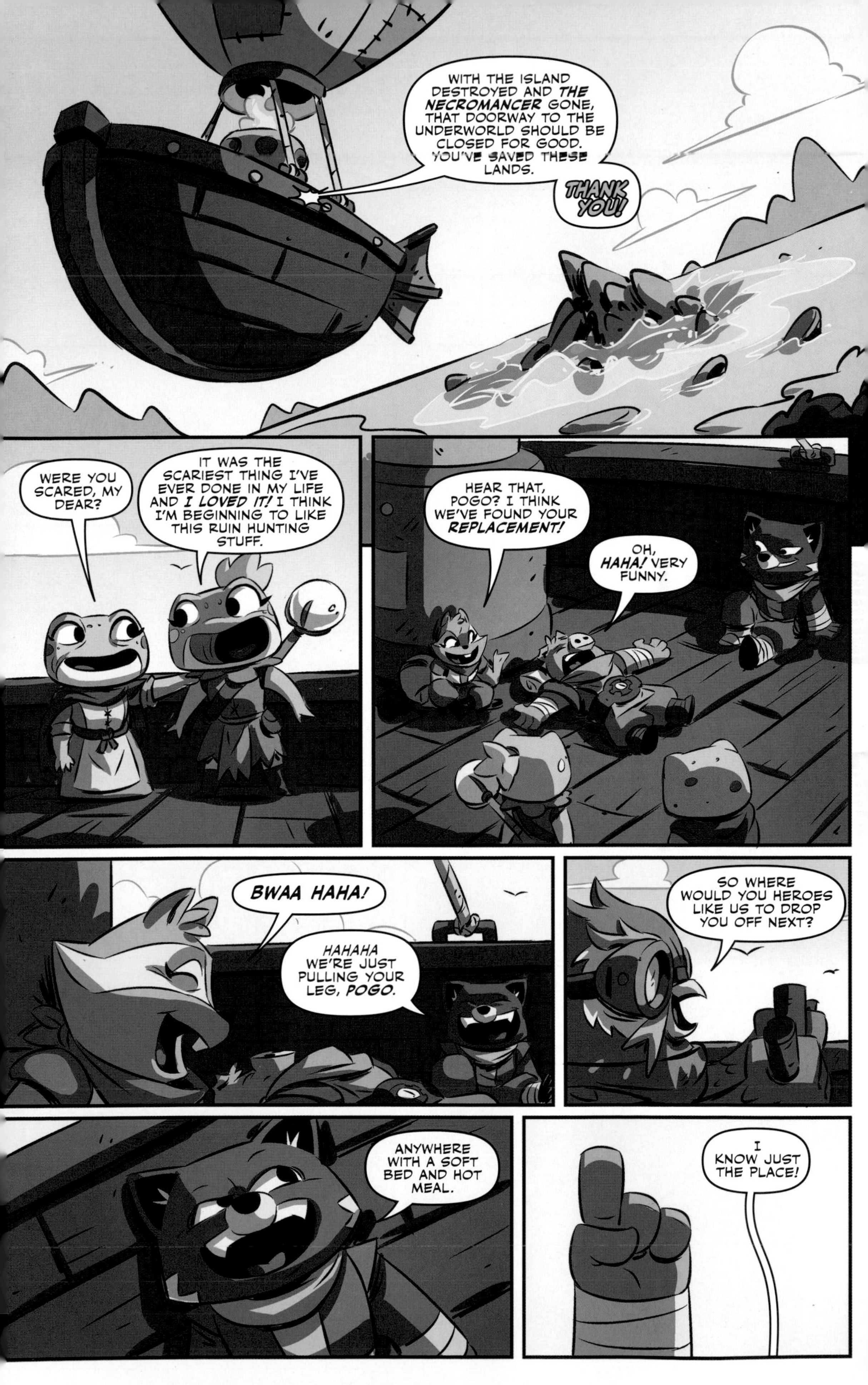
WITH THE ISLAND DESTROYED AND THE NECROMANCER GONE, THAT DOORWAY TO THE UNDERWORLD SHOULD BE CLOSED FOR GOOD. YOU'VE SAVED THESE LANDS.
THANK YOU!
WERE YOU SCARED, MY DEAR?
IT WAS THE SCARIEST THING I'VE EVER DONE IN MY LIFE AND I LOVED IT! I THINK I'M BEGINNING TO LIKE THIS RUIN HUNTING STUFF.
HEAR THAT, POGO? I THINK WE'VE FOUND YOUR REPLACEMENT!
OH, HAHA! VERY FUNNY.
BWAA HAHA!
HAHAHA WE'RE JUST PULLING YOUR LEG, POGO.
SO WHERE WOULD YOU HEROES LIKE US TO DROP YOU OFF NEXT?
ANYWHERE WITH A SOFT BED AND HOT MEAL.
I KNOW JUST THE PLACE!

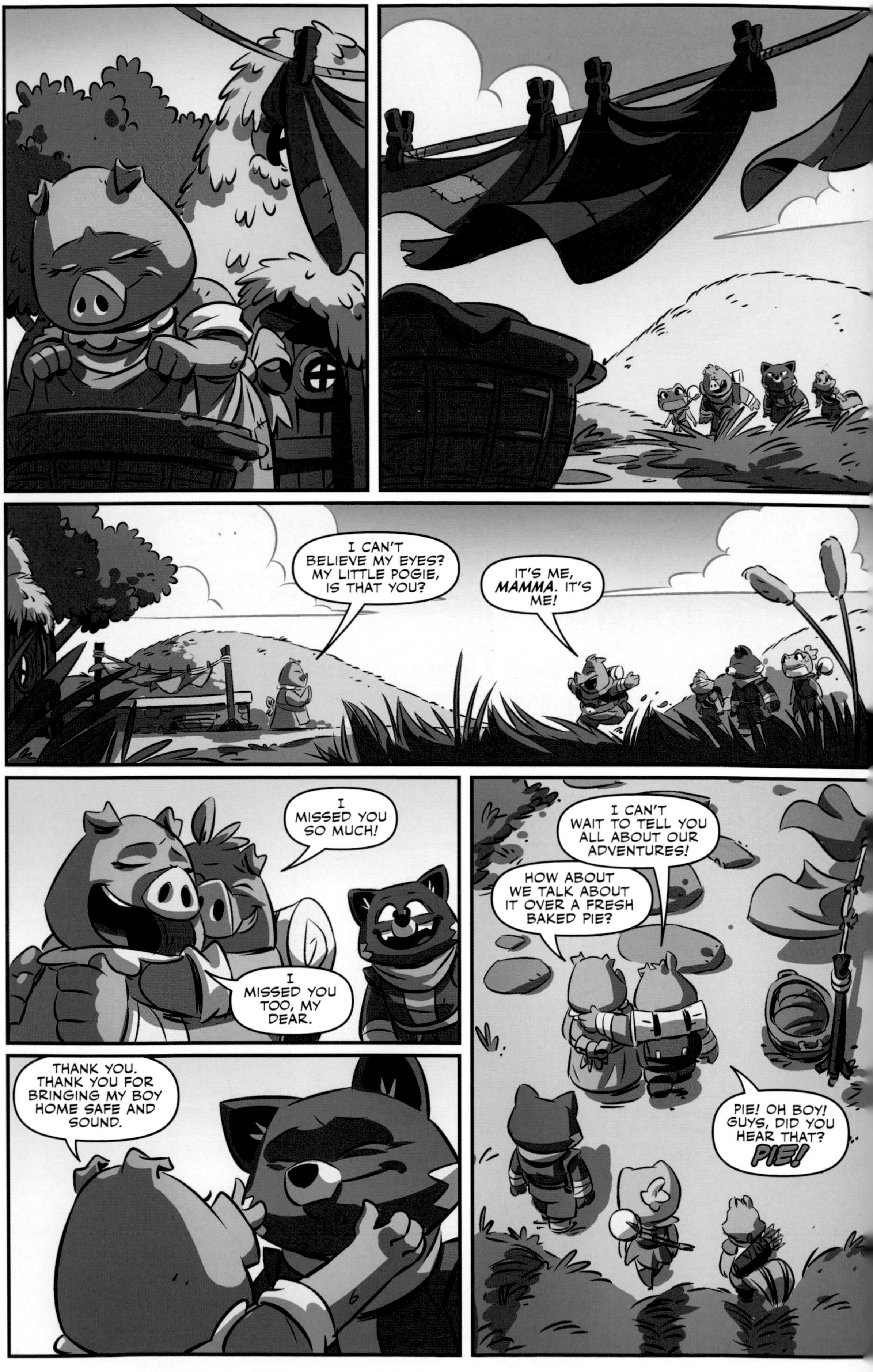
I CAN'T BELIEVE MY EYES? MY LITTLE POGIE, IS THAT YOU?
IT'S ME, *MAMMA*. IT'S ME!
I MISSED YOU SO MUCH!
I MISSED YOU TOO, MY DEAR.
THANK YOU. THANK YOU FOR BRINGING MY BOY HOME SAFE AND SOUND.
I CAN'T WAIT TO TELL YOU ALL ABOUT OUR ADVENTURES!
HOW ABOUT WE TALK ABOUT IT OVER A FRESH BAKED PIE?
PIE! OH BOY! GUYS, DID YOU HEAR THAT? PIE!

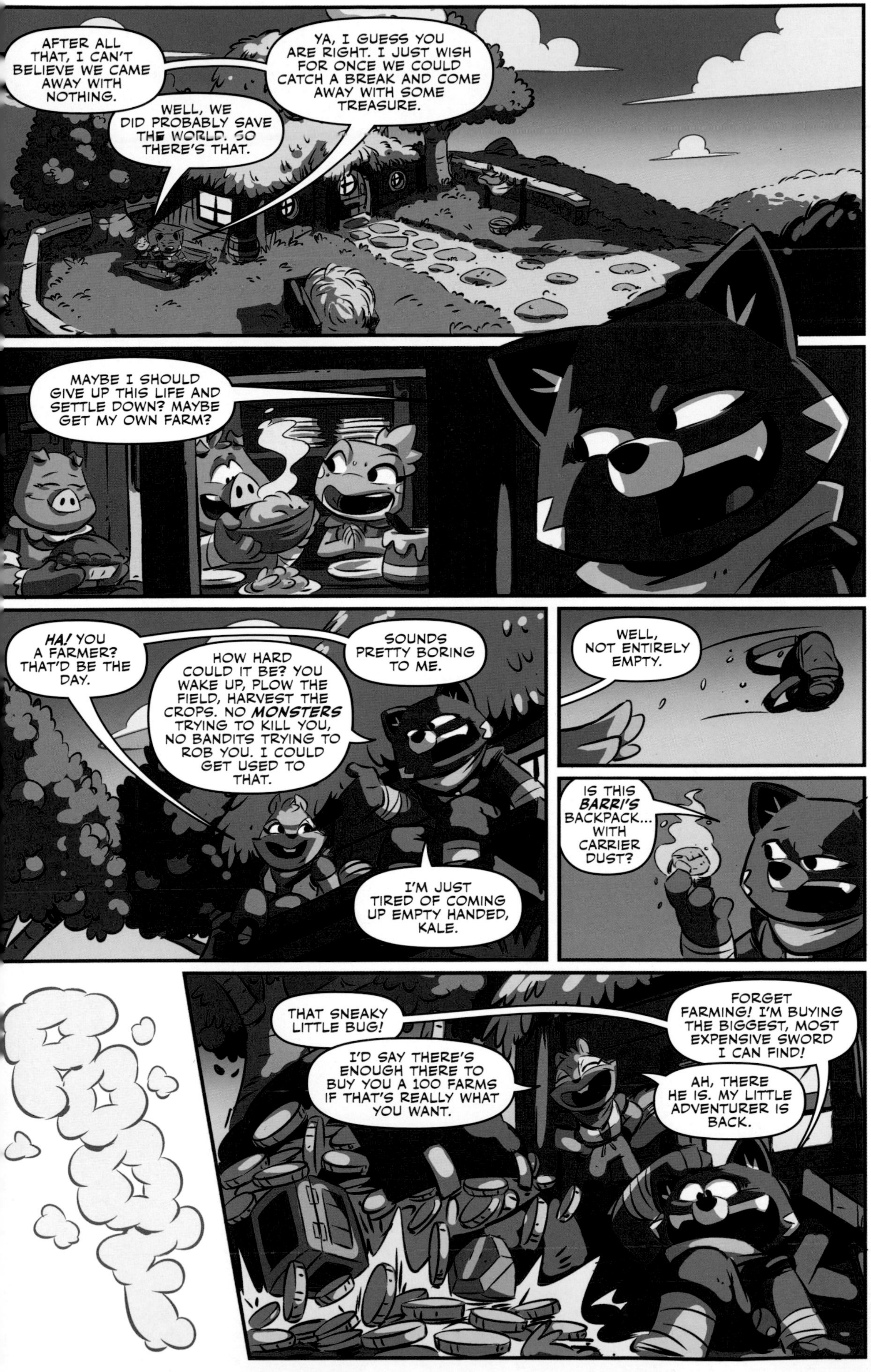
AFTER ALL THAT, I CAN'T BELIEVE WE CAME AWAY WITH NOTHING.
WELL, WE DID PROBABLY SAVE THE WORLD. SO THERE'S THAT.
YA, I GUESS YOU ARE RIGHT. I JUST WISH FOR ONCE WE COULD CATCH A BREAK AND COME AWAY WITH SOME TREASURE.
MAYBE I SHOULD GIVE UP THIS LIFE AND SETTLE DOWN? MAYBE GET MY OWN FARM?
HA! YOU A FARMER? THAT'D BE THE DAY.
SOUNDS PRETTY BORING TO ME.
HOW HARD COULD IT BE? YOU WAKE UP, PLOW THE FIELD, HARVEST THE CROPS. NO MONSTERS TRYING TO KILL YOU, NO BANDITS TRYING TO ROB YOU. I COULD GET USED TO THAT.
I'M JUST TIRED OF COMING UP EMPTY HANDED, KALE.
WELL, NOT ENTIRELY EMPTY.
IS THIS BARRI'S BACKPACK... WITH CARRIER DUST?
THAT SNEAKY LITTLE BUG!
I'D SAY THERE'S ENOUGH THERE TO BUY YOU A 100 FARMS IF THAT'S REALLY WHAT YOU WANT.
FORGET FARMING! I'M BUYING THE BIGGEST, MOST EXPENSIVE SWORD I CAN FIND!
AH, THERE HE IS. MY LITTLE ADVENTURER IS BACK.

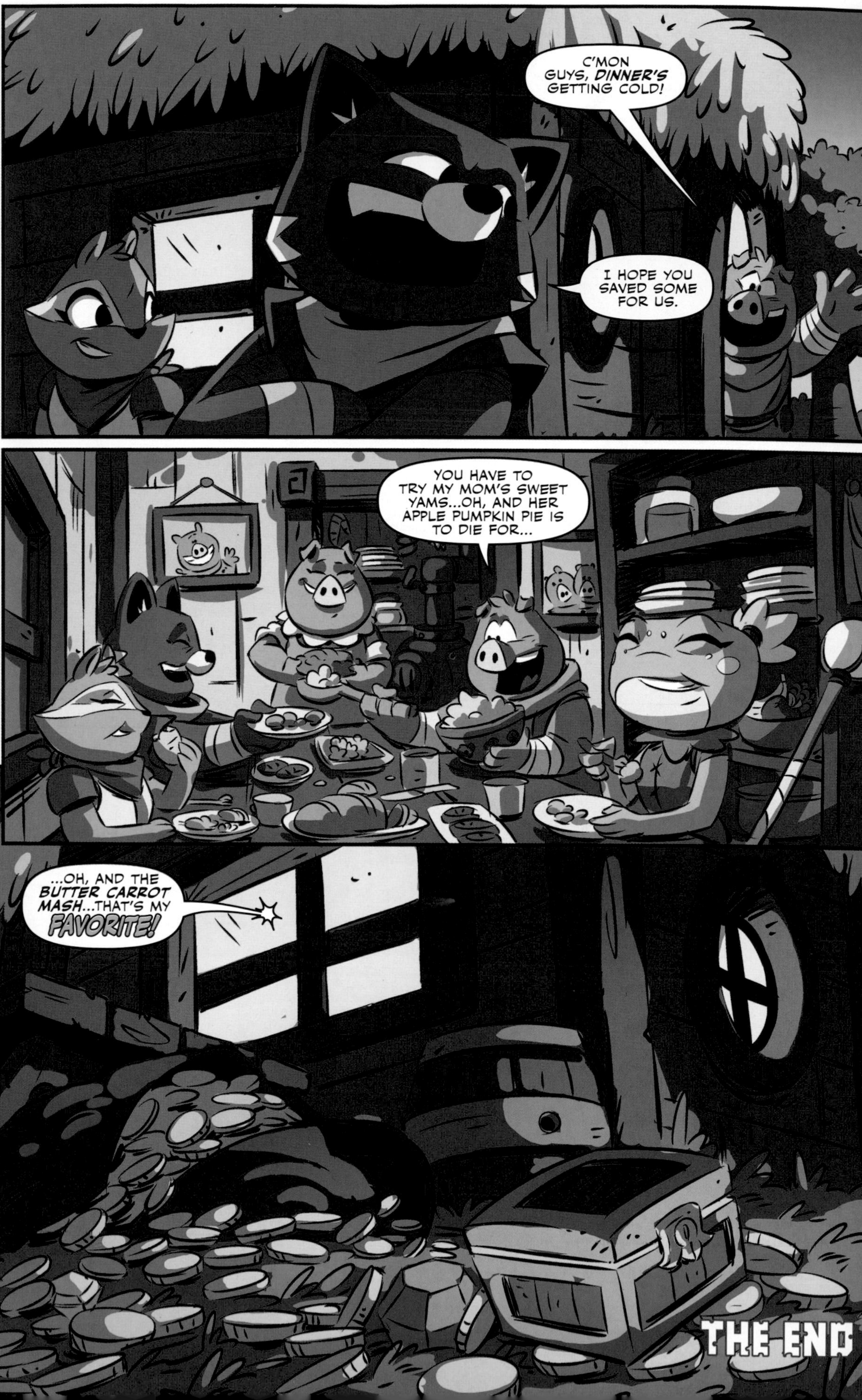
C'MON GUYS, DINNER'S GETTING COLD!
I HOPE YOU SAVED SOME FOR US.
YOU HAVE TO TRY MY MOM'S SWEET YAMS...OH, AND HER APPLE PUMPKIN PIE IS TO DIE FOR...
...OH, AND THE BUTTER CARROT MASH...THAT'S MY FAVORITE!
THE END

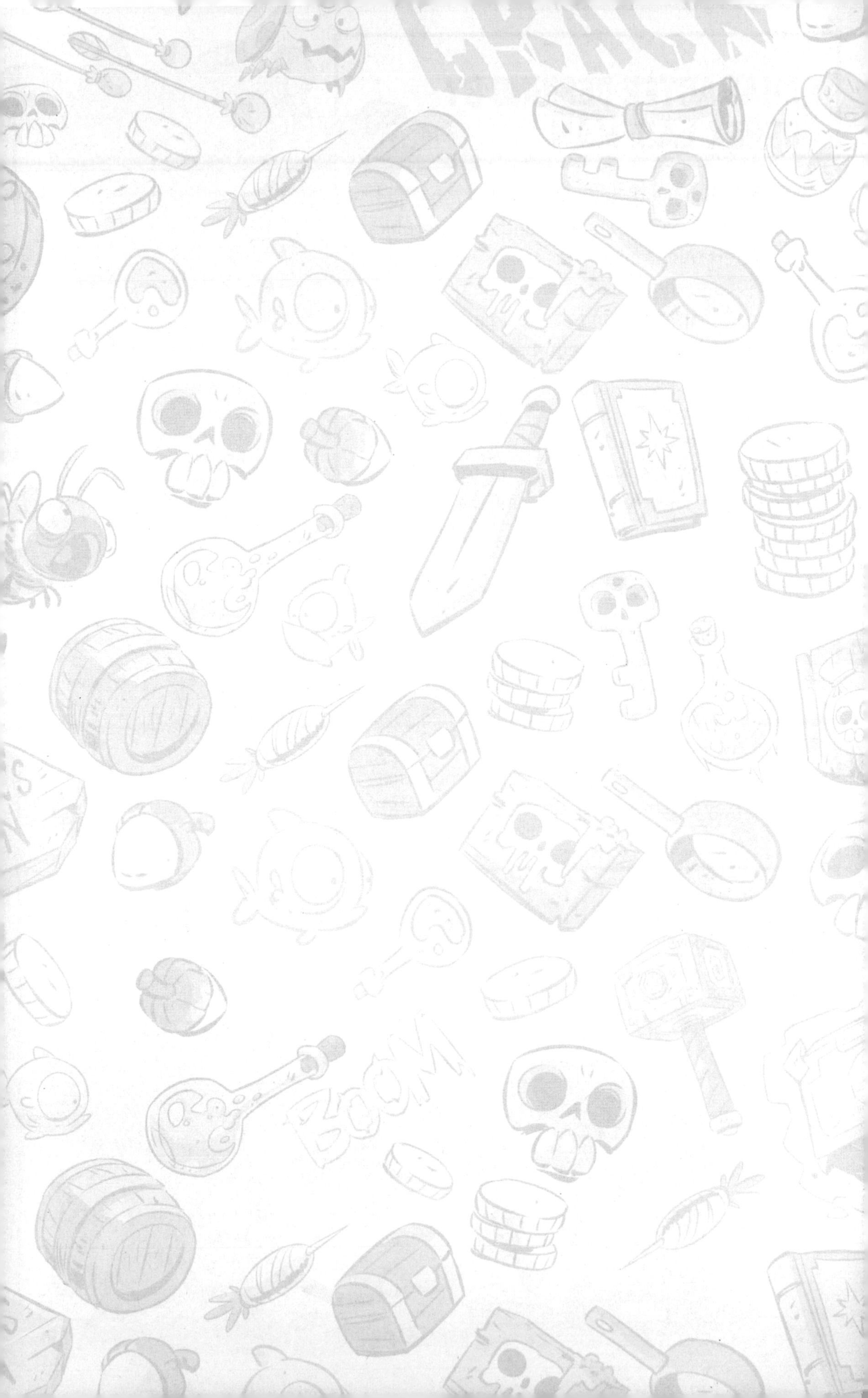
BOOM

CHARACTER DESIGNS BY DEREK LAUFMAN

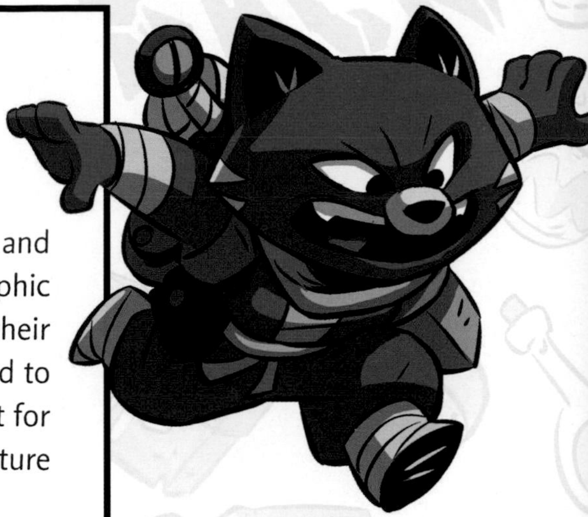

I grew up watching shows like *Looney Tunes* and *Ducktales.* I always enjoyed anthropomorphic characters in animation and how their expressions and emotions would be pushed to the max. This direction felt like a perfect fit for *RuinWorld*, a fun and action-packed adventure for all ages.

Pogo and Rex were the first two characters I created for *RuinWorld.* They set the tone for the style and really helped me imagine the world as a melting pot of animal species.

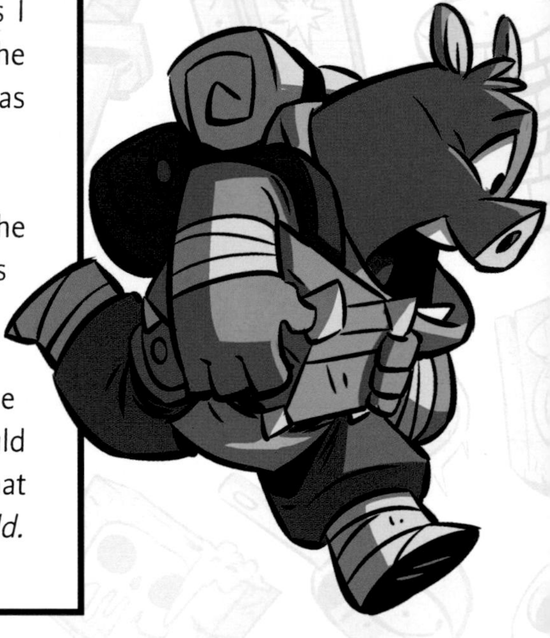

Rex was originally designed as a fox, but the design felt too much like a villain. Since he was named after my cat, I decided to combine the two animals, and the character of Rex was born. This combination also opened me up to the idea that animals in this world could be combined with other species, and how that might play into the social aspects of *RuinWorld.*

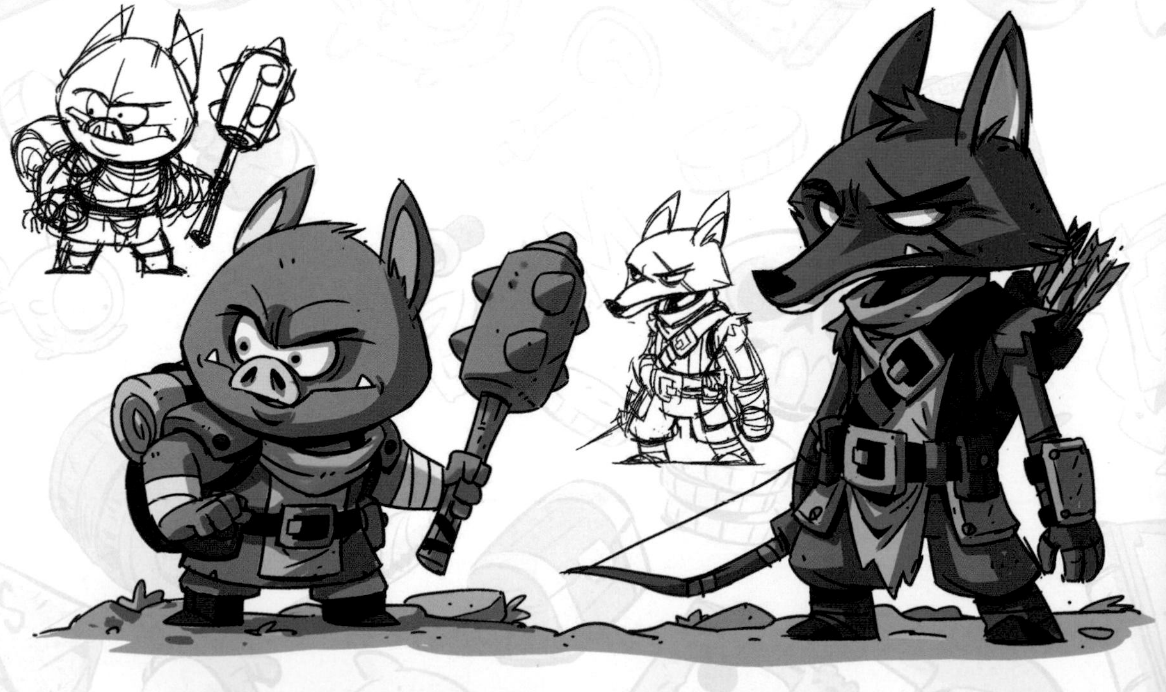

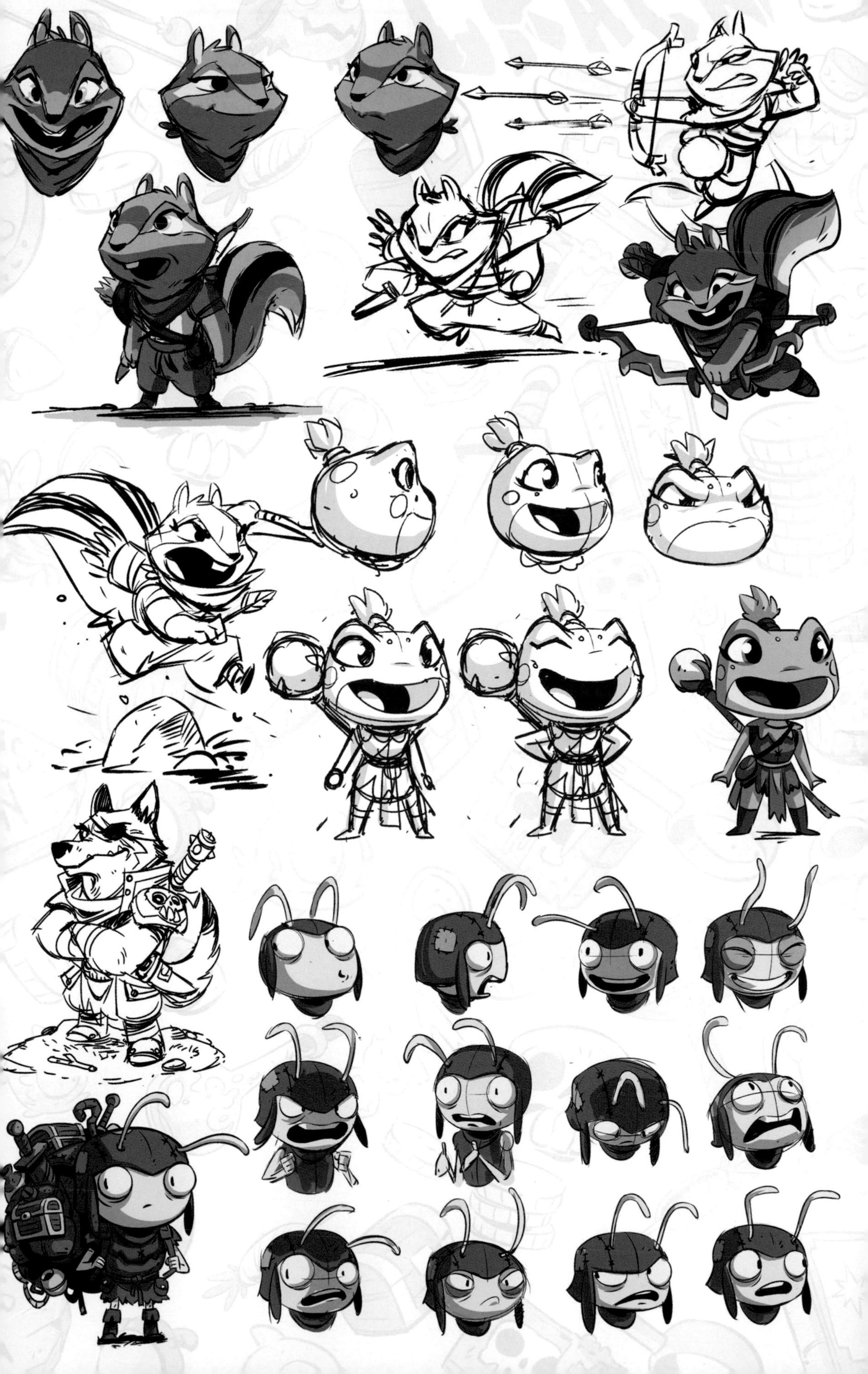

COVER DESIGNS AND CONCEPTS

Early on in development, my editor Whitney suggested that each cover should POP off the shelf, and she referenced a cover I had originally drawn for *RuinWorld* when it was an online comic. With the use of white negative space, the characters, action, and logo were really highlighted and we used this strategy throughout each cover in the series.

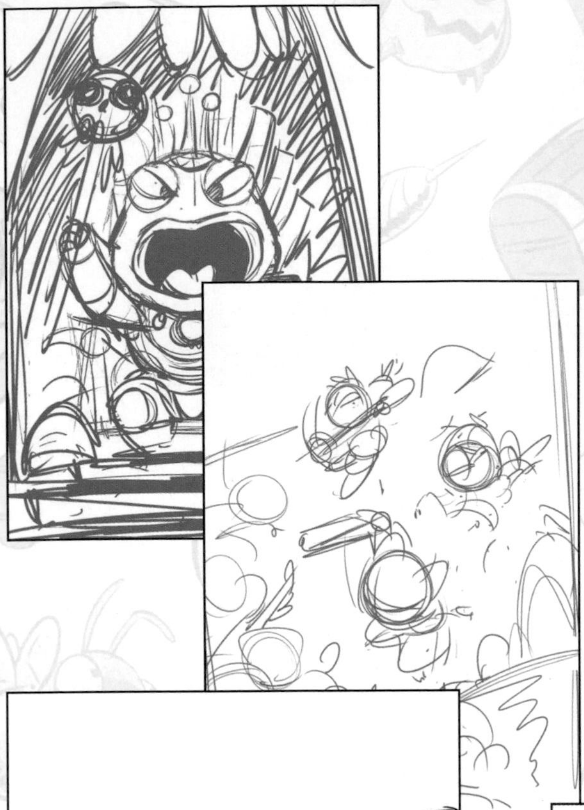

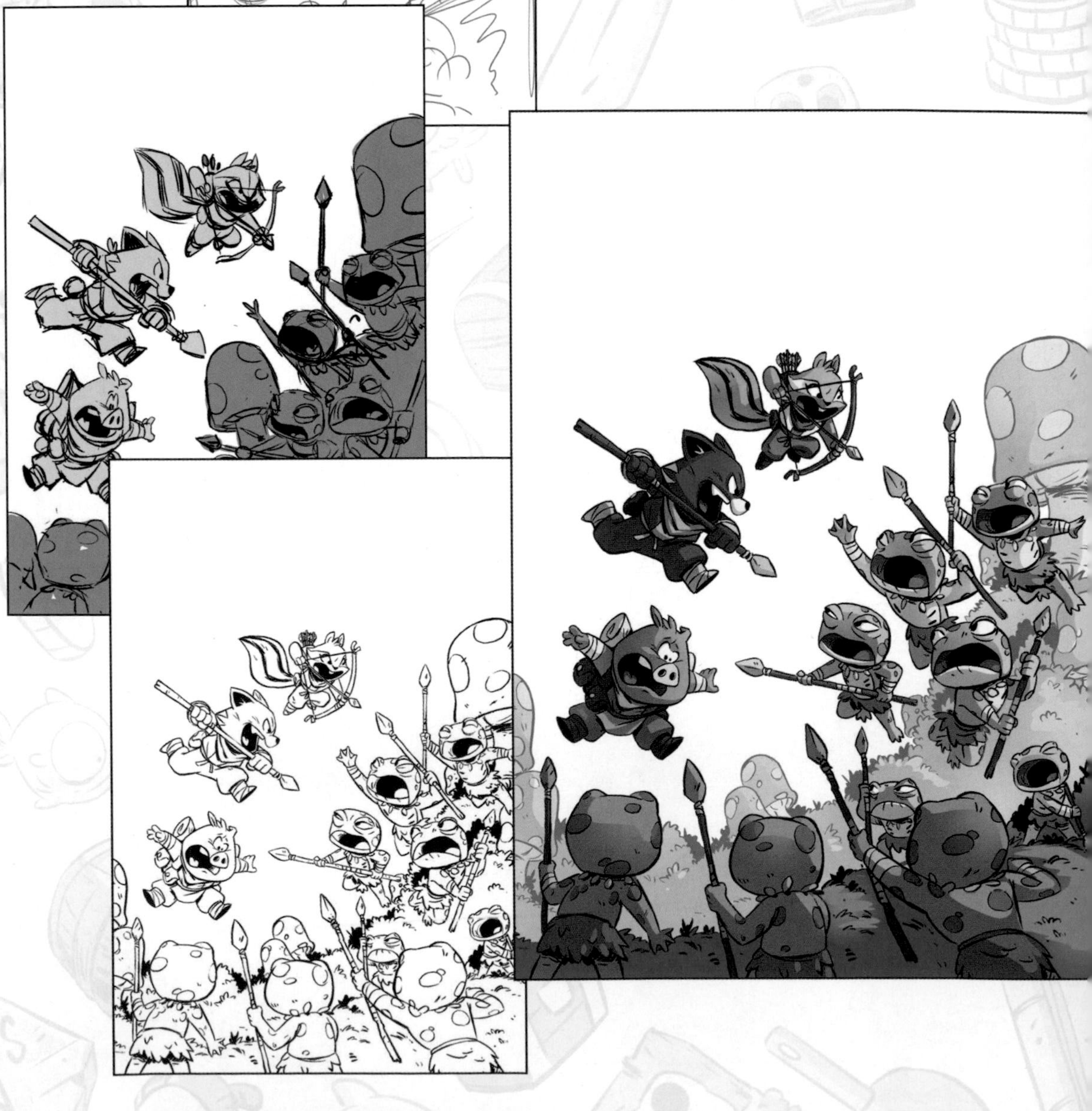

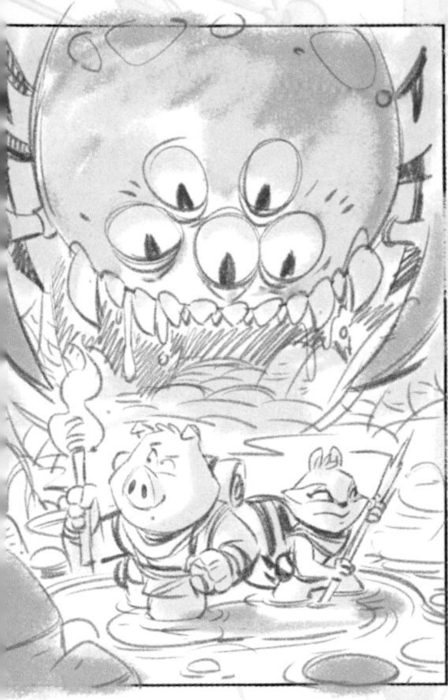
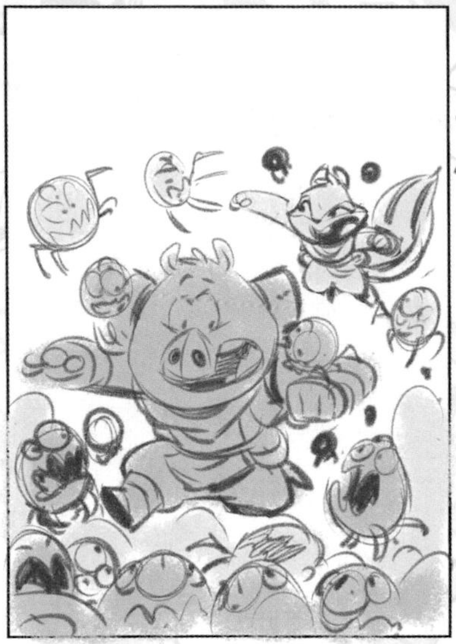
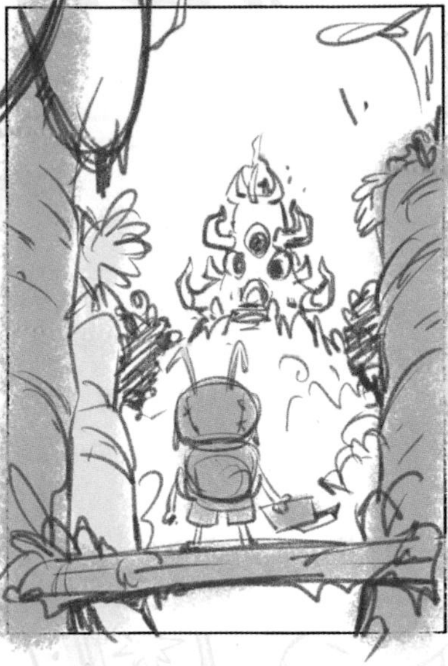
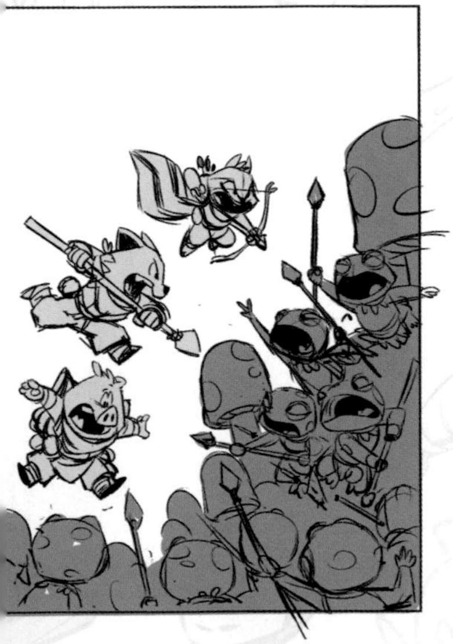
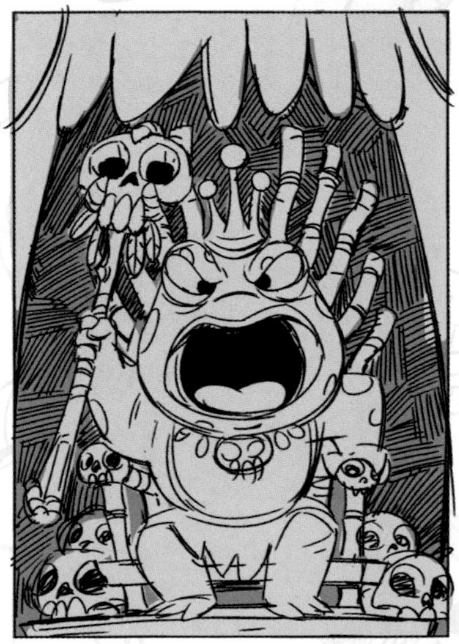
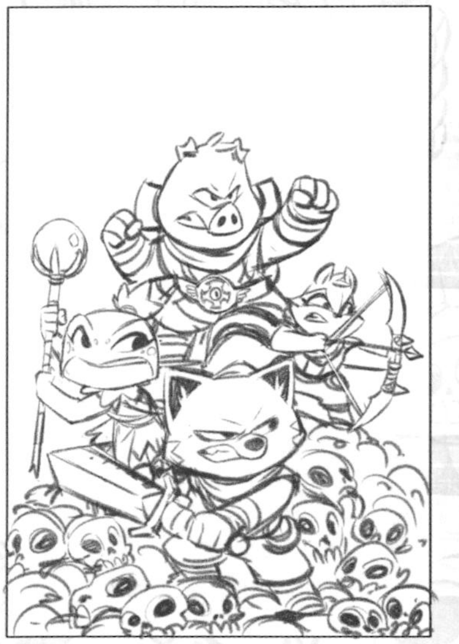
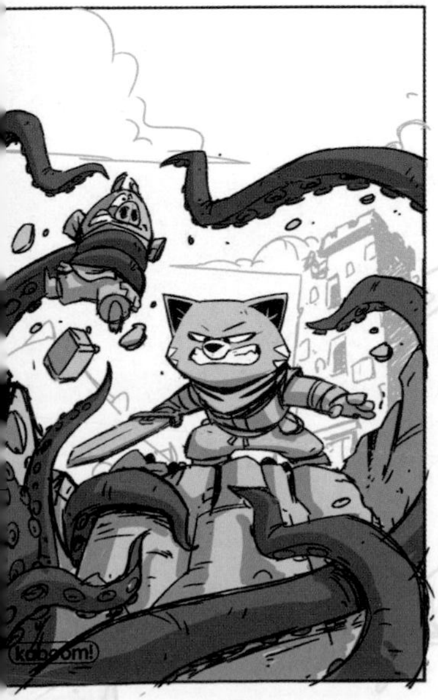
kaboom!
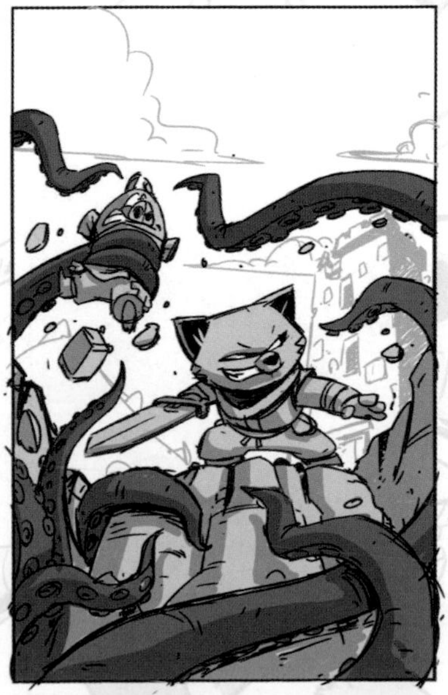
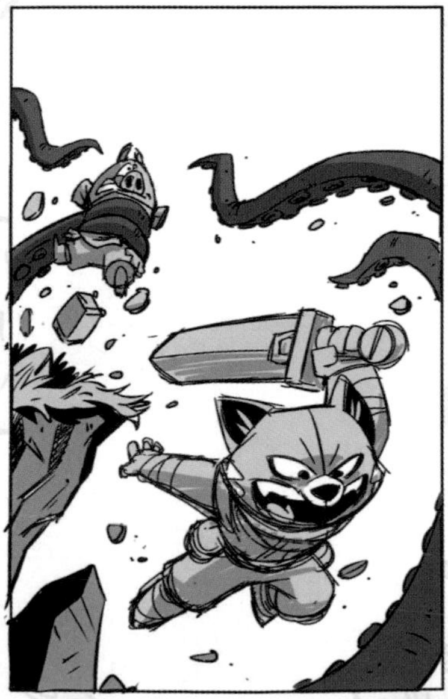

VISUAL STORYTELLING

It was very important for me to get as much emotion, acting, and storytelling into every single page. The visuals needed to flow, and every panel needed to serve a purpose. That was always a big challenge as I approached each page, and much of my time went into that process. From layout and posing, to setting the mood with color, I wanted to convey as much information as I could to the reader without the use of dialogue.

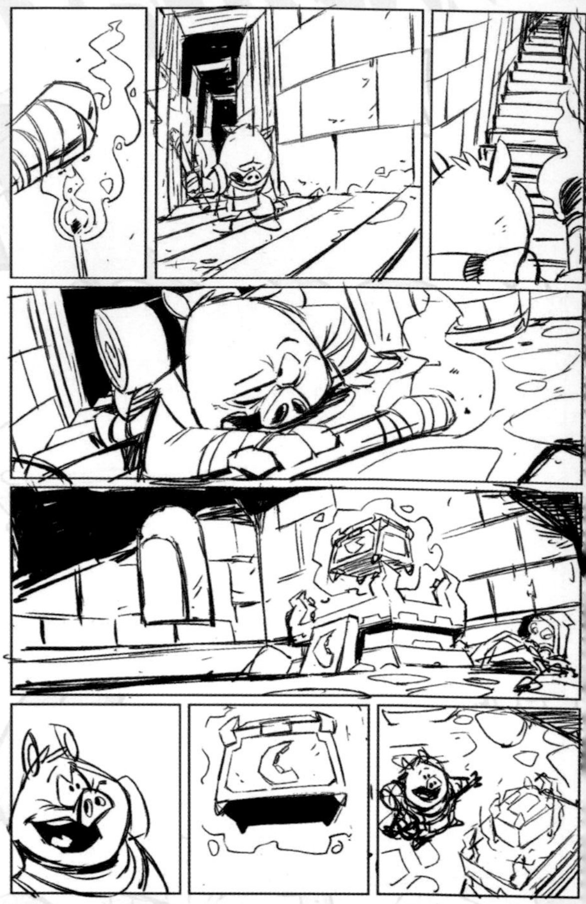

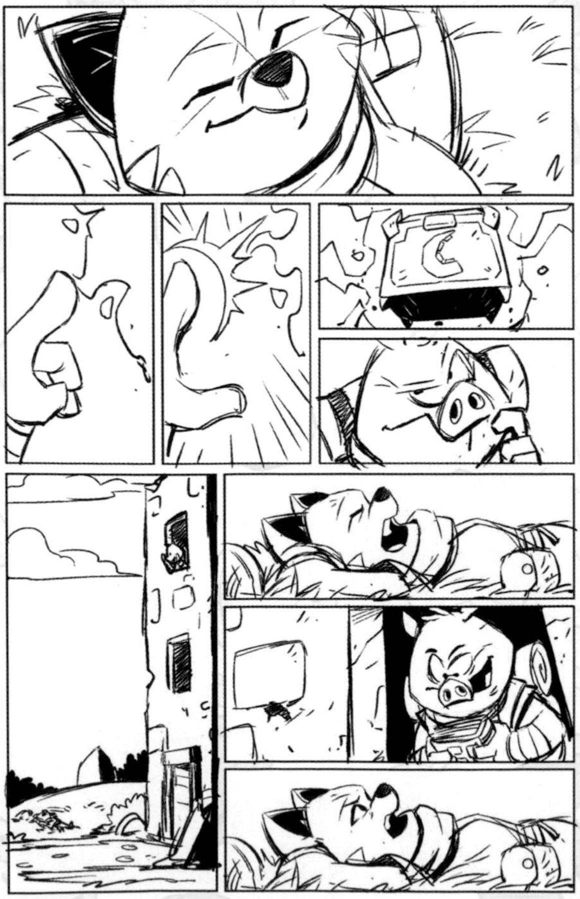

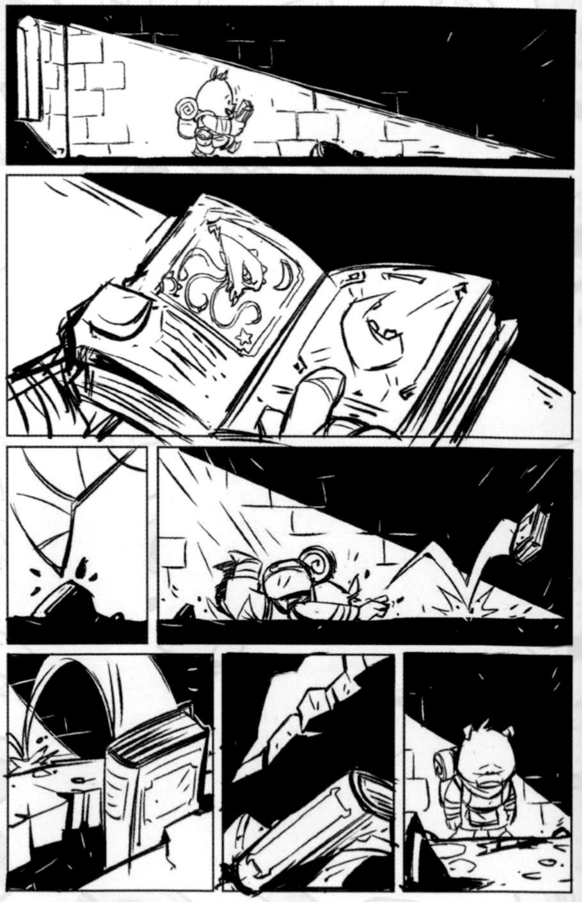

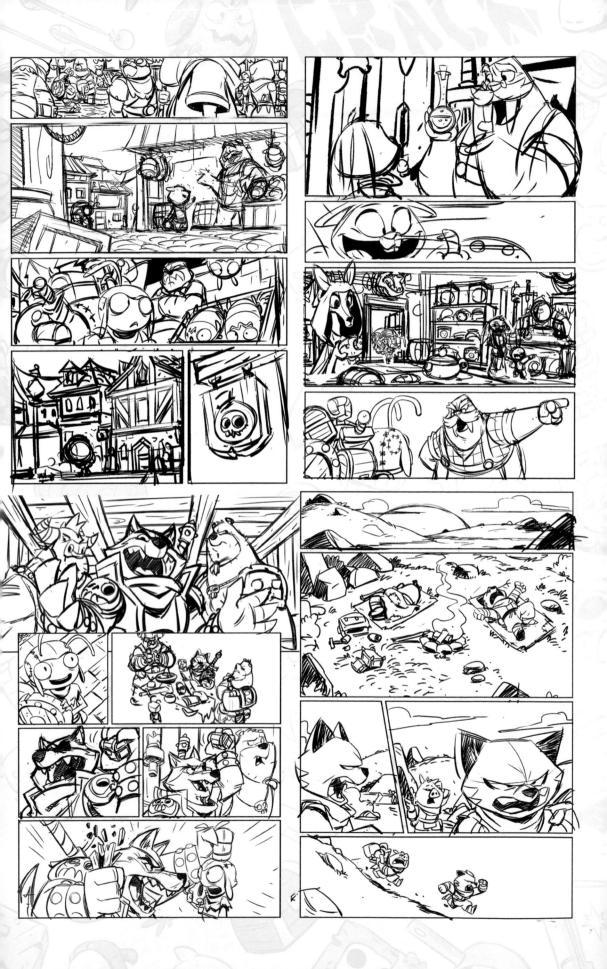

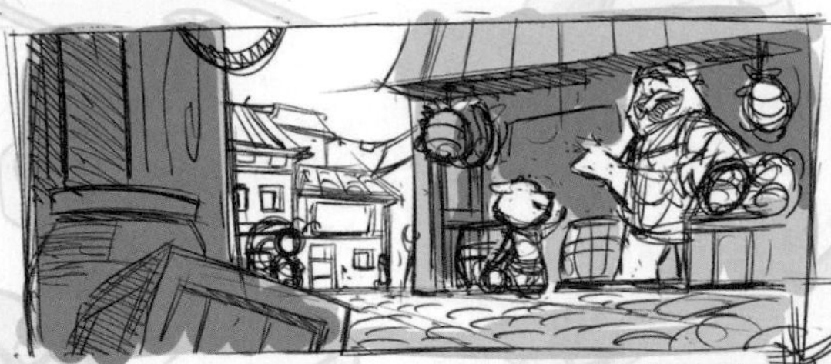

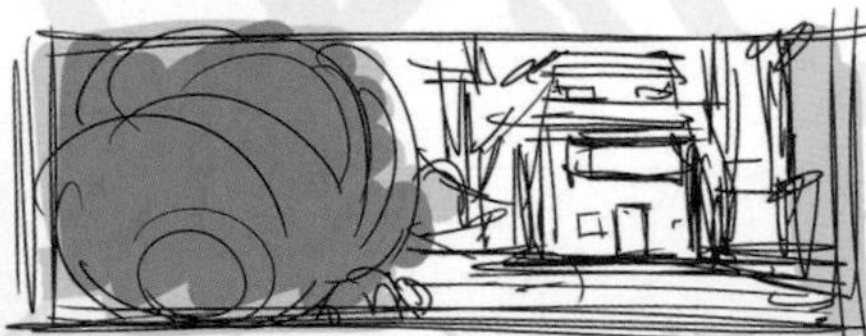

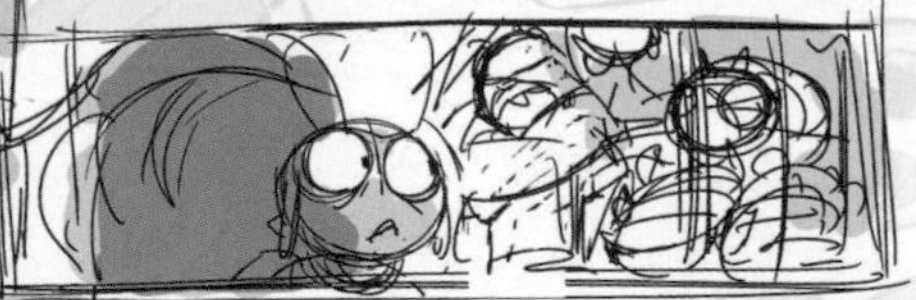

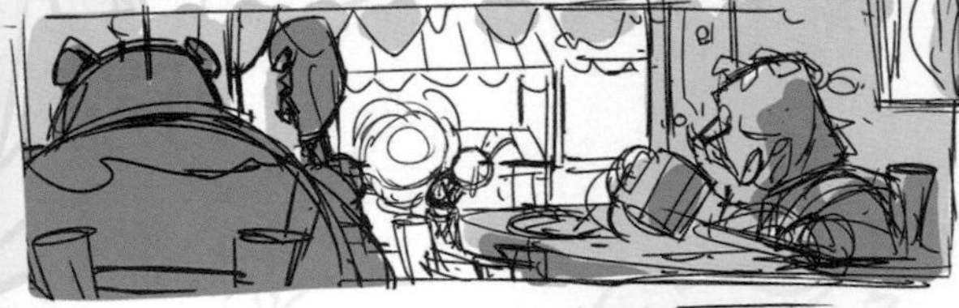

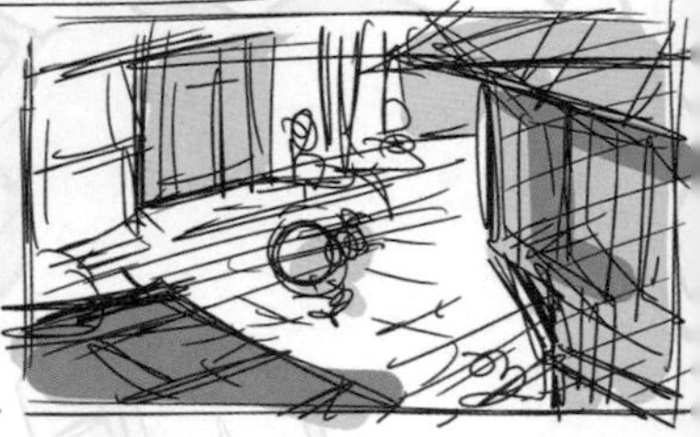

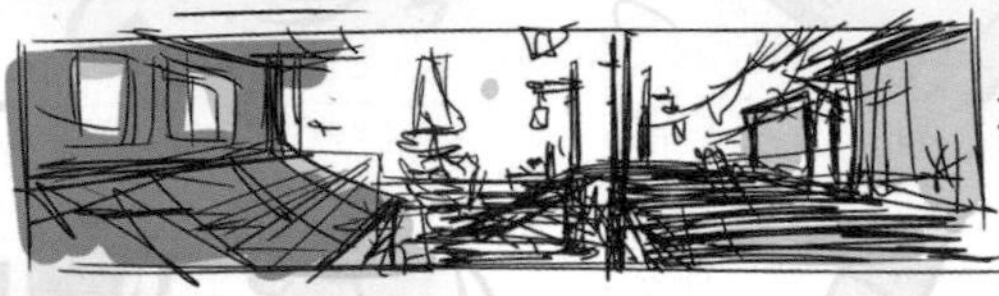

WORLD BUILDING

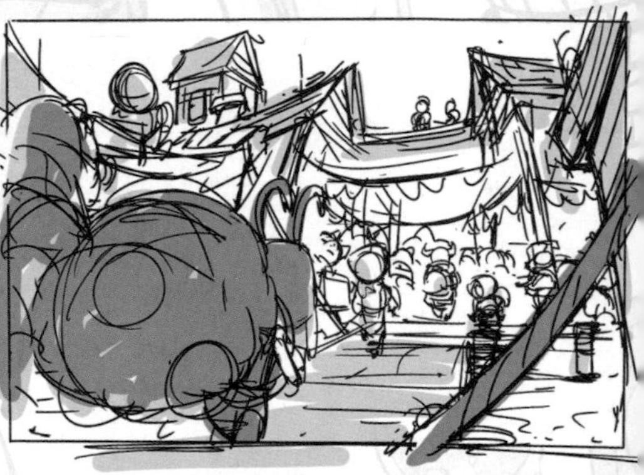

Magical kingdoms and fantastic creatures once inhabited this land, but long after they disappeared the tales of powerful artifacts and epic monsters remained. In the present day, the inhabitants of the Ruinlands are trying to discover and unlock this magic once again.

It was important for me to convey a land that is both in ruins, but also very much alive. I set out to create a world that was bustling with creatures and felt like it had been lived in for many generations.

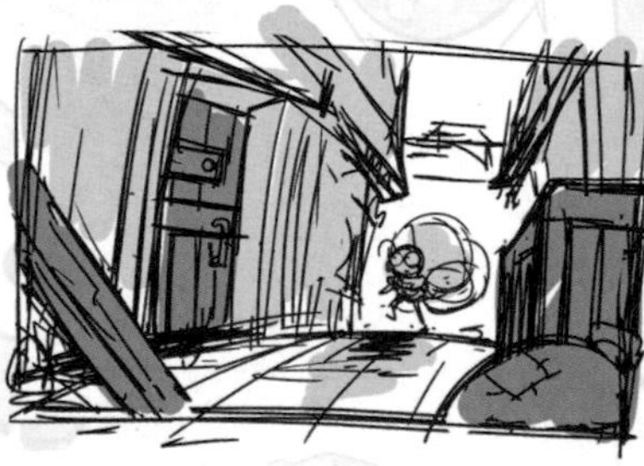

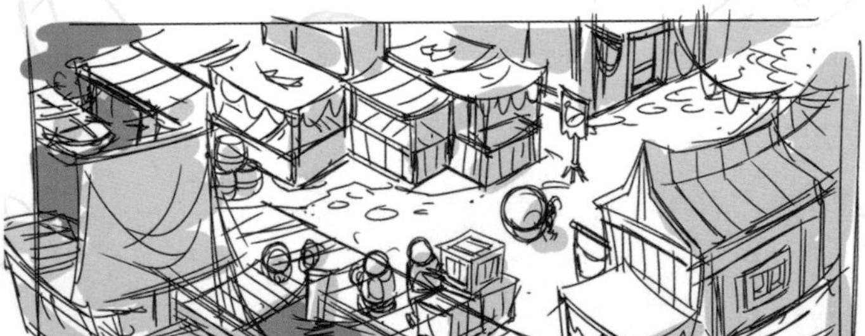

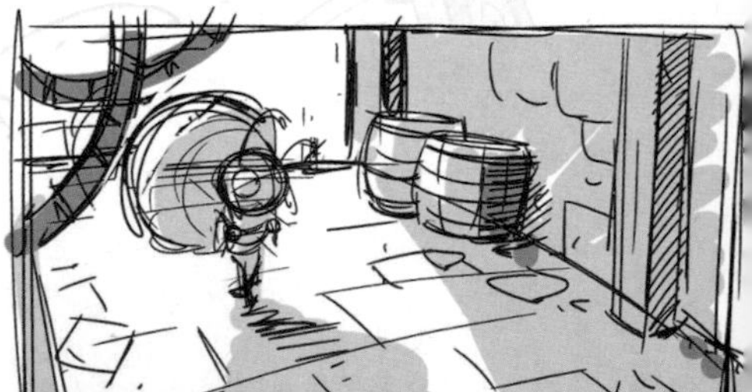

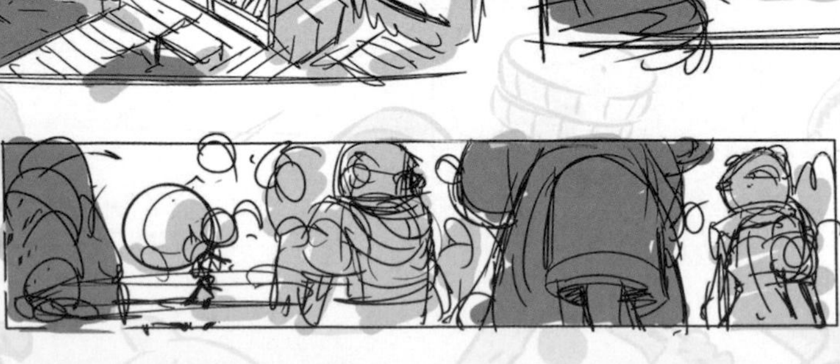

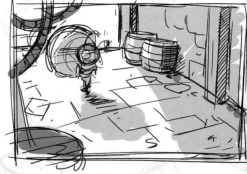

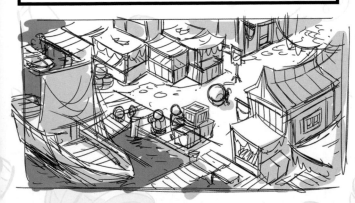